THE EYES
OF
ARCHIMEDES

BOOK THREE

Other Books by Dan Armstrong

Taming the Dragon
Prairie Fire
Puddle of Love
The Open Secret
Chain of Souls
The Eyes of Archimedes Book I
The Siege of Syracuse
The Eyes of Archimedes Book II
The Death of Marcellus

ZAMA

A Novel

Dan Armstrong

Mud City Press
Eugene, Oregon

The Eyes of Archimedes Book III
Zama
Copyright © 2016 by Dan Armstrong

Published by
Mud City Press
http://www.mudcitypress.com
Eugene, Oregon

This is a work of fiction. Names, characters, places, and incidents are either the product of the author's imagination or are used fictitiously.

The image on the cover of this book comes from an etching by Cornelis Huyberts after Cornelis Cort's, *Battle with the Elephants,* 1701-12. From the collection of Nathan and Ana Flis, New Haven, Connecticut.

ISBN-978-0-9830045-7-8

Printed in the United States

To the End of War

AUTHOR'S NOTE

The Eyes of Archimedes is a fictional trilogy set during the Second Punic War, also known as the War with Hannibal. The Second Punic War began in 218 B.C. (the 291st year of the Roman Republic) and ended in 202 B.C. (the 307th year of the Roman Republic).

The many Latin, Greek, and other foreign names used for the characters in this novel are listed alphabetically at the back of the book for the reader's convenience. A glossary containing words specific to the ancient world and/or Roman culture follows the list of characters.

Although I have made a concerted effort to be faithful to a very complex episode in ancient history, simplifications were made for the sake of readability. In the end, this is a novel. The narrator is fictitious, and his story an embellishment of the existing literature.

"Quite other instincts were loose. The red eyes of the ancestral ape had come back to the world. It was a time when reasonable men were bowled down or murdered; the true spirit of the age is shown in the eager examination for signs and portents in the still quivering livers of those human victims who were sacrificed in Rome during the panic before the battle of Telamon. The western world was indeed black with homicidal monomania. Two great peoples, both very necessary to the world's development, fell foul of one another, and at last Rome succeeded in murdering Carthage."

-H.G. Wells, *The Outline of History*

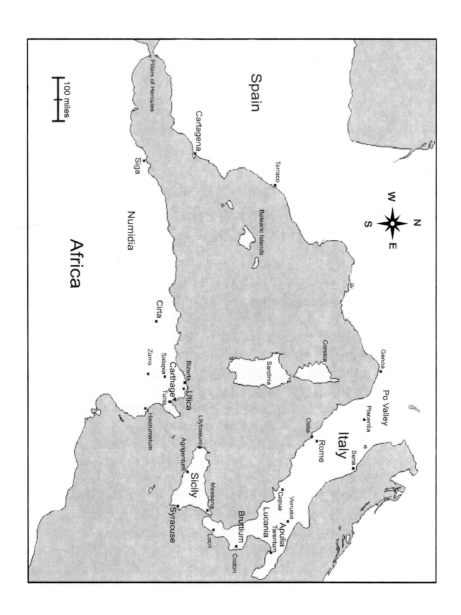

Western Mediterranean

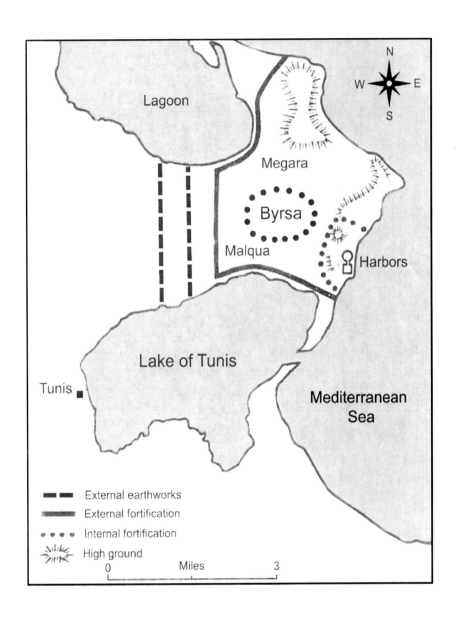

The City of Carthage

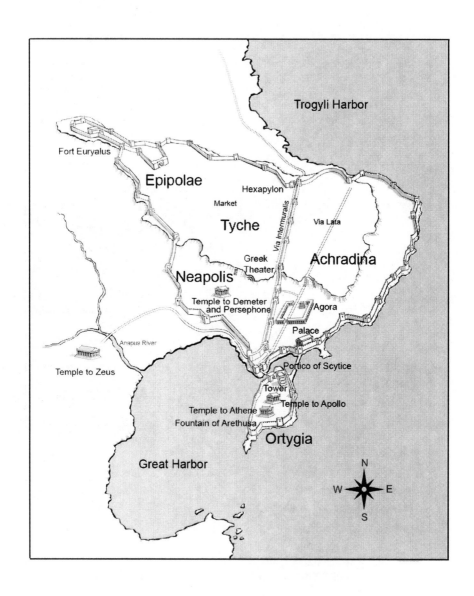

The City of Syracuse

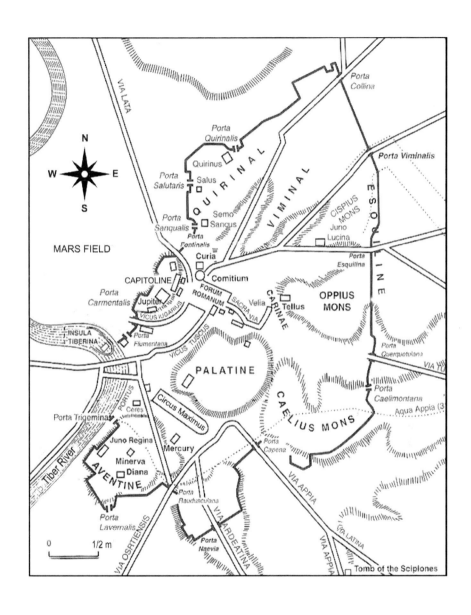

The City of Rome

PROLOGUE

I, Timon Leonidas, am now nearly seventy years old. I have spent most of my life as a mapmaker, but I have also managed to write three books recounting my experiences during the sixteen years of Rome's second war with Carthage. In the first book, *The Siege of Syracuse*, I described how my father was killed by Carthaginian agents when I was thirteen, and that my mother and I were taken from our home in Croton and sold into slavery. My mother, Arathia, ended up in Rome. I was shipped to the city of Syracuse on the island of Sicily. Despite my father's death and my kidnapping, I was fortunate even in tragedy. My master for three years was the Greek mathematician Archimedes of Syracuse, a kind man, as old then as I am now, who enabled me to greatly advance my knowledge of mathematics and geometry.

Syracuse was under siege by the Roman army during the last two years of my time with Archimedes. When the Carthaginian-controlled city finally fell, Archimedes was killed. Yet again, fortune was with me. The Roman general Marcus Claudius Marcellus took the time to question me about my master rather than turn me over to his soldiers as plunder. Marcellus immediately understood that I had learned quite a bit of science from Archimedes and gave me my freedom in exchange for tutoring his son and taking a position in the Roman army as a scribe.

In the second book, *The Death of Marcellus*, I described my first three years in Rome, my search for my mother, and three difficult military campaigns in the service of Marcellus during his fateful pursuit of the now mythic Carthaginian field marshal Hannibal Barca.

This third book covers the five years following my time with Marcellus. Two of those years were spent in Italy, prior to my going to Africa to accompany Publius Cornelius Scipio in his quest to defeat Hannibal and end the war.

I would never have thought to write these books if not for a gift I received from Archimedes. More than a mathematician, Archimedes was a remarkable inventor and engineer. His war machines were all that kept the Roman army at bay during the early months of the siege.

The day Archimedes died, he gave me two lenses, one a clear crystal disk the size of my palm, the other a bead of glass the size and shape of a lentil. The lenses were a product of his work in optics, something I had been intimately involved in. When used together, the lenses vastly improved one's eyesight. The cuts and grooves in the bark of a tree became visible from a hundred feet away. The moon seemed to drop out of the sky to within arm's reach. As intimidating as Archimedes' weapons were, the power suggested by the two lenses was arguably greater, speaking to a higher more arcane use of science. Archimedes understood this, and in his final days did not believe humankind was ready for either his weapons or the lenses. When he gave them to me, it was with a promise not to reveal them to anyone unless my life depended on it.

During my three years with Marcellus, I kept the lenses secret even though they would have had military value to this man I greatly respected and to whom I owed my freedom. Like a miser with the key to a strongbox filled with treasure, I refused to use that key when many I knew were needy.

Marcellus met his death in an ambush. I was there. Afterward I understood that I could have prevented the ambush and saved a great man's life if I had used the lenses. But I didn't. In fact, I had become so accustomed to keeping the lenses secret, it never entered my mind—until after the tragedy, and then with deep anguish and guilt, as though I were personally responsible for Marcellus' death.

The happenstance of Marcellus' death and my error of omission convinced me to break my promise to Archimedes. It was not a sudden decision. I stewed over it many months after the ambush. The entire time the two lenses hung in a leather pouch on a cord around my neck like a millstone, heavy with the weight of some terrible responsibility that I could no longer bear.

This third book is as much about the lead up to the battle of Zama that ended the war as it is about the difficulty of revealing a remarkable and powerful secret. I didn't rush out and tell everyone I knew so that I could achieve sudden fame or influence. No, this is a story about revealing something that to most would appear to be magic or some kind of trick. It had to be done with care and discretion. The taboo, my promise to Archimedes, had, in my mind, been lifted. I would open that strongbox, but I would only use the treasure in instances of absolute necessity or clear purpose.

PART I

MESSAGE FROM CROTON

"Vision, in my view, is the cause of the greatest benefit to us, inasmuch as none of the accounts now given concerning the universe would ever have been given if men had not seen the stars or the sun or the heavens. But as it is, the vision of day and night and of months and circling years has created the art of numbers and has given us not only the notion of time but also means of research into the nature of the universe."

-Plato

CHAPTER 1

I had never seen the streets of Rome so quiet. Even the Roman forum seemed subdued as I headed east across the city from the Altar of Concord to the Temple of Vesta in a light rain. Rome's war with Carthage was entering its eleventh year with no end in sight. Both consuls for the year, Marcus Claudius Marcellus and Titus Quinctius Crispinus, had been killed during the summer. Never before had two consuls died in a single season of combat. The populace read this as the worst kind of omen. Rumors in the street of Hannibal's brother's imminent arrival in Italy were as prevalent as widows of the war. Not since the Carthaginian victory at Cannae had the level of fear in the Roman people been so great.

After three years in Rome, I called it my home. I was twenty-one and stayed on a farm west of the city, owned by my friend Marcus Claudius, the son of the recently deceased consul. I had taken to wearing a toga, and now that it was winter, also with an unbleached wool himation draped over my shoulders.

I had returned to Rome in October from what had been Marcellus' last military campaign. Three anxious months had passed since then, as I waited for word from my mother, who had promised to contact me in the fall. Our last communication had been in July when I had learned she was traveling with Hannibal's army as a singer, to entertain the great general himself and act as a Roman spy. My only break from worrying about my mother and the somber mood in the Claudian household following Marcellus' tragic death, was the tutoring I did once a week. That was my destination on this day. I was going to a home on the east side of the Palatine Hill to teach geometry to the daughter of a wealthy Roman aristocrat.

Teaching fifteen-year-old Sempronia geometry was both a delight and something short of torture. I had met her two years earlier and had fallen for her immediately. By the third tutoring session, it was clear she had also taken a liking to me. Our class difference—her being the daughter of a patrician, me being a landless Greek only three years out of slavery—meant our relationship could never be more than teacher and student. It was something we both understood but never openly discussed, mostly because we were always chaperoned when we were together.

Sempronia's home was as luxurious as any in Rome. I knocked on the door and was greeted by the housemaid Dora. I could smell the fragrance of juniper burning in the braziers the moment I entered. I followed Dora into the atrium, where decoratively painted, two-story columns circuited a large, tile-lined pool containing water lilies and carp. Wall hangings from Corinth and Cyrene adorned the walls, along with some twenty wax masks—imagines—cast from past members of the Sempronian clan. Sempronia sat on a stone bench out of the rain beside a brazier. Although she didn't smile, her eyes lit up upon seeing me, and I did my best to similarly contain my reaction to seeing her.

"Timon!" squawked Ajax from the corner of the atrium, followed by the parrot's piercing array of whistles and chirps.

Dora, who would stay with us throughout the lesson, quickly covered the bird cage, then busied herself sweeping. I sat down beside Sempronia with my wax pad, a compass, a straightedge, and a bronze stylus. By some unstated agreement, we both tried to downplay how much we enjoyed our time together. Sempronia was a fabulous student, and if we had no other life together, the abstract world of plane geometry was our platonic sanctuary.

"What are our lessons about today?" Sempronia asked, glancing into my eyes briefly, before looking down at her lap.

"We'll use a compass to bisect an angle," I said. "It's one of the most basic and useful geometric constructions there is."

Sempronia watched as I demonstrated. I used the bronze stylus and the straightedge to etch two intersecting lines on the surface of my wax pad. I labeled the point of intersection with the letter "A." I set the compass to an arbitrary width and swung an arc from point A that crossed both legs of the angle created by the two lines. I labeled the points of intersection "B" and "C." I then swung an arc from each of those two points so that they intersected in the area between the two legs. I labeled that point "D."

"If I use the straightedge to connect point A to point D," I said, "the line AD will bisect the angle BAC. Can you see that?"

Sempronia nodded. "Angle BAD equals angle CAD."

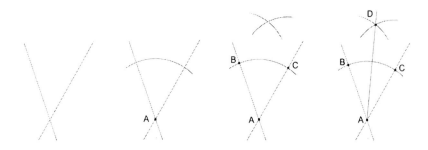

"Exactly." I smoothed the surface of the wax. "Now you do it."

As I handed her the pad and the tools, my hand touched hers. Our eyes met and held, as though we were sharing the most daring of intimacies. Sempronia blushed, lowered her eyes, then without any hesitation executed the simple construction. "That was easy," she said. "What's next?"

"Proving why that works. It's likely to take us the rest of the lesson."

During the process of going through the proof, we exchanged the wax pad several times, talking only about the geometry, but also writing short personal comments in the wax and allowing our hands to touch, however slightly, each time we passed the pad back and forth. Dora, across the garden, appeared to be deep into her cleaning and didn't seem to notice.

I etched *How are you?* in the wax.

The question brought a sadness to Sempronia's blue eyes and she wrote, *My mother spends too much of her time trying to find me a husband.*

Is that so bad? I wrote back, thinking just the opposite.

It's awful. No one will have me. Word has gotten out that I was rejected as a Vestal Virgin.

Sempronia had been selected to be one of the six Vestal Virgins a year earlier. Although this was a highly regarded honor, the pontifex maximus had chosen her as a way to deliberately block Sempronia's marriage to his political adversary's son Marcus Claudius. It was nothing more than spite. In the end, neither the marriage nor the induction to the Vestals occurred, but the rumor passed among the upper class that Sempronia was damaged goods—though she was, in fact, a virgin.

I knew the story too well, and when tears began to form in her eyes, I couldn't help myself. I leaned over and whispered, "I would marry you."

Though we both knew that was impossible, Sempronia allowed a slight smile, then kissed me lightly on the cheek, something that had never happened before.

Before my heart could leap out of my chest, Dora tromped across the atrium to where we were sitting. "What's going on here?" she demanded.

"Nothing, Dora. We're working on a proof," replied Sempronia.

Dora snatched the pad from my hand and saw what Sempronia had written. "The lesson is over," snapped Dora. "Sempronia, I will talk to your mother about this later." She glared at me. "Timon, you must leave."

Despite Sempronia's protests, Dora, who had clearly seen the kiss, escorted me through the house and out the front door, slamming it behind me for emphasis.

CHAPTER 2

I spent the next week helping Marcus with work at the farm. I went into Rome at the appointed time for the next tutoring session, not really certain what to expect. When Dora opened the door, she acted like she didn't know me.

"What are you here for?"

"I've come to give Sempronia her geometry lesson."

"There will be no more lessons. Her mother has canceled the tutoring." She started to slam the door, but I caught it with my hand.

"Can I talk to Sempronia? What does she think about this?"

"What Sempronia thinks means nothing. It's her mother's decision. There will be no more tutoring. Now please leave."

I didn't remove my hand from the door. Dora glared at me. I wanted to storm past her into the house, but instead backed away from the door stunned. Head down, a knot in my stomach, I walked across the city to get my horse. Since Marcellus' death a rift had grown between Marcus and his mother Portia. Marcus tended to stay at the villa on the farm, and Portia stayed at the Claudian residence in the city. When I came into Rome, that was where I stabled Balius.

I passed through the forum, oblivious to the speakers, then headed south past the Circus Maximus along the base of the Aventine Hill. Just before I reached the Claudian residence, I felt a hand on my shoulder.

I abruptly turned around hoping that Sempronia had escaped from her home and come running after me. Instead I saw the smirking face of Quintus Ennius, the skinny and often drunk poet, who always pestered me for a spare coin.

"Timon, I can't believe I found you so easily."

I was in no mood for Ennius or his silliness. "My means of employment has ended, Quintus. I have no money. Please leave me alone."

"Caelius wants a word with you." He looked over his shoulder, suddenly growing serious. "Come to the Community of Miracles tonight. It will be worth your while."

"I live out of town, Quintus. I can't make it." I turned away from him and continued on my way.

He hurried after me. "There's a message for you," he said as he drew up alongside of me, skipping sideways to keep up and smelling of stale wine. "Something I think you might like to know."

"Like what?"

Ennius always did this, taunting me with little secrets he might know, all leading to his needing a quadrans to buy a drink. Again he looked around as though someone might be watching. "I can't say. Just be there."

Still striding along, I faced him. "Give me one reason."

He grinned. "I can't. Caelius doesn't give reasons. I'm not in the need to know."

I stepped in front of him, bringing us both to a halt. "Know about what?"

Ennius made a face. "I've said too much already. Just be there."

"What do you mean? You haven't told me anything."

"That should tell you everything." He laughed, then darted off down the street. "I'll see you tonight," he called over his shoulder.

"No you won't," I muttered to myself before resuming on my way. But the more I thought about it, the more I wondered what message Caelius could possibly have for me.

The Community of Miracles was a collection of artists, thieves, and small time gamblers. Caelius was the ringleader. He dealt in stolen property and covered his dirty dealings by using the street theater in the Community of Miracles as a front. He was little more than a racketeer and a shakedown artist, but eight months earlier he had been instrumental in helping me find my mother. This memory made me pause.

What did Ennius mean? *He had said too much already.* All he had told me was that he was *not in the need to know.* Was there something suggested in that phrase that I should be aware of? Or was it more of Ennius' silly word play?

When I reached the Claudian residence, I went directly to the stable. Balius was in one of the stalls. I stood beside him and stroked his flank lost in thought.

Ithius, an elderly house slave and a fellow Greek, teetered into the stable. "Timon, what brings you into Rome? I saw Balius was here and was hoping to catch you before you left. How is Marcus? I never see him."

"Hello, Ithius. It's been too long." I embraced him as I would a favorite uncle. "Marcus has sunk into himself. We hardly talk. I keep expecting him to come out of his melancholy, but it hasn't happened yet."

Ithius nodded. "He's becoming more like his father. Single-minded and closed in upon himself. He hasn't been here since the funeral."

"Is Portia in the house? I was thinking of staying in Rome for the night. I could sleep in the stable."

"There's a room inside that's available, Timon. Talk to Portia. She's in the atrium. I'm sure she'll be glad to see you."

I had my own issues with Marcus' mother, but I went into the house anyway. I found Portia standing beside the atrium pool staring at the surface of the water. She looked up at me as though lost in thought, then smiled. "Hello, Timon. What brings you here?"

"I came into town to tutor Sempronia."

"How did the lesson go?" Portia was a beautiful woman, forty years old, tall, willowy, and widowed now six months. She wore a plain wool stola, with a heavy wrap over her shoulders. She had no paint on her face, and her brunette hair was pulled up in a bun on top of her head.

"Fulvia canceled it. That's why I stopped by. I wondered if you'd heard anything."

"No, this is news to me. But I do know Fulvia's getting impatient in her search to find Sempronia a husband. It's causing some tension between us. She's still angry that Marcus canceled the wedding, and I'm afraid she holds me partially to blame." She shook her head. "It wasn't me or Marcus. It was Livinius. I wish Fulvia could make that distinction."

"But she hasn't said anything about me?"

Portia tilted her head. "Not specifically, but I do know she's concerned that Sempronia thinks too much of you."

I thought of the incident the previous week.

"And that you might think too much of her," continued Portia.

I bowed my head, then looked up. "But she wouldn't cancel the lessons for that, would she?"

"She might." Portia was a complex woman. I had been totally captivated by her beauty and intelligence when I first met her, but now after three years, I knew she was too capable of intrigue and secrets.

"Do you mind if I stay here tonight? Maybe Fulvia will have changed her mind by tomorrow."

"I have no idea about that, Timon. But you're welcome to stay."

I remained in Rome that night, but I had no intention of going back to Sempronia's home the next day. After everyone else had gone to bed, I slipped out of the house and went to the Community of Miracles at the top of the Aventine Hill.

The night was especially dark. Clouds hid the stars and moon. Rome was always risky after the sun went down, the Community of Miracles more so. I had only been there twice before, and I didn't trust Ennius as far as I could throw him, but Caelius wasn't called the King of the Crooks for nothing. He had surely sent Ennius after me for a reason. I had no idea what it was, but it had been too long since I had heard from my mother, and Caelius often knew about things no one else did.

I carried a small dagger tucked into the folds of my toga and wound my way up the side of the Aventine Hill to the Temple of Minerva. I entered an alley behind the temple and followed it into a courtyard lit by torches and surrounded by rundown tenement buildings. The scene never changed. Every street poet, actor, minstrel, and common thief made a point of stopping by the Community of Miracles at least once during the night. True to form, the place was filled with the usual carnival abandon of frantic dancers, jugglers, prostitutes, and sots.

I hoped to avoid Ennius by going straight to Caelius. He held court in a little room behind the community's makeshift theater. Three drunks commanded the stage spouting lines from Euripides as I made my way through the throng of misfits.

"I knew you'd be here," slurred Ennius who staggered up to me just as I reached the curtain leading into Caelius' den of iniquity.

"Things changed," I said. "I had to stay in Rome so I thought I might as well see what Caelius has to say."

Ennius brayed like a donkey. "I don't believe a word of it. You know as well as I do that nothing in this world is as it seems. Black is white, and white is black. The wisest men in Rome aren't in the Senate. They're up here playing dice with Caelius. This is where the real business of Rome takes place."

"I thought that happened in the brothels." I pushed past Ennius and slipped beneath the sailcloth curtain into the shadowy chamber. Three torches on wooden staves provided a minimum of light. The place stunk of body odor and burning pitch. Caelius didn't notice me come in. He was on his knees on the floor, wearing a crown of cat skulls and commanding the attention of a ring of dice throwers, also on their knees. Behind them stood an unsavory crowd, waiting for a spot in the circle or simply taking advantage of the excess of bitter wine that sloshed around the room in cups and overfilled bellies.

I edged up close to Caelius, waiting for him to notice me. He shook a pair of cubed bones in his right hand and glowered at his fellow gamblers. "I've got one as against ten that my next roll shows matching dice." Caelius pushed a bronze coin into the center of a circle drawn in the dirt.

As usual Caelius was the banker, setting the odds every time a throw was made. A scruffy looking man with his goatskin cap pulled so low over his brow that I couldn't see his eyes pushed a stack of eight asses up alongside Caelius' one. "How about eight, you crook? Is that enough advantage for you?"

"Drop it to seven," said a man cloaked in shadows, "and I'll take a chance."

"I said ten," growled Caelius, scratching at his gray-streaked beard. "But I'll take eight. Who's in?"

The man who had asked for seven pushed in eight. The man beside him got a nudge from the woman standing behind him, and he did the same.

Caelius dropped a coin beside each of their stacks. He blew on the dice, then gave them a shake, calling out, "Any pair will do!" The entire room seemed to draw in its collective breath as he tossed the dice into the circle. One die stopped with a four uppermost, the other a three.

Caelius cursed as the three gamblers drew their winnings out of the circle. "See that, eight wasn't enough. Make it nine and we'll try it again!"

The seven grim gamblers around the circle eyed each other and fiddled with the coins before them. The three winners pushed out stacks of nine asses. Two of the others did the same. Caelius looked around the circle and grinned like he knew something no one else did. "One more roll. Win or lose, I'm gonna take a little break."

The only woman in the circle, though it was hard to tell with her head covered by a rough woolen cowl, peered out of the folds of cloth around her face, glanced at me, then held up a single bronze coin. "How about just one as, Caelius?" she queried. "If it's stamped with Hannibal's face?"

Everyone had heard the rumor that Hannibal was minting his own coins to pay his mercenaries, but few had ever seen one. All quieted to hear what Caelius would say.

"Let me see it." Caelius reached out to take the coin from the woman. "You sure that's what it is? Where'd you get it?"

"A friend in Croton," she said with a second quick glance at me.

That was when I recognized her. It was the same woman who had told me the previous spring that my mother was traveling with a group of pickers and that she was looking for me.

Caelius turned the coin over in his hand. "How do you know this is Hannibal? I have no idea what he looks like."

Whispers passed around the crowd. *Has anyone here ever seen Hannibal?*

"I have," I said suddenly, recalling the two times I had seen him with the aid of my two lenses. I moved up close to the circle. "I can tell you if it's him or not."

Caelius had only met me twice before, but his eyes glittered with recognition as soon as I spoke. He handed me the coin with a knowing grin. "This him?"

I took the coin and held it beneath the nearest torch. One side of the coin was engraved with the image of a date palm with a horse lying beneath it. The other side showed the profile of a man wearing a helmet in the style that Hercules had worn. It was impossible to say if it actually resembled Hannibal, but I wanted to talk to the woman who owned the coin. "That's him," I said with more certainty than I had.

Caelius looked at the woman, then placed the coin in the circle. "Fine. It's mine if I can match the dice." He pulled back the sleeves of his fleece robe, made a big show of talking to the dice, blew on them, then bounced them across the dirt. Breaths sucked in then expelled as the dice came to a stop. "Six and six," bellowed the King of the Crooks. He reached out with both hands to rake in the stacks of coins.

The other gamblers groaned and stood up. They milled around, complaining to each other about the last roll, then gradually drifted out of the chamber. I found myself alone with Caelius and the old woman. She had moved back into the shadows, clearly waiting for the others to leave. Her eyes, little sparks of light beneath her cloak, darted from side to side, then she approached me, drawing Caelius up alongside.

"You are Timon?" she asked.

"Yes."

Caelius nodded as verification.

"I remember you," she said. "Go to Croton, Timon. Go to the house that was your home."

"Will my mother be there?" I gasped.

"That's more than I know."

As she turned away to leave, I touched her on the shoulder. "What is your name, kind woman? You helped me before. How can I thank you if I don't know who to thank?"

"I have no name." She looked at Caelius. "Caelius knows how to find me if there's any thanking to do. I must go."

"And I have more money to win," stated Caelius. He glanced at me and opened his hand, revealing two dice. Six spots were on all twelve sides. He winked. "Who but a fool would throw bones with a man known as the King of the Crooks?"

CHAPTER 3

I rode Balius back to the farm the next morning. Edeco met me at the stable. The former king of Spain's Edantani tribe, fifteen years a slave, greeted me with only a nod of his head, then held the reins of my horse, allowing me to dismount.

"Where's Marcus?" I asked.

"Pruning in the apple orchard. He's likely to be there all day."

I wanted some time to think, so I decided to wait until evening to talk to Marcus instead of tracking him down on the farm. Although the message I had received the previous night held no promise of seeing my mother, going back to Croton, specifically to the house where I had grown up, had to have something to do with her. With the cancelation of the tutoring, I had no reason to stay in Rome except an unstated commitment to make maps for the Roman army. By the middle of the afternoon, I had decided to go to Croton. I had nothing to lose, and what could be more important than finding my mother?

Marcus came in from the apple orchard at dusk. I didn't get a chance to talk to him until we both sat down for dinner in the triclinium. Meda, the Thracian housemaid and cook, served the meal— two small roasted chickens, boiled chickpeas, a loaf of rye bread, and a bowl of mulsum.

With Portia living in town, only the two of us were at the table. Marcus, who had been so open and outgoing when I had first met him, had retreated into himself since his father's death. I had tutored him in geometry for three years. We used to have long conversations about science and philosophy, but the tutoring had stopped after that tragic day in Apulia. Now we passed much of our time together in silence.

Marcus dipped his cup in the bowl of mulsum, then put one of the birds on his plate. I gave him a chance to get some food and wine down before opening the conversation that had been on my mind all day.

14

"I'm leaving Rome," I said after he had devoured about half of his chicken and drained a cup of wine. I lounged on the couch directly opposite him. A single oil lamp burned on the table between us.

He pulled a wing from the carcass on his plate and looked up at me. "What do you mean, leaving Rome? Aren't you still in the army?"

"I'm not a Roman citizen. I have no commitment to the military other than year to year. I want to go back to Croton."

"That's a Carthaginian controlled city. That's like going into a hornet's nest. What could possibly be there for you but trouble?" He put the entire wing in his mouth, then pulled out the bone, drawing the meat off with his teeth.

"My mother."

"Didn't you tell me she was dead?" He dropped the bone on the plate and used his fingers to pull free a breast.

"I was deceived. I'm not certain where she is or even if she's alive, but what I was told before was a lie. I'm going back to my home on the off chance that she could be there." I had no intention of telling Marcus about my trip to the Community of Miracles.

"You said she was a slave in Rome. Why would you think she's in Croton?" He took a bite from the breast. "Seems foolish to me."

"I never knew anything for certain, Marcus. Only rumors. This is just another instance where I'm guessing as much as hoping."

Marcus took a swallow of mulsum. "That's a long way to travel on a hunch."

"I know that." I watched him lift a piece of skin from his plate. "I was wondering if I could take Balius?"

Marcus looked up. "He's yours. Do as you please."

His tone put me off. I considered him my best friend. Telling him I was leaving wasn't easy, but he didn't seem to care one way or the other. "Thank you," I said.

"Don't thank me. My father gave you that horse." He went back to eating.

I had lost my appetite. I wanted to walk away from the table. Instead I nibbled at the food and drank too much wine. I told Marcus I would be leaving in two days. "If I don't locate my mother, I'll come back to Rome."

"You're welcome here anytime." Despite the words, he said them with no emotion. His ambivalence saddened me. By the next day I had convinced myself that I was glad to be leaving.

CHAPTER 4

I went into Rome the next day to tell Ithius that I was going to Croton. When I reached the house, I saw Rullo and Julia, the twelve-year-old son and six-year-old daughter of Laelia, Portia's longtime Insubrian house slave. They were behind the stable, sword fighting with sticks. The unstated household secret was that Rullo was Marcus' illegitimate son. Although Rullo had Laelia's blond hair and blue eyes, I could see Marcus in his brow and jaw line. I waved at the children, but neither of them noticed me as Rullo lunged at his sister, poking her in the stomach with his stick, causing her to fall on her behind. I expected her to start crying, but she scrambled to her feet and went at her brother with twice the ferocity she had shown before.

I found Ithius in the peristyle watering the garden. "I'm going to Croton," I said when he looked up. "I'll be leaving tomorrow."

"What's in Croton?"

"It's where I grew up. I want to see if any of my relatives are still there."

"How are you traveling?"

"On Balius."

"Alone?"

I nodded.

"Do you know how dangerous that is, Timon?"

"After three campaigns with the Roman army, Ithius, I think I'm capable of taking care of myself. Besides, I already know many of the roads from my mapmaking. You needn't worry about me."

"But I will." He shook his head. "When might you return?"

"No telling."

"But you will be back?" he said wistfully.

"If only to see you," I laughed, then embraced him. "I thought I should let you know before I left."

"I appreciate that, Timon. May fortune be with you."

16

Despite my decision to leave, I still struggled with my feelings for Sempronia and the way the tutoring had been canceled so suddenly. In a fit of desperation, I went to Sempronia's home that afternoon. Instead of knocking on the front door, I slipped down the alley between her house and the neighbor's and climbed the fence that enclosed the back portion of the property.

I hid at the back of the yard watching the slaves come and go. I saw Dora leave the slaves' quarters and enter the house, then I saw Sempronia. She came out to the peristyle and sat on the bench where we had reviewed geometry lessons for two years. I crept up close to the colonnade that circuited the peristyle, and slipping from behind one column to the next, got close enough to Sempronia to get her attention with a whisper. I was about to say her name when I noticed Ajax in his birdcage at the edge of the atrium. If he saw me, he was certain to squawk my name and announce my presence to the entire household.

I picked up a small rock and tossed it into the rose bush beside Sempronia. The rustling sound made her stand up and look around. I tossed another stone. Sempronia peered into the rose bush, then came out of the peristyle.

She let out a soft gasp when she saw me, then her eyes hardened. "What are you doing here? Leave now or I will call the slaves to have you thrown out."

"But Sempronia..."

"No, go away. I want nothing to do with you."

"What's happened? I understand why your mother might object, but not you."

"Go," she demanded, "or I'll scream."

"Please, give me some kind of answer. What has happened?"

Sempronia pinched her face into a expression of disgust. "My mother told me about your performance at Portia's gatherings. You exposed yourself before all the women, then had sex with one of them as part of a ritual. Does that explain it?"

She spun away from me, but I caught her by the hand. "Did she tell you why?"

Sempronia pulled away from my grasp. "How could that matter? It's disgusting just talking about it."

"Something more important than my honor was at stake." I opened my toga to reveal the leather pouch that hung from my neck.

"I had lost this pouch—and what's in it changes the way we see things, and provides as important an insight into the physical world as there's ever been."

"More important than the Pythagorean Theorem?" she said with derision.

"Let me show you, and then you can tell me if what I did was a mistake." She watched me as I pried open the little pouch and withdrew the two lenses. This was not how I envisioned breaking my promise to Archimedes, but in some ways my life was at stake. I loved this woman and knew I could never be happy without her in my life—at least as a friend.

"A couple pieces of glass, Timon? That's it?"

"Yes, but wait until you see what they can do. They were gifts to me from Archimedes." I held out the larger lens. "Look at your hand through this." I demonstrated how to hold it.

She pushed it away. "No, go! Now! I want nothing to do with you. You're not who you've pretended to be. You're a dirty Greek with no modesty and no morals."

"I have no morals?" I spat back at her, losing my temper. "What about your mother? Did she tell you that the woman I had sex with was her?"

Sempronia covered her mouth in horror, then screamed at me. "That's a lie. That's a lie."

"Ask her. See if she'll deny it."

"I won't stoop to such a thing. Get out of here. I never want to see you again."

"Don't worry," I shouted at her in growing anger. "I'm going to Croton tomorrow—hopefully for good!"

Our loud voices could not be missed. Ajax began to squawk, and Dora called out from inside the house. "Sempronia! What's going on? Who's out there with you?"

I could hear the housemaid coming through the peristyle. I darted to the back of the property, hopped the fence, and ran down the adjacent alley. When I finally stopped, I put the lenses back in the pouch and began to cry. I had just made everything ten times worse.

CHAPTER 5

They say Italy is shaped like a boot. Croton is located on the instep, three hundred miles south of Rome, and deep into territory controlled by Hannibal. Most of the journey could be made on paved roads, the majority of it on Via Latina. A fast, experienced rider could complete the trip in six days if everything went well. I hoped to do it in ten.

I filled a pack with the necessities, a blanket, a leather water bag, my drawing equipment, a small tent, a sack of wheat, a few pieces of salted pork, and some dried fruit. That would be enough for me, but traveling in January meant forage for Balius would be a constant concern. I wore a linen tunic, my goatskin cap, and a wool himation over my shoulders. I kept all the money I had—ten asses and two silver denarii—in a girdle that I wrapped around my waist beneath the tunic.

Edeco met me at the stable shortly after dawn. He wished me well but said little else. Marcus had said nothing more since the night I told him I was leaving, but he came out of the house just as I was climbing onto Balius.

"Have a safe trip, Timon," he said, walking up beside Balius. He handed me a small pouch. "This might help."

I looked into the pouch. It contained two more silver denarii. "That's overly generous, Marcus. Thank you."

"You'll need money to feed Balius. And be aware that he'll be considered more valuable than you to the sorts of travelers you're likely to encounter. Taking your life for your horse will mean nothing to the desperate."

"Edeco said the same thing to me earlier. I'll treat Balius with utmost care."

"I'm sure you will. I hope you find what you're looking for."

"We'll see. If by some chance I don't see you again, please remember me as fondly as I do you and your family."

Marcus nodded, then patted Balius on the flank as I gave the reins a shake and headed on my way.

The morning was cold and the sky clear. The day warmed as the winter sun climbed overhead and I made my way south on Via Latina. The movement of large armies had left the countryside pockmarked and muddy. Broken stretches of fence traced across the land like stitching. Most of the farms I passed were vacant and had not been tended in years. The homes and outbuildings were falling apart or had been burned down. The fields offered nothing but weeds in big clumps and knots. Hannibal's marauding army had used Italy's abundant harvest as their personal pantry for ten years now and it showed.

I made a lot of miles the first four days, passing through Campania and into Lucania to the edge of enemy territory. Late in the afternoon of each day, I would seek out an empty farm building to stay for the night. One night I stayed with a farmer and his wife. I paid them generously for some oats and hay for Balius.

The morning of my fifth day on the road I woke to a light, but cold rain. Midafternoon the wind started to blow and the rain grew heavy. I began my search for a place to spend the night long before dark. I saw a thin trail of smoke rising above a farmhouse in the distance and decided to try the farmer's hospitality. As I guided Balius across a field in mud up to his forelocks, I noted the poor condition of the land and the absence of any livestock. The farmer might be living on the property, but he wasn't doing any farming. I hoped there was at least some leftover hay for Balius.

When I got close, I dismounted and walked Balius toward the small, windowless, mud brick house with a roof in need of thatching. I passed two small lean-to storage sheds and peered inside looking for any trace of animal feed. I saw nothing but spider webs and thistle. Before I got to the doorstep, I heard men's voices inside and stopped short. On the far side of the building stood four crooked crosses. Shreds of clothing blew in the wind over the rattling skeletal remains of the crucified. Whoever was in the house was likely to be squatters, not a family.

The door to the house swung open. A large man with a long, ragged beard, wearing the worn tunic of a Roman soldier, came out. He took one look at me and called into the house to others. I judged the situation to be dangerous immediately and turned to climb onto

Balius just as the man bolted from the doorstep, followed by three other rough-looking men. The first man had hold of Balius' reins before I could mount. The others took hold of me. Balius began to buck, trying to pull away, but the man held tight to his reins. The other three men dragged me into the house, then threw me on the dirt floor. I yanked the pugio from my belt and backed into a corner. The men glowered at me with eyes blank with hunger, daring me to come at them.

The fourth man stomped back into the house. "That godless horse broke away from me and ran off."

One of the other men cursed him, calling him Gaius.

Gaius glared at me. "What are you doing here?" I noticed he had only two fingers on his right hand and a long, white scar on his face.

"I'm a Roman levy just like you are," I said. "I'm traveling on my own between campaigns."

All four of the men laughed. "Who said we were soldiers," said one of them.

"Your friend's tunic."

This caused even more laughter. They were deserters on the run, the most desperate kind of men.

"Take the knife from him before he hurts someone," ordered Gaius.

I tossed the pugio on the floor, knowing I had no chance to defend myself. "If it's food you want, everything I had to eat was on that horse you chased away."

One of the men picked up the knife and moved up close to me, threatening to use it. "Food?" The man laughed, a hollow, humorless laugh, with breath heavily laced with the smell of rotting teeth. "We'd be butchering your horse right now if it hadn't gotten away."

"And you, Greek, you're the closest thing to meat we've got," snarled another of the men.

The others joined in with more ugly laughter. Gaius cut it short. "Search him. He had a horse. He must have some money. Then take him outside and have him call for his horse. Maybe it will come back."

"I have some money," I said, knowing they would find it one way or the other. I pulled the belt from beneath my tunic. "Take it."

I tossed the cloth belt at the man with my dagger. He tore it open and all coins fell on the floor. As Gaius stood back to watch the others scrambling around on their hands and knees gathering up the coins, I made a dash for the door. Gaius stuck out his foot and caught my ankle. I went flying headlong across the room. He came over and placed his knee in the center of my back, pinning me down. The pouch with the lenses had slid from beneath my tunic and lay beside me. Gaius snatched it from the floor and gave the cord a yank. It tore at my neck but didn't break. He leaned over me and pulled the cord over my head, nearly taking my ears with it. The others stood around us, eyeing each other, thinking there might be more money in the pouch.

Gaius stood up and pried the pouch open with his fingers. He looked inside, then to his fellow deserters. "How much money did he have?"

"Show us what's in the pouch first," said one of them.

"Suck Jupiter's ass, Titus," snapped Gaius. "What have you got? All of you."

I sat up as the men glared at each other. One of the men was small and wiry with bow legs and some gray in his hair. Gaius was maybe forty and a huge man, square in the chest and thick in the hips. Titus was not much smaller but several years younger. He held my knife. The fourth was blond, tall, gaunt, and probably not twenty years old. All of them were dirty and reeked. None of them had shaved in weeks.

The smallest of the men opened his hand revealing three asses. The blonde followed suit and showed an as and one of my denarii, meaning Titus had what remained. He fixed a defiant stare at Gaius. "What's in the pouch?"

Gaius wore a gladius at his hip. Titus held my pugio. If they went at each other, I was going for the door.

Gaius shook his head. "This is nothing." He withdrew the crystal disk from the pouch. "It's a piece of glass." Apparently he hadn't noticed the bead at the bottom of the pouch. He tossed both the pouch and the disk on the floor. I watched the disk roll across the dirt, cut two wide circles, then wobble, and fall on its side a few feet from the hearth.

"Your turn, Titus," said the blonde.

Titus' eyes flashed around the group, then he opened his hand. "Three silver staters," he said with a wink. "And four asses. I guess I got lucky," he smirked.

Gaius frowned. "I see eight asses and four denarii. That's two asses and a denarius for each of us."

"Yeah," said the blonde. The wiry man echoed the same.

Titus hesitated, then said, "Fine."

Instead of fighting over it, they pushed me into a corner to divide it up. When they were done, they ripped a sackcloth bag that was lying on the floor into strips and tied my hands behind my back and hobbled my feet, then led me out into the yard. It was nearly dark and the rain was harder than ever. They told me to call my horse. I called out the name *Mathos*. With the wind and rain, I doubt my voice carried very far.

When Balius didn't return, they stripped the bones from one of the crosses and tied me to the crucifix. They left me there in the wind and rain for the night and went back into the house.

The rain stopped early in the morning. Soon afterward, the sun made a hesitant appearance through the clouds. The four men took a brief look around for Balius then got ready to leave. Only the blonde bothered to check on me. I pleaded for him to let me down. He spat on me then joined the others as they headed out into the weed-filled fields and disappeared from sight.

I was sure I would die there on that cross. With little other hope, I called out for Balius until I was hoarse. I lapsed into some state between sleep and unconsciousness for I don't know how long.

I woke with a nudging at my side and a whinny. Balius stood beside the crucifix. I was so glad to see him I began to cry. But even with him there, I was still stuck on the cross. With no idea how I could get Balius to help me, I asked him outright. "If you can, Balius, pull at the rags around my feet."

And sure enough Balius gave the rags at my ankles a sniff. After a moment, he pulled the sackcloth free with his teeth, then chewed it up and swallowed it. He freed my right wrist next, which left me dangling from the cross by one arm. By kicking my feet and swinging back and forth, I managed to tip the crucifix over. Once on the ground, I pulled off the remaining scraps of cloth, then rubbed my wrists and ankles to get some feeling in them—so I could properly stroke the forelock of my loyal friend.

I went into the house to retrieve the leather pouch and the crystal disk, which had fortunately survived without a scratch. I saw a piece of the sackcloth on the floor. No wonder Balius had chewed if off. It was leftover from a bag of oats.

CHAPTER 6

The experience with the deserters gave me second thoughts about being on the road alone. With little other choice, I rode Balius a little harder and longer each day and reached Croton at dusk two days sooner than expected. I saw the walls of the city from a distance. Memories of my childhood washed over me as I directed Balius toward the main gate, wary of the fact that the city was now controlled by the local Bruttians who had sided with Hannibal in the weeks after I was kidnapped and Croton fell. The entire toe and instep of the Italian peninsula had become a Carthaginian stronghold. Last I had heard, Hannibal wintered on the coast in Metapontum not far from Tarentum and about one hundred miles west of Croton.

Croton had once been a large and prosperous city enclosed by twelve miles of walls, but seventy years earlier, during Rome's war with Pyrrhus and the Tarentines, Croton was besieged by the Romans. The city was never the same. The river that ran through the city now split it in half—one side was inhabited, the other was a desolate wasteland.

Four guards appeared on the wall above the gate as I rode up. One called down to me, asking what my business was. I replied in the Bruttian dialect. I told them I was coming home to Croton. I had been taken as a slave six years earlier and had recently been given my freedom. I had returned hoping to find my mother.

I was an unarmed lone rider and clearly Greek. Rather than open the main gate, they directed me to a postern gate farther east along the wall. I dismounted and led Balius. A guard opened the gate from the inside.

"Things have changed in Croton since you were last here," the man said. "Most of the Greek populace was transported to Locri after the city went over to Hannibal."

"Yes, I'm aware of that. If I don't find my mother here, I plan to go to Locri."

The guard shrugged. "Just be aware that the Senate no longer makes the laws here. A military tribunal of Carthaginian officers runs everything." I thought of my time in Syracuse under similar circumstances. "Stay clear of the Carthaginian officers," continued the guard, "and you'll be fine."

I crossed the city warily, leading Balius by his reins. The friendly warmth of the Croton I had known as a child had transformed into an icy chill. Carthaginian soldiers were everywhere. The Bruttians, who had been second-class citizens when I lived there, were now the controlling populace. Greeks were far and few between. When I neared our old home, I began to hurry, certain my mother would be there. I knocked lightly on the door, then in a storm of mixed feelings, let myself into the room where I had seen my father killed. The room was empty, so I headed to the atrium and called out my mother's name.

"Who's that?" shouted back from the peristyle. Lucretia, a slave who had known me since I was an infant, came running from the garden as though she were expecting me.

I caught her in my arms and embraced her. "Do you believe we're finally home?"

Lucretia was well over fifty years old. She carried a little extra weight in her face and hips, and her hair was entirely gray, making her look like a grandmother, but her eyes remained strong and radiant. She held me at arm's length and looked into my face, tears streaming from her eyes. "It seems like a lifetime since we spoke outside the Roman camp last summer."

"Where's my mother? I must see her."

Lucretia lowered her head. "She's not here."

"Then what was the message I got?"

"That was from your mother. We didn't know if you'd received it or if you were coming."

"But where is she?"

"Metapontum."

"What?"

"Hannibal requested her company shortly after she sent the message to you. It's been three weeks."

"I don't get it. I thought he was letting her go after the campaign."

"He secured this house for her and issued an order to the garrison commander that she's to be treated with utmost care. I live here with her. And there's another slave, a young woman, Ava, who was a gift from Hannibal. She's with your mother now."

"He's given her back *our* house. That's some gift. And she goes to him whenever he demands? Lucretia, that bastard still owns her!"

Lucretia gave me a sad look. "I know it must seem strange to you, but trust your mother."

"Trust her? I want her entirely free from that Carthaginian ogre."

"But that's not what she wants. You'll have to talk to her." Lucretia looked around as though someone might be listening. She lowered her voice. "She still hopes to pass information on to the Romans."

"I know that must seem noble to her, and gives her the satisfaction that she's avenging Father's murder, but it seems too extreme and too dangerous to me."

"Then you can tell her that. She told me if you arrive while she's gone to take you to her."

"To Metapontum? What's she going to do, introduce me to Hannibal?" I said derisively.

"Yes, that's exactly what she plans to do."

CHAPTER 7

Lucretia made the travel arrangements the next day with the garrison commander. Three days later we set out for Metapontum in a two-wheel carriage, accompanied by a Carthaginian officer on horseback and ten soldiers on foot. It didn't exactly feel like we were free, but the word was that we were guests of Hannibal and that we should be treated as such. It all seemed impossible at the time, but I was about to see my mother and that was all that mattered.

We followed the coastline all the way to Metapontum. It rained the first two days of the six-day trip. We camped at night. The soldiers set up three large tents—one for the officer, one for the soldiers, and one that I shared with Lucretia. The dear woman had said almost nothing about my mother during our time in Croton, but once we began the trip, she wouldn't even mention her name, leaving me with absolutely no idea what to expect in Metapontum. As far as I knew I would end up in a prison cell.

The morning of the sixth day a squadron of Numidian cavalry, perhaps sixty riders, swarmed out of the forest alongside the road and quickly surrounded us. Hannibal always gave his Numidians free rein in the winter, allowing them to forage and plunder on their own. They were known for their brutality and their insatiable appetite for women. The way they rode up and flashed around us on their horses suggested the worst, but the officer in charge of our little party called out to them in what I imagined to be the Numidian language. The captain of the squadron of cavalry promptly acknowledged the officer, and after a short exchange with him, signaled to his charges to reassemble in formation. There had been reports of small bands of thieves in the area. The Numidians would escort us the rest of the way to Metapontum.

We reached Metapontum late that afternoon. Like Croton, or almost any city of size, it was surrounded by a formidable stone wall designed to repel an army. With the Numidian captain in the lead, the gates opened at our approach and we were soon within the city.

I had never been to Metapontum, but my father had spoken about it many times. Like Croton, Metapontum was a Greek colony, older than either Rome or Syracuse. Legend said it had been founded by the man who built the wooden horse during the siege of Troy. Now it was a wealthy city of greater standing than Croton, known for the quality of the surrounding farmland and its plentiful wheat harvest. Pythagoras had fled to Tarentum and then to Metapontum when his school in Croton came under attack. According to my father, Pythagoras was revered in Metapontum, and after his death, his home was turned into a temple to Demeter.

Metapontum was also the first large city to go over to Hannibal after the battle of Cannae. It had one of the largest granaries in Italy, and in recent years had become Hannibal's sanctuary when he wasn't on a campaign.

Our escort took us to a large villa on the south side of the city. Ten armed guards stood on duty out front. The officer who had arranged for our trip dismounted and spoke briefly to the lead guard.

"This is where Hannibal stays," whispered Lucretia. "The soldiers here are members of his Sacred Band and act as his bodyguards. Be wary of them. Also be aware that Hannibal will not be what you expect. He's a rough one, to be sure, but he's also a clever man with a subtle intellect. Be on your toes. He can be quite charming."

The lead guard told us to get out of the carriage. He searched us both. I had lost my dagger to the deserters a week earlier and carried no other weapon.

This same guard then led us into the villa. Despite being in an enemy city, and expecting to meet the man responsible for the war, I was excited by the prospect of seeing my mother—though I didn't really know when that would happen.

With my heart pounding, we were taken through the atrium to the back of the villa. It was larger and more luxuriously furnished than Sempronia's. Paintings hung on the walls. Greek sculptures were situated throughout the atrium. Black figure vases from Athens stood on the tables or sat in the corners filled with fresh flowers. Ornaments of gold and silver seemed to be everywhere I looked.

The peristyle, really a huge ornamental garden with fruit trees and exotic plants, was tiled with large squares of pink granite and enclosed by a colonnade with an arch that led to a stairway. We followed the guard up the stairs to an elevated patio that looked out on the city's wharf and a stunning panoramic view of the ocean. My mother was seated on a stone bench beside the balustrade that circuited the patio. She stood immediately on seeing me and rushed across the porch with her arms outstretched. Both of us burst into tears of joy and relief as we embraced. I squeezed her up close to me as if she would suddenly vanish if I let her go. I told her in a whisper how much I had missed her and had worried about her.

After a moment we held each other at arm's length. She appeared more beautiful than I remembered. She leaned into me and kissed me on the cheek. "Timon, I was afraid I'd never see you again. If I were to have no other wish in my life, the one I wanted most has just been granted." She touched my face to feel the stubble on my cheek, then looked into my eyes. "You're a young man now. And judging from your eyes, just as intelligent as your father."

"I spent three years as a slave, Mother. But I was lucky. My master was Archimedes of Syracuse." She knew his name. "He taught me so much my knowledge of geometry nearly equals Father's now."

We embraced again. When we finally did release each other, Hannibal was leaning on the balustrade, looking out at the turquoise sea and a clear winter sky. He wore a plush, collarless black robe, embroidered in red at the cuffs, hem, and neckline. The full beard he had worn when I saw him in Apulia had been trimmed close, with the hair above his upper lip shaved clean in the traditional Carthaginian style. The guard who had brought us had left, but four more of the Sacred Guard stood at intervals around the patio.

Hannibal faced us, and with a smile, addressed my mother in perfect Greek. "So Arathia, this is your son, Timon. I can see the joy his presence brings you. I expect that I will hear it in your voice when you play for me this evening." His voice was deep, but soft and thoughtful. He tipped his head in my direction, peering at me with his one good eye. A black patch covered the other. "Did I hear you say your master was Archimedes?"

"Yes, sir," I said, bowing my head. "I was his slave for three years."

I had seen Hannibal's face through the lenses twice, outside Numistro during my first campaign with Marcellus, and during the third campaign, when I had used them to find my mother. His black hair showed more gray, and the lines in his face had sharpened, etched deep around his eyes and in parallel furrows across his brow. Even with the patch over his right eye, there was a mournful sentiment in his left that brightened when he smiled as he did now.

"Were you in Syracuse during the Roman siege?" he asked coming closer. Physically, he was a younger, taller version of Marcellus. The thickness of his body, the width of his hips and chest, suggested tremendous power. He was clearly a formidable man with a sword and buckler.

"I was part of the plunder, sir, and taken to Rome. Only recently have I bought my freedom. That's why I'm here now. I came to buy my mother's freedom. Unfortunately the silver I carried was stolen from me on the road, but the knowledge I accumulated with Archimedes is more valuable than silver or gold. I can tell you things that no one else knows. Perhaps we can make a trade."

Hannibal grinned and nodded his head. "So what might you tell me—in exchange for your mother?" As he said this, an older man, who I judged to be Greek, came up the stairs from the garden onto the patio, followed by a Bruttian girl carrying my mother's Lyre. This was Ava, the slave Hannibal had given my mother as a second attendant.

Hannibal smiled as the man approached us. "Here's the man you must impress with your knowledge, Timon. He's the scholar, not me. Sosylus," he said, "meet Timon, son of Arathia and student of Archimedes. He says he can tell you something you don't know and is worth his mother in trade."

The bald, white-bearded Sosylus appraised me with skepticism. "Archimedes? What might he know that I don't?"

"That the Earth is round and is moving. Even now as we stand here, it's spinning and circling the sun."

Sosylus gave me a wry grin. "Aristarchus wrote such a thing. He put it in a book which I have read. Many are aware of his work."

"But is that true? Is the Earth moving, Sosylus?" asked Hannibal intrigued by what I had said. "I have no sense of that. All is still."

"It is written by a wise man, General, but I don't know if it's true or if it can be proven," said Sosylus. "It's merely one man's speculation."

"Archimedes said it could be proven, sir, with the Babylonian's records of the stars. And there is no doubt that the Earth is round. You can see it for yourself if you look closely enough."

"How's that?" asked Sosylus, taken aback by my confidence.

"Watch any ship that leaves the harbor. Look closely as it reaches the horizon. You will see that the ship disappears from bottom to top, as though it's following the curvature of a sphere."

Hannibal nodded. "I appreciate, Timon, that I have not heard this theory of the heavens. It all sounds quite fantastic." He smiled warmly. "But I am a solider, not a philosopher. Can't you tell me something more concrete with such a treasure as your mother in the balance?"

I lifted the leather pouch from beneath my tunic. If the motion of the planets wasn't good enough, then perhaps a demonstration with the lenses would be. I pried open the pouch and for the second time prepared to reveal what I had promised to keep secret. It was not something I had planned to do, but I was caught up in the moment, and freeing my mother from Hannibal's leash meant everything to me. I took out the two lenses. "With these," I held them out to both Hannibal and Sosylus, "I can see farther than any man by ten." I pointed to a ship along the wharf below. "Do you see that merchant ship? And the crates stacked on its deck? Can you tell me what they contain?"

Hannibal looked to Sosylus, who shook his head. "It's too far away. I have no idea what's in those crates."

I held the lenses up, one in each hand. "With these, I can tell you."

Hannibal laughed as though he thought I might be clever, but not profound.

I held the bead to my right eye and the magnifying lens out in front of me with my left arm fully extended. With some effort I focused the lenses on the deck of the ship. "I can see that the boxes are marked with Greek lettering"—though it was backwards and upside down— "which says they are a shipment of wine—from Corinth."

From the looks on both men's faces, they clearly doubted that I could even see that there were markings on the boxes, much less read them. Hannibal traded a look with my mother, even she seemed skeptical. Hannibal laughed as though it were a parlor game. "How do we know what you're saying is true?"

"See for yourself."

I handed the lenses to Hannibal, then step by step, instructed him how to use them, also telling him what he saw would be upside down. He made a good effort, but it was difficult, and after several tries, he handed them to his scholar. "Upside down or not, I see nothing but haze, Timon. Perhaps my one eye is not so good. Sosylus might do better."

Sosylus was nearly as old as Archimedes had been and probably with eyesight just as bad. He tried the lenses, but gave up quickly. "Everything I see is blurred. These are nothing but pieces of glass." He handed them back to me, shaking his head.

I knew it would be impossible to convince them of the lenses' value if they couldn't actually see through them. I thought of my last months with Archimedes. He had never been able to make them work. Determined to make some kind of breakthrough with Hannibal, I demonstrated the magnifying glass alone. I showed Hannibal the back of his hand, which of course impressed him. Then I used the lens to coax some smoke from a pile of dry leaves.

Again Hannibal found this curious, but Sosylus frowned. "This is nothing new. I have known of the burning glass since my childhood."

Hannibal smiled easily, clearly enjoying my efforts. "These are cute trinkets, Timon, and fascinating, but what of those stories I heard coming from Syracuse at the time of the siege? Hippocrates reported of fantastically accurate catapults and ballista. He mentioned something about an array of mirrors that could concentrate sunlight into fire. What of those things? Can you tell me anything about them? Do you have enough knowledge to instruct my engineers how to build such weapons?"

"I can't, sir," I said fully distressed. "I know what you're referring to, but I don't have that knowledge. The design of those weapons is difficult, and as far as I know, something only Archimedes could do."

"What a shame. But it doesn't matter." Hannibal's eye lit with deep pleasure. "I couldn't trade your mother for those things even if you had them with you." He looked over at her lovingly. "Especially since I don't own her and she is already free to go at any time."

"But she must come when you call."

"Only if she wishes."

I'm sure my mouth fell open.

Hannibal laughed. My mother smiled at me, clearly happy that I was there.

"Your mother is a treasure, Timon. At least to me. Her singing is the one pleasure I allow myself. Her voice soothes me in the evening and allows me to sleep. Her songs are better than drink, better than whoring. I pay her for her time. I've made sure that she can return to her home in Croton, and that she's protected whenever she's there. Even if I were so greedy to think such a treasure could be mine, I would want to share her with everyone I knew." The look he gave my mother made me shudder. "You are fortunate to have such a woman as your mother. And I see her in you. You have her courage and intelligence."

While I had tried to impress Hannibal, several other men and women had assembled on the patio. Slaves brought out a table and filled it with food—bowls of fruit, loaves of bread, a plate of grilled tuna, stacks of lamb chops, five kinds of cheese, snails dressed with cumin, flamingo tongues in honey, and several amphorae of wine. My moment to speak to Hannibal, it seemed, had passed as more important people settled in around him, lying on couches, passing food and drink.

My mother sat beside Hannibal. Ava, a skinny girl who I guessed to be no more than thirteen, stood behind her. I sat next to Lucretia at the far end of the table and had no real chance to talk to my mother. She seemed distant and focused on things other than my arrival. I noticed that Hannibal didn't drink, though most of his guests did. As the men talked, I recognized the names Carthalo and Maharbal, both cavalry commanders. And Mago, Hannibal's youngest brother. The women, it seemed, were there as ornaments, hired to add to the festivities.

Midway through the meal, as the sun was going down and wisps of clouds began appearing in the west, Hannibal asked my mother to play for the group. As much as I loved her singing, all I wanted was a chance to be alone with her, to learn more about what was going on and her relationship with Hannibal. I hadn't seen him touch her or take the slightest liberty with her, but I knew too little of what confidence games my mother might be playing or what she might have already told him about me. As things were, I just wasn't sure what to say or think.

But all of these concerns melted away once my mother began to play and sing. Her eyes swung to me often as she sang one after another of my favorites poems. It was as the woman in the Community of Miracles had said, my mother had the kind of voice that caused all around her to stop and listen. And only the setting sun, blushing the undersides of the clouds lavender and tangerine, could match the loveliness of her songs.

After my mother had stopped singing, and the meal wound down with the onset of darkness, Hannibal left with his brother and several other men, including Carthalo and Maharbal. I took the opportunity to sit beside my mother. She put a finger to my lips, then motioned to Lucretia and Ava that it was time to leave. The four of us went down to the garden and back through the house to my mother's chambers off the second floor of the atrium.

As we walked, my mother leaned up close to me and whispered, "I'm sorry, Timon, until we return to Croton, measure every word you say."

When we reached her chambers, which were quite luxurious and included several rooms, Lucretia suggested that she and Ava get some bedding. We would all be staying there that night.

My mother and I went into her bedchamber and sat on the bed. She embraced me again, her tears now flowing freely. "After all that has happened, Timon, it seems impossible that we're finally together again."

"The war has made a mess of everything, Mother. I have been fortunate, but have also seen too much tragedy." I hung my head thinking of Marcellus and Archimedes, then looking up, I lowered my voice. "Tell me what's going on here? When can we go back to Croton?"

She nodded slowly. "Be patient. I know there is much to explain. We will return to Croton in a few days, but now that we have this moment, there are a few things you must know."

"Like what Hannibal means to you? Why did you let him tease me when I asked to buy you?"

Again she nodded. "It's all theater. Be aware of that. Even your visit. I had you brought here with a purpose." She looked around as though the walls had ears, then whispered. "Revealing my private life to Hannibal, introducing him to you, whom he knows I have been looking for since I was kidnapped, increases his trust in me. And as I get closer to him." Her eyes narrowed, and again she looked around the room. "I can pick up information about the war, perhaps learning something that could help the Romans."

"But Mother, why should it be you who takes such a risk? Let's just go back to Croton. Let's leave this life and this war behind."

She looked at me sadly. "That can't happen until Hannibal is gone and the war is over. What I'm doing, if the gods allow, can hasten that."

"I spent three campaigns with the Roman general Marcellus. I saw the war up close. I don't want any more of it. For you or for me!"

"No one wants the war, Timon. But I have this chance, and we're never to speak of it unless we're alone."

"What about Lucretia?"

"She knows all."

I nodded, then asked what I had to. "Has Hannibal bedded you?"

She lowered her head, nodding the affirmative.

"Are you sure you know which side of the war you're on?"

"I hear the accusation in your voice. Trust me on this, Timon. Hannibal is a man of elevated intelligence and insight. Like no other I have known. Woman are not that important to him. He has a wife and a son. He regularly turns down the young women his men bring him, and on a few occasions, only a few, he has requested—requested not forced—close company with me. I think it's because we are the same age, and he wants more than the physical in his intimacy."

"And it gives you a special leverage with him?"

"Please, Timon." She touched my face, pained by my intimations. "Yes, and I hope to make good use of it. Now never mention it again."

I didn't like it, but I agreed. "Answer me this, then. Why did you communicate with me through the Community of Miracles? Who are Caelius and this woman with no name?"

"The community is not what it appears to be."

"What do you mean?"

She took a moment to answer. "Ennius is a Roman military officer."

I immediately pictured the crazy poet with the wild hair. "Impossible."

"He uses Caelius' network of criminals as the foundation for an underground of spies. Knowing them is what makes what I'm doing possible—and actionable. I have a means of transferring information."

"And Ennius takes it to the Roman command?"

She nodded.

"Have you been able to help? Have you learned anything important?"

"Did my advice about Marcellus' signet ring help?"

"Yes, of course. Anything else?"

"No." She touched my face and looked into my eyes, being as honest with me as she could. "Perhaps you're right to question what I do, Timon. Maybe I'm fooling myself that I can help the Roman cause. Maybe all I'm really doing is entertaining a man who should be my enemy."

"So let's go back to Croton tomorrow."

"Not tomorrow, but soon enough. All of us. But I will come back again. There's something I am fishing for, something important. Have patience."

I heard Lucretia's voice. She came into the outer chamber with Ava. Both of them carried blankets and pillows. I kissed my mother on the cheek. "We'll talk of this again." We both stood and went out to the front room to help with the bedding.

CHAPTER 8

We stayed in Metapontum three more days. I didn't have an opportunity to talk to Hannibal again, but my mother spent part of each day with him, usually in the evening. I saw Sosylus in the garden the second day. He immediately approached me.

"I'm curious about those pieces of glass you demonstrated to Hannibal and me. I went down to the wharf this morning to check on those crates you pointed out. They did contain wine from Corinth. Did you see that through the pieces of glass? Or had you seen what was on those ships earlier and hoped to trick us?"

I had not wanted to show the lenses to Hannibal at all. I had made the offer out of desperation. And after I had learned that my mother was free to come and go, I was relieved that neither Hannibal nor Sosylus had been able to make them work. But Sosylus' question put me in a pinch. I didn't want to reveal anything more about the lenses, but I didn't want Hannibal thinking I had tried to deceive him in any way.

"The lenses work, Sosylus. I did see the writing on the boxes from the patio. Archimedes gave those lenses to me the day he was killed, but they are difficult to use. They can be very frustrating." As I said this, I knew making them easier to use was something I would work on when I got back to Croton.

"They were certainly frustrating to me. I saw nothing. May I try them again?"

I did not want to show Sosylus the lenses at all, but how could I say no? I got them out trusting that Sosylus, like Archimedes, would not have good enough vision to use them. He took a lens in each hand, then looked up and down and this way and that with no success. Finally he shook his head and gave them back to me.

"If this is some kind of trick, young man, I warn you, be very careful what you do or say in the company of Hannibal. He's a generous and remarkably thoughtful man, but he doesn't like being made a fool of. He can be very quick with retribution."

CHAPTER 9

My mother, Lucretia, Ava, and I returned to Croton, escorted by the same contingent that brought Lucretia and me to Metapontum. Carthaginian officers made periodic stops by our home to see if everything was all right, but it really did seem that my mother was free to do as she pleased.

My mother had been paid extremely well during her time with Hannibal, and there was no pressure on her or me to bring in any income. This allowed me to return to my study of geometry and mathematics on a full-time basis, something I had never been able to do before. Several of my father's old papers remained in our home, and though someone had clearly gone through them, presumably looking for seditious writings, I used his work to extend what I already knew.

It seemed that mapmaking was destined to be the way I would make my living, so I concentrated on methods of triangulation. I also began to assemble my own writings, which until that time had been little more than diary entries. This was when the first book in my trilogy began to take shape, mostly as a chronology of my time in Syracuse.

Life in our home was almost normal. Of course the absence of my father remained the unspoken hole in the household, but this made me cherish the time with my mother all the more. After six years of wondering where she was, not knowing if she were even alive, seeing her each day seemed the greatest gift I could hope for. Yet all too often my thoughts drifted off to Sempronia. Our last day together had not gone well. I felt awful for my admission about her mother. I had spat it out in a moment of anger. I couldn't help wondering if Sempronia ever thought of me or if there was any way we could repair the damage we had already done to our friendship.

Life outside our home was definitely not the same as it had been. Croton had suffered only the slightest damage during the change of regimes. There had been no siege, no battle, but the aristocrats had holed up in a citadel overlooking the ocean. Rather than root them out, Aristomachus, working with Carthaginian agents, arranged for them to be given housing in Locri. After a relatively peaceful evacuation, the local Bruttians were allowed to move into the city. Aristomachus acted as the mediator between the Bruttians and Carthaginian officers who imposed martial law. It reminded me of my time in Syracuse during the reign of Hieronymus. I was an outsider in the city where I had grown up. Nothing felt safe. Often I was stopped in the street and questioned. Early on in my stay, I saw one of the Bruttians who had come to our house the night my father was murdered. It was the man who had stabbed him. I kept my eyes out for him throughout my time in Croton with some vague hope of exacting revenge on the man.

After six weeks of relative bliss in Croton, my mother got another request from Hannibal to come to Metapontum. I had begun to feel like the man of the house and immediately confronted her.

"Say no to him," I demanded. "Give this up. It's dangerous and it's not clear that your efforts will bring any reward."

"I'm sorry, Timon," she replied, denying the authority I thought I had gained. "My mind is made up. I'll be leaving in two days. The arrangements have already been made."

"Cancel them. If what Hannibal said while we were in Metapontum were true, you can do as you please, and I would hope that my wishes outweigh his."

"My choices are political, not personal. You were young at the time of the Carthaginian takeover. You couldn't possibly have understood all your father and I talked about, but he, particularly, was adamant in his resistance to the Carthaginians. Croton had a good relationship with Rome. Yes, we paid a tribute and supplied levies when needed, but with the Bruttians in charge, Croton is a mere shadow of what it was ten years ago. The democracy your father so valued is gone. There is no city council. No forum for the people to voice their opinions. These were important issues to your father, and things I still feel very strongly about."

"Yes, of course," I pleaded, "all of what you've said is true, but from what I saw, Hannibal has influence over you that is more than information about the war. You told me he's bedded you. That troubles me and suggests that there's something more to your leaving than you say."

"You're simply wrong about that." For the first time anger crept into her voice. "I admit that the man can be charming and that I can enjoy his company, even his bed, but I will never forget who he is, what he's done, and what his intentions are. If I prostitute myself in any way, it's for a cause—Greek Italy and your future. I am not a brazen street walker. I'm doing something I believe in."

I shook my head. "You're fooling yourself, Mother. I can hear it in every rationalization you make."

My words did nothing but create tension between us. She left two days later with Ava. Lucretia and I remained in Croton.

The time that my mother was gone seemed interminable. I continued with my studies and writing, but I also began to apply myself to the task of building a mechanism that would make the lenses easier to use.

I sought out an old craftsman by the name of Furius whom my father had known and whose shop I had visited as a youth. His mother was Bruttian, his father Greek, and he had been allowed to stay in Croton when others in the city had been sent to Locri. I found him in his shop, down the same alley it had always been. We spoke about my father. He deliberately stayed clear of politics. I asked him if he could make three wooden tubes, with diameters that allowed them to fit one inside the other. He said that he was too busy at the time, but he could give me the instruction, materials, and tools to make the three tubes myself. I enjoyed working with my hands and readily agreed to his offer.

I bored out the tubes with a hand drill and fitted the sleeves as tightly as possible, so that their combined length could be adjusted by twisting them in or out. I mounted the crystal disk at the end of the tube with the largest diameter and the glass bead at the end of the tube with the smallest.

With the perfection of these wooden tubes, I was able to use the lenses for longer periods of time, and with considerably more ease and clarity of vision. The power and value of lenses became more evident, and anyone could use them. The lenses did, however, lose some of their security with the addition of the tubes. If someone had found the lenses in the pouch, using them in combination was not at all obvious. They were hard enough to use even with my assistance. Mounting them at the ends of the tubes gave the secret away. Should anyone find or steal the device, learning to use it was not so difficult to figure out. But the positives outweighed this one negative. The lenses were easily focused by sliding the tubes in and out, and the tubes held the lenses steady and in line, which was so difficult without them. Because of the fantastic nature of its visual effect, almost like looking into another world, I thought of the device as my magic wand, capable of bringing a profound awe to anyone who used it. I kept the device, my "spyglass" as I called it, with me at all times, tucked in the folds of my toga—looking more like a extendable walking stick than a scientific tool.

I felt a greater temptation to show the lenses to others now that they were so easy to use. If the lenses had been mounted in the wooden tubes when I had tried to show them to Sempronia, maybe then she would have understood why I had gone to such extremes to recover them when they were lost. I planned to show the spyglass to my mother when she returned from Metapontum, but no one else, even Furius. For the time being, I would remain highly selective, waiting for the right person and the right time. Hannibal had not been that person, and I knew it. In that instance, I was fortunate I hadn't made the wooden tubes yet.

CHAPTER 10

My mother returned to Croton after three weeks in Metapontum. I showed her the spyglass one afternoon when we were in the peristyle at the back of our house.

"Mother, do you remember when I showed Hannibal the two pieces of glass?"

"Yes, I do. I had been meaning to ask you about that. I'm afraid I didn't understand what you were trying to do."

I nodded. "Afterward I realized I had to do something to make them easier to use." I withdrew the spyglass from my toga and pointed out the lenses at each end, then demonstrated how the tubes slid in and out. I held it out to her. "Try it. Hold the end with the small opening to your eye. It's really quite surprising what you'll see."

She held the spyglass in both hands and twisted the tubes to get a feel for how they worked, then she lifted the device to her eye. With only the slightest assistance from me, she was able to focus on a distant portion of the city wall."

"What is this?" she asked lowering the spyglass. "The wall appears so close—and upside down."

"Ignore that it's upside down, and try focusing on that guard in the parapet." I pointed to the man. He was little more than a stick figure from where we stood.

It didn't happen without some effort, but when she saw the man's face through the lenses she gasped. "That can't possibly be the man patrolling the battlements? Can it?" She lowered the spyglass to verify what she was looking at.

"It is, Mother. The lenses were something Archimedes was working on while I was with him. His eyes weren't good enough to appreciate what he'd made, but mine were. He gave me the lenses the day he died and told me never to show anyone how they worked—unless my life depended on it."

43

"But you showed them to Hannibal and now to me?"

"Something happened." I bowed my head, remembering the day Marcellus was killed. "After holding them in secret for three years, I concluded Archimedes was wrong, so I've decided to show them to a few select people. I only showed them to Hannibal because I had nothing else to trade for your freedom. I showed you just now because they are something Father would have appreciated, and I thought you might also."

She lifted the spyglass to her eye to target another guard on the battlements. After a moment, she lowered the spyglass and looked at me, awed by what she had seen. "Is this some kind of magic, Timon? Is that the reason for the secrecy?"

"No, it's not magic. It's applied geometry, nothing more. But you're not to say anything about the device—to anyone. The secrecy is necessary because there isn't another one like it—anywhere—and it's valuable. My experience with the lenses has made me realize that this device, which I call a spyglass, can be highly useful in warfare. It allows a form of spying that doesn't risk the life of the asset."

My mother acknowledged my reasoning, but ignored my not-so-subtle suggestion.

Later that night I took my mother to the roof of our house for another demonstration of the spyglass' power. The night was clear and the moon nearly full. Even after her limited experience with the spyglass in the afternoon, she had no trouble focusing on the moon's surface. She was instantly captivated by the details of the lunar landscape, and stared at the cratered surface for so long I had to direct her to other parts of the sky so she could appreciate the vast depth of the heavens.

My mother was an intelligent woman. She had lived almost twenty years with my father and had often heard him expound on the size of the universe and the various planets and their relationship to the stars. She understood the implications of what she was seeing almost immediately. On concluding her brief tour of the heavens, she lowered the spyglass and looked at me. "For all the beauty of what I have just seen, and the marvel of this device, I think I understand why Archimedes wanted you to be so secretive with these lenses. After using this spyglass, I feel differently about who I am. Think how insignificant we must be in so large a universe. And what this suggests about the gods?"

"And why would we bother to fight wars? Why would we as Greeks choose one side or the other—Roman or Carthaginian?"

She knew where I was headed. She shook her head. "Your father and I chose to support Rome because the thing we believed in most was Greek democracy. Rome had learned to stay clear of the business of our senate, but that was the first target of the Carthaginian agents. I believe in the process of a democratic government and hope that one day women will be allowed to take part more actively in politics—and the war. Maybe I can't be a soldier, but I can help—of that I'm more certain than ever." She looked out over the roofs of the other houses in the neighborhood. Although no one else was in sight, she lowered her voice. "I have recently gained access to military information with my lyre that even this spyglass could not have discovered."

She took my hand, then knelt down drawing me with her, so that we huddled close together on our knees. "During the time that I was gone," she whispered, "I learned what I had hoped to. And I need you to deliver a message."

"To Ennius in the Community of Miracles?"

"No. To Claudius Nero, the recently elected Roman consul."

"How can you know that?" It was the first of May. The elections had taken place six weeks earlier. "I haven't heard anything here in Croton about the election."

"Hannibal knew right away. I heard him talking about it with his brother. The other consul is an older man named Marcus Livius. He'll be stationed in the north to contain Hasdrubal when he arrives. Nero's coming south with two legions as we speak. Hannibal said that Nero was one of the commanders under Marcellus. Did you know him?"

"He's not a very pleasant man, but I know him and he knows me."

"He's planning to join up with another Roman general and two more legions somewhere in Apulia, specifically to confront Hannibal."

"What's your message?"

My mother took another glance around. "I know when Hasdrubal will arrive in Italy and what route he will take to join Hannibal. I give you this information with the same confidentiality you requested regarding your spyglass. Tell Nero, and no one else—and *say nothing to Nero of your source*." She narrowed her eyes to emphasize this final point.

I nodded.

"Last winter Hannibal sent Hasdrubal the best maps of Italy he could acquire. Through a series of letters, they agreed on a location to meet and the route Hasdrubal should take to get there. He is due to arrive in northern Italy very soon. Once he descends from the Alps and gathers more mercenaries, he will follow the Po River from Placentia to the coastal branch of Via Flaminia, then head south along the Adriatic coast to meet Hannibal in Apulia."

I knew the region from my own mapping. "That's the most obvious route. The Romans will be ready for that."

"Which, of course, Hannibal also knows. So in the days following Hasdrubal's arrival, Hasdrubal will send a team of messengers to south Italy, supposedly seeking Hannibal. They will let themselves be captured by the Romans, and they will reluctantly reveal the sealed message they were instructed to deliver to Hannibal. The message will describe a completely different route south for Hasdrubal, a much riskier one that takes Via Flaminia across the Apennines into Umbria toward Rome, as though the two brothers intend to advance together on the city walls. It will be a deliberate falsehood to draw the Roman's attention to Umbria and to facilitate Hasdrubal's taking the faster and easier coastal route south."

My mother's knowledge surprised me, not just her message, but her understanding of the war. "So you want me to go to Nero and tell him that when these messengers are caught, the note they have is part of a ruse and should be ignored, and that Hasdrubal will be traveling down the coast on Via Flaminia."

"That's right. The message is a trick." My mother looked around, and we both stood. "You should leave tomorrow. The sooner Nero knows the better."

We climbed from the roof and retired for the night. Despite my objections, my mother had gone about her work and discovered something of value. Right or wrong, it didn't stop me from worrying about her.

CHAPTER 11

My mother and I ate oat porridge and sipped a cup of kykeon together shortly before daybreak the next morning. Neither Ava nor Lucretia were up yet. The plan was that I would give the message to Nero and return to Croton. I might be gone as long as a month. Should Hannibal request my mother's presence in Metapontum, she would go, meaning she may or may not be in Croton when I returned. Before leaving I embraced my mother a little too long. Both of us knew the dangers both she and I would face. She began to cry, and then so did I.

I packed up Balius and rode out of Croton just after sunrise. The trip from Croton to Apulia afforded two routes. I could take Via Latina north to Calatia—at least a week of travel—then turn south by southeast down the Appian Way to Apulia, another five days—depending on the weather. Or I could go north on Via Latina for four days, then cut directly east across the low hills of southern Italy to Apulia, only four days, but of much rougher travel. I knew the area from my campaigns with Marcellus. I had mapped all of it over a period of three years. I could still see the maps in my head, every road and ravine in Apulia and Lucania. I decided to take the faster but more difficult route.

The coming of spring and the season of war unleashed waves of refugees up and down the peninsula. The anticipated four days on Via Latina stretched out to five with the heavy traffic—carts, livestock, and whole villages of people on foot hoping to find a well-fortified city for refuge. Food was in short supply for this army of travelers, but an early spring had brought forage for Balius, and I soon detoured off the paved road into the hills of Lucania.

Two days later, while crossing a piece of open farmland, I noticed some commotion on the horizon. I took out the spyglass and quickly deciphered the cloud of dust as a raiding party of Numidians headed my way. I was surprised they were this far north, but because of the advantage of the spyglass, I managed to avoid them by slipping off into the hills.

Fortunately the weather was better than what I had experienced in January. I bedded down in the forest and did my best to stay out of sight from anyone, often scanning the distance with the spyglass to be as careful as possible. Half a day from Venusia, I woke up in the morning surrounded by a turma of Roman cavalry. When I was prodded from my blankets by the tip of a javelin, I saw that one of the men held Balius' reins.

"What are you doing out here?" demanded the decurion who led the thirty-man contingent.

I warily stood up, realizing immediately that without some quick talking I was likely to lose Balius, and if I said the wrong thing, perhaps my life as well. "I'm looking for the Roman camp in Apulia." The troops in this region were very likely the same two legions that Marcellus had commanded a year ago. I took that chance. "I'm hoping to find the Eighteenth legion."

"And why would that be?" continued the decurion, clearly suspicious.

Knowing I couldn't mention the message I had for Claudius Nero, I lied. "I spent the last three years as a scribe for the Eighteenth. I want to sign up for another campaign."

"We're from the Eighteenth," snapped the decurion, who then turned to his men. "Do any of you recognize this man?" The decurion touched my chest with his lance. "I don't."

No rider spoke up for me. The man holding Balius' reins summed it up. "I think we have more need for this Greek's horse than another scribe."

Several of the soldiers laughed. This inspired a crude comment from the back of the group and more laughter. The decurion jabbed me with his lance, not so hard to puncture my skin, but with enough force to cause me to fall backward on my rear. This got them laughing even more. I wasn't certain where this was headed. I tried to stand, but the decurion jabbed me again, causing me to fall back to the ground.

"Not so fast, Greek. How do we know you're not a spy, scouting our position for the Carthaginians? Convince me otherwise."

"Do you know a veteran soldier known as Pulcher? He's a sub-centurion in the second maniple of first cohort of the Eighteenth."

The riders exchanged looks, clearly recognizing the name. The decurion lifted his lance. "How do you know this man?"

"I was in his tent unit," I said, finally getting a chance to regain my feet. "Take me to your camp. He'll speak up for me."

The decurion thought about this a moment. "I'm not convinced, but we'll take you back to camp anyway. Expect the worst if no one knows you."

They tied my hands behind my back and hefted me up on Balius. Another rider held the reins and led Balius and me all the way to their camp. We arrived in the middle of the afternoon. One of the riders took Balius to the corral at the back of the camp. The decurion and two of his turma escorted me, my hands still bound, into the camp and down Via Principalis. The decurion put out a call for Pulcher while I stood outside headquarters deciphering the standards before each row of tents. I noticed that both the Eighteenth and Twentieth legions were in the camp. I couldn't help but wonder if Marcus would be there as well. That would certainly make all of this a lot easier.

Before Pulcher arrived to verify who I was, Claudius Nero, wearing the purple cape of his consulship, came out of the headquarters' tent accompanied by two of his commanders. I decided not to wait for Pulcher and called out to Nero. "Consul! Can I have a word with you?"

The decurion slapped me for shouting out, but Nero heard me and abruptly turned to see who had spoken. He didn't recognize me right away. Being bound and guarded by two soldiers didn't help matters. He was not a pleasant man, and he glared at me. "Who is this prisoner who dares address me? Ten lashes for impudence," he snarled.

"Please, Consul, I'm the mapmaker from your campaign last summer. You recommended me to Publius Scipio."

"The Greek!" I heard Pulcher call out as he strode up Via Principalis toward headquarters.

Nero, who had started to walk away, suddenly stopped and stared at me. "Timon Leonidas?"

"Yes, sir."

"Why are you here and bound? What's going on?"

The decurion spoke up. "We found this man half a day's ride from here. He told us he was looking for our camp. He wants to enlist."

"You want to enlist? I would have thought you would be in the north with Marcus Claudius."

"No, sir. I have been in Croton. And if possible, I would like a word with you?"

"Say what you will. Make it quick."

"In private, sir. It must be that way."

Always impatient and in a hurry, Nero looked around at the other men. "There's no time now. Come back this evening." He turned to the decurion. "Untie this man," he ordered, then continued on his way flanked by his commanders.

When the bonds had been removed, Pulcher approached me. "So, Greek, you've come to enlist? I didn't expect to see you without your friend Marcus."

"Things change, sir. I've been with my family in Croton."

"Need something to eat? Come with me. The unit is putting together a meal right now."

I followed Pulcher to his tent. I saw Decius first, sitting with three soldiers I didn't recognize. He scowled as I walked up. "Where'd you find this useless Greek?"

"In front of headquarters, talking to the consul—for who knows what reason."

Troglius emerged from the tent. The huge, awkward man, who I had considered my closest friend among my tent mates, bowed his head as though he thought I might not remember him.

"Troglius, how are you? I didn't know if I'd ever see you again."

Troglius peeked up at me, shy and reticent as always, then allowed a weak grin.

"Oh, isn't this cute." Decius shook his head. "Troglius can actually smile."

The unit shared their wheat gruel and flat bread with me. I hadn't eaten all day and wolfed the food down. I spoke briefly with Troglius, but he had never been much for conversation. I still enjoyed seeing him and I'm sure the feeling was mutual.

After the meal I went out to the corral to look for Balius. I walked around the edge of the enclosure and called his name several times. I was relieved when he appeared out of the mass of horses and wandered over to me. Much like Troglius, he was glad to see me but didn't have much to say.

At dusk I went to headquarters. Two centurions stood on either side of the tent's entrance. I told them my name and said that I was there to see the consul. The men looked at each other, then one reluctantly stuck his head into the tent to announce me. I heard Nero shout back, "Tell him to wait."

Long after nightfall, three officers emerged from headquarters. A short while later, another officer came out of the tent. After a bit more time passed, I asked one of the centurions to announce me again.

"He'll call for you when he wants to see you."

"He could have forgotten."

"Someone like you?" The soldier laughed and nudged the other guard in the ribs. "Think the consul could have forgotten about this skinny lad?"

Their laughter was cut short by Nero's voice. "Send the Greek in."

I slipped into the tent uncertain how to present my mother's message. The tent was luxuriously furnished. Persian carpets covered the floor. Eight individual oil lamps perched on ornate bronze stands provided light. A couch and several chairs were arranged around a small dining table. Glittering swords and shields hung from the tent posts. Nero stood at a table looking over some documents. He wore a white tunic trimmed in purple and girdled with a wide leather belt. His gladius hung at his hip. "This better be important," he said without looking up.

I approached the table. He was looking at maps that I had drawn during my campaigns with Marcellus. When he continued to study the maps, I realized that I had to earn what attention he gave me. I got right to the point.

"I have information on Hasdrubal's route south."

Nero was a large, square, muscular man—a patrician born to privilege who had trained for war since childhood. He was known for his arrogance, brusque manners, and capacity to kill in battle. I had seen him in action when he was one of Marcellus' prefects. The memory only added to his physical intimidation. His eyes lifted at the mention of Hasdrubal's name. "Go on."

"In the coming weeks, you will intercept a message coming from the north. It will be from Hasdrubal. Though the message will appear to be written for Hannibal, it will be meant for you."

Nero's head came all the way up. He was handsome in a rough way. His facial muscles accentuated his mouth and cheeks.

"The message will say that Hasdrubal will take the west branch of Via Flaminia across Umbria."

"Towards Rome."

I nodded. "Suggesting that the two brothers will join in an attack on the city—something certain to create a strong reaction in the Senate—like concentrating Roman forces outside Rome. But it will be a trick, designed to allow Hasdrubal to proceed upon a completely different prearranged route."

Nero stared at me, thinking over what I had said. "Where did you get this information?"

"I can't say."

He tilted his head. "Then why should I believe you?"

"Because I have no reason to mislead you."

"What route will Hasdrubal take, if not the one described in the message?"

"Instead of taking the west branch of Via Flaminia, he'll take the east branch that follows the coast to Apulia."

"The fastest route."

"Yes, and thus the reason for the ruse. Hannibal is never one to use the obvious or the easiest way of doing things. But in this case he wants to. The intercepted message is designed to throw you off."

Nero walked away from the map table and paced across the tent, stood a moment in silence, then recrossed the tent. "I need to know where you got this information. If I'm to act on it, it can't be wrong. And I just don't see how you could possibly know this."

I thought of my mother's safety. "I'm sorry, sir, I can't reveal my source."

Nero looked at me as though he might beat it out of me. "What's this of wanting to enlist?"

"Something I told your decurion so he would bring me to your camp. I don't want to enlist. I wanted to talk to you in private. Now that I've given you the message, I plan to go back to Croton."

"Croton?" Nero frowned. "That's Bruttian controlled."

"Yes, but my family is still there."

Nero didn't seem to understand. "When will this message arrive?"

"I don't know."

Nero went back to the map, clearly perplexed. "Hasdrubal is in north Italy right now. He's besieging Placentia. I think he's wasting his time. Is there any reason he hasn't already come south?"

"I can't say. Perhaps the message will be sent just before he leaves to join his brother, but these are not things I really know."

Nero came up close to me. "Who's your source?"

I looked him in the eye. "A spy in Hannibal's camp. I have promised not to reveal his name for fear of giving him away."

"Tell me something more."

"Do you recognize the name Quintus Ennius?"

He lifted his head in thought, then turned away, striding across the tent and back again, frustrated by my demand for secrecy, but also captivated by what I was saying. "Are you willing to stay with this army until the message is intercepted?"

It was his way of testing me. I would be something short of a hostage. I reluctantly agreed.

"This message will have to arrive soon if Hannibal intends to meet with his brother this summer. It can't be more than a few weeks. You can work on these maps while you're here. I will pay you as a scribe, but you won't be enlisted for the entire campaign—just until your information is verified."

"Fair enough."

CHAPTER 12

Shortly after I settled into the Roman camp with my old tent unit, the Roman general Gaius Hostilius arrived with two more legions and word that Hannibal had been seen near Grumentum, about fifty miles south of Venusia. Nero now had four legions containing forty thousand men at his command. He didn't hesitate. We broke camp the next day and headed south.

Nero understood that Hannibal was not likely to accept battle, but he wanted to keep him in the south, as far away from his brother as possible. The best way to do this was to stay between Hannibal and all routes north or, if possible, keep him in sight.

We reached Grumentum in three days. Hannibal was camped unusually close to the walls of the city. We set camp a mile away. Hannibal offered battle the next two days, but Nero didn't answer. This general, who had once been so critical of Marcellus, was now being as cautious as his former commander. The only action occurred between foraging parties and the small squadrons of Numidian cavalry that rode up to the walls of our camp daily to taunt us. During this time, Nero made a thorough assessment of the ground. Well before dawn of the third day, he sent two thousand men to hide behind a rise east of the city. When Hannibal's troops lined up for battle that morning, Nero answered.

Many of Hannibal's troops were hastily raised levies from Bruttium. They'd had little if any training and no experience. They assembled slowly and their lines were muddled. Nero didn't wait, he sent his cavalry directly into their confusion, causing more disturbance in the rest of Hannibal's formation. Nero then ordered his first line forward.

The beginning of the battle was all about the Carthaginian army regaining order amid our advance. Hannibal rode furiously back and forth behind the line, bringing some semblance of discipline to his ranks one unit at a time. Just as it seemed that Hannibal had gotten control of his men, Nero signaled for the two thousand troops hidden on Hannibal's left flank to attack. Hannibal had used similar tactics against the Romans many times earlier in the war. He sensed the difficulty of the situation immediately and called for a retreat. Only the proximity of the Carthaginian camp prevented a rout.

Hannibal had been outmaneuvered by Nero, but he did not lose that many men. Knowing his most important task was joining with his brother, he slipped away from Grumentum quietly that night, leaving a few Numidians behind to man the walls and light the morning campfires so that it appeared his army was still there.

Nero was fooled. Not until late afternoon did our scouts venture up to the walls and discover that Hannibal was gone. Nero was furious. We had lost a whole day, but with forced marching, unlike anything I had ever experienced with Marcellus, we caught Hannibal four days later camped near Canusium. Three weeks had passed since I had arrived in camp.

The situation in Canusium was similar to that in Grumentum and began as a standoff. Hannibal was well camped, but there were forty thousand men in front of him. His troops numbered thirty thousand, but they contained the least experienced collection of soldiers he had ever had. The entire future of the war hung on his making contact with his brother. After the experience in Grumentum, he was in no mood to fight it out with Nero.

Three days into the standoff, a trio of soldiers arrived at our camp on horseback with a message from Tarentum. Two Numidians and four Gauls had been captured outside the city. They had just ridden the length of Italy looking for Hannibal and had accidently gone to Tarentum instead of Metapontum. When they were searched, a message written to Hannibal was found on one of the Numidians. It was signed by Hasdrubal. The trio of soldiers had brought Nero the original piece of writing and a translation from Punic into Latin. Nero read the translation once, dismissed the messengers, and called for me.

He was alone when I entered headquarters. He was pacing back and forth and suddenly stopped. "The message from Hasdrubal has been intercepted." He handed me the translation. "Is this real or is it a ruse? The direction of the war depends on it."

Nero returned to his pacing as I quickly read the message. Hasdrubal would leave his position outside Placentia in one week. He would cross the Apennines on the west branch of Via Flaminia and meet Hannibal in Umbria east of Rome. Exactly what my mother had told me. "It's a ruse, sir," I said. "I couldn't have known about this ahead of time, if it wasn't. That's the only way to interpret it. I also don't believe Hasdrubal will wait two more weeks. I believe this message is a signal that he's already left or soon will."

Nero eyed me from across the tent, thinking about what I had said. He strode up close to me. He was twice my size. His entire presence was physical, but he had been educated by Rome's best tutors and he had a good mind. "I think you're right," he said. "I've been thinking about this every day since you first mentioned it, wondering if it could be true and what I would do if it were. Your horse is in the corral. You're free to go."

"What are you plans, sir?"

He shook his head. "Why would I tell a man who is going back behind enemy lines? Why would I tell a spy?"

CHAPTER 13

Claudius Nero took a chance and accepted my interpretation of the message. Hasdrubal was not headed to Rome. He was going to take the fastest and easiest route to meet his brother, down the coastal branch of Via Flaminia. In a strategic move that only Rome's ten years of war with Hannibal allowed him to conceive, Nero immediately assembled his best six thousand foot and best one thousand horse and left camp in the middle of the night, headed north to help the other consul, Marcus Livius, stop Hasdrubal. Hostilius and the rest of the troops remained in the camp outside Canusium, carrying on business as though nothing had changed, and hoping that Hannibal would not notice that Nero had left. The Roman military mind was evolving, and at this stage of the war, Claudius Nero and his friend Publius Scipio were the preeminent examples.

Nero and his seven thousand men made one of the most famous marches in all of military history, traversing the Italian peninsula from Canusium to Sena, some two hundred and fifty miles, in seven days. He sent messengers ahead on horseback to inform both the Senate and Livius what he was doing. Along the way, Latin villagers gave his army food, water, and extra horses to ease the strain of the march.

By this time Livius had already positioned himself in Sena with thirty thousand soldiers on the coastal branch of Via Flaminia blocking Hasdrubal's march south. The two armies, Hasdrubal's swollen to forty thousand with recently recruited Gallic mercenaries, were camped half a mile apart south of the Metaurus River. Livius had declined battle with Hasdrubal twice already, concerned about the enemy's greater numbers. Nero's arrival would make the numbers nearly equal, but the quality of Nero's contingent would give the Romans a sure advantage—the reason for the march from the beginning.

Hoping to prevent Hasdrubal from noticing the influx of new troops, Nero arrived at night. His soldiers shared tents with Livius' men rather then setting up a second camp. When the Roman lines formed the next morning, Hasdrubal answered, thinking he outnumbered his adversary. Early on in the fray, however, he realized that Rome's second consul was on the battlefield with what he assumed was an additional legion. Thinking this meant Hannibal had suffered a major setback in the south, he fought the battle defensively through the rest of the day, barely holding his own before retreating to camp. He evacuated his camp that night, hoping to get away from what he understood to be a superior force.

Hasdrubal's retreat took him north to the Metaurus River, which he hoped to follow to the east branch of Via Flaminia. Unfortunately his army got dispersed that night in the unfamiliar territory. When the Romans caught up with him the next afternoon, he struggled to get his troops into any kind of battle formation at all. The battle went badly from the start. Hasdrubal did all that he could to inspire his over-matched troops, but by the end of the day, Hasdrubal was dead and the entire Carthaginian army was either destroyed, taken prisoner, or lost in the surrounding forest.

Immediately following the victory, Nero assembled his men, and again marching night and day, returned to Canusium—this time is six days. Although he was gone two weeks, Hannibal never noticed that the consul had left or knew that the battle in the north had taken place.

The day following his return, Nero, who had taken the head from Hasdrubal's corpse as a victory trophy, ordered a turma of cavalry to ride up to the walls of Hannibal's camp and throw the head over the ramparts. A Carthaginian soldier recovered the head and brought it to Hannibal. Although he hadn't seen his brother in ten years, he recognized the head immediately and knew what it meant. The momentum of the war had turned against him. His chances of bringing Rome to her knees were all but nil.

CHAPTER 14

I had returned to Croton by the time Hasdrubal's head sailed into Hannibal's camp. I learned about it in the Croton forum several weeks later. Nero's mad dash north had changed the course of the war, and he had acted on the information I had gotten from my mother.

When I told her the news, I also apologized for doubting that she could make a difference, but added that I didn't want her to continue seeing Hannibal. "Rome seems certain to win the war now. I think it's time for you to stop."

"Don't you think that might cause Hannibal to wonder if I cut off my visits so soon after Hasdrubal's defeat?" Although we were in the atrium, she glanced around as though someone could be listening. "But perhaps you're right. I should begin letting go of Hannibal. I could be free of him by the end of the winter."

"That could mean several more visits."

"And the least possible suspicion." She put her finger to her lips. "Timon, please, keep your voice down. Croton is not the city it used to be. The less said about this the better, even in our own house."

Six weeks after Hasdrubal's defeat, Hannibal retired to the security of Metapontum. Shortly afterward, he called for my mother. I begged her not to go, telling her she was taking unneeded risk, but she went anyway. Ava traveled with her. Lucretia stayed in Croton with me.

While my mother was gone, I continued to advance my mapmaking skills and to work on the narrative about my time in Syracuse. I tended to stay at home. Occasionally I made trips to the agora, either going to the market or listening to the speakers in the forum, hoping to gather information about the war and events in Rome.

During one of my trips to the agora, I saw the man who had murdered my father for a second time. I began to look for him in the

59

crowds. On several occasions I followed him, learning where he lived and the drinking establishments he frequented. I had no plan, but I was intent on revenge of some sort.

One afternoon, as I walked home from the forum, I deliberately chose a route that would take me past the man's favorite tavern. When I was still a short distance from the establishment, I saw him stumble out of the building and teeter down the street. I decided to follow him.

He was a large man, as tall as I was, but heavier and older, your typical thug. His path took him in the direction of his home. I sped up my pace, closing in on him, knowing we only had a little ways to go before reaching his apartment.

Buried in the folds of my toga was a dagger that I had bought to replace the one I had lost to the deserters. When he entered a narrow alley and I was just a few steps behind him, I slid my hand over the dagger's handle. He wavered drunkenly through the alley, twice using the side of a building to keep himself upright. My chance for revenge could not have been better, but I could not draw the knife. I suddenly stopped and watched him stumble out the far end of the alley. I was no murderer. I had killed a man in self-defense after the battle of Numistro, but even that had felt wrong when it shouldn't have.

I wandered back to the house, cursing my weakness.

CHAPTER 15

Two weeks later my mother returned to Croton with Ava. Lucretia made a big dinner the first night they were back, grilling a tuna she had bought at the market and filling out the meal with lentil stew, a loaf of rye bread, and a bowl of mulberries for dessert. Afterward my mother got out her lyre and sang for us. The music transported me back to my childhood and happier times.

"You know," she said to me when the session was over and Ava and Lucretia had retired to their rooms, "there's quite a difference between playing for money and playing for my family."

"You mean playing for Hannibal and playing for your family?"

"Even more so for Hannibal, but I also played for money when I was in Rome. It allowed me to buy my freedom, but it always seemed to demean the music when I was paid. Remember how your father spoke of it as something sacred."

"Oh, yes, Plato would have considered your singing for money the ultimate adulteration of the music of the spheres."

My mother nodded and smiled, having heard the sentiment many times from my father.

"I never believed that, Mother. How could something so elevated and beautiful be wrong?"

"It does seem silly," she said, looking lovingly at her lyre, the same one my father had given her years ago, though the polished tortoise shell body had acquired a few nicks and bruises along the way.

"Mother, will you go back to Metapontum again?"

She lowered her eyes then looked up at me. "Maybe another time or two."

"Is that necessary? Isn't there some chance he might begin to suspect you?"

"I sensed nothing of that when I was there, Timon. I appreciate that you worry about me, but I'm proud of what I did and what it led to."

"But isn't that enough?"

"Perhaps. Hannibal does seem to understand that he will never take Rome. But he has no immediate plans to leave Italy. He feels that he's been mistreated by his own people and has little reason to return to his homeland."

Ava entered the room. "Arathia, would you like me to turn down your bed?"

"Yes, please, Ava. I'll be right there."

After Ava left, I turned to my mother and in a soft voice asked, "How much does Ava know?"

"Nothing, and I'm trying to keep it that way. She's young and may talk more than would be advised. Lucretia knows everything, but don't say a word to Ava."

"I have no intention of saying anything to anyone. Let's not mention it again."

"Yes, let's not," she said standing. "And please understand if I must make a few more trips to see Hannibal," she leaned over and kissed me on the forehead, "it's only to make my break from him less suspicious."

CHAPTER 16

My mother became ill in the weeks following her return. At first she suffered from stomach cramps and nausea. She struggled to keep her food down, and as a result had no energy. She began to stay in bed late into the morning and retire earlier and earlier in the evening. Ava and Lucretia did their best to take care of her. They made soups and provided her with warm compresses, but little seemed to help.

When a message came from Hannibal asking her to come to Metapontum, she was in no condition to travel and had to say no. One of the garrison commanders came to our house a week later, most likely on orders from Hannibal. She had grown so weak and thin it was all she could do to get out of bed to talk to the man. The seriousness of her condition was obvious. He made no effort to change her mind about going to Metapontum.

At the time, I almost considered the illness a blessing. I didn't want her to see Hannibal again, but I had also seen many sick and invalid during the last few years. I recalled those who had died when the plague struck Syracuse in the second year of the siege. I remembered soldiers dying in my tent when I traveled with the Eighteenth and Twentieth legions. I began to worry that my mother would not recover. The one Greek doctor we had known in Croton had evacuated at the time of the Bruttian's takeover. I knew nowhere else to turn.

Two weeks passed and another request came from Hannibal asking my mother to come to Metapontum. When she declined for a second time, Hannibal sent a doctor from Metapontum to our home. He had no answer for my mother's illness. Her symptoms suggested nothing he could recognize. He left us with a collection of herbs and strict instructions for their use. Ava and Lucretia followed the doctor's orders, and my mother seemed to get slightly better. She played the lyre and sang one night. She sang with such delicacy and beauty, I thought it was a sign of her recovery.

My mother made steady progress for a week or so, but then fell back into a state of delirium that was worse than before. Lucretia woke me one night, long before dawn, and anxiously hurried me into my mother's bedroom. A single oil lamp provided the only light. My mother had grown so thin she was barely a wrinkle beneath her covers. I knelt down by her head and stroked her forehead which had become damp with fever.

She turned her head to face me and reached out with her hand to hold mine. A weak smile graced her face as she gazed into my eyes. "Timon, I fear I will not last much longer. I feel so fortunate to have found you after our separation. I never thought I would. Now I've had nearly a year with you. My life has been good, but this last year has meant more to me than any other."

Tears streamed down my cheeks. I could only choke out that I felt the same way. She let go of my hand and ran her fingers through my hair and stroked my cheek. "I don't know if you remember, son, but long ago I asked your father to place a lyre string in an urn with my ashes should I die before him. He's been dead now nearly ten years, so to you I make this same request."

I took her hand in mine and pressed it to my cheek, then nodded. I remembered the request. Oh, how I remembered it—recalling the falsehoods I had been told by Paculla Annia during my time in Rome.

"If it's not too much trouble," she continued, her voice barely audible for her weakness, "take the strings from the lyre your father gave me and put them all in my urn. I would so love to continue playing music in the underworld."

Lucretia and I stayed with her through the night. In the morning my mother felt well enough to sit up. Ava brought her a bowl of wheat porridge. She took a few spoonfuls from Lucretia, but refused any more.

After Ava had returned to the kitchen, I took a spoonful of the honey sweetened porridge for myself.

"What is it?" asked Lucretia when I seemed to puzzle over the taste.

"This is sweet, but it leaves a bitter aftertaste. Try it. See what you think?"

Lucretia tried a taste and immediately frowned. She took the bowl of porridge back to the kitchen and spoke with Ava. When she returned, she was visibly disturbed.

"Ava said she might have scorched the porridge while making it." Lucretia shook her head. "But I wasn't tasting burnt gruel. It was something else. Maybe the wheat has become rancid. I'll look into it a bit more."

Lucretia sent Ava to the market that afternoon to get wheat from another source. Without telling me, Lucretia searched Ava's room. She found a small mortar and pestle and a ceramic jar containing dried flowers beneath the bed and brought them to me.

"These flowers are foxglove. They contain enough poison to kill an infant or someone very old, but not someone as healthy as your mother," she said, trembling with what she was thinking, "unless it were in her food every day." She looked up a me.

"Are you saying Ava has been slowly poisoning her?"

She took a deep breath and nodded.

"But why?"

Lucretia lowered her voice. "Ava was a gift to your mother from Hannibal. Maybe she acts as his eyes and ears. Your mother had this suspicion from the beginning and was always careful in her presence."

"But Ava couldn't have known that my mother was passing on information." I recalled how she had entered the room the night I had asked my mother not to go back to Metapontum. "Could she?"

"Only if she were very attentive and very secretive, listening when we didn't know she could hear us."

When Ava returned from the market, she put what she had bought in the kitchen then went to her bedroom. I followed her into the room and confronted her with the flowers. She denied everything, increasing my anger. I took hold of her by the wrist. "I don't believe you," I screamed. "You're working for Hannibal. He's paid you to poison my mother." I leaned into her face. "Why? What did you tell him?"

Lucretia heard us and came running to the bedroom doorway. Ava's eyes flashed to Lucretia for help. Lucretia came all the way into the room. "What did you tell Hannibal, Ava?"

"I didn't tell him anything!" she shouted defiantly. "And he didn't pay me either. The poison was my idea."

"But why?" I demanded. "Why? She's treated you well."

"Because I knew she must be some kind of informant. She had Hannibal completely fooled. She cast a spell on him with her singing. He thought she was some kind of goddess. He even preferred her caresses to mine despite her being so old. He would never have listened to me." She began to cry. "So I took it on myself to protect him."

I backed away from her, my hands in fists, so upset I didn't know what to do. I turned to Lucretia in absolute frustration. "What should we do with her?" I glared at Ava. "I can't do what she deserves."

"I can." Lucretia strode across the room toward Ava. I saw that she held a kitchen knife behind her back. She slapped Ava once across the face with her free hand then buried the knife in her belly. Ava didn't see the knife until the last moment. She gasped instead of screaming. Sweet and gentle Lucretia, the woman who had cared for me as baby, pulled the knife from Ava's stomach and stabbed her three more times until the girl slumped to the floor dead, leaving a wide smear of blood on the wall behind her.

Lucretia faced me with a look so intense I didn't recognize her. "She had it coming," she snarled, then stomped out of the room.

CHAPTER 17

Lucretia and I wrapped Ava's body in the blankets from her bed, then went to my mother's room. We told her everything. My mother began to sob and shake. Lucretia held her, trying to calm her down. "We'll begin a three-day purge right away, Arathia. I don't know what else to do. Without the regular doses of foxglove, your health is certain to improve—and as soon as you have the strength," the loyal slave turned to me, "we must leave Croton."

I knew she was right. Eventually Hannibal or one of his officers would ask about Ava. Whatever we might say would lead to greater complications. There was no good reason for us to stay in Croton.

That night at the evening meal, Lucretia, proving to be shrewder than I had ever imagined, hatched a plan. She leaned across the table, her face lit by the oil lamp, and spoke very softly, just above a whisper. "Tomorrow, we'll tell the neighbors that Arathia has died. We'll put Ava's body in her bed, covered by a sheet. We'll notify the garrison commander and stage a funeral as soon as possible. He will pass the news on to Hannibal. He knew that she was sick. It won't be a surprise. We'll say you freed Ava and that she returned to her home. Then the three of us will leave as soon as your mother is strong enough to travel." She took a quick glance around the room. "With all the gold and silver your mother's saved, we can go anywhere."

I had known Lucretia all my life. I thought of her as family, but never could I have imagined her covering up a murder, done by her own hand. "We'll go to Rome, Lucretia. I know Rome and have friends there that can help us."

"Rome is a long way, Timon. Your mother is weak. It will be a hard trip for her."

"Where else could we go? It has to be to the north, out of the region controlled by Hannibal. And we would be strangers anywhere else we went. We wouldn't know who to trust."

Lucretia drew back from the table, thinking. After a moment, she nodded. "You're right. We'll go to Rome. Let's move your mother to Ava's room and tell her what we're doing. I'll talk to the woman next door as soon as the sun is up. With her mouth, the entire neighborhood will know of your mother's death by noon."

CHAPTER 18

My mother showed me her savings the next day. Hannibal's generosity had made her wealthy beyond my wildest dreams. The money made everything easier. No one asked questions when you paid in gold.

Though Ava's corpse was covered, Lucretia dressed her in my mother's clothing and wove some of my mother's graying hair into Ava's for the trip to the crematorium. We made a big deal of the funeral. I placed the urn in the Pythagorean School's mausoleum alongside my father's. I tearfully added the seven lyre strings to the urn, while the captain of the Carthaginian garrison and those few neighbors who knew my mother stood by.

Once the purge had been completed, and my mother was eating untainted food, her health began to improve, but she remained weak and uncommonly thin. We worried that Hannibal would send someone looking for Ava, so we felt it was important to leave no more than a week after the funeral. I bought a two-wheeled carriage. Balius would draw the carriage, and I would drive.

The day before we left, inspired by Lucretia's courage to do away with Ava, I decided to complete some unfinished business of my own. I knew that the man who had killed my father drank in excess every night. I went to the establishment where I had seen him last. He sat at a table with two other men. I watched him drain one cup of wine after another. I had two cups myself to strengthen my resolve. The man got into an argument with the men at his table. He suddenly stood up and stormed out into the street. I threw down what was left in my cup and followed him.

His route was the same as the last time. We passed through the same narrow alley as before. The situation was perfect for what I had in mind. I gripped the dagger beneath the folds of my toga, determined to avenge my father's murder, but before I could make a move, two men stepped from the shadows, one in front of my target, one in back. As soon as the first man confronted him, the second struck him from behind with a club. When he fell to the ground, the thug clubbed him two more times, while the other spat on him, then kicked him. Even in the dark I recognized the men as the ones he had been drinking with. They hurriedly rifled his pockets. I heard one curse, perhaps at the absence of money. They both added another kick for good measure, then took off at a run down the street, never having seen me.

I quietly slipped down the alley and knelt beside the man lying in a heap on the ground. He was still alive. He looked up at me with no idea who I was. His face was broken and bleeding. He took hold of my toga and pulled himself up close to me. "Help me, please," he muttered. His hands lost their grip, and he sank back to the ground. I thought to finish the job with my dagger, but recalled the only time I had killed a man. It was after the battle of Numistro, and that man, much like this man, was in no shape to defend himself. I couldn't bring myself to do it again. Instead, I remained at his side and watched him die. I'm not sure how long I was there, but when I left, my revenge felt tarnished and incomplete.

That night as I lay in bed unable to sleep, I realized my time in Croton had come to an end. We would leave the next morning just before daybreak so that no one would notice our leaving or see that two women sat in the carriage, not just one. Once we were out of Croton no one would notice or care.

CHAPTER 19

Everything went as planned the next morning. We took very little with us. We wrapped my mother in blankets to make the ride as comfortable as possible, and were rolling out of the gates of Croton just as the first rays of sunlight appeared in the east. I had built a secret compartment beneath the carriage to carry my mother's gold and silver coins, and we did our best to make ourselves blend in with the other travelers on the road north. I wore a plain tunic, and both my mother and Lucretia had on bleached wool chitons of the most common variety.

It was midwinter. None of the armies had been dispatched yet. Fortunately the weather was mild as we traveled through Lucania headed to the west branch of Via Latina, approximately five days of rough travel on little more than rutted dirt roads. My mother struggled with the uneven ride, but we were able to find comfortable inns to stay the night.

Outside Grumentum, still a day from Via Latina, I noticed that a contingent of riders was coming up the road behind us. I took out the spyglass and quickly realized that the riders were Numidians. They gained on us quickly. I had little choice but to stay the course. Suddenly they were right behind us, their black mantles draped around the faces and shoulders, only their dark eyes visible. Then they were alongside the carriage, forty dark-skinned Numidians shouting what could only have been ugly propositions to my mother and Lucretia in a language none of us could understand. They rode small, agile horses called garrons and darted up close to us in swarms, hooting and laughing, then scampered off again. One rider leapt from his horse onto the back of the carriage. Two other riders rode up close to Balius, took hold of his bridle, and brought us to a stop. Just like that we were surrounded. Some of them remained on their horses, others dismounted, crowding in around the carriage aggressively. My mother

71

and Lucretia, their scarves covering their faces, huddled together to avoid the grasping hands.

With no plan other than a request for mercy, I addressed them in Greek. They erupted with more laughter and incomprehensible, sneering remarks. Four Numidians, who had lagged behind the others, rode up. The men around us suddenly quieted and backed off to allow one of the four, a young man with his mantle pushed down from his face, to approach us. By the cut of his tunic, his gold-handled sword, and the silver trappings on his horse, this man, perhaps five years older than I, was surely the squadron captain.

The man was uniquely handsome and confident in his manner. He appraised me with green eyes as piercing as arrows, then addressed me in perfect Greek. "I'm sorry for the actions of my men. We mean you no harm. We are looking for someone. We only want to search your carriage."

Even with this polite opening, because of the needs of the war, I expected the Numidians to take Balius and the carriage. "How can we make this easier for you?" I asked.

"Have the women get out of the carriage and reveal their faces."

I looked at my mother. She nodded. I helped her climb from the carriage, then gave a hand to Lucretia. Both women removed their scarves as two of the riders searched the carriage—though not beneath.

When they were done, the captain thanked us for our patience, then explained that they were looking for a young Bruttian woman. A slave by the name of Ava. She was a runaway. Her owner, a ranking Carthaginian officer, wanted her back. "Have you seen such a girl?"

I told the man that we had just left Grumentum. It was our first day on the road, and we had not seen anyone. The captain took me at my word. He called out an order in Numidian. The riders quickly gathered into a loose group and galloped off down the road in the direction we were headed.

My mother looked at me. "Hannibal must have expected Ava to report to him in Metapontum. It seems he gave her a week before sending out his men."

Lucretia nodded. "It's likely he doesn't know that we've left Croton. After learning of your death, Arathia, he would have little reason to be looking for Timon or me."

"I hope you're right," I said. "The garrison commander saw the funeral. He knew how long you'd been sick. I don't think he had the slightest inkling that the body we cremated was Ava's. He may not have even known she was a plant."

"Let's get going," said my mother. "The sooner we're in Rome the better."

I gave my mother a hand into the carriage. She collapsed into the blankets exhausted by the incident. Lucretia crawled in beside her.

Before climbing onto the driver's seat, I patted Balius on his neck and leaned up close to his ear. "I just hope we don't see those Numidians again," I whispered. "I'm sure you noticed how they looked at you."

I felt fortunate that our encounter with the Numidians had not been worse. I suspect we would have been treated quiet differently by any other squadron. But the young man, their captain, was exceptional. I sensed it immediately. I could hear it in the accuracy of his Greek. As I would learn later, he was a wealthy Numidian prince by the name of Masinissa who had been educated in Carthage. His father Gala was king of the Masesulii, one of the two most powerful Numidian tribes in the region west of Carthage.

Masinissa was in Italy at the time of the incident just described to be trained by Maharbal, Hannibal's superb cavalry captain. Two years later, he would change sides in the war. He and I would meet in Africa and become friends. Even these tens of years later, I still know and see Masinissa. As a source for my writing, he has been invaluable. He told me parts of this story I could not have otherwise known.

CHAPTER 20

Once we reached Via Latina the trip became considerably easier. On a good day we could make twenty miles. The traffic on the road varied. At times we were alone, no one else as far as we could see—even using the spyglass. At other times, hordes of travelers, on foot, on horseback, in carts or carriages, filled the road and dropped our speed to that of those walking. Finding a place to stay each night became easier as we proceeded north. One night it might be a farmer's barn, the next it could be a lodging in a walled city. We stayed in Nola and Catalia, but paid in silver rather than bronze.

We had just passed Capua and were alone on the road, making great progress, with the worst of the trip over, when the iron felloe on the carriage's right wheel broke from fatigue, causing two spokes to splinter, bringing us to a complete halt.

I disconnected Balius from the hitch, then unloaded everything from the carriage. I dragged it to the side of the road and fiddled with the broken wheel hoping somehow to fix it. But we had nothing to work with, no tools or materials. I looked at my mother. "This carriage is done for. If Lucretia and I walk, do you think you could ride Balius?"

"I think so," she said.

Lucretia nodded. "It will be all right, but we'll have to give her regular breaks."

"It will double, maybe triple the time it takes to get to Rome, but we can't just stay here hoping someone will come along to help us. I suggest we retrieve the box of coins from beneath the carriage and get on with it. Most of this other stuff we'll have to leave behind."

My mother and Lucretia were gathering up the blankets to put them on Balius' back for a softer ride, when I noticed that something large was coming down the road from the north. The women looked up at the same time I did because of the clanking sound it was making.

I got out the spyglass, thinking it was some kind of military equipment on wheels—siege apparatus or a catapult. I could see that six oxen were pulling an amorphous mass about the size of a small ship. All three of us stared down the road as the slow moving vehicle trundled into view.

The six oxen towed three large farm wagons, each one stacked precariously high with all manner of junk scavenged from the debris of war. A fat man in a dirty wool tunic sat at the reigns of the lead wagon. His black hair stuck out from his head in all directions. It was full of knots and curls and matched his beard in length.

I guessed that he was a Latin, and as the wagons drew closer, I called out to him. "Kind sir, do you have anything that might help us fix this carriage?"

I didn't think the man heard me for all the rattling of the items piled in his wagons, but all of a sudden, just as the third wagon reached our carriage, he called to his oxen to stop. From what I could see in his ragged collection of junk, he had a little bit of everything from garden statuary and wall hangings to military armor and weapons. Household goods, ceramic ware, tools, I scoured the lot of it, looking for a wheel.

As the heavyset junk collector came down the line of wagons, two of his fellow scavengers, apparently walking on the other side of the caravan, appeared from between the wagons. They were a rough-looking bunch, swarthy Italians, likely three brothers. The heavyset driver was the oldest, perhaps forty years of age. He approached me grinning, showing a lot of broken teeth and smelling of garlic and stale wine.

"You could use a new wheel," he said, sidling up to me, looking closely at my mother, who was still quite frail and sat beside Lucretia on a blanket they had laid on the ground. Our few belongings were piled beside them.

I wasn't sure if these men were a threat or not, but I knew we were no match for them if they became aggressive. "Any chance you have something that might fit our carriage?"

The man closed one eye and studied me with the other. "How far you going?"

"Rome."

He seemed to think about this, then said, "I've got a wooden cart. I'll trade it to you for your carriage. The cart will make it to Rome, but the going will be slow."

He showed me a rough wooden cart that was being towed behind the third wagon. It was only big enough for one. Lucretia would have to walk. Even with a broken wheel, the carriage was worth ten times what the cart was. The difference was my mother riding on a horse or in a cart, and an extra three days on the road either way. "Unhook it," I said. "Let's see how it rolls."

He turned to his assistants and jerked his thumb. They untied the cart from the wagon and pulled it down the road about thirty feet. The solid wooden wheels appeared more oblong than round. Clearly the ride would be rough even on Via Latina, which would take us all the way to Rome. I looked at my mother.

"I think it's better than the horse, Timon."

Just as I accepted this dubious trade, I realized that the box containing my mother's wealth was still strapped beneath the carriage. Removing it in front these men would likely lead to suspicions about what was in it. If they saw the number of gold coins we carried, they would surely kill us and take it all. I explained the situation to the women in Greek so as not to reveal our problem to the junkers, who were standing there gawking at us.

My mother understood right away. Without any hesitation she reached for her lyre, which lay on the grass beside her. She placed it on her lap and ran her fingers over the strings, then deftly adjusted the tuning, drawing the attention and wonder of the three men. When she began to play and sing, they were immediately captivated and moved up close to listen. Even weak from the poisoning and the travel, my mother's voice filled the air like the fragrance of spring. No one could resist the beauty of her songs. The three men stood spellbound before her watching her fingers on the strings, clearly transported by the Greek poems though they didn't understand the words.

I quickly took the opportunity to slip over to the carriage. Pretending to inspect the broken wheel, I reached beneath the frame and freed the small box of coins. The men didn't even turn their heads as I slipped the box beneath our pile of blankets, and then sat on the ground to listen to my mother.

My mother sang three songs. Not a word was said throughout her performance. When she stopped, she spoke to me in Greek. I translated for the three men awed by her talent. "My mother sang those songs as thanks to you for coming to our rescue."

Although clearly vagabonds of dubious character, they bowed to my mother to show their appreciation. With little else said, they disassembled the carriage and loaded it in pieces onto their wagons. We packed the cart and made it into a bed for my mother.

What could have been a difficult confrontation was over. The team of oxen was prompted into motion with the crack of a whip, and the three wagons disappeared like a ship over the southern horizon. I harnessed Balius to the cart, and we went the other way to Rome.

CHAPTER 21

After what had been too long a trip, more than three weeks on the road, we reached Rome. I avoided the city proper and went west to the Claudian villa. Marcus had no advance knowledge that we were coming. He may or may not be at the farm when we arrived. At the very least, I expected Edeco and Meda to be there.

I saw the carriage out front of the stable as we came down the dirt road to the house. I hoped it didn't mean that Portia was there. The creak and clatter of the wooden cart brought Edeco out of the stable.

"Edeco, this is my mother, Arathia, and her slave, Lucretia. We've come from Croton and hope to stay here for a while. My mother's been sick. I'm concerned the long trip has been too hard on her. Can you help me get her and her things into the house?"

My mother had regressed in the last week. Traveling in the cart hadn't helped. Edeco lifted her from the cart without any questions.

"Who's here, Edeco?"

"Portia and Meda. Marcus is in Rome. He should be back tomorrow."

"Does Portia stay here now?"

"No, it's rare that she's here at all. She comes out occasionally to take things back to the house in Rome. That's why she's here now. I'll be taking her to Rome in the morning."

With Edeco leading the way, I assisted my mother to the house. Lucretia followed behind.

Portia met us as we came through the door. I introduced her to my mother and Lucretia. Portia, like Marcus, thought my mother had died several years earlier. Instead of asking questions, she assured me that all of us were welcome at the villa and that we could stay there as long as needed. She told Meda which bedroom to use, and Lucretia and Meda took my mother off to bed. I worried that I had taken her on the road too soon, but if anyone could nurse her back to health it would be cranky old Meda. She warmed up some soup, but when she took it to the bedroom my mother was asleep.

Edeco and I carried the few things we had brought from Croton into the house. Afterward, Portia found me in the atrium. She was a lovely woman, and though I had many issues with her, I always found her beauty disarming.

"I thought you found your mother's urn in the Aemilii tomb?" she asked, sitting down beside me at the edge of the pool.

"I spoke to Marcus Aemilius Lepidas at your party a year ago. I asked him about the urn in his family's tomb, and it became clear that it was not my mother's."

"But you didn't say anything to me?"

I bowed my head, then looked up at her. "I should have, but the discovery made me suspicious of Paculla, and I knew that you would resist anything negative I might say about her."

Portia sat up straight. "You think she's making it all up? That's she's a fake?"

"Yes."

"But what about the other reading? Didn't that help you find your lenses?"

"She sent me to the Community of Miracles, Portia. It's a society of thieves and beggars at the top of the Aventine Hill. What I learned there was that she was a sham, and that she often came to the Community of Miracles for information."

Portia became indignant. "So what's that make me?"

"Portia, we all believe what we want to believe. I would say be careful. I'm worried that Paculla's playing a game with you and the other wealthy women."

Portia stood up and took three strides away from me, then turned and came back. "There's more to her than readings and rituals. She's shown us the Greek tragedies and opened us up intellectually."

"Yes, I've seen that, and you're right, that's good, but at the same time, she used her so-called readings to manipulate me and, most likely, you also."

Portia glared at me. "So where was your mother?"

"It's a long story, but in the end, I found her in Croton. In our old home."

"Well, thankfully she wasn't dead," she said coolly. "I'm sorry if Paculla had it wrong. I was trying to help you." She turned away, but I stopped her.

"Portia, for the time being, don't mention that my mother is here."

"Why would that matter?"

"I can't say."

"Oh, that's right. You don't trust me."

"I never said that, Portia."

She just stared at me.

"Do you still speak to Fulvia?" I asked.

"Why would you care?"

"I worry about Sempronia. How is she?"

"Still unmarried," she said, then turned abruptly and walked out of the atrium to the back of the house.

CHAPTER 22

Portia left the farm early the next morning. Marcus returned at noon. I went out to the stable as soon as I saw him arrive. He was clearly surprised to see me. He leapt from Euroclydon and embraced me like a brother.

I told him I had returned from Croton with my mother and her slave, and that they were inside. I made him swear to secrecy, then recounted what had happened in the months since I had last seen him, including the trip to Hannibal's winter headquarters in Metapontum, and the message I had passed on to Claudius Nero.

"You gave him that information? That may have won the war!"

"My mother deserves the credit, but I'm concerned that Hannibal will learn that she was the source, and that the funeral we held was staged. I came here hoping we could hide her at the farm until we know something more. Will that be all right with you?"

"Of course. You and your mother are welcome here as long as you like."

I looked around anxiously "It's important that no one knows my mother is here, but Portia saw her yesterday when we arrived, and I—I..."

"Don't trust her?"

I hung my head.

"I don't either, Timon. It's all right. She has intrigues of her own going on. I rarely see her anymore."

"She knows that my mother is here, but not about her activities in Hannibal's camp."

"I wouldn't worry. Her friends won't care about your mother or about you. She's not likely to say anything because it's not relevant to her position in society. It will be fine."

Marcus and I shared a few cups of mulsum with dinner that night. My mother didn't join us. Lucretia ate with her in the bedroom. Marcus had been in the north with Marcus Livius during the summer. He was there at Sena when Nero arrived to help defeat Hasdrubal.

"I saw Hasdrubal die." Marcus took a swallow form his cup. "I give the man credit. Once the battle's outcome became obvious, he waved his sword over his head and rode directly into a cohort of hastati, all of them eager to say they'd taken the Carthaginian general down. He made a few of them pay, but they cut him to pieces. I think a centurion had the idea of cutting his head off. Nero decided to make it a gift to Hannibal. I can't say I agree with the sentiment."

"Neither can I. Hannibal gave your father a military funeral, and from what I've heard, Aemilius Paullus got the same after Cannae. Hasdrubal deserved better."

Marcus nodded. "Nero's not my favorite. But his march was genius. We might have beaten Hasdrubal without him, but it was certainly easier with him." Marcus grinned. "It was a tactic taken straight from Hannibal. You surely recall when Hannibal did that to us—secretly sending half his cavalry to Locri while we camped opposite him, waiting for him to accept battle."

"I spent a month with Nero last spring. He's still as coarse as he always was, but I think his time with your father did him well. He did his share of chasing Hannibal around Apulia. He was all caution, and in the end, he made it work." I lifted my cup over my head and drained it. Marcus refilled his and mine.

"The elections are coming up. Who are the candidates for consul, Marcus? Have you thrown your hat into the ring?"

Marcus smiled warmly. "In a few years perhaps, Timon, but not yet. I'm thinking about running for tribune of the plebs." He took a studied sip from his cup. "Publius Scipio is making a push for a consulship. He's still stationed in Spain, but I expect we'll see him in Rome in the next week or two. He's made no secret of his political ambitions. His clients have been out in number. And you know what they've been saying."

"Invade Africa."

PART II

CARTHAGE

"Six hundred years before Hannibal's march through the Alps, the Phoenician princess Dido founded the colony of Carthage on the north coast of Africa. The colonists who joined her came from a long line of highly successful Semitic sea merchants, and following in that tradition, sent their ships all over the Mediterranean and beyond. Carthage quickly became the most important seaport in the western Mediterranean, and as wealthy a city-state as any in the world."

-Nicoledes of Croton, Letters.

CHAPTER 23

From the jubilation in Rome after Claudius Nero's and Marcus Livius' defeat of Hasdrubal and their ensuing triumphant march into the city, the first Roman triumph of the war, one would have thought that the war was over. In some ways it was over in Italy. Hannibal had settled into Metapontum for the winter for the third year in a row and showed no sign of coming north. The beast outside the walls was gone and Rome could finally breathe again. The farmers were told to go back to their land and to return to the business of growing food.

Across the Mediterranean in Carthage the tables had turned. While the central motive of Roman life was war, the Carthaginian aristocracy focused on the accumulation of riches and a level of luxury only experienced by royalty elsewhere. In a system of government not unlike Rome's, one hundred and four of these wealthy merchants made up Carthage's Council of Elders. An assembly of the people annually elected two leaders, sufets, who presided over the Council of Elders and a special legislative body of thirty judges. From the colony's inception, it had maintained a strongly mercantile society where wealth determined social standing and the primary goal of the government was to enable commerce. Now, following Hasdrubal's defeat, many of the elders were growing tired of the war and wanted to get back to the business of making money, and it was causing a serious split in the Council of Elders.

This war of incredible cost, human and fiscal, was the work of the Barcid faction of the Council—the war party. Their leader Hannibal, once praised as a hero, was now being characterized as a problem by the opposing faction, known as the peace party. This was not something new. Throughout the course of the war, the Council had been slow to respond to Hannibal's needs in Italy. Reinforcements and warships came late or not at all. The war effort in Spain had gotten more support than Hannibal. In many ways, he had fought the war in

Italy by himself. Now that the momentum of the war had swung to Rome and Scipio was threatening an invasion, many of the elders were ready to cut Hannibal off completely. His daring idea to invade Italy had become a dismal failure, and they wanted nothing more to do with him or his pursuit of the war.

CHAPTER 24

Hasdrubal Gisgo entered his plantation manor like an angry bull, shaking his shaggy head from to side to side as though looking for a target to ram. He was just back from a day of arguing in the Council of Elders and a rough ten-mile carriage ride to his country estate south of the city. He may have achieved what he wanted, but it had not come easily, and he was still seething from the opposition's political tactics.

Hasdrubal had returned to Carthage a month earlier after two years of disappointing military operations in Spain. Shortly after his return, he was elected to one of the sufet positions for the year. A member of the Barcid faction, Hasdrubal had spent his first week as a sufet in an ugly verbal sparring match with the other sufet, an older man by the name of Hanno, a capable orator from the peace party. The topic, of course, had been Scipio's invasion and the direction of the war. Hanno argued for immediate withdrawal from Italy. In his opinion, the war had effectively ended with the death and defeat of Hasdrubal Barca. It was time to cut their losses and sue for peace. Hasdrubal Gisgo, and about half the Council, wanted none of this. Didn't they still have Hannibal, the greatest military mind the world had ever known? The war was not over as long as he was alive and had soldiers to lead. There were sources of troops yet untapped. Carthage was wealthy enough to pay mercenaries for ten more years of war in Italy as well as protection from an invasion at home.

After many tense days of debate, Hasdrubal had finally gathered enough votes to pass a resolution that empowered him to travel to west Numidia to seek a military alliance with Syphax, king of the Masaesyli tribe. The other choice, as he said to the Council prior to the vote, "was to sit inside our homes and wait for the Roman army to encamp outside the city's walls."

Hasdrubal was a heavy-set man with a full beard except what was shaved off above his upper lip. At fifty-five, his hair was still black, and worn long in the Canaanite style of oiled ringlets. He crossed the house in long impatient strides, kicking at the fringed hem of his white linen robe. A bare-chested Ethiopian slave, wearing a red felt cap and a thigh-length skirt of striped silk, appeared like a shadow from the interior of the house and followed his master into the courtyard.

"Vangue, bring me some raisin wine," Hasdrubal ordered without any other acknowledgment of the man. "An amphora and a cup."

The slave vanished as quickly as he had appeared. Hasdrubal advanced to the colonnade that enclosed the south end of the courtyard. He stared out between the fluted columns at his vast plantation. All the land as far as he could see belonged to him. His farm produced wheat, barley, dry beans, oats, figs, flax, and olives. He ran a large oil press and a bagging plant in Carthage's industrial region of Malqua to process his harvest. He managed a fifty-ship merchant fleet to send his products around the world. He owned a bank in Carthage with partners in Rhodes and Cyprus, and he had just built a second home in the city with all the most modern innovations in plumbing and heating. At this moment in time, he was arguably the wealthiest man in Carthage, and also someone who still believed in Hannibal. Now he had the task of raising an army to protect his property and his wealth.

Hasdrubal drifted back to the center of the courtyard and settled down on his favorite couch. He put his feet up and stretched out, trying to push the past week out of his mind. Vangue appeared at his side with a silver tray, carrying a crystal goblet, an amphora of wine, and an amber bowl filled with dates and fried grasshoppers. Vangue put the goblet on the table beside the couch and filled it.

Hasdrubal selected a grasshopper from the bowl and put it in his mouth. He crunched the insect into small pieces then washed it down with a long swallow of wine. "Baal," he called out to the heavens, "why have you cursed me with the creation of this man Hanno?"

Vangue was a smart, rather oily man, with ebony skin and a set of eyes that always seemed to be moving. He stood a few feet from his master watching him lounge like a water buffalo on the couch, waiting for that moment when Hasdrubal would want his goblet refilled. "All men must have an opponent in their life," the slave said. "They are necessary to make one a better man."

Hasdrubal looked up at him. "The Roman Scipio should be enough for anyone." Hasdrubal had suffered badly in Spain at the hands of the young Roman general. The battle of Ilipa had been more a whipping than combat.

After Vangue had filled the goblet for a third time, Hasdrubal sat up, and with visible effort, swung his thick legs to the floor. "Have Sophonisba brought to me. Tell her to wear the gown I like so much."

Vangue nodded and headed off to Hasdrubal's daughter's suite of rooms on the second floor. He had heard the chambermaids talking earlier and knew that Sophonisba would be bathing. Vangue went out to the patio through the bedroom.

Sophonisba sat up to her shoulders in soap suds in a bath sunken into the marble surface of the patio and shaded by a silk awning. Two young Numidian slaves, Nycea and Gaia, knelt in the water on either side of her, washing her hair. A third slave, an older Numidian woman, Zanthia, Sophonisba's personal handmaiden, stood beside the pool, supervising. A cheetah cub named Felicia slept in the sun on the far side of the patio. Four large porphyry vases, each containing a dwarf lemon tree, stood at regular intervals along the balustrade. The dull blue silhouette of the Atlas mountains stretched across the horizon well beyond the plantation's expanse of grain fields.

The two young slaves saw Vangue first. They quickly closed in around Sophonisba for her privacy. Zanthia held up her hands to stop the man from coming any closer. "You may be a eunuch, Vangue, but you can't come in here unannounced. The lady of the house is not dressed."

Vangue was the top slave. With Hasdrubal's wife dead three years now, he ran the house, but Zanthia supervised the women slaves and had her own source of power in the household. She ushered him out the way he came in. "What do you want?"

Vangue gripped her by the forearm. "Continue to talk to me like that, you old whore, and I'll find a whip for your backside. Tell Sophonisba her father wants to see her in the courtyard. She's to wear the gown he considers his favorite." He released Zanthia's arm, spun around, and strode back through the suite of rooms.

Sophonisba passed the intrusion off as something well beneath her acknowledgment. Though only seventeen, she had gained a reputation in Carthage for her beauty and the elevated manner in which she presented herself. When the two slaves finished rinsing her hair, she stood from the bath wearing a shimmering veneer of water. Her hair, black like her father's, was straight, long, and lustrous, matched by a thick patch of maiden hair that rose in a thin trail up to her navel. Her breasts stood out unsupported like two halves of a melon, each crowned with a small, dark nipple. The curves of her hips beneath a silk gown could stop a man at a hundred feet and suggested all the unstated mystery of a woman's sensuality. Her skin was opalescent with the luster of youth, a stark white compared to the glistening brown of her chambermaids, who were dotted here and there with puffs of white soap bubbles. But Sophonisba's real beauty was in her face, beginning with her eyes—a startling aquamarine, almost luminous in the dark like a she-wolf's, and deep with the intellect and melancholy of a poetess—and culminating with her lips—the color of cinnabar, and perpetually poised in an unfathomable, beckoning pout.

The maids quickly dried Sophonisba with white linen towels. Then Zanthia held out a matching robe so she could step from the bath into the soft garment.

"Your father has requested your presence, Sophonisba," said Zanthia. "He's downstairs in the courtyard. I'll put out the gown you're to wear."

Sophonisba pulled her robe around her and strode, slow and languid like a cat, out to the patio to let the warm winter sun dry her hair. She sat on a stone bench beside the napping cheetah and distractedly reached down to pet the kitten her father had given her for her seventeenth birthday. The little cat lifted its head at her touch and nuzzled against her leg. Gaia stood behind Sophonisba, combing her luxurious hair that reached nearly to the patio surface, while Nycea manicured her fingernails.

Zanthia leaned on the patio balustrade and watched the maids at their work. She had been Sophonisba's handmaiden since the young woman's mother died. She had grown to love Sophonisba and talked to her at night like a mother, comforting her with stories of her own past and speculations on the young woman's future.

When the maids were done, Sophonisba's hair had been braided and coiled on top of her head in a spiral tower. The three slaves escorted the young woman to her bedroom to finish the task of preparing her for her father.

Hasdrubal stood by the courtyard pool, watching a variety of small fish, each with a ruby embedded in its dorsal fin, pass in and out of sight beneath the lily pads. Vangue hovered in the shadows off to one side of the courtyard watching his master, then turned as Sophonisba appeared. She wore a pale-blue, one-shoulder gown of fine silk that clung to her hips and torso like a second layer of skin. A teardrop of amber hung from a gold chain around her neck. Smaller, matching amber teardrops were suspended on gold chains from her earlobes. A streak of antimony colored her eyelids. A gloss of olive oil moistened her lips. Her slippers were gold lamé, just visible at the hem of her dress as she walked. An unseen chain of gold stretched from one ankle to the other, preventing her from taking too long a stride.

On reaching the pool, Sophonisba embraced her father and kissed him on both cheeks. He placed his hands on her waist and held her back to admire her beauty. Aside from his money and power, he enjoyed nothing more than the sight of his daughter. As he leaned in to kiss her on the forehead, his hands slipped to her hips, then slid around to her backside to stroke her haunches affectionately like he might a thoroughbred horse.

He took her hand and led her to an alabaster bench beside the pool. He settled onto the bench and drew her down beside him. For a moment he simply gazed at her. She reminded him of her mother at the same age. Elissa had not been as lovely as Sophonisba, but she had graced her daughter with the same sensual manner of movement and a nearly numinous sense of sexuality. In Hasdrubal's eyes, a woman was born for one thing. His daughter embodied it. He laid his hand on her knee as though touching her were irresistible.

"It's time I found you a husband," he said, captured by her eyes. "For my own reasons I have wanted to put your wedding day off as long as possible," his hand rose up from her knee to pat her lightly on the thigh, "but the hour glass is running out. The time has come."

Sophonisba bowed her head. She had been educated in Carthage by the best tutors money could buy. She knew Greek and Latin and Numidian, had studied arithmetic and astronomy, had read Euripides, Sophocles, and Aeschylus, and wrote poetry to the goddess Tanit to free her from the troubles of the world. She had known from childhood this day would come.

"The war has taken a turn for the worse," said Hasdrubal. "You and I have already spoken of this."

Sophonisba nodded. Her father talked frequently with her about the war and politics. He considered it part of her education.

"The fate of Carthage is in jeopardy. The Council of Elders anticipates a Roman invasion in the spring. In the next few months, I will seek an alliance with one of our neighboring African nations. Should I not be able to reach an agreement on political grounds, I will offer your hand in marriage as further inducement."

Sophonisba again was not surprised at what her father was telling her. She had been groomed for this all her life. She expected it.

Her father continued. "Because of your beauty and your ancestry, you are considered one of the greatest prizes in Africa. I would rather you marry a Carthaginian of standing, but the situation may dictate otherwise." He paused thinking of the two potential husbands, Syphax and Gala, both Numidian kings of great wealth. "You're likely to be made a queen, and your children will share the blood of royalty."

Sophonisba didn't hesitate. "I am ready, Father. There is no greater honor for a Carthaginian woman than to wed for the sake of the state."

Hasdrubal embraced his daughter. "You are the daughter all fathers want. You are brave and intelligent, and more lovely than you know. By the lord of the skies, Baal Shamin, I have been blessed." He stroked her back tenderly. "You may go now. There will be more talk of this in the coming weeks."

As Sophonisba stood, she noticed Vangue for the first time, standing in the shadows. His eyes met hers. She looked away but his eyes followed her until she passed out of sight.

CHAPTER 25

Zanthia suddenly clapped her hands. Nycea and Gaia hurried out of the bedroom. Zanthia went over to Sophonisba sitting on the side of the bed and began to gently brush the young woman's hair. With each stroke its luster heightened so that it shone like polished obsidian.

"Why the sad eyes tonight, Sophie?"

"My fate is one of melancholy." She spoke to her slaves in their native language. "It is who I must be."

"What do you mean by that? You have more wealth and beauty than any woman would dare to ask for."

"What good is wealth and beauty when my maids have more freedom than I?"

"You don't know what you're saying. Trust your well-traveled handmaiden. The gods have been very good to you."

"I don't mean to sound ungrateful, Zanthia. I do honor my father and hold nothing above the well-being of Carthage. It is my duty to fulfill his wishes. But I fear I will never know a romance of my own. I yearn for what you must know. I want to know what men are really like."

"If you follow the example of your mother, the art of knowing men will be your strength."

"I did not miss her art with men. But that's not what I long for. I want to know from you, a woman of honest lust, what real love is?

"A woman of honest lust?" Zanthia, a brown skinned woman of forty years, chuckled softly. "Is that an honor or a disparagement, my lady?"

Sophonisba took Zanthia's free hand and held it between both of hers. "Oh, Zanthia, an honor of course. To know men is a wisdom of which I am all too ignorant. I want to know what it's like to be touched by a man," she let go of her maid's hand, "who's not my father."

Zanthia's look was one of wisdom. "At least he has not spoiled your virtue as many a father might have with a daughter as tempting as you. Be thankful your father has had the sense not to tamper with your honor."

Sophonisba hung her head thinking about it.

Zanthia embraced her as though she were her daughter. "Men are something else, Sophie. Especially those with power like your father. Just know that love is rarely what we want it to be. The fabric of fate is a tricky weave. Prepare yourself for more than you imagine."

Sophonisba stood and strode across the room. "Cavalry is the only thing my father talks about. If his talks go well, I'm destined to be a Numidian queen."

"I was a gift from King Syphax to your father the day your mother died. If he should be your father's choice, you would be queen of one of the most spectacular kingdoms in all of Africa. Certainly there are worst fates than that."

"If not Syphax, than Gala, a man of seventy or more years."

"And another large kingdom."

Sophonisba turned away to stare off into the dark recesses of her bedroom. "A king might be something any other woman would die for," she whispered to herself, "but is dead dry obligation to me."

CHAPTER 26

Hasdrubal Gisgo paced anxiously on the bow of a Carthaginian trireme, watching the six triremes ahead of him navigate into the harbor at Siga on the African coast in west Numidia. Hasdrubal was there to talk to King Syphax about a military alliance between Carthage and the Masaesyli people. He would offer his daughter in the arrangement, but only if it could not be avoided.

Hasdrubal watched the first of the seven triremes being towed onto the beach. Once all the ships were secured, he would be escorted to the palace to talk to the king. They had met before, but under less pressing circumstances. If he could not reach an agreement with Syphax, his next trip would be to east Numidia, to speak to King Gala of the Maesulii tribe.

A sailor high on the mast suddenly shouted out that there were warships on the horizon. Hasdrubal and all his commanders turned to the open sea. Just barely discernable from the deck were two Roman quinqueremes, clearly intending to come into the harbor. Hasdrubal, thinking he had the advantage with seven ships, ordered his commanders to come about and attack. The Roman ships, powered by five tiers of oars and two large sails, caught a favorable breeze and glided into the harbor before the Carthaginian ships could turn around. Knowing that a sea battle in his host's harbor would work against any efforts to reach an alliance, Hasdrubal canceled his orders and watched the Roman ships run up onto the shore.

Hasdrubal was not the only one courting the tribes of North Africa in preparation for an invasion. Publius Cornelius Scipio, the youngest of the Roman generals, had recently evicted all but a few scattered Carthaginians troops from Spain. The siege of Cartagena, followed by innovative victories over Hasdrubal Barca at Baecula and Hasdrubal Gisgo in Ilipa had added to Scipio's reputation as an up and coming military commander.

While Fabius and the controlling faction in the Roman Senate still argued against an invasion of Africa, Scipio proceeded on this path as though it were already settled. Three weeks earlier he had sent his naval commander and closest advisor, Gaius Laelius, to Siga laden with gifts, to see if King Syphax would be open to negotiating an agreement of friendship with Rome. Syphax, yet to be approached by Hasdrubal Gisgo, said that he was not against the idea, but that he would only enter into a serious discussion if it was face to face with the dashing, young Roman general.

Scipio, then stationed in Tarraco on the east coast of Spain, made the trip with Laelius in two quinqueremes, and as luck would have it, arrived in the harbor at Siga the same day as Hasdrubal.

Unaware that the Roman commander was Scipio, Hasdrubal went ashore first with twenty armed soldiers. Shortly afterward Scipio and Laelius followed with a squadron of legionnaires. The two parties were just realizing they were there for the same reason when the Numidian king met them at the wharf with his entourage. Syphax, honored to be visited by generals from the two most powerful nations in the Mediterranean region, invited the men into his palace for a feast. The circumstances could hardly have been more awkward for his guests.

Syphax, who could speak passable Greek, was no fool. Concerned that a Roman invasion would be difficult for all African nations, he decided to take the opportunity to offer himself as a mediator between the two warring republics. He began the sumptuous dinner by proposing a treaty between Rome and Carthage.

Scipio respectfully rejected the idea. While he had no personal grievance with Hasdrubal, and he respected the wisdom of his host, for peace was always a better option than war, he could not enter into any kind of treaty without guidance from the Roman Senate.

Scipio's manner and elevated sense of diplomacy, particularly with regard to his handling of Syphax's offer, made a strong impression on the barbarian king. Even Hasdrubal, who Scipio showed the utmost courtesy, was impressed by this man he had faced across a battlefield several times, but now shared a dining couch with.

Scipio tactfully directed the conversation away from the war or any other divisive issues, then proceeded to charm both Syphax and Hasdrubal with his knowledge and graciousness. Hasdrubal knew before the meal was over that he had no chance of winning over Syphax the way Scipio had. He had planned to offer Syphax his daughter's hand in marriage as a last resort, but to suddenly offer Sophonisba to Syphax now, when the king was so clearly under the influence of Scipio, was disrespectful to his daughter. He decided against it. The trip to Siga had been for naught. He left for Carthage the following morning, knowing his only other source of military support would be King Gala. He would make the trip inland to Gala's palace in Cirta as soon as he could.

Scipio, on the other hand, stayed two more days in Siga. During that time, using even greater delicacy than he had shown at the dinner table, he reached an agreement of friendship with Syphax that included a promise that the king would give no monetary or military assistance to Carthage. Syphax responded by offering Scipio the use of his cavalry when he came to Africa. It was exactly what Scipio had sought.

After his return to Tarraco, Scipio left for Rome to inform the Senate of his treaty with Syphax and to advocate for a consulship in the coming election.

CHAPTER 27

Sophonisba sat in the window seat of her bedroom reading the poetry of Sappho with her little cheetah cub in her lap. On the far side of the room, Zanthia plucked at the strings of a kithara. Commotion in the yard below attracted Sophonisba's attention. From the window, she watched two of her father's house guards swing open the compound gates for ten men on horseback. A handsome Numidian warrior, riding a beautiful black garron with no saddle and only a rope halter, led the contingent into the compound. The young man dismounted with such flourish Sophonisba could not help but watch him. He was clean-shaven and wore a white linen robe. A brilliant blue mantle wrapped around his head and lay about his shoulders. A short sword hung from a belt at his hip.

"Zanthia, quick, come to the window!" As her handmaiden came across the room, Sophonisba put the kitten on the floor and stood to allow Zanthia to look out the window. "Do you know who that man is?"

They both watched a stable boy take the halter of the man's horse, then lead the horse and the other nine riders to the stable to water and feed their mounts. One of the house guards approached the Numidian and bowed. A few words were exchanged, then the guard escorted the man to the house.

"That's Prince Masinissa of the Maesulii tribe. Your father invited him here to talk. He's an envoy for his uncle, King Oezalces."

"He's a handsome man."

Zanthia looked at Sophonisba, surprised by the young woman's comment. She smiled. "Yes, you could feel his presence from here. He would be a prize for any woman even without his royal blood."

"Help me freshen up, Zanthia. Somehow the prince must see me before he leaves."

After fighting bravely and with initiative for the Carthaginians in Spain, gaining the attention of officers on both sides of the war, Masinissa had been sent to Italy to train with Maharbal. That was when I first encountered him and had been so impressed. Shortly after that, he had returned to Spain only to learn that his father, King Gala, had died and that the crown had been passed on to his father's younger brother, Oezalces, who, unfortunately, was also in poor health. Masinissa immediately left Spain for Cirta. Soon afterward, Oezalces was contacted by Hasdrubal, asking for an opportunity to talk with him. Instead of inviting the Carthaginian sufet to his palace in Cirta, the new king sent his nephew Masinissa to Carthage. Hasdrubal requested that the young man come to his country estate.

Vangue met Masinissa at the door and escorted him to Hasdrubal's study. Hasdrubal knew Masinissa from his time in Spain, but had never spoken to him. Hasdrubal opened the conversation with several compliments to Masinissa's late father, then quickly proceeded to the topic of interest. He described the situation of the war in much better terms than truly existed. He told the young prince that the Council of Elders anticipated a Roman invasion in the spring and that any Roman presence in Africa represented a threat to all of Africa, including the tribal kingdoms in Numidia. He told Masinissa that Carthage sought a full military agreement with his uncle and that such an alliance would be beneficial to the security of both nations. Carthage would pay the cost of all military operations if King Oezalces could provide an army in the neighborhood of thirty thousand foot and ten thousand horse.

Having spent several months in Italy, Masinissa understood the circumstances of the war better than Hasdrubal might have thought. He knew what had happened at Metaurus, and he knew that Hannibal was struggling. He even knew that Scipio was the Roman general set on invading Africa. Scipio had approached him right after his return to Spain and had asked the young cavalry commander to change sides and to take part in the invasion. Still an active member of the Carthaginian cavalry, Masinissa made no commitment at the time. Soon afterward, he learned of his father's death and left for Cirta without any follow-up to Scipio's proposition.

Now he was in Carthage with a much more substantial offer. Knowing how ill his uncle was, and that he or his cousin was next in line for the crown, Masinissa listened as though the proposal were being made to him. With offers from both warring nations on the table, he understood that he was in a position to do something important for his people. "Hasdrubal," he said, "I am honored by your offer, but I can give you no answer today. I will take your message back to my uncle. Only he can make such a decision."

"Yes, of course," said Hasdrubal, "but you know that the Romans have contacted Syphax recently and made an agreement."

Masinissa lifted his head. It was not something he knew. The two Numidian tribes, the Maesulii and the Masaesyli, were longtime enemies, constantly skirmishing at their borders. Never would they fight for the same side. "That's worth knowing," replied Masinissa. "I'm sure that will figure strongly in my uncle's response."

Hasdrubal was a successful merchant, who made deals of all kinds. Again he did not immediately offer his daughter's hand as part of the arrangement. He felt Syphax's alliance with Rome would be more than enough incentive for Oezalces to side with Carthage. If not, then he would offer the king his daughter and a large dowry as further inducement.

Hasdrubal's villa was surrounded by an extensive formal garden. Pink paths of powdered coral twisted through beds of exotic flowers, interspersed with native cactus, jujube trees, and date palms. Exquisite stone fountains, imported Greek sculptures, and religious shrines hid in grottos or populated the open spaces. Enclosed by a ten-foot stone wall, draped with purple wisteria, the property resembled a palace more than a home. Hasdrubal paid a private battalion of guards to patrol the grounds day and night.

Sophonisba and Zanthia were in the garden picking flowers near the front door, when Vangue escorted Masinissa out of the house. Sophonisba wore the pale blue, single-strap gown that was her father's favorite. Although a young woman with no experience with men, she knew full well why her father liked the gown and wanted to make certain the young prince had the opportunity to see her in it.

Sophonisba inspected several rose bushes with her back to the door, pretending to be unaware of the young man who was waiting for his horse. Zanthia whispered that the young man was watching her. Sophonisba leaned over to cut a flower, presenting herself to him in a way that was impossible for the prince to ignore. She added the rose to those already in her hand, then suddenly turned to face him, looking into his eyes as though reading his thoughts.

It may have been her figure from behind that first caught Masinissa's attention, but Sophonisba's beauty, particularly that first look she gave him, struck him like a thunderbolt. Not a shy man, he approached her boldly, "You must be the daughter of Hasdrubal Gisgo," he said in perfect Greek. "My name is Masinissa, son of Gala. Is there any chance you're picking those flowers for me?" His nostrils flared with excitement as he looked her up and down, his brilliant smile as disarming as her aquamarine eyes.

Sophonisba, as taken with his Greek as she was with his confident manner, seemed to double in radiance. She motioned with one hand to the flowers all around. "As you can see, we have plenty. These were for the house, but take them if you like." She extended the bouquet to him. "Please call me by my name. I am Sophonisba."

Masinissa came up close to her to take the flowers, captivated by the color of her eyes and the poetic rhythm of her voice. "Sophonisba, a name as lovely as you," he said, breathing in the fragrances that encompassed her.

Although ten years younger than the Numidian prince, and hardly more than a girl, Sophonisba didn't blush at his compliment. She knew what her beauty did to men, and that ignoring their pretty words as though they were nothing only increased her allure. "What interest does a warrior like yourself have in flowers?"

"I will give them to the one I love, of course."

"Then you have a wife?" asked Sophonisba, having already been told by Zanthia that he didn't.

"No, my dear Chthonia means more to me than a wife."

"A courtesan?"

Masinissa laughed. "Better!" He glanced over his shoulder. "Here she comes now."

The stable boy crossed the grounds leading Masinissa's jet black garron by the halter. The riders that had accompanied the prince trailed behind on their horses. Masinissa held out the bouquet to his horse. Chthonia took them in her mouth and began chewing.

Sophonisba knew she was being teased. "I have always heard Numidian men took to their horses more seriously than they took to their women." She turned her body to accent the curves in her figure and pushed her hair behind her ear. "Now I know it's true." She tipped her head. "How sad for the Numidian women."

Masinissa laughed freely. "What a shame Sophonisba is not so drawn to Numidian horsemen as her father." He suddenly swung up onto his horse, then turned to her with the arrows of his eyes. "Maybe one day she will be." He stroked and patted his horse's rump affectionately, as though it could be a woman's.

"It's unlikely," she replied, already glowing with evidence to the contrary.

Their eyes met and held for a moment. Masinissa abruptly turned his horse and galloped from the courtyard, leading the other men out through the gate.

Zanthia approached Sophonisba from behind. "I thought you wanted to know something about men?"

"What do you mean?"

"What is there for me to tell you? That man is already in love with you."

PART III

RETURN TO SYRACUSE

"Scipio advised the people that they would never drive Hannibal and the Carthaginians out of Italy except by sending a Roman army into Africa and so bringing danger to their doors. By persisting strenuously and persuading those who hesitated, he was chosen general for Africa and sailed forthwith to Sicily."

-Appian of Alexandria, *Foreign Wars of Rome*

CHAPTER 28

Publius Cornelius Scipio returned to Rome in February with ten transports loaded with plunder collected in Spain. The day following his arrival he went to the Temple of Bellona to make a report to the Senate on his five years in Spain. With his desire to be elected to a consulship behind every word, he recounted his capture of Cartagena, his victories against four different Carthaginian generals, his subjugation of the Iberian tribes, and finally his complete elimination of all Carthaginian forces from the region. In conclusion, he proudly stated that Spain was now a Roman province, then requested a triumph, admitting that he was well aware that triumphs could only be granted to elected consuls, which he had not been while in Spain.

Although his achievements were impressive and his reputation as a field marshal was rising as rapidly as his popularity among the populace, he was not granted a triumph. Two days later, he entered the city with a long train of treasure from Spain that included a donation of fourteen thousand pounds of silver to the treasury.

A week later, on the eighteenth of February, in an election presided over by the current co-consul Lucius Veturius Philo, Scipio was unanimously elected to his first consulship. His friend Publius Licinius Crassus was chosen as his co-consul, also his first consulship. On a more personal note, Marcus Claudius was successful in his bid to become one of the five tribunes of the plebs. It was his first official position in government, and we celebrated at the villa that night.

The two consuls were inaugurated twenty-seven days later on the ides of March. Following the sacrifice of two white oxen at the Temple of Jupiter, Scipio and Licinius convened the first Senate meeting of the three hundred and fourth year of the Roman Republic—the fourteenth year of the war with Hannibal.

I went into Rome that day with Marcus to attend the meeting. Anyone paying attention knew that the invasion of Africa would be the central issue of the day, and this inspired a huge turnout from the populace. Marcus stood with the other four tribunes to the left of the assembly of senators. I squeezed in with the mass of citizens who were so tightly pressed up against the walls around the perimeter of the Curia that many others spilled out into the forum.

The meeting began when Scipio and Licinius entered the chamber to a loud roar of approval. They took their seats in the two curule chairs and faced the amphitheater of three hundred senators. The poulterer came to the center of the Senate floor with a wooden cage containing two chickens. Fabius, as the senior augur, accepted a handful of feed from the poulterer and raised his hand for silence. When the hubbub of the room quieted, he sprinkled the feed into the cage. After a moment, Fabius announced to the Senate and those in the audience that the chickens had eaten with vigor. "The auspices are favorable. Let this meeting of the Roman Senate begin."

As was the law, the two consuls took turns presiding over the Senate meetings. Licinius offered the younger Scipio, now thirty years old, the honor of being princeps senatus for the first meeting.

Scipio had let his hair grow unusually long in Spain. He combed it back from his face so that it fell in blond waves onto his shoulders. In the bright white toga pretexta, the handsome consul appeared some other species of man in the room full of dark Latins and elderly men with white beards. Although he spoke with a well-practiced humility, his high opinion of himself was evident in everything he said.

"I would first like to thank the citizens of Rome for electing so young a man as myself to the position of consul. I am truly honored, and will do everything in my power to earn the trust and respect of those who put me in office. That said, I am not here to simply oversee the continuation of our war with Hannibal. In my opinion, it has gone on far too long. After the business of the day is completed, my co-consul and I will offer a plan to end it."

This brought another round of thunderous approval from the audience who knew this meant invading Africa.

Following several long reports on the finances of the state, representatives from the various Roman provinces made statements. An ambassador from the city of Saguntum, on the coast of Spain, was the last to come forward. The war had begun when Hannibal initiated a siege of Saguntum prior to his march through the Alps. The ambassador thanked the Roman people for protecting them from the Carthaginians and the Roman Senate for honoring the promises of their longtime alliance. The ambassador concluded almost tearfully with thanks to Publius Scipio. After reciting a litany of superlatives to describe the newly elected consul, he retold the story of Scipio's father and uncle being killed in Spain, and Scipio's coming there at the very worst of times, and taking a general's command though only twenty-five. "With courage and intelligence, Scipio systematically cast the Carthaginians out of Spain and brought the most violent of the Iberian tribes to heel. Saguntum owes him everything. We believe the Roman people could not have elected a better man to the position of consul."

Standing at the edge of the room, watching over and between the heads of those in front of me, I almost laughed at the ambassador's extended praise of Scipio, knowing it was all part of a well-orchestrated prelude to introducing the most important topic of the day. But the ambassador's statements were also true. The young officer had proven himself to be a field marshal of the highest caliber, and now he was leading the Senate.

The next piece of business was the assignment of commands and the distribution of troops. This began with the two consuls drawing lots for their provinces of duty. A flamen came to the floor of the Senate with an empty ceramic bowl and a half-filled pitcher of water containing two wooden lots—one for the province of southern Italy and one for Sicily. The standard practice required one of the consuls to pour the water from the pitcher into the bowl until one of the lots fell into the bowl—that lot would name his province.

Licinius stood from his chair and addressed the Senate. "Senators, citizens of Rome, as all of you know I am the pontifex maximus, and as such, I will have religious duties to attend to in Rome throughout the year. Because of this, I believe it would be in the best interest of the state that my command be the province of southern Italy. There will be no need to draw lots if my co-consul will accept the province of Sicily as his command."

Licinius' request was not out of the ordinary. No one in the Senate objected, though Fabius looked at the floor and shook his head. In retrospect, this may have been something that Scipio and Licinius had worked out prior to the election, knowing that Scipio sought the province of Sicily for staging an invasion of Africa.

When Licinius returned to his chair, Scipio stood and turned to Licinius. "Consul, I would be honored to take the province of Sicily, and nothing could be a more appropriate preface to introducing what, in my opinion, is the best military strategy for the coming year."

Scipio advanced to the first row of the Senate amphitheater, then strode confidently back and forth along its length, assessing his audience before continuing. "While many here today contend that the central theater of the war this year will be in southern Italy, my co-consul and I are of a different opinion. As I said earlier, we believe that we were elected to consulships not merely to conduct the war but to end it—and that can only be achieved by invading Africa."

This was what the audience was waiting for, and again the boisterous crowd erupted with an enthusiastic demonstration of support. And yet, despite this response, and the fear of a Roman invasion already brewing in Carthage, the decision was by no means settled among the senators.

Scipio glanced briefly at Fabius sitting on the left side of the amphitheater. "I have visited Lilybaeum in Sicily and determined it is the best port for transporting an army to Africa. My tribune Gaius Laelius has scouted the north coast of Africa and found several possible locations for staging an invasion, and I have recently secured assurances from King Syphax of Numidia that he will not provide support of any kind to the Carthaginians. I plan to go to Africa as soon as I can raise the troops. I will besiege Carthage and by doing so force Hannibal to return to his homeland." His eyes lit with the intensity of his purpose. "I realize there will be strong objections to this strategy from some my colleagues, so if I cannot gain the Senate's approval today, I will go to the People's Assembly tomorrow to ask for the authority to circumvent the Senate's position."

Scipio's final words were spoken directly to Fabius, who had led opposition to an invasion of Africa for the past three years. The room became completely quiet in anticipation of Fabius' response. The grand old man of Rome stood slowly, showing his eighty years. He had been directing Rome's military since the war's second year, and now with Hannibal pinned in Bruttium, some would argue Fabius' strategy of tactical defense had already won the war. Although his words no longer held the influence they once had, he responded to Scipio with the calm and reason that had made him one of the most respected Roman statesmen in the history of the Republic.

"Many of you here today may feel that the subject we are about to debate has not already been settled, and that the question of fighting in Africa remains an open question. This is not the case. There has been no resolution in the Senate stating that Africa will be a theater of military operations in the coming year, and our young consul insults the Senate by presuming to assume a command that has yet to be approved.

"I realize that my opposition to invading Africa will be heavily criticized on two counts. The first is that my natural tendency is to avoid impulsive actions, which some attribute to indolence or cowardice, despite what my strategic methods have proven in practice. The second objection will be that I am simply envious of the daring young consul and his growing desire for glory, and that I wish ill will for the man." Fabius looked directly at Scipio. "Nothing could be further from the truth. My reputation is not in question. I have been elected consul five times. I served as dictator in the second year of the war, and I have received the highest accolades a soldier and a statesman can achieve. If this were not enough recognition for any man, then my age surely speaks against such jealousy. How could I possibly hope to compete with a man who is younger than my son? Why would I now, at the end of my career, enter into a petty rivalry with a man in the very flower of his manhood for the prize of an African campaign? Should I successfully stop his effort, the command to confront Hannibal would certainly not be given to me. No, my days of conquest are over. My defensive tactics have prevented Hannibal from taking Rome. Now it is for those of you who are young and strong to finally bring him to his knees."

A light applause arose from about half the senators.

"For me, Consul," continued Fabius, "the welfare and glory of Rome has always been more important than what others might say of me. So excuse me if I don't rate your achievements in Spain, which the ambassador so graciously described, above the security of Rome itself. If there were no war in Italy, if there were no enemy on our soil, I would be the first to send you off to Africa. But our enemy is Hannibal, and he still occupies Bruttium and Lucania and his army is still intact. Would you not be just as satisfied with the glory of defeating Hannibal here in Italy, as in Africa? Why not focus your efforts on defeating this still formidable enemy where he is now?"

Fabius shook his head in obvious displeasure. "Don't promise what you can't possibly know, Consul. We have no real assurance that when your army arrives in Africa that Hannibal will follow. And why take the risk of transporting an army across the sea? March directly to where he is at this moment and fight him there. Let us first bring peace to our homeland before we take the war to Africa. Could you not just as well defeat Hannibal in Italy, and then go to Africa to complete the task of taking Carthage? Even should another be responsible for that invasion, wouldn't the man who defeated Hannibal still be granted the greatest fame and glory?

"Above and beyond your own grand plans, it is a fact that public funds cannot support two separate armies—one in Italy and one in Africa. Imagine the danger, if, with our resources stretched to the limit, Hannibal should regain traction in Italy and march again on Rome. How would we defend ourselves with half our military across the sea?

"I heard you say that you had received a pledge of loyalty from the Numidian King Syphax. Have we not already learned the fickle nature of barbarian allies? The enemy did not defeat your father or your uncle until they were betrayed by their Celtibarian friends. And did you not have as much trouble with the Indibilis and Mandonius tribes in Spain as you did with the Carthaginians generals? Yes, you might say that the Numidians, whether the Maesulii or the Masaesyli, are just as jealous of Carthage as they are of each other, and that these people are in a constant struggle among themselves for control of North Africa, but should another nation suddenly invade their country, might we not expect that their mutual danger would bring them together against a foreign foe?

"Be aware, Consul, your success in Spain will be but child's play compared to fighting the Carthaginians on their own soil with their own walls and gods to protect. And even with all your recognized talents, did you not allow Hasdrubal to slip out of Spain? After you had promised to this same Senate two years ago that you would prevent that. In my opinion, you are still being educated in the art of war and are not ready for such an invasion.

"Not even you can deny that the very head and seat of the war is wherever Hannibal is. Wouldn't it be easier to defeat the man here on our soil, where he is boxed into the toe of Italy and his resources are stretched to nearly breaking, than in his own backyard with all of Africa at his back and his knowledge of the land and the customs of the people so much greater than yours? This, Scipio, is an odd sort of strategy for winning a war.

"It appears to me that you want to go to Africa because you believe it will increase your fame and glory—not Rome's security. To make matters worse, you have told us you will do this even without authorization from the Senate." The old senator wagged his head, then turned to face his fellow members of the Senate.

"In my view, gentlemen, Publius Scipio has not been made consul for his own personal benefit but to serve the country and to serve us, the Senate. Our armies have been raised for the protection of Rome and Italy, not for arrogant generals who believe they can whisk away to any part of the world they please to accumulate trophies. Please, Consul, reconsider your demands." With these final words Fabius sat down to extended applause from the senior senators and a scattering of catcalls from those in the audience who had been captured by the gallant Scipio's adventurous spirit.

Scipio, who had remained standing in the center of the Senate floor, made the slightest acknowledgment to Fabius, then answered his critic.

"Fabius prefaced his speech by saying that his stand against the invasion of Africa and his disparagement of me will lead to accusations of envy. Although I would never make such a claim against a man as great as Fabius, I don't believe that suspicion has been entirely washed away. As you will recall, he listed his own accomplishments, which are many, as a way to clear the air, and assure you that he in no way considers my achievements to date comparable to his. The implication—*how could such a man be jealous of me?*—is fair enough. But he also noted his age, and that in no way could he pretend to be in competition with a man younger than his own son. I don't see how this applies to the argument.

"A man's glory, if it is real, is not limited by his age or his lifetime. Great deeds are remembered without regard to time. They live on in the memory of posterity. If you will forgive my saying so, Fabius, I do not wish to rival your fame. My ambition is to surpass it." He stared directly at the man. "And I imagine that with your great wisdom, you must surely see this is the way we should want all Romans to be. That every man should hope to be greater than those who came before him. How could it be otherwise? Older generations could not want those who follow to be lesser men. That would be no way to make a nation greater."

Several in the audience shouted out, "Of course not," or "How could it be otherwise?"

Scipio nodded at these comments, then continued. "When Fabius referred to my desire to go to Africa, it seemed that he might actually be worried about me personally. That my youth and my lack of experience would lead me into a situation that I would not be prepared for and that might be disastrous for my career and for Rome. Why did he not show the same concern when my father and uncle were killed in Spain, and only I, among all Romans, though a mere twenty-five years old, stood up and asked for a command that no one else wanted. I was far less experienced than I am now, and no one spoke out then about my youth or the enemy's strength or the difficulty of the task at hand. Can anyone truly say that the situation in Spain is that much different than the one in Africa? Will I not fight the same generals? That is, until Hannibal is forced to return to his homeland.

"Yes, it is easy enough to disparage my achievements in Spain— the utter defeat of four Carthaginian armies, the subjugation of countless fierce barbarian tribes, the conquest of the entire country all the way to the Atlantic Ocean, a complete victory as expressed by our guest from Saguntum." Scipio motioned to the man standing off to his left. "It might be just as easy, should I return victorious from Africa, to diminish that achievement, as a danger grossly exaggerated by an old man simply to keep a young man at home."

Scipio began to pace back and forth before the Senate. "More than once during this debate, which has been going on for three years now, we have heard of the horrible outcomes that befall a general when he takes an army to a foreign land. We are reminded of the Greek's invasion of Sicily two hundred years ago. Or our own Regulus who disastrously invaded Africa in our first war with Carthage. But the successes were never mentioned. Did Agathocles of Syracuse not successfully invade Africa? Did Pyrrhus of Epirus not have success in his invasion of Sicily? But why go back in history at all? Why not admit the truth? Has not Hannibal brought an army to our own country and for fourteen years successfully ravaged the countryside with pillaging and destruction?"

Scipio, now radiant with the energy of his words, stopped pacing and turned briefly to the audience around the perimeter, then back to the three hundred senators seated before him. "Does the courage of war not burn brightest in the invader, not the defender? Does it not take a braver man to venture into the unknown of another land with the dream of conquest? When many of our allies deserted us because of Hannibal's victories, we stood strong with our citizen soldiers and those allies who did not renege on their allegiance. Carthage has no such federation of city-states. They are tyrannical masters who are always at odds with their African neighbors. The defeat of Carthage will only mean greater freedom for other African peoples. Carthage will find no support at home and doesn't have the citizen soldiers that are the backbone of our military.

"No, I believe Africa will be an easier task than Spain, and at the moment you hear that I have crossed the sea, and that Carthage is ablaze, you will learn that Hannibal is preparing his ships to leave Italy. Expect more frequent and more encouraging dispatches from Africa than you received from me while in Spain. Yes, I shall rely on the loyalty of Syphax and other barbarians that I may bring to our cause, but as Fabius so aptly warned, I should also be careful and protect myself by anticipating treachery. Which I will—so that I can cut it off before it begins.

"Don't worry, Fabius," Scipio continued, nodding in Fabius' direction. "I will have the antagonist you want to bow before. But that man won't keep me here. Instead I shall draw him away to fight him on his own ground with the prize of victory Carthage, not a handful of dilapidated Bruttium towns. Think of it! The destruction of Carthage would heighten Rome's reputation in the eyes of kings and princes everywhere. They will know that we are no less courageous than brazen Hannibal. That when our country is attacked, the enemy must expect the same for their homeland.

"Italy has long suffered. That we all know. Let her have a rest. Let Africa be the theater of war. For fourteen years all the horror of combat and the terror of defeat have fallen on us; it is now Carthage's turn to suffer the same. She must be destroyed!"

Despite the spirit and energy of Scipio's speech, and the enthusiastic way the audience responded to his high-handed manner, it was not received well by the Senate. Scipio's earlier threat that he would ask the People's Assembly for permission to go to Africa if the Senate refused him had not been forgotten. Quintus Fulvius, four times a consul, stood up. "Consul, please, for the Senate's sake, call for a vote to settle this issue—yes or no. But first tell me, so that our time is not wasted, if the answer is no, will you abide by that decree?"

"I will do whatever is in the best interest of the state," replied Scipio.

"In other words, Consul," continued Fulvius, clearly angry at Scipio's evasive answer, "you are not really consulting the Senate at all, merely sounding it, and unless we promptly grant you what you want, you have a bill ready to present to the people to override our refusal."

When Scipio made no comment, Fulvius turned to the five tribunes of the plebs. "If that is the case, tribunes, can you protect the integrity of the Senate's decision?"

The five tribunes conferred quickly. One of them, not Marcus, stepped forward. "If the consul allows the Senate to assign provinces, he must abide by the Senate's decision. And should he resist, we will not allow a bill to the contrary to be brought before the people."

Scipio lifted his head indignantly, then abruptly returned to the chair beside his co-consul. He whispered something to Livinius, then told the Senate that he would like a day to discuss the options with his colleague. He called for a recess and announced that the Senate would reconvene the next day.

I had never witnessed the Senate in so ugly a mood as when the senators filed out of the Curia that afternoon. Scipio didn't stay around to listen to the senators complain. Marcus found me outside. He was more amused than angry.

"Scipio has some gall, don't you think?" he asked with a wry grin.

"There's no denying that. What do you expect will happen?"

"Scipio and Livinius will confer with the senators who support the invasion. They will get a head count and make a decision whether they feel they have sufficient numbers to ask for a vote."

"How do you see that going?"

"I would vote with Scipio, and I think many of the senators feel the same way, just to avoid the rancor at a time when we need to think as one. The older senators will fight it. Fabius will certainly make his own head count. Three years ago he had the votes he needed. Tomorrow, I don't think he will."

CHAPTER 29

Licinius ran the meeting the next day in the Senate. When he gave the floor to his co-consul, Scipio made a major concession by addressing Fabius' concern about the cost of his plan. Should the Senate grant him permission to go to Africa, he would not request any money from the treasury for the new ships he would need nor for his soldiers' pay. His army, he said, would be all volunteers, drawn to his campaign by the potential for enormous plunder in Carthage. Licinius then put the matter to a vote.

The vote was close. Scipio's promise not to dip into the treasury was a surprise and may have been the deciding factor. Scipio was granted the province of Sicily, but was given no army. He would have the use of the thirty warships already in Syracuse. He would be allowed to raise a volunteer army, and to the wild approval of the audience, he also had permission to cross to Africa—if he judged it to be in Rome's interest.

Even without the troops, this amounted to a huge victory for Scipio, and really a victory for Roman unity, as an ugly confrontation between the Senate and a stubborn but popular consul was avoided. Licinius was given the province of southern Italy and two legions to command. Caecilius Metellus, the previous consul, would join Licinius in Bruttium, also with two legions. They would be charged with keeping Hannibal in the south.

Afterward I waited outside the Curia for Marcus. I expected him to be in good spirits. I was standing on the perimeter of the comitium when I saw him come out. He was with Scipio. I could see that they were talking.

Marcus saw me and came my way. Scipio remained at his side. I had never met the man. Marcus introduced me. As determined and full of himself as he had been on the floor of the Senate, he seemed quite charming up close.

"My friend Claudius Nero speaks highly of you, Timon," said Scipio as though we were equals. "I hope you remember the note I sent you after Marcellus' funeral."

It had been two years. His note had asked me to be his mapmaker if he went to Africa. I had received the note at a time when many other things were on my mind. I had never even mentioned it to Marcus. "Yes, of course, Consul, I remember. I was honored that you would contact me at all."

Scipio smiled, a genuine, confidant smile. "The time has come," he said. "Will you come to Sicily with me? I will need a mapmaker in Africa."

I wasn't quite sure what to say. I had little interest in reenlisting in the army. With too much spinning through my head—my mother's health, returning to Sicily, the grind of military life—I looked to Marcus.

Marcus grinned and put a hand on my shoulder. "If you plan to make a career of making maps, this is the opportunity of a lifetime. Take it. Think of the reputation you will have should Scipio defeat Hannibal."

"When I defeat Hannibal," said Scipio with irresistible confidence.

"My mother is ill, Consul. I must make arrangements for her before I can make a commitment."

Marcus interrupted. "Her arrangements are already made. She is welcome in my home for as long as you are gone. Nowhere else could she get better care."

Scipio smiled and nodded as though it were already decided.

I bowed my head, trying to gather my thoughts. How had my life become so entangled in ebb and flow of the war? Something about it seemed unavoidable, predestined. I lifted my eyes to Marcus', then turned to Scipio. "I would be honored, sir. When do I report?"

"Tomorrow. Mars Field. Daybreak."

CHAPTER 30

I arrived at Mars Field in time to watch the sun rise over the walls of Rome. Many thousand Roman citizens were already there. The situation reminded me of my first spring in Rome when I served as a scribe for Marcellus while he raised and trained two new legions of Roman recruits at Mars Field.

The day began with the obligatory religious rituals. The chickens were fed and they ate with vigor. Both consuls sacrificed a bull outside the Temple of Mars, then went inside the temple cella and, as all new consuls did, shook the spear held by the statue inside.

Licinius was there to put together two new legions of recruits. Scipio, because of his bold promise to build his army without assistance from the Roman treasury, did not have permission to raise troops from the Roman citizenry, as was the usual process. His army would have to be volunteers from existing Roman troops or from Roman allies. He had been given the thirty warships already stationed in Syracuse, but any additions to his fleet would also have to come from donations made by allies or from his personal resources.

Scipio was in the early stages of putting together a plan for raising troops when I found him that morning. He was in a large tent on the east side of the exercise field, sitting before a desk covered with scrolls and writing equipment. The consul looked up as a centurion opened the flap to the tent to announce me. I noticed the strong fragrance of burning frankincense as soon as I entered, something very unusual in a military tent.

Though clearly deep into his work, Scipio immediately stood. Seven years my elder, he greeted me warmly and with little formality. "Timon, just what I need. A competent scribe who's adept with numbers. I'm so grateful you have accepted my request to go to Sicily. My friend Nero recommended you with the highest praise. And he's not particularly quick with a good word for anyone." He smiled easily, as though we had known each other for some time. "We have quite a bit of work to do before going to Sicily—and even more before we depart for Africa. I'm sure you're up to it."

"Thank you for your kind words, Consul. I'm honored to be of service."

"As I said yesterday, I'm primarily interested in your capacity as a mapmaker. I have already begun a search for maps of the African coast and have been sorely disappointed. The maps are both sketchy and inconsistent. What one map shows is contradicted by another. I will give you all that I have found for your perusal, but I imagine that the real work won't begin until we get there."

I nodded.

"Until then, you will work with a team of scribes as we assemble and enlist volunteers. At the same time we must acquire the materials to build thirty new warships, transport that material to Ostia, and then supervise construction. Right now most of my problems are logistical. I need men with good minds more than anything else."

"Yes, sir."

With every word he said, I was measuring the man, probably just as he was me. He may have wanted accurate maps, but I had something more to give him. I was not carrying the spyglass that day, but once I had a fair chance to appraise Scipio, who Marcus had warned was far more complex than his charm suggested, I would decide if he were the right man to show it to.

Scipio surprised me by asking me about my life. His interest seemed sincere, but I also understood it was a way for him to gain my trust. I told him all that was appropriate, beginning with my kidnapping in Croton. His line of questioning gradually moved from issues of casual interest to the most important things on his mind. When I recounted my time with Marcellus, he peppered me with questions about tracking Hannibal and how it had happened that Marcellus was ambushed. Then he asked me about the warning I had given to Nero. "What else can you tell me about that?"

This caught me off-guard. I had hoped that Nero would not tell anyone about my part in the intrigue, as it could only lead back to my mother. For the first time in the interview, I had to test the edge of my new superior. "Yes, sir, I was the messenger. That's all I can say."

Scipio tilted his head. "But how did you come by that information? You must know how important it was?"

"Yes, sir."

"Many months have passed since Hasdrubal's defeat. Surely you can reveal something of your sources by now? Do you know a spy embedded in Hannibal's army?"

Again this was something I had told Nero. I wasn't pleased. "I'm sorry, sir. Despite the time that has passed, there's nothing more to say."

Scipio smiled as though he might let the matter go. "Of course, I understand the need to protect those involved. A leak could compromise further information or that source's life. But you will be working very closely with me the next year or so," he said fixing his eyes on mine. "I must have the highest trust in you, and you me. Secrets get in the way."

"Yes, sir. I understand that."

He nodded pleasantly but continued to press me. "As you must know, I'm fully aware of the Roman spy networks. The name of Quintus Ennius is not unfamiliar to me."

"Yes, sir."

Scipio stalked across the tent and back, clearly irritated by my reluctance to reveal anything more. "Are you part of the Roman network, Timon? There's no reason you couldn't reveal that to me— unless of course you were spying on me to report back to the Senate?"

Although this confrontation had already become uncomfortable, I had no idea how far Scipio would go. "I'm not a member of any network, sir. And I'm certainly not an internal agent for the Senate. I'm a mapmaker intent on helping you win the war. Only once have I been privy to information of importance to Roman military matters. My source on that occasion demanded silence about his identity for his own safety. There may be a time in the future when I can reveal that identity without endangering the agent, but please allow me that. When the time comes, I will tell you all you want to know. Then, I believe, you will understand why I have maintained my silence now."

Scipio sat at his desk and stared downward for an extended moment. He tapped the surface of the desk with his forefinger, clearly annoyed, then looked up at me. "Fine."

"Thank you, sir."

Scipio was not pleased. No one said *no* to him. He changed the subject and briefed me on the work he wanted done that day.

CHAPTER 31

The next two weeks were filled with paperwork. I was one of four scribes making lists of the things that we needed, where those items could be procured, and what they would cost. I saw Scipio each day, but only briefly and never with an extended conversation. I did have some time to myself, and for the most part I spent that out at the farm with my mother.

One evening, after a meal in the triclinium, I showed my mother Archimedes' terrella that Marcellus had brought back with him from Syracuse. It sat on a table in the corner of the atrium. I told her it replicated Aristarchus' model of the universe, which placed the Sun at the center, while the other planets, including the Earth, revolved around it. I filled the ceramic tank beside it with water and demonstrated the way the little water wheel could propel the smaller brass globes around the larger one. Of course she found it fascinating, and listened with interest when I told her how the terrella had initiated my first real conversation with Archimedes.

We sat down on a bench beneath the colonnade. A light rain was falling, and as we watched the circular wavelets spread out across the surface of the pool, I told her about Sempronia.

"I want to see her before I leave for Sicily," I confessed after telling her everything, including the politics around Sempronia's being selected to be a Vestal Virgin and the events that took place at Paculla's readings. "I'm likely to be turned away if I go to her home," I said. "Would I be a fool to try anyway?"

"You have only been her tutor, Timon," she said. "She's patrician, a different class than you, and her mother has already made her position clear on that. I suggest you forget this woman." The sparkle had returned to my mother's eyes, but there was still a dim yellow cast to her skin.

"But she loves the numbers and the geometry. I'll never find another woman with both her beauty and her subtlety of mind."

She looked at me sadly. "I think you've already made up your mind. I see heartbreak ahead."

"But what if no one will marry her? What if the Vestal Virgin incident means no aristocrat will touch her? Wouldn't that make an ordinary man like myself eligible?"

"Does it matter how I answer these questions, Timon?" She wagged her head and chuckled. "It's clear what you will do. I appreciate that you have asked me for an opinion, but no mother should expect her son to follow all of her advice. Do what you must."

And of course I did. One afternoon, when I had completed my work earlier than expected, I decided, against all my better judgment, to visit Sempronia. As evidenced by the fact that I had told my mother about her, I clearly felt deeply about this young woman and wanted to try explaining myself to her one more time before I left for Sicily.

Instead of going to the front door, I went down the alley and entered the property from the back. I stayed out of sight, watching from behind the slaves' quarters, hoping to see Sempronia alone in the garden.

It had rained that morning, but the sun had come out at midday. The smell of wet earth hung in the air. Everything in the garden that wasn't a flower was bright green. And flowers were everywhere, scores of fragrant roses, of all colors. Dora came out shortly after I arrived to collect a bouquet for the house. Not long afterward Sempronia appeared with a bowl of bird feed for the parrot. She wore a stark white stola with a pale saffron scarf covering her hair and shoulders. She glided up to the bird cage like some kind of ethereal being. I heard her greet Ajax in a little child's voice, as though he were fully capable of conversation.

"How are you today, Ajax?"

"Very well, thank you," the bird answered.

"Are you hungry?"

"Always.".

As Sempronia sprinkled feed into the cage, I crept across the yard to get a little closer.

"Thank you," said the bird as it hopped from its perch to the floor of the cage to peck at the broken kernels of wheat. After a moment, the bird sat up and spoke again. "How are you today?"

"Thank you for asking, Ajax," Sempronia said politely, then in a voice I could barely hear, added, "a little lonely."

I was close enough to whisper, "So am I."

"Timon," squawked the bird.

Startled by my sudden appearance, Sempronia quickly covered the cage before Ajax could squawk again, then turned on me. "You shouldn't be here." But I could see it in her eyes, she was glad I was. "I thought you went to Croton?"

"I've just returned, but I'll soon be leaving with the army for Sicily. I could be there a long time." I advanced a little closer. I could smell that she had sprinkled herself with rose water. "I wanted to see you before I left." Sempronia glanced over her shoulder toward the house, clearly anxious that someone might see me. "And I can't bear your being angry at me."

"For claiming you—you had intercourse with my mother!"

"But you didn't allow me to explain why it happened."

She glared at me. "How could that matter?"

I withdrew the spyglass from the sleeve of my toga. "Let me show you something." I held the device out to her. "It will change how you see everything—even this issue with me and your mother."

Sempronia eyed the spyglass before taking it in her hands. "This is why you're here?"

"Yes. I believe you and I have made an important connection through geometry, and I don't want to lose that. This device might even convince you to return to the tutoring."

"I doubt that will ever happen," she snapped, but I could see that she was intrigued by the spyglass.

"Remember the two lenses I tried to show you before I left for Croton? They're mounted at the ends of this device to make them easier to use." I pointed to the Temple of Minerva at the top of the Aventine Hill. "Tell me what's inscribed on the pediment."

Sempronia looked off to the temple. "That's impossible. I can hardly see the pediment, much less read the inscription."

"Try the device. Hold the small end to your eye and point the wide end at the temple."

She looked confused.

"It's easy. Just lift it to your eye. You'll be surprised."

Sempronia took a quick glance back toward the house, then lifted the spyglass to her eye and pointed it at the top of the Aventine Hill.

"Now twist the tubes, one inside the other, to make the device longer or shorter. It will increase the clarity of what you're seeing—and it will be upside down."

"What do you mean?"

"Just do it."

It took her a moment to get a feel for it, but the tubes made the lenses so much easier to use she hardly needed any instruction. "There it is," she gasped. "I don't believe it. Oh no, I've lost it." She twisted the tubes a bit more, one way then the other.

"Oh my! How can this be? I *can* see the inscription. It's upside down and backwards, but I think I can figure it out, yes—courage, wisdom, strength!" She lowered the spyglass and looked up at the Aventine Hill without the spyglass, then at me. "This is miraculous!" she exclaimed, looking at both ends of the spyglass, then lifting it to her eye again. "This is truly miraculous."

"Look at the moon." The moon sat just above the horizon in the west, a white ghost against a pale blue sky.

Sempronia aimed the spyglass at the moon. After a moment, she lowered the device, even more amazed than before, and looked at me. "What are these—these lenses? How do they work? And why is the image upside down?"

"It's all in the geometry. The lenses demonstrate an application of geometric principles called optics. It was something Archimedes was working on in the last years of his life. He gave me the lenses, but then I lost them. That's when I went to the women's group. I thought their teacher, Paculla Annia, could help me find them with her magic. What happened between your mother and me was part of a ritual linked to Paculla's effort to locate the lenses. It happened in the dark. I didn't even know it was your mother at the time. But finding the lenses was more important than any mark against my reputation. I was willing to do anything to find them. Can you see why?"

Sempronia stared at me. "My mother denied it, Timon."

"But she told you that I exposed myself to the group. Exploring sexuality is part of what that women's group does. It is!"

"Stop! This is disgusting. I don't want to hear any more about it."

"I was desperate, Sempronia. I wanted these lenses back. At the time I thought the rituals were nonsense, but I went through with it anyway."

"Then the priestess told you where the lenses were?"

"Not exactly, but I did find them. Only recently did I put them in the tubes. You're only the second person I've shown—but you can never tell anyone."

"Why?"

"Because they're that important. Because they're proof of the value of applied mathematics and suggest things so powerful that they will change the world completely."

"Then why have you shown them to me?"

I bowed my head then looked up at her. "I wanted you to know why I did what I did. That's why I came here today. I didn't want to lose you as a friend. I felt it was that important."

Sempronia shook her head sadly, then lifted the spyglass to her eye and aimed it at the top of the Caelius Hill. "This device is very powerful," she said, scanning the distance. "And amazing. I can't deny it."

"You should see the moon at night. And the stars."

She lowered the spyglass. Her hands shook with excitement as she returned it to me. She stared into my eyes, as serious as I had ever seen her, weighing the moral value of the lenses against the trespass against her mother.

"I'll be taking this spyglass with me when I go to Sicily. Publius Scipio has taken me on as a mapmaker. It's a position of honor and offers good pay. Our ultimate destination is Africa. That's where Scipio needs the maps. It's very exciting, and this device will make it all easier and my maps more accurate. Sempronia, can you find it in your heart to forgive me?"

Now she bowed her head. When she looked up, our eyes met. "My mother stills hopes to find a patrician husband for me, but the episode with the Vestal Virgins has proven to be a problem. Apparently I am not a virgin." She looked at the ground as though just saying the words hurt. "Perhaps when you return from Africa, when the war is over, and Scipio is victorious, and you have great piles of booty," she chuckled, "then we might talk again. You have shown me much that confuses me today. I need a little time." She reached out and held my hand briefly, then let go.

"That's all I really wanted, Sempronia. When I come visit you again, perhaps two or three years from now, I will be riding in a golden carriage and I'll use the front door."

Sempronia laughed. A voice from inside the house shouted, "Sempronia! Who are you talking to?"

"Ajax," Sempronia called back, now giggling.

"I'll be back," I whispered, then scampered to the back of the property and out into the alley.

CHAPTER 32

Publius Scipio would rise to mythic heights in his career as a Roman military officer. He would be cited for his nobility, his courage, his ingenuity, and his field tactics. Rarely mentioned are his organization skills. In forty-five days, starting from scratch, he assembled a volunteer army and doubled the size of his fleet. His success in Spain and his youth attracted donations of all variety. The city of Caere gave him grain for his troops. Populonium brought him iron, Tarquinii sailcloth, Volaterrae timber, Arretium three thousand shields, three thousand helmets, and five thousand pikes, plus equal numbers of shovels, axes, and sickles. Perusia, Clusium, and Ruselle provided storage buildings for his accumulation of grain. Volunteer soldiers came from everywhere—Nursia, Reate, Amiternum, and all across the Sabine territory. But it was more than the volunteers and donations. It was Scipio's attention to detail that made him a superior military officer. By the end of April, seven thousand volunteer troops, thirty brand new warships, and all the provisions the campaign would need were in Ostia, ready to go.

I spent almost all of my time in Ostia during the weeks before our departure. I did manage to get one day free during the last week. I went to the Claudian farm to see my mother. She had recovered from the poisoning, but she would never regain her full vitality and color.

It was midmorning and warm for the first of May. We walked through the olive orchard for quite some time before I got to the point of my visit. "I won't see you again, Mother, until the campaign is over. I'm not sure when that will be. It's possible we could return from Sicily during the winter, but once we go to Africa there's no telling. It could be years."

My mother looked at me with sadness in her eyes. "I knew it would be a long campaign the moment you told me of Scipio's offer. I think a mother would normally cry when her son goes off to war, but this war has gone on for so long, it just seems to be what life has become, and we've learned to accept it."

"Maybe Scipio will be successful and end the war."

"After all that's gone on, Timon, it's hard to be hopeful. But he may at least draw Hannibal out of Italy. That would be something."

"And I wouldn't be so worried that he might find you here."

We walked on a little farther in silence. Neither of us wanted to admit how difficult another separation would be.

"Are you all right living here, Mother?"

She finally smiled. "Yes, I feel comfortable here. Marcus is a good man. Meda and Edeco have been exceptionally kind to me. I don't foresee any problems—other than missing you. I know some people in Rome if I get too lonely."

"Don't go into Rome." I stopped walking to impress my point. "Don't go to the Community of Miracles. You're supposed to be dead."

"I know people there I can trust, Timon. It will be fine."

"I know that some of those people are your friends and have the highest opinion of you, but you've no reason to revisit people like Caelius or Quintus Ennius."

"Those people helped me when I needed it the most. I can't just forget them."

"But you should. At least until the war is over. Promise me that."

"Promise me that you will come back."

"You know I can't. Please, just stay out of Rome. It's all I ask. I'll be back as soon as I can. Then you can go wherever you want."

Neither of us spoke again until we had returned to the villa. Just outside the house, I embraced her. Tears rolled down my cheeks. I couldn't say a word without sobbing. She had no tears, but squeezed me as tightly as she could. When we finally released each other, she brushed the tears from my cheeks and looked into my eyes. "Your maps could be the difference between victory or defeat. Make your father proud."

I nodded, wishing now that I had never promised to go to Africa. There was too high a probability that I would never return.

Marcus came into the stable as I was preparing for the ride back to Ostia. Edeco would accompany me on another horse, so that he could return with Balius.

"I'm not sure when I'll see you again, Marcus," I said, putting the bridle on Balius. "With a little luck, the war will be over the next time we meet."

Marcus looked at me with a confident grin. "I wish I were going with you. After two months as a tribune, I've concluded I'd rather be a soldier. Instead I have a year in Rome."

"What do you think, Marcus, will Scipio's strategy work? Will he draw Hannibal back to Africa?"

"He just might. The more difficult question is whether Scipio will be able to defeat Hannibal in his own backyard. Scipio may surprise us, but it's impossible to predict. Did you know he's acquired a good number of his volunteers from the Eighteenth legion? He wanted men with combat experience against Hannibal. Men who weren't in awe of him."

"I hadn't heard that. My work has been focused on provisions rather than soldiers. I wonder if I know any of them?"

"I know none of the specifics. But I believe it's several hundred men."

"We only had seven thousand volunteers at last count. That can't be enough. I wonder what Scipio's got planned for our time in Sicily."

"Raising more troops. He needs twenty thousand men at the very least. Thirty thousand would be better. Expect to be in Sicily for a while."

Edeco stood stoically outside the stable with the horses.

I embraced Marcus. "Thank you for allowing my mother to stay here."

"You know it's no trouble. May the gods be with you—and Scipio."

"With all of us," I said, walking off to join Edeco.

CHAPTER 33

We sailed out of Ostia four days later with thirty new warships and fifty transports. The voyage took nine days. We followed the west coast of Italy south through the straits of Messana, then continued along the east coast of Sicily past Mount Etna to Syracuse. I had made the same trip, going the other way from Syracuse to Ostia, six years earlier. As I stood on the bow with the wind in my face, five tiers of oars pulling at the water, I felt myself fill with emotion when the outline of Syracuse's massive walls appeared in the distance.

We sailed along the edge of Trogyli Harbor where I first landed in Syracuse nine years before. I had been in chains, cargo on a slave ship at the age of thirteen. A flood of bittersweet memories welled up in me. I remembered being stripped of clothing then auctioned off like livestock. The experience still stood out as the most humiliating moment in my young life. Two years later, during the Festival of Artemis, I was drinking wine with Moira, a young Sicilian woman, gazing out at the harbor from the battlements, the stars and moon reflected off its surface like a sheet of glass, both of us lost to the innocence of young love.

As we skirted the east wall of the city, about to enter the Great Harbor, I saw the tower where I had spent so much time with Archimedes. I recalled the long hours of letter copying, the experiments with rays of light, and the mornings in the tower basement, drinking kykeon with the kitchen staff. Hektor and Lavinia had been victims of the siege. I wondered if Agathe and Eurydice had survived. It all seemed ancient history to me now as we entered the harbor and the ships glided onto the beach to begin the process of unloading.

We built a fortified camp in an elevated field just south of the city. Behind the camp was what remained of the Temple of Zeus. Arguably the largest and most impressive temple in Sicily, it had been entirely dismantled. Only the huge stone plinth marked the spot. Broken limestone blocks and rubble from the deconstruction lay scattered across the plinth or half-buried in the weeds around it.

As one of ten scribes attached to the legion of volunteers who had come from Ostia, now named the Twenty-third, my work began early in the morning the day after our arrival. All that was on the transport ships had to be inventoried and stored. What we hadn't brought with us would have to be obtained in Sicily. Scipio sent squadrons of men off in all directions, pressing the locals for supplies and volunteers.

Scipio's first order of business was the change of command. He met the current praetor, Gaius Servilius, at a large home within the city that he had converted into his headquarters. I wasn't there, but I got a report the next day. Servilius, twenty years older than Scipio, had taken to gluttony during his year in Syracuse. He was grossly overweight. His paperwork was incomplete, and the problems of the local populace had been ignored. Fortunately for Servilius, Scipio didn't understand how bad things were until the man had sailed for Rome.

I accompanied Scipio into Syracuse a week later. Following the siege, Marcellus had stripped the city of its finest art and limestone. Six years later the place was just as he had left it—a battle zone. Refugees from the war wandered the streets. Lawlessness ruled after nightfall. The situation was so bad Scipio was forced to temporarily put off preparation for the invasion. He set up a court in the forum to listen to complaints against Servilius. Many of the Syracusans claimed they had been better off under Carthaginian rule.

The hearings took a full week, during which time the locals quickly understood that Publius Scipio was not Gaius Servilius. Scipio's greatest talent off the battlefield was handling people. His manner, his efficiency, and his common sense when it came to legal matters served to calm a city full of angry people. Foremost were property claims. Promises made by Marcellus and edicts made in Rome were often at odds. Two men, sometimes three, would make claims for the same piece of land. Scipio went through each complaint one at a time, showing patience and insight, when he might have used force.

Along with these legal actions, he put two cohorts to work cleaning up the city. Other officers would have considered this a waste of time, a secondary concern compared to pursuing the war. But in much the same way that Scipio had gained the respect of the tribal leaders in Spain, he won over the people of Syracuse, and it wasn't just the native

Greeks. Word of his elevated sense of justice spread throughout Sicily during the first month we were there. Suddenly the air of hostility that had filled Syracuse on our arrival had changed to one of friendship and common purpose. Communities all over the island began to make contributions to Scipio's war effort. Rather than a waste of time, Scipio's judicious approach saved him both time and money.

As Marcus had said to me upon leaving, Scipio's seven thousand volunteers were not nearly enough men to invade Africa. Scipio knew this better than anyone, and once he had settled things in the city, he focused on increasing the size of his army.

Something that Scipio might have anticipated prior to leaving Rome was the presence of the survivors from the battles of Cannae and Herdonea, soldiers who years earlier had been exiled from Italy for cowardice and sent to Sicily. Marcellus had enlisted these men while besieging Syracuse. Although he was later reprimanded by the Senate for using them, they made a significant contribution to his success. Arguably these exiles represented some of the most experienced legionnaires in the Roman military. Scipio had been there at Cannae. He knew what had happened. He understood the rout that day was more the work of headstrong officers, not common soldiers. Scipio made recruiting these men one of his highest priorities. His trust in these men would make them some of our most loyal and dependable legionnaires.

A legion of Cannae survivors, the Fifth, was stationed in Syracuse. Another, the Sixth, though not a full legion, was in Messana. Other survivors were scattered across the countryside in small clusters or as individuals who had taken up permanent residence in Sicily. Once Scipio put the word out, they came from all over the island. The legion in Syracuse enlisted as a unit immediately. The legion in Messana did the same two weeks later. Another thousand locals filtered into Syracuse over the next month. Six weeks into our stay in Sicily, our numbers were approaching twenty thousand.

Raising a cavalry out of thin air was not as easy. It took money to own and care for a horse. Scipio used pure ingenuity to solve the problem. Early on in the process, he had chosen three hundred of the best men from his volunteers and put them aside. These men trained with the other troops, but were not given specific duties, weapons, or placement in a cohort.

In the weeks after our arrival, Scipio put a call out to the wealthiest families in Sicily, asking for three hundred volunteers to form a contingent of cavalry to go to Africa with him. It was no secret that the duty would be difficult and dangerous. There was considerable reluctance among the families to part with their sons because of the risk. It took a few weeks, but three hundred young Sicilian noblemen, all skilled horsemen, did come to Syracuse on the appointed morning. Each man came with his own horse, tack, and military gear. I was there at a desk with two other clerks, signing them up as they arrived. Also present were the three hundred volunteers who had yet to be armed or assigned a duty.

Scipio had the noblemen assemble on their horses in three lines, one hundred across. He sat on his beautiful, blond-maned roan and watched them move into formation. When the commotion settled, he rode down the line talking to the three hundred men as one.

"I've called you all here this morning to assemble a cavalry. Thank you for coming. I do believe that the outcome of this war is as important to the people of Sicily as it is to the citizens of Rome. In many ways you are volunteering to fight on your own behalf as much as Rome's. And it's appreciated.

"That said," he continued, "I want to clarify that the campaign to Africa will be demanding. Judging from your youth and bearing, I might guess that some of you are not necessarily looking forward to going. You have lived a good life, and may not feel yourselves prepared for the kind of expedition we are about to make. If anyone is thinking these kind of thoughts, I would rather know now then at sometime later when I have to depend on you in battle. So please, speak out. Let me know what you're thinking."

Many of the young men looked around at their compatriots, but no one spoke out.

"Are you sure?" continued Scipio, riding slowly down the line of horses, looking into the faces of the riders. "Anyone? Better now than later."

One man advanced his horse two steps from the line. "Consul, if I'm really free to choose, I would prefer not to be here."

Scipio nodded as though he thoroughly understood. "Because you have spoken openly and have not concealed your feelings, I will find a substitute for you." The young man could not help smiling at this welcome news. "But," continued Scipio, "you will have to give him your horse and your equipment, and also take the time to train him to ride."

When the young nobleman gladly agreed, Scipio called for one of the three hundred volunteers who were standing in formation nearby. The two men, the Sicilian and the Latin volunteer, were paired and the training began.

Scipio faced the remaining two hundred and ninety-nine young noblemen and asked once again if there were any among them who had second thoughts about what lay ahead. Five men came forward, followed by ten more, all accepting Scipio's terms—to equip and train one of the volunteers. Before we could complete the paper work on these fifteen men, all the others had made the same decision. A month later, Scipio had a cavalry of three hundred riders, all equipped and trained at no cost to Rome or himself.

CHAPTER 34

During the first six weeks in Syracuse I saw very little of Scipio and spoke to him even less. Although I had been enlisted as a mapmaker, while in Syracuse I was but one of a squadron of scribes who spent almost all of our time cataloguing supplies and men, trying to verify that we would be ready for the voyage to Africa by the end of the summer. It was nearly July, and at least in terms of our numbers, Scipio had more recruiting to do.

One afternoon I had the tedious job of transcribing the original list of volunteers who had traveled with us from Ostia. The men had signed their names and described their previous duties in the military so they could be assigned to the most appropriate maniple and cohort. The handwriting was not the best. Many of the names were impossible to read. More often than not the descriptions of the men's duties were left blank because so few of them could write anything more than their names.

I came upon one name that was especially poorly written and followed by a word that I concluded was "hastatus" and the number eighteen. I immediately wondered if this man had served in the Eighteenth legion at the same time I had. I spent quite a bit of time trying to make sense of the name that was scrawled on the piece of papyrus. It was just a single word that I was certain began with the Latin letter "T."

When I couldn't figure out a name, I would assign the man a number and hope that eventually we could connect each number with a name. I was about to assign a number to this entry when I realized that the scribbled name was *Troglius* or something very close. I noted that he had been assigned to the first maniple in the fifth cohort of the Twenty-third legion.

When my work was completed that day, I wound through the camp looking for the first maniple in the fifth cohort. I found the standard stuck in the ground before a long row of tents, then walked down that row looking for Troglius.

I didn't find him on my first try, but I returned to the row of tents later that night during the evening meal. Five tents down the line, I saw Troglius sitting at a campfire with his tent mates, eating the standard fare of wheat gruel and flat bread.

Although I had seen him a year earlier in Nero's camp in Venusia, he made no sign of recognition when I approached the little circle of soldiers. A few of the soldiers looked up at me—a Greek in the tunic of a scribe. One spoke out roughly. "What are you looking at scribe? Don't they feed you Greeks?"

Before I could answer, Troglius interrupted. "That's my friend, Timon." Though no one in the tent unit had yet to see Troglius on the battlefield, it was clear by their reaction that he had already made a positive impression on them.

"Then give the man a bowl if he's hungry," said one of the other soldiers.

"Oh, no," I said. "I've eaten. I was looking for Troglius. We served together in the Eighteenth a couple of years back. I just learned that he was one of the volunteers. I wanted to let him know I was here in Sicily also."

Troglius was a curious kind of friend. You didn't just sit down next to him and begin a discussion. If what you said did not pertain exactly to what he was doing—eating a meal, sharpening his gladius, whatever it might be, he had little to say, if anything at all. Often the effect was like talking to yourself. Still I felt close to this man, who had never once asked me about my life or my personal interests, yet who had protected me on several occasions from bullying soldiers during my time in the Eighteenth. Though Troglius might not have much to say, this huge, awkward man, with eyes that seemed to look in different directions, had a good heart and made for a loyal, if quiet, friend. He also owned the reputation of being one of Rome's best men in combat.

After the meal, he and I walked through the camp. I told him that Scipio had enlisted me as a mapmaker, and that I had been on one of the warships during the voyage from Ostia. I reflected on the day Marcellus was ambushed, his funeral, and finding my mother, though I made no mention of her connection to Hannibal.

Troglius showed little interest in what I said and had even less to say about himself. I wasn't offended. It was who he was, and in spite of that, I enjoyed his company and the opportunity to talk to someone I knew.

"Why did you volunteer for duty with Scipio?" I asked him, hoping for some insight into this man of such a simple nature.

We walked down an entire row of tents before he answered. "I wanted to go to Africa."

"Why's that?"

Troglius shrugged, then muttered, "It's the best way to win the war."

I smiled. "I hope you're right."

CHAPTER 35

Troglius was not the sort to seek me out. If I didn't stop by his tent at meal time, I would never have seen him. But I did. Somehow talking to Troglius in our one-sided conversations was important to me. If nothing else, he was a set of ears to listen to my trials and tribulations when there was no one else who would.

About a week after I had located him, I discovered he and I had some free time that overlapped. I told him that I had lived in Syracuse for three years and that I had only gone into the city once since arriving. "I'd like to go again and look around a bit. Are you interested in coming with me?" I wanted to go to Ortygia. I wanted to visit the tower where I had spent so much time with Archimedes, just to see how much things had changed.

Troglius surprised me by saying he would go. We hiked from the camp to the city's south gate. We both wore Roman tunics and had no trouble entering the city. We walked due north on Via Intermuralis, the main artery in the city, following the wall that separated Syracuse into an eastside—the Tyche district—and a westside—Achradina. Even after the clean-up that Scipio had ordered, Syracuse was not the city I had known. The stunning temples were either gone or partially deconstructed. All the Greek statuary was gone. Homeless people with hungry eyes wandered the streets just as they had during the siege. Street thugs hung out on the corners waiting for night to fall. The city didn't feel safe. That was one reason I had asked Troglius to accompany me. He appeared more beast than man and wasn't the sort to pick a fight with or attempt to rob.

When we reached the north end of Via Intermuralis, I showed Troglius the entrance to the tunnels beneath the city. They dated back two hundred years and hadn't been used in decades. We retraced our route on Via Intermuralis to Achradina. The gate was open and had no guards so we went in. The agora no longer had a market. The Altar of

Concord had been removed from the forum after the siege. Only its base, a large rectangular block of limestone, remained. A man stood on it and spoke out against Roman rule. Before we had crossed the agora, two soldiers had come and hauled him away.

Access to Ortygia was at the south end of the agora. The narrow island was separated from the rest of the city by a canal and a fortified gate. It served as a sanctuary of last resort should the city be besieged. I knew this only too well. I had lived on the island during the last six months of the Roman siege. The gate was open, but guarded by Roman soldiers. Wearing our red tunics, we were allowed to pass without a question. During my time there, the gate had always been closed and entry highly restricted.

The island was no different than the rest of the city. Stone from deconstruction was everywhere. A visitor who had never been there before would not know if the city were being built or taken apart. The entire scene filled me with a profound sadness. It had once been my favorite part of Syracuse.

I led Troglius to the six-story tower where I had lived. As we crossed the yard, I saw a gray cat sitting in the sun. I was sure it was my old friend Plato, but when I tried to approach it, the cat ran off. Either it wasn't Plato or the war had turned him skittish.

The tower door was open. We walked right in. It was much the way I had last seen it, filled with the leftover debris of a complete sacking. I climbed the stairs to the top floor with Troglius trailing behind. I didn't try to explain what I was feeling when we entered the vacant workshop.

The broken tools and furniture scattered around the chamber had not been touched in the six years since the Roman takeover. This room, once a laboratory at the leading edge of Greek science, was now little more than a wasteland. I was so saddened by the condition of the workshop, and the memories I associated with it, that I was reduced to silence. I stood before the east facing window just staring out at the sea, recalling the first time Archimedes told me to watch a ship disappear over the horizon as verification of the curvature of the Earth. Africa was two hundred miles across the sea to the southwest.

When I turned away from the window, trying to push through my emotions, Troglius asked me, "Is this where the magnifying glass came from?"

"Yes," I said, surprised that he might have made such a connection. He was one of the few people I had shown it to. "It was a gift from my master, Archimedes."

"You were once a slave?" It was the first question he had ever asked me about my life.

"For three years. Marcellus freed me after the siege."

"Where's the lens? I don't see the cord that's usually around your neck."

Troglius thought the lens' was magic and found it tremendously fascinating. While tent mates, he had slipped the leather pouch from around my neck while I was asleep. It was a point of contention that we talked about afterward. That short conversation had proven to me that Troglius was a more thoughtful man than most realized. It was also the beginning of our friendship.

I had the spyglass with me, hanging on my belt in open sight, as though it might be a drafting tool. I had shown it to my mother and Sempronia, asking them never to mention it. For reasons I can't truly explain, I wanted to show it to Troglius. "Can you make a promise to secrecy?" Archimedes had asked me the same question in this room six years earlier.

Troglius came across the room, his eyes looking off in two directions. One then the other met mine. "Yes, I can keep a secret."

I took the spyglass from my belt and showed it to him. "I call this device a spyglass." I touched the fat end of the device. "The magnifying lens is here."

He looked and nodded.

I touched the narrow end. "A smaller lens is here. When they are used together, they can be quite powerful. Watch how I use it." I put the small end to my eye and aimed it out the north window toward the city. I gently twisted the tubes to focus on a parapet across the moat. "Do you see what I am doing? Turning these tubes one inside the other?" I handed the device to Troglius. "It clarifies what you see."

He held the tube to his eye and did as I had instructed. I talked him through the entire process. I could see it in his body when the upside down image in the glass came into focus. He became very still, then lowered the spyglass and turned to me in question.

I nodded. "Yes, the lenses together can make things in the distance appear closer and upside down."

He put the tube to his eye again and aimed it at Mount Etna. Its snow capped peak was just visible above the horizon to the north. It took him a moment to find his target and bring it into focus. When he lowered the spyglass a second time, he gave it back to me as though it was too much for him to hold, like it was a precious gem or a piece of Jupiter's robe. "I don't understand," he said with a mixture of anxiety and awe. "You have said the lens is not magic, but it must be if it turns everything upside down. How else can this be explained?"

"It's simply a tool that makes use of the natural properties of glass. That's all I can tell you. It's not magic, but it is powerful. I believe it could be useful to a field marshal."

Troglius looked out the window to where he had aimed the spyglass, then back to me.

"I have thought about showing it to Scipio." I probably shouldn't have said this, but if Troglius was to be a friend, I had to trust him. "It could help win the war."

Troglius shook his head. "No, we can win without magic. Keep it to yourself. I will never say a word."

"So said Archimedes, Troglius. Perhaps you're right." But I had already made up my mind. Once I felt Scipio was the right man—and I hadn't determined that yet—I would show him the spyglass.

From the tower, Troglius and I headed farther south on the one-mile spit that was Ortygia. Suddenly we were outside the tenement housing where Agathe had lived. It was the one part of Syracuse that had not been heavily plundered. The Temple of Apollo and the Temple of Athene were gone, taken away stone by stone, but all the lesser buildings were intact.

I was curious if Agathe were still alive, but she was not someone I really wanted to seek out and visit. We continued south to the Fountain of Arethusa at the southernmost end of the island. We got a drink of water from the spring and watched the waves crash on the rocks.

On our way back I saw a young boy, no more than seven years old, standing outside the tenement housing. He had unruly red hair and a lightness about his movement that caught my eye. If I wasn't mistaken, this boy was Eurydice's son Gelo, the illegitimate offspring of Syracuse's last king.

I called his name. The boy looked up. I approached him, speaking in Greek. "Do you remember me?"

The boy shook his head as his eyes strayed to Troglius standing behind me.

"My name is Timon. I'm here as a friend."

The boy eyed the two of us suspiciously.

"Do you live with your mother?"

He nodded reluctantly.

"And Agathe, is she here too?"

Gelo looked over his shoulder. An older woman, thin as a rail and not nearly as pretty, came out of the nearest building. It was Agathe. She saw us talking to Gelo, surely noted our red tunics, and came right over to us, placing her hand on the boy's shoulder. I had grown from a boy into a man since last seeing her and wore a closely trimmed beard.

"What do you want?" she demanded angrily, not recognizing me. "Leave this boy alone. Next you will want to recruit him."

I struggled not to laugh. Agathe had not a changed a bit. Even Troglius had not scared her. "Agathe," I said, "don't you remember me? Timon, Archimedes' slave."

She squinched up her face and gave me a long, hard look. "So what?" she said. "You're wearing Roman red. Why are you here?"

"I'm a scribe with the army. My duties brought me to Sicily. I chanced to see Gelo as I walked by. How is Eurydice?"

Gelo called out his mother's name.

"Quiet, boy," snapped Agathe. "Eurydice is fine. Why would you care?"

"She was once a friend. That's all."

Eurydice came out of the tenement. She was only a few years older than I, but her face seemed older. The times had been hard on her. She was still an attractive woman, but she had once been gorgeous. "Gelo, what do you want?" she asked, viewing Troglius and me as intruding Romans.

"This man asked about you," said the boy.

Eurydice gave me a second look. "Timon!" All of her radiant beauty returned with her smile. "It—it—it is you!" She opened her arms and embraced me.

I remembered the last time I had seen her. She had been victimized by the plundering Romans after the siege. She had been a hollow shell of herself and hadn't said a single word to me. Just hearing her voice now—even with the stutter—filled me with joy, reminding me that time did have healing powers.

I told Eurydice the short version of my time in Rome, and how good it was to see her. She had no stories to tell, but said that she and Gelo lived with Agathe. The reunion was, as I would have expected, bittersweet. Syracuse had not fully recovered from the siege, nor had the inhabitants.

On the way back to the camp, Troglius commented on Eurydice's beauty. "Is she married?" he asked, a man of silence suddenly inquisitive.

"I don't think so," I said.

"And her father, is he alive?"

"She was sold into slavery as a child."

"She looked at me without turning away. I think she's a good woman. When we return from Africa rich with plunder, I will ask her to marry me." Though he faced me, his eyes stared off in opposite directions. He was about as ugly a man as I had ever seen. "Please don't tell anyone."

"One pledge is worth another. I won't say a word," I tapped the spyglass at my hip, "if you never mention this in the company of others."

Troglius nodded.

"And please, don't let anyone take it from me."

CHAPTER 36

In the days following my trip to Ortygia, I found myself thinking about all the people I had known during my first stay in Syracuse. I knew for certain that several of them had not survived. Excepting Agathe, Eurydice, and Gelo, I didn't know anything about the others. One of them was the Sicilian girl Moira. She was my age and had been my closest friend when I lived in Syracuse. Unfortunately our friendship had come to an ugly end after the siege when I learned that she was supporting her ailing grandfather by selling herself to the Roman soldiers. At the time I could barely face her. I left Syracuse hating her. In the years since I had seen more of the war, its collateral damage, particularly to women, and the extreme measures one might have to pursue to survive. Now, despite the heartbreak she had caused me, I felt I owed her an apology for the things I had said to her. I decided to look for her, and should I find her, admit that the war made all of us do things we wouldn't under other circumstances—myself included. I was twenty-three. She would be twenty-two. Maybe we were older and wiser and could find some peace between us.

The first chance I had I went back into the city. Moira's grandfather had owned a small farm south of the city and sold his produce at the market in the Tyche district. Moira might have returned to her grandfather's farm. Perhaps I could find her at the market, where I had first met her, selling "the best figs in Sicily." I didn't ask Troglius to accompany me. If I should find Moira, there was no telling how she would react, and I wanted to take that on alone.

I entered the city through the south gate and headed north on Via Intermuralis. The street climbed onto the plateau in the northwest portion of the city known as the Tyche district. When I had been in Syracuse the first time, there had been two markets, one in Achradina, with luxurious merchandise and high prices, and one in Tyche, where produce and more common goods were sold. This was where I went.

The market was busy, but the number of vendors was considerably less than before the siege. I explored the market one aisle at a time. I went slowly, but methodically, assuming I would recognize Moira though six years had passed. I had always enjoyed going to this market, saturating myself in the sounds and smells and bustle of everyday life, but I didn't find Moira. I had known the odds were slim. I went back to the camp thinking I would try again on another day.

A week later I had a free morning. It was a warm sunny day. A few billowy thunderheads drifted like warships across the sky to the east. I decided to head south into the farmland instead of going into Syracuse. Moira had once pointed out her farm to me from the steps of the Temple of Zeus. I had never been there, but I knew the general location. I followed the dirt road that wound through the small farms and pastures with no real expectation of finding Moira, just glad to get away from the camp.

Not long into my walk I noticed two young men coming the other way on the road. They appeared to be farmers. One of them had a sack of something—potatoes as it turned out—over his shoulder. When they got close, I acknowledged them with a nod of my head. The man with the potatoes took one step and swung the sack with all his might into the side of my head, shouting, "a god insulting Roman," as he connected.

I was knocked to the ground and was further kicked and beaten by the two men. Clearly it was the wrong day to go anywhere without Troglius. They left me lying in the weeds along the road with a bloodied nose, a split lip, and a pounding headache. When I finally managed to climb to my feet, I spit out a thick wad of bloody saliva, then opened and closed my mouth to see if my jaw still worked.

Seven or eight cows grazed in the pasture beside the road. I could see several farm buildings and an orchard beyond the pasture. Maybe I could find some water there to clean myself up before returning to camp. I crawled through the rail fence, lost my balance, and fell to the ground.

Gaining my feet, I weaved across the field to the closest farm building and found a trough of water. There was a well beside it. I used a rope to pull up a bucket of water and washed the blood from my face and hands. As I was standing there, looking for a way to dry my face without soiling my tunic any worse than it was, a woman shouted at me. "What are you doing at my well?"

The woman crossed the yard from what appeared to be her home, with a little girl gripping the hem of her chiton and a slightly older boy trailing behind.

"I'm sorry," I said turning to face her. "I met with some difficulty on the road."

My condition didn't seem to faze her. Perhaps she hated Romans also. "What can you pay for that water?" she snapped getting closer.

That's when I recognized her. "Moira...?"

She stood back, suspicious that I should know her name.

I realized that with my beard and the wounds she might not recognize me. "It's me, Timon. Don't you remember me?"

She tilted her head, appraising me from a distance. She took a few steps forward, both children now hanging onto her dress. "Timon? Archimedes' slave? You left for Rome years ago."

I smiled. "That's right." She was a woman now, not an impish girl. Her hair was pulled back in a long brown ponytail. Light beads of moisture dotted her forehead. Even wearing a worn, wool chiton, towing two dirty children, she was the picture of pastoral beauty. "I returned two months ago. I'm a mapmaker in the army."

She came up close to me. "It looks like you've taken a couple of bad hits."

"From two of your neighbors. Must have been my tunic," I said, looking at the ground.

"Come to the house. We need to do something about those cuts on your face."

The house was a one-room, mud brick structure with a thatch roof. I sat on a stone wall with a child on either side of me, while she went in to get a clean towel. She used water from the well to reclean the wounds. As she dabbed at my face, I could smell her, not some fragrant perfume, but the sweat of a woman who worked all day in the sun.

"Is this your grandfather's farm?" I asked.

"It was. He died shortly after I last saw you. I sold it to the neighboring farm to survive. They own the orchards, but I manage them for a portion of the profits."

"Do you still grow the best figs in Sicily?"

This didn't elicit the smile I had hoped for. "Probably not," she replied, now using the towel to dry my face.

"Do you still sell them in town?"

"One day a week."

"I came out here hoping I might find you. I didn't think it would happen quite this way."

"You came looking for me?" I saw that she still had a smattering of freckles across the top of her cheeks.

"I wanted to apologize for the way we parted."

"What do you mean? I'm the one who should apologize. I wasn't honest with you."

I shook my head. "The times were bad. I didn't quite understand your predicament."

Tears began to form in her eyes. She abruptly turned away, and without facing me, said, "I'm glad I was able to help you, but I have work to do."

I stood up. "Of course. Can I pay you for the water?"

She wiped the tears from her cheeks, then faced me. "Don't be silly. I should never have said such a thing."

I could see how poor she was. I had a few coins with me. Apparently my attackers weren't thieves, just angry locals. I took a coin out of my tunic pocket. "Please, take this. I would feel better if you did."

Moira hesitated then took the coin. "Thank you," she said looking at the ground, embarrassed by her situation.

"What day do you go into the market? I will come find you and buy some figs."

"It's never the same," she said quickly. "Work at the farm dictates when I go." She took her children's hands and turned away, walking toward the orchard. She stopped to call over her shoulder. "One day is as likely as another. Look for me—every sale counts."

"Then expect to see me," I called back. I watched her enter the orchard, then I headed back to the road. On the way, I realized in a panic that the spyglass wasn't hanging from my belt.

I didn't understand how badly I had been beaten until I tried to hurry across the pasture. I found the spyglass lying in the weeds. It must have caught on the fence when I had crawled through. I checked the lenses, then aimed it toward the orchard, but Moira and her children had disappeared into the trees.

Seeing Moira affected me in ways I wasn't expecting. She wasn't rich or blond like Sempronia. She likely had no interest in geometry or numbers—beyond the price of her figs—and she wasn't the laughing, adventurous girl who had stolen my heart years earlier. She was something more. I couldn't put my finger on it, but I knew I would seek her out again, just to make sure it was her, not the blows I had taken, that was causing my head to swim.

CHAPTER 37

Two days later I was called to headquarters. Scipio, wearing a toga, which I had never seen on a Roman officer in camp before, was looking at a scroll spread out on a large table when I entered. His naval commander and friend since childhood Gaius Laelius stood beside him, wearing a bronze breastplate, no helmet, and a gladius at his hip. I had seen him speak on several occasions in the Senate, but I had never met him. He was tall, about the same age as Scipio, and not particularly handsome, with a long narrow face, thick brown eyebrows, and bushy hair that receded somewhat at the temples.

Scipio introduced me as a scribe and mapmaker and motioned for me to come forward. The two men were looking at a map of the African coastline.

"This is a map that Laelius has been working on," Scipio said. "He's been to Africa several times in the past three years. You will notice it has no inland detail."

"I have focused on the coastline," said Laelius. "Much of this comes from direct observation. I have no real mapmaking skills." He ran his finger along the coastline. "This is no better than a rough approximation."

Scipio nodded. "I'm sending Laelius to Africa for further reconnaissance as soon as he's ready to go."

"Perhaps a week," said Laelius looking at me.

"You will be going with him," said Scipio. "I want you to work on this map. Laelius will give you all the help you need."

This was the first I had heard of the voyage. My heart immediately began to pound. "Yes, sir."

"Laelius expects to be gone three weeks to a month. Do all that you can in that time. You will have other opportunities when we all go to Africa, but whatever you can map now will serve as the basis of our invasion strategy later."

"I will advise you about the depths of the water and the currents," added Laelius. "We'll try to determine the best possible location for a landing."

I nodded.

Laelius continued. "I was told you can make maps that allow distances to be accurately translated into miles. This would be of immeasurable value to everything we do."

"Yes, sir. Of course," I said, then I was dismissed.

As soon as I learned that I was going to Africa, and that the trip might last as long as a month, I knew I needed to see Moira before I left. A question had been stuck in my head since going to her farm. I hadn't seen anyone else while I was there. Where was the father of her children? I went to the market the following two days, hoping to ask her this question. I walked every aisle and didn't see her either day.

I got three days' notice before our departure for Africa. I got up before dawn the day before we left and hiked out to the farmland. I wore an old wool tunic to blend in. I reached Moira's farm as the first rays of sunlight appeared on the horizon.

I stood in the pasture a good distance from her farm and watched her come out of the house to begin the chores of the morning. As the light increased, I used the spyglass to watch all that went on, looking for evidence of a man. I only saw Moira and her children.

I waited for the sun to get a little higher before approaching her house. I helped her carry four buckets of water as a way of apologizing for the intrusion.

"I'm leaving for Africa tomorrow," I said. "I'll be gone a month or more. I wanted to get some of your figs before I left. I didn't see you at the market so I came out here to purchase them."

"Are you making that up?"

I took a deep breath. "Not completely. I do want the figs, but I also wanted to see you before I left." I lowered my eyes, then gave her a sheepish look. "Mostly I came to see you."

Her eyes narrowed.

I pawed at the ground with my foot. "Do you have a husband?"

"So you can insult me if I say no." Her youngest called to her from inside the house.

"No, no, of course not. I apologized for that kind of thinking when I came here the first time. I simply wanted to know if I should come by again when I return."

"Why's that?"

"Maybe you could use some help."

She gave me a grim look. "Do you have time to help right now? There's plenty to do."

"No, I barely have time to be here at all. But I would stay if I could."

"I've heard that before. I have two children to prove it." The little girl called for her again. Moira turned to go into the house.

I called after her. "Any chance I could get some figs?" She continued to the house. "I want a bag. And I've got a piece of silver to pay for it."

She stopped in the doorway and faced me. "A bag?"

"I need a month's worth." I held out a silver half-stater.

The coin got her attention. She retrieved a bag of figs from one of the outbuildings and gave it to me.

"Thank you," I said, handing her the coin.

"This is way too much, Timon—but I'll take it."

"Good. You should."

She wagged her head and walked away like she didn't understand.

"I'll be back," I called to her.

She didn't even turn her head. "I won't hold my breath."

I had to laugh. In spite of the sarcasm, I heard some of the old spark in her retort. She was a tough one for sure. She always had been. But powers beyond reason were at play. I wanted to see her again.

CHAPTER 38

I had never been so far out at sea that I couldn't see land. Most Mediterranean shipping routes followed the shoreline, always keeping land in sight, and for the first part of our voyage, Laelius guided our fleet of thirty triremes west along the coast of Sicily around Cape Pachynum to Lilybaeum. It took three and a half days. From Lilybaeum, it was a hundred and twenty-five mile, two-day voyage across the open sea to Africa, something rarely done in the winter, and only with caution in the summer.

During our second day at sea, with everyone anxious for the sight of land, I stood at the bow of the lead ship, periodically using the spyglass to look for signs of the African coast. The first few times I did this I made an effort not to be noticed, but I quickly realized that no one paid much attention to me anyway. I began to use the spyglass like it was just another sighting tool. And the more I used it, the more I understood how valuable it was at sea.

As I had told Troglius, I intended to show the spyglass to Scipio, but only after I had gotten to know him well enough to trust him. I had not reached that point yet. I had hardly spoken to him since our first conversation, and there had been tension then. With this voyage being a reconnaissance trip, however, I couldn't help thinking how useful the spyglass would be to our captain. What about showing it to Laelius? What better opportunity would I get to demonstrate its powers?

I didn't know Laelius any better than Scipio. I had met him when I was told about the trip to Africa, and I had spoken briefly with him during preparation for the voyage. He seemed like a good man to me, but showing him meant Scipio would also have to see it. I decided to take more time before making a decision, then raised the spyglass to my eye again. As I scanned the southern horizon, expecting to see more boundless ocean, I caught sight of something. I looked up to the crow's nest. The man with the best view other than mine didn't appear to have seen anything yet.

I raised the spyglass and took another look. It was land. I was sure of it—and at a very great distance. Despite my earlier hesitance, I was so excited about what I was seeing that I immediately sought out Laelius. I found him at the stern watching the progress of the other ships in our flotilla.

I didn't know how much longer it would be until the man in the crow's nest would see what I had, but I wanted to show Laelius the spyglass before that happened. I came up alongside of him. "Sir, may I have a few minutes of your time."

Laelius was nearly ten years my senior. He had the look and feel of a veteran officer, stolid, physically superior, and not overwhelmingly outgoing with enlisted men. He turned to me with little interest. "Yes, scribe, what is it?"

"Come to the bow with me." I lifted the spyglass. "I believe this sighting tool will be of value during the voyage. I want to demonstrate it for you."

Laelius took a brief glance at the spyglass. "Another time, scribe, we're close to land." He looked up at the man in the masthead and shouted. "Sailor, have you seen anything yet?"

The man called back that he had not.

Laelius, clearly anxious, took a deep breath and let it out. Being out of sight of land overnight made everyone nervous—even a veteran of many such voyages.

I touched his shoulder. "I have seen land, sir."

Laelius turned abruptly, somewhat irritated by my persistence.

"Through this device, sir," I said quickly.

Laelius shouted at the sailor in the masthead again. The response was the same. "No land in sight, sir."

"Come with me to the bow, sir. Trust me in this."

A scribe rarely talked to an officer in this way. Some would judge it insubordination, but I had come to Laelius with the highest recommendation from his superior, and rather than snap at me, he paused. "And you will show me land?"

"Yes, sir."

Laelius followed me to the bow. "Watch how I use this device." I lifted the spyglass to my right eye, and describing everything I did, aimed it where I had seen a dark spot on the horizon. It took a moment, and some twisting of the tubes, but I refound the dot of land. The passage of time had only brought it closer. If I had any doubts before, I didn't anymore.

I handed the spyglass to Laelius. Thankfully it was not just the two lenses. On board a ship they would have been impossible to aim and hold steady. He struggled with the device as it was. He first drew a bead on a distance piece of open sea. He lowered the spyglass and turned it around to look at the wide end. "What did I just see, scribe? It appeared to be at the end of this tube. What is this?"

"There's nothing at the end of the tube but clear glass, sir. Try it again. It allows you to see farther. Try to focus on the horizon."

Intrigued by what he had already seen, he reapplied the spyglass to his eye. I watched him adjust his line of sight and twist the tubes, now clearly understanding how to focus it. When he lowered the spyglass a second time, I could see the amazement in his face. "What am I seeing? The water is above the sky?"

"That's right. The device flips things over. Ignore that and look closely."

Laelius nodded, seeming to understand. "Where did you see land?"

I pointed. "It's only a shadow on the horizon. Have patience."

Laelius raised the spyglass to his eye and scanned the horizon for quite some time without lowering the glass. Suddenly he hushed in amazement, "I see it. Yes, that's what it is." He lowered the spyglass and shouted again at the man in the crow's nest. "Any sight of land, sailor?"

"No, sir."

"Are you certain, sailor?" He used the spyglass as his pointer and aimed it in the direction of what we had seen. "Look where I am pointing."

"Nothing, sir."

Laelius turned to me somewhat confused. "Is this an illusion? Some trick you've learned?"

"No, sir. Of course not. The glass lenses," I pointed to each of them, "were a gift to me from Archimedes. This spyglass is an optical tool. What you're seeing is real. Given time, the sailor is sure to verify what we've seen."

Laelius continued to use the spyglass and watch our progress. He spotted two other points of land. "I believe I've located two islands— islands that I know should be there, but why are they only visible through these tubes?" He stared at the spot on the horizon where he had seen the islands. "Without this device, I see nothing."

"Land ho!" shouted the man in the crow's nest. The sailor pointed to the location we had already identified.

Laelius handed the spyglass to me as though it were a golden scepter. "Who else knows about this?"

"A few close friends and you. I suggest we keep it quiet, but not overtly veiled."

He tilted his head,

"I always carry the spyglass at my hip, like you do your gladius. I use it without concern for who sees me. If anyone asks, it's a sighting device. And it is. With this tool I can make some very accurate maps. Am I out of line to ask for your confidence in this?"

"What about Scipio?"

"I'll show it to him when we return to Syracuse. But only after I've made enough progress with the map to demonstrate what I can do with it."

Laelius shook his head as though bewildered by what he had seen, then grinned, as he never had before in my presence. "I want to be there. I want to see his reaction."

"Wait until tonight," I said. "We'll turn it upward to the heavens." I nodded at him to emphasize what I felt was the most stunning use of the lenses—viewing the stars.

I spent the rest of the day on the bow, making sightings and writing down numbers. My mapping of Africa had begun. I had been lucky. Laelius had proven to be a curious man. Revealing the lenses to him had not been a mistake. The more he understood what I was doing, the better he could assist me with the map.

CHAPTER 39

We landed unnoticed that evening at dusk and quickly made our camp at a location known as Bizerta, about seventy-five miles of winding shoreline west of Carthage. The next morning Laelius took a raiding party into the surrounding countryside. He stormed and looted several small villages that were totally unprepared for marauding Roman soldiers. By the next day news of our arrival had reached Carthage. The number of soldiers and ships was badly exaggerated, suggesting that Scipio had landed and that the invasion had begun. The same kind of hysteria that had gripped Carthage six months earlier in anticipation of Scipio's arrival ripped through the city again. The Council of Elders immediately decided to hold a levy within Carthage and throughout the nearby countryside, enlisting every able-bodied man to help defend the city. Stores of grain were brought in from the farmland, iron plough shares were forged into swords, and a fleet of ships was prepared to send to Bizerta.

Shortly after these efforts were put in motion, a second, more accurate report reached Carthage. The invading force was not Scipio, but a small raiding party. While this provided welcome relief in Carthage, the Council of Elders knew that the threat of an invasion was real and countered with several strategic moves of their own. Despite Syphax's previous commitment to Scipio, envoys were sent to Siga in hopes of reversing that pledge. Another delegation went to Greece promising King Philip, a known enemy of Rome, two hundred talents of silver to stage an attack on Sicily to distract Scipio—an offer he did not accept. Six thousand infantry, eight hundred cavalry, and seven elephants were sent to Hannibal's youngest brother Mago, who was in Corsica assembling an army. His orders were to take his troops to northwest Italy to enlist more barbarian mercenaries, and then to head south to join his brother.

At our camp, one raiding party after another returned, steadily filling our ships with booty. Early in the morning of our fourth day in Africa, a contingent of perhaps sixty Numidians on horseback rode up to the edge of our camp. I was immediately reminded of the sorties Hannibal's Numidians had launched against our camp while I was with Marcellus. A state of heightened alert raced through the camp. Helmeted legionnaires appeared at regular intervals all along the palisades. The riders came to a halt outside the range of our weapons. Defying all sense of danger, their captain, wearing a black mantle wrapped around his head and shoulders, cantered up to the gate flanked by two of his men and asked to see Laelius.

The guards sent a runner to headquarters. When the runner returned, the three men were admitted to the camp. The rest of the Numidian contingent watched from their horses.

A short time later I was called to headquarters. Laelius' opinion of me had greatly increased since I had shown him the spyglass. He seemed to recognize my intelligence and began to give me the same kind of respect I had received from Marcellus.

Two centurions stood guard outside headquarters. The two Numidian soldiers who had accompanied their captain knelt on the ground nearby. The centurions knew who I was. One stood aside while the other lifted the tent flap and announced my arrival.

I recognized the Numidian captain as soon as I saw his piercing green eyes. It was the dashing Masinissa, whom I had encountered during the trip to Rome with my mother and Lucretia. Laelius introduced me to the Numidian as his scribe. Because Masinissa's Latin was limited, he spoke Greek, and I interpreted for Laelius.

"I've heard that Syphax has pledged Masaesyli loyalty to Rome," said the Numidian prince. "In no way should you trust him. He has recently invaded land that is rightfully mine, and with the assistance of a man by the name of Mazaetullus, installed my cousin, who is no more than a child, on my throne. This boy is little more than a puppet for Mazaetullus, and Syphax now believes that all Numidia is his." Masinissa, I would learn, always expressed himself with tremendous passion, very much the antithesis of the stoic Roman officers.

"Syphax was assisted in all of this by the Carthaginian Hasdrubal Gisgo." His eyes flashed with intensity and intelligence. "He has promised Syphax my kingdom as a way of drawing him away from Scipio. Mark my words. Syphax cannot be counted on for anything.

"While in Spain, Scipio asked me if I would consider offering my services to Rome as an allied cavalry commander. You were there, Laelius. I didn't answer at the time, but the loss of my kingdom has prompted my decision. I would never fight on the same side as Syphax, but should he turn traitor, as I promise he will, I will put everything I have behind the Roman cause."

Laelius nodded his approval. Both he and Scipio had recognized the young man as a valuable asset.

"The Carthaginians are currently scrambling to assemble troops, and courting Syphax is only part of it," continued Masinissa. "Tell Scipio he is wasting time. Your raiding party should have been a full invasion." Masinissa, at this time, was twenty-seven years old. He was making demands of a Roman officer several years his senior.

Laelius' response was measured. "Syphax has been cooperating with the Carthaginians. That's something you know for certain?"

"Cooperating! They're fighting as one against my people. Against me! Is that something I know?" He laughed in derision. "Twice I have raised troops to counter Syphax's actions. Each time I was greatly outnumbered and defeated." He lifted his robe to his knee, revealing a large, recently healed wound. "Is Syphax's collusion with Carthage something I know for a fact? Absolutely. The boy on my throne just married the daughter of Hannibal's sister. Syphax, Mazaetullus, and Carthage are all in this together against me and will soon conspire against Rome!" Masinissa was an impressive and confident young man, remarkably bold for his years. Something told me I was witnessing a great and dynamic man very early in his life.

Laelius listened to my translation and took a deep breath. "This is important information, Masinissa. I assure you I understand that. I will make certain the consul understands also. But you must realize that preparation for such an invasion is vast. We are not ready yet. My visit is necessary reconnaissance."

Masinissa shook his head when I passed on Laelius' response. "Every day that passes is a day wasted," he snapped. "Tell Scipio that even though I have been driven from my kingdom, I can bring a considerable force to the Roman side." He pounded his chest twice with his fist. "Tell him a Roman victory in Africa is also a victory for me. That is the kind of loyalty he can count on."

"I will pass that on to Scipio," said Laelius, showing remarkable patience with the fiery young man, but also, like myself, impressed by the confidence of the Numidian prince.

Masinissa paced across the tent several times to cope with his vast energy. He stopped suddenly and faced Laelius. "You would be wise to be gone within the week. Carthage is preparing a fleet as we speak to prevent your ships from leaving shore."

The information gave Laelius pause. If true, it demanded immediate action. "We need three more days to finish packing the ships, Masinissa. Then we will leave. But I have one request to make of you, if you are willing."

Masinissa lifted his head.

Laelius looked to me. "My scribe is a mapmaker. One of our objectives while we're here is to prepare a map of the area around Carthage. The scribe has made some initial sketches." He motioned to the map table on one side of the tent. "Would you look at what he's done so far?"

Masinissa went to the map table and studied my rough drawing. "This is done quite nicely," he said, looking directly at me for the first time, studying my face as though remembering our encounter in Italy. "Maps have always fascinated me. I can certainly point out a few rivers and specific mountain peaks as references. But I can do better than that. Can your scribe ride a horse?"

I nodded.

"Give me two days with your scribe, Laelius, and I will give him a tour on horseback so he can add some detail to the inland regions."

Laelius was all for it. "A good map will be invaluable to the invasion. You can have him immediately."

It was a great opportunity, but it meant my taking off with a contingent of Numidian cavalry for two days. "I'll need a horse, sir."

"I'll have one readied for you."

Masinissa looked at me and tilted his head. "Your face is familiar to me, scribe. Have we met before?"

"Yes, in Italy. I was traveling with two women."

His eyes lit. "One was your mother. She was ill."

"Yes. That's right."

"Such things are not accidents. Trust me. We have met for a reason."

CHAPTER 40

Masinissa and I became friends almost immediately upon meeting the second time. He was a highly energetic and well-educated man, more at ease on a horse than at any other time. He hurried me from the tent leaning on my shoulder, excited to be assisting me with the map. His studies in Carthage had included rudimentary geometry and some modest introduction to numbers and the work of Pythagoras. By the time I had acquired a horse, he was asking me if I would come to Cirta after the war to help him map his kingdom. He was passionate, intelligent, and thirsty for knowledge. If I had any worries about riding off for two days with sixty Numidians, they were gone by the time we left the Roman camp.

Masinissa introduced me briefly to his men, then told them where we were going and what we were trying to do. Without any further delay, we rode off at a gallop headed inland. In the distance was the ragged silhouette of the Atlas Mountains, a range that stretched a thousand miles across North Africa from the Pillars of Hercules to Carthage.

I rode a Roman war horse, four palms taller than Balius. The Numidians rode their little garrons, charging and challenging each other to ride faster. It was thirty Roman miles to the outskirts of Carthage, and it seemed Masinissa was determined to be there before the sun set that afternoon. I had never tried to cover so much ground at such a speed on horseback before. It was all I could do to keep up as we raced southeast across the rising plains with no conversation beyond the hoots and yelps of the Numidian riders.

Well before sunset we crested a series of low ridges and came to a halt. I was exhausted from riding. We had only stopped twice briefly for water. Masinissa pulled up alongside me and grinned. With his horse pawing at the ground, he pointed to the north. "That's Carthage at the tip of that tongue of land. The elevated area in the center is

159

Byrsa, crowned by the Temple to Eshmoun. The river you see is called the Bagradas." He smiled broadly, showing his teeth.

From where we sat on our horses, the ground sloped downward into Carthage's rich agricultural land, second only to Egypt's in its production of fruits and grains. Huge farms and luxurious plantation manors stretched out for miles on the fertile plains of North Africa. Brilliant green fields of wheat, oats, and barley were interspersed with orchards of olives, figs, almonds, and pomegranates, and crisscrossed with intricate irrigation systems. The Romans were farmers who grew food for themselves. The Carthaginians were agriculturists whose harvests were targeted for export.

Beyond the farmland, some ten miles off, was the concentration of walls and buildings that defined the city of Carthage. Farther off on the horizon stretched a narrow strip of aquamarine that was the Mediterranean Sea. With the sun low in the west, the entire expanse was tinted to the hue of a pale red wine.

Masinissa watched me as I took in the view. "Carthage is noted for its two harbors. Can you see them? One is rectangular and the other circular."

"Yes, just barely."

"They are said to be the most advanced in the world. The rectangular one is dedicated to merchant ships and commerce. There's a gate at its east end for access to the sea. A heavy iron chain can be drawn across the opening to seal it off from outside traffic. The circular harbor is for the Carthaginian navy. I've heard it's three thousand feet in diameter. That elevated island in the center," again he pointed, "is where the fleet admiral lives. The sea wall that surrounds the harbor has two hundred individual quays on the inside, with stone pillars at the entrance to each berth, creating a colonnade all the way around the harbor's interior. It's quite impressive."

It was difficult to see all that he described, but I had heard of the harbors before. I would use the spyglass to get a better look the next day when I did the surveying and no one would notice what I was doing.

Masinissa climbed from his horse. "We'll camp here for the night, and use this location as our base of operations tomorrow."

"One full day here should be all I need. Thank you, Masinissa, this is extremely helpful."

We made an open camp for the night. Several of the riders went hunting for our dinner and returned with three antelope and a wild boar. The meal was nothing short of a feast. I sat at one of the four campfires with Masinissa and fifteen of his men, gnawing on meat-laden bones and passing around a leather bota bag filled with fermented goat's milk.

Masinissa and I spoke in Greek, which none of the others could understand. He told me the remarkable story of his last few months. His uncle, Oezalces, who had replaced Masinissa's father on the throne, died four months after his coronation at a time when Masinissa was in Spain. Oezalces' eldest son, Capussa, took the throne. Mazaetullus, a man connected by blood to the royal family, immediately contested the crown and inspired a popular revolt against Capussa. In the ensuing uprising, Capussa was killed. Rather than taking the crown himself, Mazaetullus installed Capussa's ten-year-old brother Lacumazes on the throne. Knowing that Masinissa would be infuriated by what had happened, Mazaetullus prepared himself for the prince's return by enlisting the aid of Syphax with the promise of a large portion of the Maesulii kingdom.

"I returned to find that my father's kingdom had been stolen and that there was a price on my head." Masinissa held an antelope shank in his right hand. He bit into it with the anger of his words and pulled free a huge piece of meat with his teeth. Talking and chewing, he told me of raising two armies to reclaim his land and being defeated twice by Syphax.

"Following the second defeat, I got away with only thirty of my men and hid in the hills." Masinissa shook his head, remembering the day. "Syphax ordered his most able officer, a man by name of Bucar, to seek me out with a contingent of five hundred foot soldiers and two hundred cavalry. They surprised us one morning at our camp in the hills. All but five of us were killed in the ambush. Bucar and his cavalry chased us across the open plain on horseback, gradually using their numbers to hem us in and direct us into a cul-de-sac formed by a bend in the Chelif River." Masinissa spoke with such intensity it was difficult to tell if the flash in his eyes was a reflection from our campfire or the spark of his passion.

"Bucar's men killed two of mine with javelins during the chase. I received a bad wound in the leg. When we reached the river's edge, it looked hopeless. The water ran fast and deep. With two hundred riders intent on making my head a trophy, we lashed our horses and leapt into the river." Masinissa raised the shank above his head and shouted across the fire. Two men answered with a series of piercing yips, which set off a chorus of yips and whistles from around the other campfires.

"Bucar assumed that we had all drowned. He returned to Syphax with the mutilated head of one of my men, claiming it was mine. Soon it was common knowledge that I was dead." He nodded his head and grinned. "My men pulled me out of the river and hid me in a cave in the Atlas Mountains, where they nursed me back to health over a period of three weeks. Little by little, we gathered other men that were loyal to me. We began raiding Masaesyli villages, stealing horses and weapons." He grinned again, lighting his eyes with the passion of his tribe.

"Many of my people still believe I'm dead. I have made no effort to dispel that belief. Syphax will find out soon enough, and he won't be pleased. The men you see here tonight are some of my closest friends." The flames from the campfire lit his face. His eyes glowed like embers. His teeth flashed as he spoke. "I will use this loyal core to build yet another army, and if you ever have the ear of Laelius or Scipio, let them know I won't give up until I have regained my kingdom."

Masinissa squirted some of the goat's milk into his mouth, then handed the leather bag to me.

"Timon, I have done a lot of talking about myself. Tell me something about yourself. What is deepest in your heart tonight?"

I lifted the leather bag over my head and squirted a stream of the fermented milk into my mouth, then passed it on to the man beside me.

The goat's milk was stronger than the mulsum I was accustomed to, and though I had tried not to drink too much, I had. Without the drink, I would have said the deepest thing in my heart was geometry. I would have gone on about the numbers and Archimedes' vision of the heavens. On this night, however, Masinissa's question struck a deeper chord.

"I'm in love with two women," I said, an admission I had yet to make, even to myself.

Masinissa's face lit with affirmation, and he nodded. "Yes, yes, go on."

"One," I said, "lives in Rome. Her hair is the color of sunlight and her eyes blue like the sky. She is sweet and kind, and like you, captured by the mystery of the forms and the figures. Her name is Sempronia. A name as lovely as she is." I said it again. "Sem-pro-nia. But she is wealthy, and I am not. Her family is of the highest rank in Rome. I was once a slave."

Masinissa lifted his head, considering my words. "And the other?"

"Her name is Moira. She's a farm girl. A dark Sicilian with a fiery temper and a will of iron. While Sempronia is an ethereal, intelligent woman, Moira is the earth, as lovely and complex as life itself. She has no money, two children, and needs a man to help on her farm." I reached into my tunic and withdrew a handful of the figs that I had brought with me. I opened my hand to Masinissa. "These come from her orchard."

He took several figs and put one in his mouth. "Almost as good as the figs we grow here," he said as though that was the highest possible compliment. "And who will you choose?"

I put a fig my mouth. "It may not be for me to choose. Sempronia's mother won't let her see me. And Moira is too proud to admit she might need me."

The prince laughed and tossed another fig in his mouth. "Given the choice, who would you take? What in a woman means the most to you?"

"A month ago I would have said Sempronia. Tonight, I can't say." I tapped my chest. "Your question strikes me square in the heart, Masinissa. I just don't know who I would prefer."

"Become a Numidian," he replied, gently giving my shoulder a shove. "Marry them both." Then he burst into laughter. He called out something in his native language. The men around the fire laughed, presumably at me.

Masinissa sobered and gathered my eyes. "I love but one woman, Timon," he said, more serious than at any time I had seen him, even when addressing Laelius about the prospect of an invasion. "Her name is Sophonisba—as lovely a name as any there is," he added, as though there might be a competition between us. "Her skin is pale as milk. Her hair as black as this night. Her eyes are the color of the sunlit sea and shine like some light originates behind them. I have seen her only once. A year ago. And unless I am horribly mistaken, she feels the same way about me."

"And will you marry her and make her your queen?"

Masinissa stared at me in a way he hadn't before. There was anger in it, a fierce glare. "She's Hasdrubal Gisgo's daughter. The wealthiest Carthaginian of them all. He could not have a blacker heart. He's as much to blame for the problems I'm having now as Syphax. To affirm their dark alliance, Hadrubal is sure to offer his daughter to my gravest enemy." He paused and stared into the flames. "Sophonisba can only be mine if the Romans defeat Carthage and I win back my kingdom. She is the plunder that I seek."

CHAPTER 41

We rose with the sun the next morning. I began the day by using the spyglass to scan the area looking for prominent landmarks from which to begin the process of triangulation. When Masinissa saw me using the device, he asked me what it was. I was tempted to show him, but I decided against it. I told him it was an instrument I used for sighting that increased the accuracy of my measurements. He let it go at that, then gave orders to his men to help me with the day's work.

I needed two types of measurements, distances and angles. I sighted straight lines to five different landmarks, then used my compass and a straight edge to approximate the angles between them. I had a thirty-foot length of chain with me for measuring stretches of ground. I used the chain to measure several much longer pieces of rope that I gathered from the Numidians. I then sent teams of riders to each of the five landmarks. Using these lengths of rope, stretched out end to end, they made rough approximations of the distances between the landmarks and also from the landmarks back to where I sited the angles.

We went to several locations to measure additional sets of angles and distances. What might have been two weeks of work for me alone had been completed in one day. We planned for more of this work the next day, but when we awoke in the morning, and the sun illuminated the African plains and Carthage in the distance, Masinissa noticed an increased amount of activity in the harbor. He interpreted this as a sign that a Carthaginian fleet was preparing to leave, quite possibly the one he had warned Laelius about. I used the spyglass to look for myself and concluded the same. By the time we had eaten, we could see the warships leaving the harbor one at a time. I counted forty triremes.

Instead of making more measurements, we decided to ride back to the Roman camp to tell Laelius he was running out of time. The voyage along the coast from Carthage to Bizerta was about seventy-five miles into the wind. The warships would have to stop once for the night before reaching Laelius' camp. Riding fast we were there before sunset. Laelius had the men work through the night loading the ships with plunder so that we could leave at dawn the next morning.

Masinissa and his men stayed the night, giving me a brief chance in the morning to thank him for his help. "I will be returning with Scipio at the time of the invasion," I said after a parting embrace with this man whose friendship had come so easily.

"Then you will see me again, Timon. As I said, what I want most," his eyes sparked with his desire for Sophonisba, "can only be achieved with the assistance of the Romans. Impress Scipio of this and that he must act soon."

Once at sea, I joined Laelius at the bow of the ship taking turns with the spyglass to scan the eastern horizon. Almost immediately we spotted the lead ships in the Carthaginian fleet, meaning they were close but not yet aware of us. Laelius changed our course to a westward direction to assure that they didn't see us. By midday he adjusted that to north by northeast, headed to Lilybaeum.

The trip from Syracuse to Lilybaeum to the coast of Africa had taken seven and a half days. The voyage back was slowed by a steady easterly wind. The trip took ten days. Laelius went straight to headquarters when we landed. I didn't accompany him, but I learned later that Scipio was particularly interested in what Laelius had learned from Masinissa. The consul had met the young prince before and had also recognized the man's intelligence and talent. He was pleased that Masinissa had offered to take part in the invasion, but he dismissed the warning that Syphax would break his alliance with Rome. It was mid August. Scipio set a goal of leaving for Africa in four weeks.

PART IV

SOPHONISBA

"It was those nuptial torches which had set Syphax's palace aflame; she was the poison in his blood, the avenging fury, who with her soft words and caresses had alienated his wits and sent him astray."

-Livy, *The War with Hannibal*

CHAPTER 42

Even knowing of Syphax's commitment to Scipio, Hasdrubal Gisgo had not given up his effort to court the Masaesyli king, now undeniably the most powerful tribal leader in the region. Hasdrubal had coaxed him into taking advantage of King Gala's death and wresting the Maesulii kingdom from Masinissa. But this was only the beginning of the courtship. Hasdrubal had become desperate and was now willing to do what he had resisted before. He knew that Syphax had a weakness for women and that he had expressed interest in Sophonisba, though he had only seen her once, when she was but a child. With all Carthage quaking with fear of an invasion, Hasdrubal sailed to Siga, and during a long evening meal, offered Syphax his daughter's hand in marriage to change sides in the war. The proposition threw Syphax into deep moral anguish, forcing him to weigh his word to Scipio against the pleasures of a woman who would make him the envy of all men. After one sleepless night of turmoil, he chose lust over loyalty.

Upon returning to Carthage, Hasdrubal went to his new home in Megara, where he had moved Sophonisba and his house slaves when Laelius' arrival on the African coast was mistaken for a Roman invasion. He immediately informed Sophonisba of the arrangement he had made with Syphax. She responded in the same way she had when he had first told her that her marriage was likely to be political. There were no tears, no pleas to be released from the arrangement. She told her father that following his wishes was her only desire and that she was honored to give herself in marriage for the security of Carthage and the Carthaginian people.

Sophonisba rose from her bed late that night and slipped out of the house to go into the garden. Wearing a thin, white sleeping gown, she glided like a ghost past the neatly arranged flower beds to a circular temple at the rear of the garden. The limestone temple to Tanit, mistress of the moon, had been built by Hasdrubal specifically for his deeply devout daughter.

Sophonisba climbed the temple's seven stairs and entered the internal chamber, where an alabaster statue of the goddess stood with its arms lifted to the heavens. Sophonisba recited a short salutation to Tanit, then prostrated herself on the stone floor and prayed for the strength to endure a marriage without love.

Sophonisba had learned a month earlier that the young prince, who in one brief encounter had stolen her heart, had been tracked down and killed by one of Syphax's henchmen. His head, she'd heard, had been delivered to Syphax in a glass jar. She cried for a week afterward and expected from that day onward to be promised to the man who had ordered Masinissa's murder.

Sophonisba remained prostrate in the temple until daybreak. After her prayers for strength, she had prayed that her life would be short so that she could soon join the young Numidian warrior in the spirit world. Only then would she know peace.

On returning to her room, she threw herself on her bed and began to cry. Her cheetah, now a year old, leapt up on the bed and lay down beside her. Sophonisba looked into the cat's big yellow eyes and stroked her head. "I don't want to be married to a barbarian like Syphax, Felicia. I don't want to live alone in desolate Numidia."

Sophonisba heard the door to her bedroom open. She immediately sat up and wiped the tears from her eyes. Felicia jumped from the bed and swayed across the room in long easy strides to greet Zanthia as she came in. The handmaiden sat beside Sophonisba and used the hem of her dress to dry the tears that Sophonisba had missed.

"My dear Sophie, why the tears after the strong face you showed yesterday afternoon?"

"You know the reason as well as I, Zanthia. My life has come to an end only days before my eighteenth birthday."

Zanthia wrapped her arms around the young woman to comfort her. After a moment, she released Sophonisba and touched her cheek. "You may want to mourn your fate and live behind a mask, but the other choice is to know your fate and make the most of it."

"What do you mean?"

"More often than not women are left to the mercy of men in this world, but that does not mean they are without influence in their lives."

Sophonisba's face remained a question.

"If true love is not to be part of your life, Sophie, you must make use of the power your beauty provides. Subtle guile can often surmount ten thousand lances. You may recall that I spent several years in Syphax's court through three of his five marriages. He let no woman who struck his fancy go untouched. I was younger, and I was delivered to his bedroom on more than one occasion."

Across the room, Felicia had found a slipper to chew on. Sophonisba snapped her fingers. The beautiful spotted cat let go of the slipper and came over to the bed to lie down at the her mistress' feet. "Go on, Zanthia."

"Part of the reason Syphax sent me to your father was his interest in you. He sought to gain favor with your father on the off chance it might lead to a marriage—just as it has. But what you must realize is that when a man, especially a Numidian, reveals that kind of interest in a woman, it puts the woman in a position of power."

"How's that?"

"Even should Syphax chain you to his bed, remember, at bottom, it is how you treat him in bed that determines who's in control."

Sophonisba's eyes narrowed with interest. "Tell me more."

"You are an intelligent and cultured woman, Sophie, but there are things to be known that are not taught by Greek tutors." Zanthia paused to glance around the room, as though someone might be listening. "A woman as smart and beautiful as you can wrap any man around her finger if she has the courage to learn the art." Zanthia nodded and a little grin crept over her face.

"Were your situation anything but what it is, I would never dare to tell you the secrets I'm about to divulge. However, the circumstances are what they are. Innocence can longer be the way of your world. And if anyone can tell you the wants of Numidian men, particularly Syphax, it is I. I spent enough time pleasing Syphax to know exactly what he likes. There are some things that you may find difficult to do at first, but if you learn to do these things with skill and with passion, he will be at your beck and call."

"Truly?"

Zanthia nodded very slowly. "Truly."

CHAPTER 43

A fleet of warships took Hasdrubal and Sophonisba to Siga three weeks after the agreement with King Syphax had been made. Siga, as most large cities of the time, was designed as a fortress. It was built on an elevated site a mile from the coast and was protected by precipitous cliffs on the north and east sides and massive stone walls on the south and west. When the Carthaginian flotilla entered the harbor at Siga, a welcoming party was already there to greet the ships and escort the bride and her attendants to Syphax's palace. Two columns of Numidian soldiers, wearing ceremonial armor, led the procession into the city. Hasdrubal rode in a curtained cedar litter carried by eight slaves. Sophonisba and her three attendants followed in a second litter. A squadron of cavalry in brilliant white tunics trimmed in red, riding four abreast, brought up the rear. The entire populace came out to watch, filling the streets all the way to the palace, hoping to get a glimpse of their new queen.

As Sophonisba's litter entered the city gates and made its way through the crowd, Zanthia pulled back the edge of the curtain so that Sophonisba could get a view of the city.

"Soon this city and the rest of Syphax's kingdom will be yours, Sophie. The king has a palace here and has acquired another in Cirta. Yours is not the worst of fates."

Sophonisba, who had maintained a stoic face throughout the journey from Carthage, made no acknowledgment of the splendor of the city and simply said, "All is politics."

Zanthia smiled. "I hope it's a little more than that. Syphax may believe he's a god, but he's a good king, a valiant warrior, and a passionate man with a heart."

"Then at least one of us will have one," replied Sophonisba, pulling back the curtain.

When the two columns of soldiers reached the palace, they paraded into the great hall, split into individual files, and stood at parade rest on opposite sides of the vast chamber with their javelins at their sides. A red carpet ran between them from the vestibule to the throne, where the bearded Syphax sat bare-chested, wearing a vest of gold chain, blue silk pantaloons, and an ornate crown in the shape of a cobra's hood. On either side of the throne were galleries filled with the king's family and his guests.

Hasdrubal was met in the vestibule by Bucar, who had gained prominence in Syphax's court since chasing down Masinissa. Two slaves helped Hasdrubal from his litter, and it was carried away to make room for the bride's arrival. Bucar did the honors of pulling back her litter's curtain. Zanthia came out first, then Nycea and Gaia, and finally Sophonisba, wearing a white wedding dress and veil. Bucar, reacting to her beauty, offered her his hand as she stepped out of the litter.

Syphax's palace was luxurious in the style of the partially civilized Numidians, a peculiar mix of tribal hunting trophies and oriental wealth. The hides of zebras, wildebeests, and leopards hung on the walls between the stuffed heads of elephants and lions. Shields covered with the skins of hyena or jaguar, extravagant leather headdresses, long wooden spears festooned with ostrich feathers and talismanic bones provided the central theme throughout the palace, all intermixed with wall hangings of richly-colored cloth, embroidered with precious gems or threaded with strands of gold.

Sophonisba's three attendants, dressed in high-necked, white chitons and carrying bouquets of flowers, led the procession down the center of the hall. Hasdrubal, with his daughter on his arm, followed ten steps behind. Looking like a fashionable bear with his full beard and head of curled hair, he wore a long maroon robe with black fringe at the hem. Sophonisba's wedding gown was made of a dense white lace. It was cut tight at her waist to accent her figure and billowed out at her knees with so many layers of cloth she appeared to be walking on a cloud. Her veil was of a finer white lace, transparent enough that Sophonisba's face could be seen behind, but only vaguely. An honor guard of twelve, wearing white tunics trimmed in red, vermillion chainmail vests, and red plumed helmets, marched up the aisle two by two to complete the procession.

Syphax, a well-chiseled man of forty-plus years with dark penetrating eyes, rose from his throne as the entourage proceeded up the red carpet, drawn in by the mystery and allure of his bride's appearance. When the attendants reached the throne, Zanthia and Gaia turned to the right, Nycea to the left. Syphax descended the three stairs from his throne's elevated platform to receive Sophonisba. Hasdrubal presented his daughter to the king by offering him her hand. Syphax, staring into the face behind the veil, reached out, almost as though he were afraid to touch the fairy creature before him, and gently touched her fingers.

A Numidian priest, who had been standing beside the throne with his arms folded within the wide sleeves of his purple robe, came forward with a jewel encrusted silver goblet and stood before the couple, now side by side and holding hands.

The priest recited a long traditional Numidian marriage poem, then concluded by saying, "Of all the gods of the Numidian people, of all the gods of the Carthaginian people, we ask the blessing and protection of the union of King Syphax of the Masaesyli tribe and Sophonisba, daughter of Hasdrubal, son of Gisgo."

The priest presented the goblet to Syphax. Syphax took a sip, then held it out to Sophonisba. She took it in both of her hands, and Syphax lifted her veil so that she could drink. Sophonisba wore no paint or makeup so that the bloom of her youth was not diminished and the subtle colors of her skin were not dimmed. Syphax went down on one knee as though her beauty had commanded it. He lifted her right hand and slid a ring on her finger with a diamond so large it seemed to be a source of light in itself.

Syphax then stood and embraced Sophonisba. They kissed and the priest pronounced them husband and wife. A slave came forward with a red pillow, carrying a golden diadem set with emeralds and rubies. Syphax lifted the diadem from the pillow and placed it on his queen's head. The soldiers on either side of the red carpet raised their javelins and held them out, touching the tips of the javelins opposite them, forming an arched pathway from the throne to the vestibule. Syphax, beaming with pleasure, took Sophonisba's hand and walked her down the aisle with the soldiers falling in behind as they passed. The guests followed the soldiers out of the palace to a huge outdoor feast that was open to the entire populace of Siga.

While Sophonisba maintained a smile throughout the proceedings and seemed to enjoy the celebration, Syphax glowed with joy. He could not have been more pleased with himself or the woman he had married.

CHAPTER 44

When the sun sank behind the mountains west of the city, Sophonisba left the feast that would go on all night. Four guards accompanied the bride and her attendants back to the palace. The guards directed Sophonisba to the royal chambers on the palace's second floor and the bedroom where the marriage would be consummated.

Gaia and Nycea both gasped upon entering the vast bedroom that had been decorated specifically for that night. Ten oil lamps on gold stands provided the light. A four-poster bed dominated the room. Curtains of gauze hung on three sides. The fourth side was a black maple headboard, carved with the images of birds and wild animals. Huge bouquets of flowers covered the bed and overflowed from ceramic vases all around the room. Along with the king's spears, shields, and hunting trophies, tapestries embroidered with landscapes of Africa hung over the stone walls. Gold necklaces, earrings of silver or gold or ivory, and two more jewel encrusted diadems were set out on the bride's dressing table as gifts from the king. Royal robes, evening gowns, ornamental dresses, and other clothing accessories filled a black maple cabinet set against the wall adjacent to the bed.

While Nycea and Gaia spun around the room overwhelmed by the jewelry and artwork, Sophonisba stood at one of the room's two large windows and watched the sunset transform from brilliant orange into purples and reds. Zanthia instructed Nycea to turn down the bed and arrange the pillows, then told Gaia to help Sophonisba change from her wedding dress into her nightgown.

When the attendants had completed their work, Zanthia dismissed them to be alone with Sophonisba. Sophonisba had said nothing since entering the room. She stood before the mirror stoically, appraising herself. Her gown clung to her like a lover. No detail of her body was hidden by the nearly sheer, white silk. Her black hair, brushed to a glossy ebony, hung free over her shoulders well past her waist.

Sophonisba watched Zanthia approach her from behind in the reflection of the mirror.

"No man in the world could resist you, Sophie. Be confident. And smile!"

Sophonisba continued to gaze into the mirror.

"Smile, Sophie, it's your wedding night."

Sophonisba turned to face her handmaiden. "It's not a wedding, Zanthia. It's a political arrangement."

"Regardless of what you call it, you must learn passion—if only as an act. Do not be afraid."

"I'm not afraid."

"Then why are you shaking? Remember that you are a queen now. You cannot show fear, particularly tonight when you share the king's bed. Syphax, all Numidian men, dreams of bold, imaginative women."

"How can I be bold and imaginative when I've never been with a man before, never even kissed a man other than my father?"

"Pretend. Imagine that you are an animal. Use your mouth. Use your hips. Tonight especially, do the things I've told you to do. In the order that I said to, in the ways I've instructed. And do it with pleasure and heat—even if you don't feel it. In return he will worship you. When you touch him, when you hold his phallus, imagine that the scepter to his kingdom is in your hand."

Sophonisba frowned at the thought.

Zanthia sighed. "You're right, Sophonisba. It's politics, not love. You are here to win the war and nothing less. In no other way should you imagine it. It's politics, and it's politics you need to take advantage of. Take control of Syphax tonight and you will always have him under your thumb."

Sophonisba walked across the room to the south facing window. Her stride was long and slow like a big cat. She was starting to feel the significance of what had just transpired. The bright colors had drained out of the sunset and the sky was a steel blue. The moon was low in the east, a crescent, sitting on its back, a big grin in the heavens. "For my father, for Carthage, for Tanit, I will learn the science of pleasure tonight," she whispered to herself.

Three knocks sounded on the door. Zanthia slipped out the room's back door, dousing half the oil lamps as she went. The door swung open. Syphax stepped into the room wearing a long golden robe. He noticed that the bed was open but empty, then he saw

Sophonisba, a silhouette before the window, with the moon over her left shoulder. She stared at him for an extended moment before swaying across the room, slow and deliberate. She stood before him and opened his robe. She lifted it from his shoulders and dropped it to the floor behind him. Syphax was transfixed. She took his hand and drew him into the bed.

CHAPTER 45

Syphax was not seen until late in the afternoon the following day. He strode from his chambers with Sophonisba, looking both tired and pleased. The new couple wore matching crowns of gold and purple robes threaded with gold wire. Sophonisba's eyelids were painted silver with antimony and her lips were painted red. They were escorted to the great hall by the twelve honor guards who had stood outside the king's chambers throughout the night. A second throne had been installed for Sophonisba since the wedding.

Hasdrubal, who had waited all morning in a guest room, was notified that the king and queen were ready to receive him. They were seated beside each other when he came into the hall.

Hasdrubal bowed before his daughter and Syphax. Sophonisba appeared calm and contained behind her mask of makeup. Syphax radiated masculinity fulfilled.

"I trust you both enjoyed your wedding night," said Hasdrubal.

Syphax's answer was a big smile. Sophonisba merely met her father's gaze with a look of strength and confidence that he had never seen in her before.

"I cannot remember a happier moment in my life," replied Syphax. "What business do you wish to conduct?"

"Before I leave for Carthage, Your Majesty, I have one last request of you to complete the agreement yesterday's wedding celebrated."

Syphax looked at Sophonisba and smiled. "Whatever you like, Hasdrubal. What can I do for you?"

"I would like you to send an envoy to Scipio in Syracuse."

Syphax cocked his head in question.

"I want you to tell Scipio that you cannot fulfill the promises you made to him a year ago. Tell him that you have married my daughter and are now bound to Carthaginian interests by blood, and that your best advice to him is to remain in Italy to protect his homeland."

Syphax frowned. "Is it not good enough, Hasdrubal, to say nothing to Scipio and turn away his envoys when he arrives in Africa?"

"No. He should know immediately. I'm hoping it will be enough to dissuade him from coming to Africa at all. That would be the best for all involved."

Syphax was not happy with this request. He glanced at his queen. "I will have an answer for you tomorrow."

"I had hoped to leave today, Your Majesty, but I will remain one more day, trusting that your decision will reflect the significance of the gift I have just given you."

Syphax remained in the great hall to conduct business for only a short time before returning to his chambers with his queen. Women, of course, are as different in their individual makeup as men. Some women, as some men, are more predisposed to sexual intimacy than others. Some exude this quality in their every movement, in every expression they make, whether intended or not, and heat up the conjugal bed in ways that would be shocking to others. Sophonisba's mother, who was also a woman of noted beauty, was a palpably sexual woman. It was in her blood and her being. Sophonisba had these qualities also, though prior to her marriage she didn't really know what that meant. When her time came, a panther-like sensuality came naturally to her. Her deep intellect allowed her to use her body with a vicious kind of detachment that drove Syphax wild with craving for her.

Upon reaching the bedroom that afternoon, Sophonisba removed Syphax's crown, and he hers. They each then disrobed the other, Syphax hastily, Sophonisba with a slow, purposeful grace. When Syphax embraced her, she whispered, "Why would you not be willing to tell Scipio of our marriage? Am I not a woman you would want to boast of?"

Syphax placed his hands on her buttocks and pulled her hips into his. He kissed her on the neck over and over, hardly hearing her words for the desire that encompassed him.

"Did I not please you last night?" asked Sophonisba softly.

Syphax lifted his head from her neck to look into her eyes. "Oh, yes, Sophonisba, more than you can know. And certainly I am proud to show you off to every man alive. In your company, I feel as though I can conquer the world."

"Then why the reluctance to tell this to Scipio? He will learn of our marriage eventually. Show him that you are not afraid of him. Show him that Rome is nothing to you compared to your love for me and for Carthage."

"I need to think it over. There should be a diplomacy to it—to save face."

Sophonisba took hold of his hand. "Please," she said, "please your queen. Prove to her that Scipio is nothing to you." She kissed down his chest, taking his left nipple in her mouth until it became hard, then dropped to her knees, pressing her cheek against his belly. She looked up at Syphax and wet her lips. "Pleasing each other, isn't that what marriage is for?"

Syphax agreed to Hasdrubal's request the next day. That afternoon, after Hasdrubal had left for Carthage, Syphax and Sophonisba, sharing a litter, led an extravagant procession from the city to the Siga River. Musicians played flutes and rang bells. Slaves strew flowers or waved staves tipped with burning incense all the way to the edge of the river, where an extravagant three-hundred foot cedar barge lay at anchor, its two rows of gilded oars standing upright on each side, ready to put the barge into motion. Syphax helped Sophonisba from the litter, and taking her hand, guided her down the ramp that led from the river bank to the barge deck. A long train of attendants followed them, carrying provisions and wedding excesses.

With two floors of living space and banquet rooms, featuring a gym, a copper bath, stables, and an aquarium, the barge was more like a floating palace than a ship. Brightly painted, two-story cypress columns lined both sides of the deck. One hundred soldiers in white tunics and polished bronze armor stood at attention along the colonnades. Two solid gold thrones sat on an elevated stage in the center of the ship to allow the best view of the river and the shoreline. An enormous purple silk awning stretched overhead, from colonnade to colonnade, for protection from the sun. The gunwales were inlaid with silver and gold. Polished bronze accoutrements—windlasses, cleats, ladders, anchors, boat hooks, and chains—sparkled everywhere, dazzling the eye.

One hundred trumpets announced their departure. The oars dipped into the water and began their rhythmic pull to the slow beat of a drum. The barge would proceed down the river at a leisurely pace for a week, then would reverse direction and come back to Siga, a two-week honeymoon cruise that would have made even an Egyptian queen jealous.

CHAPTER 46

"So, Sophie, you have had five days and five nights with your husband, what do you think?" Zanthia brushed Sophonisba hair in the privacy of one of the royal barge's bedrooms. She had chased off the other girls to have this conversation with the young woman she cared for as much as a daughter. "Has my instruction been helpful to you?"

Zanthia stood behind Sophonisba, who sat in a chair before a large bronze mirror. The new queen had transformed herself into someone she would not have recognized prior to her arrival in Siga. She had always been somber and withdrawn. Only Zanthia had been privy to her thoughts and her turmoil. But her solemnity had deepened in the past week. She was growing into her persona as a queen and it became her and added to her beauty. Now, when she might have blushed in response to Zanthia's question, she answered with the calculated cool of an assassin.

"Your words have changed me forever, Zanthia. I feel no shame in the animal pleasures that once frightened me, and Syphax can please me in ways I did not anticipate. But I cannot give myself completely to a man I do not love—a man who ordered the murder of the only man I have ever wanted."

Sophonisba stared into the mirror and revealed the depth of her anguish. "I can rouse passion in myself and in him because I must. I consider everything I do with Syphax an act of political necessity. I can see that I am pleasing him, and your advice has enabled me."

"You're more than pleasing the king, Sophie. It's as evident as the sun in the morning sky. The man worships you. Next," her eyes narrowed, "you must make him understand that you are smarter than he is. Engage in the politics of his kingdom."

Sophonisba eyes met Zanthia's in the mirror.

Zanthia nodded. "Rule the bedroom and the rest of the empire will follow."

CHAPTER 47

Syphax took Sophonisba to Cirta following their honeymoon on the river. Cirta had been the largest and most important city in Masinissa's kingdom. Sophonisba was well aware of this, and found it painful to be there, but she made a point of being in the palace's great hall each day when Syphax discussed affairs of state, made legal judgments, and conducted the everyday business of running a large kingdom. Much of this was dull routine. Although only eighteen years old, Sophonisba had decided that she would try to understand it all.

Their third day in Cirta, three weeks into their marriage, Sophonisba attended the morning session of state when small claims were assessed. Syphax had gone through three cases—two involving street vendors and one grazing rights—when a local man, in a dirty linen tunic, came running into the hall. The honor guard that accompanied Syphax whenever he was in public quickly stopped the man well short of the throne. The man screamed that he had information for the king that he would want to hear. Syphax told the guards to bring the man forward. Four guards ushered him down the aisle and pushed him onto his knees before the two thrones.

"What have you to say?" bellowed Syphax, a man whose image of himself was that of a warrior. He was king because of his capacity as a soldier and as a procreator.

"Masinissa is alive. I saw him outside Bizerta when the Romans landed last month."

Syphax immediately stood from his throne and screamed for Bucar. Sophonisba felt herself grow warm. Word traveled fast through the palace. It wasn't long before Bucar came striding down the hall's central aisle in full armor. He knelt before the king. "You called for me, Your Majesty."

"Six weeks ago you brought me the head of Masinissa."

"Yes, sire."

184

"And you were certain the head was Masinissa's?"

"Yes, sire. I cut the head off his body with my own hand."

"And you are certain that the body was Masinissa's? And that there can be no doubt of that?"

"Well, sir, the body was retrieved from the river. It was battered and swollen."

"Would you stake your life on the claim that Masinissa is dead?"

"I—I am not—yes. Yes, sire."

"You don't seem as certain as the day you collected the reward for his head."

"It's the way that I have been summoned and the questions you have asked that shake my certainty."

"As well they should." Syphax pointed to the man standing off to one side of the hall in a dirty tunic. "This man says Masinissa is alive. What do you say to that?"

"Ask my men what they saw. We surprised Masinissa and thirty of his men one morning. We killed all but Masinissa and four other riders before they were out of their bedrolls. We caught two of those five, then chased Masinissa and the others to the edge of the big bend in the Chelif River, where it runs fast and deep. All of them leapt into the river while still mounted and went beneath the surging water with their horses. We searched the river bank downstream for miles. We found three dead horses and one body, Masinissa's. The others could not have survived."

"Someone bring me the head," shouted Syphax. He had brought it to Cirta as verification to the locals of his position as their new king.

Syphax motioned to the guards. They stepped in close around Bucar as the king waited for the jar to be retrieved.

A slave came into the hall carrying the glass jar that was said to contain Masinissa's head suspended in olive oil. Beads of perspiration broke out along Sophonisba's hairline, fearing she might cry.

"Who's head is in this jar?" demanded Syphax.

Bucar bowed his head without giving an answer.

Syphax held the jar up with both hands and peered into the murky oil. "I can't see a thing in his light." He angrily threw the jar on the stone floor. It shattered in front of Bucar. The head rolled up to his knees, face uppermost.

"Is that Masinissa, Bucar? Is it? Your life depends on it."

Bucar bowed his head.

Sophonisba couldn't stop herself from standing to get a better look at the poorly preserved head. One of the guards kicked it with the toe of his sandal so that it rolled a quarter turn and faced directly at the king and queen. Sophonisba took a breath. She had not seen Masinissa in more than a year, but she was certain the head was not his.

"That's not Masinissa," said the guard.

Syphax took three steps closer. "You're right. It's not."

Bucar sat up on his knees, hands upraised, seeking mercy. Syphax pulled a sword from the scabbard of one of his guards and in a single long stroke decapitated Bucar. The head rolled across the aisle, stopping at the feet of one of the guards. The corpse fell forward, blood pulsing from the severed neck.

"Masinissa lives!" Syphax shouted to the gods. "What could be worse?"

Only being married to you, thought Sophonisba, her heart split in two by the news.

PART V

PROBLEMS IN LOCRI

"If you are ruled by mind you are a king; if by body, a slave."

-Marcius Porcius Cato

CHAPTER 48

Scipio might have achieved his goal of reaching Africa before the end of the summer had Africa been the only theater in the war, but Carthage had been anticipating Scipio's arrival for almost a year and was continuing to do whatever she could to stop him or slow him down, part of which had been sending Hannibal's youngest brother, Mago, to northern Italy.

Unlike Hasdrubal's march through the Alps two years earlier, Mago left Spain by sea. He took thirty warships, carrying twelve thousand foot and two thousand horse, to the Balearic Islands and then to Corsica to recruit more soldiers. Shortly after Laelius arrived in Africa for reconnaissance, Carthage sent Mago additional ships and troops with orders to immediately sail for Italy. He landed north of Rome in Liguria with approximately twenty thousand men. Within a week, Mago had taken the city of Genoa. Suddenly he was a looming threat in Italy. The Roman Senate responded by sending four legions to Liguria, with orders to keep Mago in the north and to prevent him from joining forces with his brother. Only a year earlier the war in Italy had seemed to be winding down. Now it was heating up again, not only in the north but also in the south.

About the time of Laelius' return from Africa, Scipio received word that a Roman cohort had gained access to one of the two citadels in Locri, a Carthaginian stronghold since early in the war. After Marcellus' siege of Syracuse, Locri had become Hannibal's closest port to Carthage and one of his most important sanctuaries in southern Italy.

When Scipio learned that Hannibal was headed to Locri to prevent a Roman takeover, he decided to put the invasion of Africa on hold to take the two-day voyage to Locri. He put Laelius in charge of Syracuse and set sail the following day with a small fleet and the Fifth legion.

Up until this point, I had worked nonstop on the map of Africa and had no time for Moira. With Scipio gone and some of the pressure off completion of the map, I decided one morning that I simply had to see her. I went to her farm but was disappointed to find no one there. As far as I knew, she only left the farm to go into the market, so that's where I went. I stopped at the camp on the way and ran into Troglius. I told him I was looking for a woman I was very fond of and asked him if he wanted to accompany me into the city. He had some free time and agreed to join me.

We went straight to the market. Uncertain where she might be, I started at one side of the market and worked my way to the other. Halfway through, I spotted Moira at the far end of an aisle, standing in front of a cart of fruit with her two children. I immediately thought of my conversation with Masinissa when I had admitted that I was in love with two women. I knew I would be comparing Moira to Sempronia every time I saw her from now on.

Troglius followed me down the aisle and stood back when I approached Moira. "How can I help you?" she said as though I was just another customer. Her children stood on either side of her, both with dirty faces and soiled tunics.

"I've been back for two weeks, Moira. I just haven't had any free time to come see you."

"I thought it might be another five years."

"Thankfully not," I replied, feeling her resistance. "I see you have more than figs. I'd like two of your melons and about fifty of the figs."

Moira needed sales more than anything else and this elicited a smile. She directed her son to pick out two melons while she counted out fifty figs and dropped them into the sackcloth bag I had brought with me.

"You've never introduced me to your children," I said when her son, not more than four years old, laid two melons at my feet. "What's this young man's name?"

"That's Donato," she said as she accepted my payment for the fruit. She reached over and used the hem of her chiton to wipe his nose. "And this little one," the girl, perhaps two, reached up to grip her mother's dress, "is Rosa."

"It's nice to meet you both. I'm Timon." Rosa slipped behind Moira when I looked at her. Donato was starring at Troglius several feet behind me. "Donato, meet my friend Troglius," I said turning to

Troglius, who was only slightly less shy than Rosa. "He's a man revered for his strength and courage."

Troglius glanced around like he didn't know who I was talking about.

"He has a funny head," said the boy, not sure what to think of the huge misshapen man.

Moira put her hand over Donato's mouth and looked up to the sky. "Excuse my son, sir," she said to Troglius, "he has no manners."

Troglius aimed one eye at Moira and the other at Donato. "Funny is a nicer word than many have used." He turned his split gaze to me with an expression so sad I could feel his confusion and pain.

I put a hand on his shoulder. "This is as fine a man as I know," I said to Moira and the children, more for Troglius than for them. "He has saved me more times than I can count."

"And in my opinion," said Moira, still trying to make up for Donato's comment, "strength of character is what makes a man."

Two Roman officers, both centurions, heard her as they walked by. One stopped and sized up Troglius. "Even one as ugly as this?" he said with a cruel grin. Then he appraised Moira and her two street urchin children. "Selling anything besides fruit, sweetie?" He laughed and poked the other centurion in the ribs.

Moira spit in the man's face. The soldier grabbed her by the arm and pulled her up close to him. "You little..."

Before he could get another word out, Troglius yanked the man around by the shoulder and punched him in the jaw. The centurion fell to the ground and lay there motionless. Moira and I backed away stunned. The other centurion drew his gladius and stepped forward. "You're under arrest, soldier, for striking an officer. You had better hope he's not dead."

Troglius looked around in absolute confusion, then took off running into the crowd.

The centurion let him go. "He won't get away with this. I'll see to it that monster is court-martialed. What's his name?"

Moira looked to me.

Donato answered. "Troglius."

The centurion knelt beside his friend, whose eyes fluttered then opened. The centurion and I helped the man to his feet. I was enlisted to assist the officer back to camp. I had no chance to say anything more to Moira. She called to me as we moved away through the crowd. "Let me know what happens."

CHAPTER 49

Word went out immediately from camp that Troglius had been arrested and then escaped. Search parties were sent into the city. Days passed with no sign of Troglius. I had no idea what to do and felt responsible for him He should never have struck the man, but if he hadn't, I would have. It could just as easily have been me who was arrested.

Six days after the incident, I went into Syracuse despite needing to work on the map. I remembered showing Troglius the tunnels beneath Syracuse and wondered if he might be hiding underground. I wandered through the market first, on the off chance that I might see Moira, but she wasn't there.

I walked from the market to the tunnel entrance at the north end of Via Intermuralis. I removed the stone that covered the opening and peered down into the darkness. There was a ladder. I climbed down some twenty feet to the tunnel floor. All was black except for the diffuse light coming in through gratings in the street. I had explored these tunnels somewhat with Moira, but they were an incredibly extensive network, stretching out beneath the entire northwestern portion of the city. The only way to find a person hiding in these tunnels would be a systematic search carried out by several teams of men with torches. I doubted that would ever happen. I didn't even know if the Romans were aware these tunnels existed. In frustration I called Troglius' name as loud as I could. No one answered. I walked in farther and called out again, only to get the same empty response.

I felt certain that Troglius believed he had killed the centurion. If that had been the case, his punishment would be execution. But the centurion had not died. The punishment would be something less. Somehow I needed to get the message to Troglius that the centurion had survived.

I stayed beneath the city streets as long as I could. I didn't dare venture very far without a torch. I shouted Troglius' name many more times before finally giving up. As far as I knew, he might have left the city entirely to disappear into the Sicilian countryside, but with Troglius it was impossible to guess what he would do. Saddened by the events of the last week, I wandered back to camp to resume work on my map.

CHAPTER 50

During this time the events in Locri came to a head. The Carthaginian garrison was concentrated on one side of the city, and the invading Roman cohort was on the other. For over a week the two contingents had exchanged attacks on each other's strongholds, with the Locri residents trapped between the two groups of warring soldiers. When Hannibal arrived with reinforcements, some two thousand men, he used an agent to get a message into the city, telling the Carthaginian garrison to make a diversionary attack on the Roman stronghold at daybreak the next morning, while at the same time sending a squadron of men to open the gates for Hannibal. However, the Carthaginians' sortie was met by strong resistance, and they were forced back into their camp almost immediately, leaving the Romans to man the gates and prevent Hannibal's entry. His troops fought outside the walls all morning, but could not get in.

Scipio arrived late that afternoon by ship on the opposite side of the city without Hannibal's knowledge. Determined to secure Locri, Hannibal decided to attack again the next morning, this time with scaling ladders and siege equipment. When his men reached the walls, the city gates swung open and five thousand Roman soldiers burst forth.

Hundreds of the Carthaginians were killed almost immediately. When Hannibal learned that Scipio was there, he called for a retreat before incurring any greater losses, then sealed himself in his camp. The following morning he sent a message to the Carthaginian garrison that he was leaving and that they were on their own. That afternoon the Carthaginian garrison set fire to their camp, and in the ensuing confusion, made a break from the city. Many were killed in the effort, but those who survived eventually caught up with Hannibal's retreating army.

Although the confrontation between Hannibal and Scipio had never really materialized, Scipio's quick action had turned the tide, and yet another important city had come under Roman control. Scipio stayed in Locri a few more days to put the city in order. He began by reprimanding the Locrians for having gone over to Carthage. Then, following a public trial, he executed those who had helped the Carthaginians. Prior to his departure, Scipio doubled the size of the Roman garrison and put a tribune by the name of Pleminius in charge of the city. Scipio sailed into Syracuse's Great Harbor two days after my failed attempt to find Troglius in the tunnels.

Scipio called me to headquarters the morning after his return. He wanted to see what progress I had made on the map. I wasn't quite finished, but I showed him the map anyway. Laelius was there with Scipio. Laelius wore his red tunic with a wide leather belt and his gladius at his hip. Scipio, as had become his custom, had draped himself in a white linen toga. I had hardly spoken to him since my return from Africa. He addressed me as soon as I entered the tent.

"Timon, so good to see you."

"The pleasure is mine, sir." The unfinished map was on the map table, rolled up like a scroll. I acknowledged Laelius with a tip of my head.

"Laelius told me about the sighting device you showed him on the voyage to Africa. He said it defied description, and that only by seeing it could I possibly understand what it was or its significance. What is this device?"

After showing the spyglass to Laelius, I had known it was only a matter of time before I would have to show it to Scipio. I had wanted to finish the map first, but I was not overly surprised that Laelius had already revealed what was supposed to be a secret.

"As Laelius said, it's a sighting device, sir. It enhances vision. I call it a spyglass." I put my hand on the device hanging from my belt. "I would be honored to demonstrate it for you, but that would be best done outside. Let me show you what it's allowed me to accomplish before we do that."

"Certainly, if that's what you prefer."

I walked over to the large table at one end of the tent and unrolled the scroll. Scipio and Laelius stood beside me as I described the general layout of the map. "I have done my best to make this as accurate as I can. It's drawn to scale so that any measurements you take from this map can be translated into Roman miles. I have included some topological enhancement, showing the hills and rivers, but I'm still working on that."

"And this coastline is accurate also?" asked Scipio as he studied the map.

"Yes, thanks to Laelius," I tapped the spyglass at my hip, " and this sighting device."

Scipio nodded without looking up from the map. Laelius joined him in examining my work. They muttered back and forth between themselves, clearly impressed with the map and how they could make use of it.

After a short time, Scipio looked up. "Excellent, Timon. This is far beyond what I imagined. Laelius has said that Masinissa took you inland to make some of the measurements. What did you think of the man? Can I count on him?"

"Masinissa was a tremendous help to me. I think very highly of him." I remembered what he had said about recovering his kingdom and securing the woman he loved. "We spent two days together. He believes by working with you he can regain his kingdom. Nothing is more important to him. I believe you can trust him."

Scipio nodded, seeming pleased by my appraisal. He turned to Laelius. "And he told you that Syphax is completely untrustworthy?"

Laelius nodded. "This is one of the problems with going to Africa or any foreign region, sir. We don't know the interrelations of these men and their tribes. I have met both Syphax and Masinissa. Syphax commands far more territory and troops. Masinissa, it seems, has lost much of his kingdom. I judge him more trustworthy than Syphax, but not as valuable."

"But his skills on a horse would be difficult to match. He would make a fine leader of a cavalry unit."

"Especially if he can recruit another thousand Numidians to ride with him."

"Which he led you to believe he could do?"

"Yes."

Scipio thought about this a moment, then returned to looking at the map. He was likely planning the invasion as we watched.

After a while he straightened up and turned to me. "This map is invaluable, Timon. Thank you." He nodded to emphasize his sincerity.

"Now what about this device, the spyglass, that Laelius has been raving about. Let's have a look."

"As I said, sir, we should go outside. I would suggest out behind the camp on the hill to the west."

The three of us left camp from the rear gate. I led them up to the stone plinth that had once held the Temple of Jupiter. It was the perfect place to demonstrate the compound lenses. To the east was Syracuse's Grand Harbor stretching out before us to the sea. To the north was the fortress of Syracuse, and to the south was lush, green Sicilian farmland as far as you could see. I showed Scipio how the tubes fit one inside the other, then pointed out the lenses at each end. "The lenses came from Archimedes, sir. He gave them to me the day he died."

I held the spyglass to my right eye and aimed it at the tower where I had lived with Archimedes. I demonstrated how twisting the tubes, lengthening or shortening the device, brought clarity to what one saw. I warned Scipio that the image would be upside down, then handed him the spyglass as Laelius stood by. His experience was much like everyone else's. It took him a while to bring an image into focus, and then when he did, he didn't know what to make of it. He lowered the spyglass from his eye and looked quizzically at the wide end.

Scipio glanced at me then lifted the spyglass to his eye again. He progressed rapidly from there, targeting several different locations in the distance. He caught on faster than anyone else who had used the device and immediately understood the value of the spyglass' application to warfare. Clearly impressed, he handed the tubes to Laelius, who took the opportunity to view the landscape for the sheer fascination of it.

Scipio came up close to me while Laelius stood some distance away peering through the tubes.

"I have never seen anything more remarkable, Timon. I would say that it's magic if I hadn't studied enough Greek science to know that it's not. Do you ever look into the heavens with this device?"

"It's even more impressive at night, sir. Archimedes considered the lenses so powerful he asked me not to show them to anyone."

"And yet you have?"

"I didn't for a long time, then I began to understand it could help Rome in its war with Hannibal. Maybe even bring an end to the war more quickly and save thousands of lives."

Scipio nodded slowly, his eyes distant, as though measuring my words. "Yes, I see many possibilities for your spyglass."

Laelius returned to our company and handed the spyglass back to Scipio, who lifted it to his eye and stared straight out to sea. When he lowered it, he faced me. "Don't show this to anyone else." He looked at Laelius. "Who have you told?"

"Only you."

Scipio looked at me. "I think it would be wise if I keep this, so that it's safe."

My stomach tightened. "I may have broken my promise to Archimedes by showing the spyglass to you and Laelius, sir, but I'm still its entrusted keeper. I can promise to keep it secret, but it must remain with me."

I saw a little flare of anger in Scipio's eyes. He clearly understood the spyglass' significance, and he wanted it for his own. But his eyes immediately softened, and he gave it back to me. "Then I suppose I should be grateful that you showed it to me at all."

"Yes, sir. Thank you."

CHAPTER 51

What Scipio saw in my map, and even more in the spyglass, changed how he saw me. When he first interviewed me, he was pleased with the extent of my knowledge and recognized immediately that I would be a valued asset. But after that day at the deconstructed site of the Temple of Jupiter, Scipio brought me into his inner circle, that included Laelius and his younger brother Lucius, who had not yet arrived in Syracuse. Scipio called me to headquarters periodically for advice. He asked me more questions about my time with Archimedes and my three campaigns with Marcellus. I think he now saw me as an intellectual equal—something rare for him—and someone he enjoyed talking to about philosophy and literature. He had been highly educated, more than any other Roman general I would ever meet. At times he would reveal his deep belief in patrician superiority, which he tended to cloak with his manners and charm. This more difficult side of Scipio was something I only began to see after I had gained his confidence, when he spoke more freely in my presence and allowed his arrogance and ambition to show. He thought very highly of himself and, like Marcellus, his destiny. But he affected a certain numinous quality in his person that Marcellus would have found far too self-serving. Scipio liked to say that he was in communication with the gods through his dreams, and when he spoke to his soldiers, he would often reveal these dreams, and the omens they forecast, invariably predicting the army's success and other great things ahead. He was good at this. He used it to inspire his men, but it was also a kind of confidence game that he played.

Laelius told me a story from Scipio's siege of Cartagena. He had learned through extensive reconnaissance that when a low tide coincided with strong wind from the north, the lagoon to the west of Cartagena became shallow enough to march through and provided access to the least defended side of the city. When his men were assembled at the edge of the lagoon and the wind began to blow, he told his men that Neptune had spoken to him in a dream and told him this would happen. It was a psychological ploy, a way to make his troops believe in him and in themselves. And in Cartagena, of course, it proved out. As Scipio or any experienced general would tell you, an army's mindset was just as critical to its success on the battlefield as its weapons.

The situation in Locri set us back several weeks, but Scipio still hoped to set sail for Africa by the beginning of October. I focused on finishing the map, while also attending to my other duties as a scribe, mostly creating inventories of the supplies needed for the campaign. I worked long hours with few chances to get away. I hadn't seen Moira since the incident with Troglius, who was still missing, and I wanted, no I needed to see her. Ever since my conversation with Masinissa, I felt that it was important for me to know exactly what I thought about Moira before I left for Africa.

One afternoon, though still overloaded with work, I changed from my red tunic into one of unbleached wool and headed off to her farm. I saw Moira from a distance. She was in the fig orchard with Donato and Rosa, picking figs and putting them into baskets. She saw me coming, but made no acknowledgment of me and continued to work. I came up alongside of her, and without saying a word, began picking figs.

After a long silence, Moira let down her guard. "Thanks for helping, Timon," she said with only the slightest glance at me. "Have you heard anything from Troglius?"

"Not a word," I said, dropping a handful of figs into a basket. "It's been two weeks. I think they've given up searching for him. There's no telling where he is."

"I feel responsible."

"You shouldn't. If anyone's to blame, it's me. I put Troglius in a bad situation, and he simply reacted. No one should fault him for what he did. The centurion was out of line."

As Moira moved from one part of the tree to another, Rosa, still wary of me, clung to her mother's dress. Donato was the opposite. He picked up the figs that fell to the ground while keeping a close eye on me.

"I went down in the tunnels looking for him," I said. "I had showed them to him a few weeks before the incident."

"I remember showing them to you." She looked directly at me for the first time.

"How about the time you brought the ball of yarn?"

"The night of the Festival of Artemis."

"When Corax and his gang chased us. What a night!"

Moira and I had made love that night. When I looked at her, I'm sure she was thinking the same thing. She allowed the impish grin that had captured me many years earlier, then turned away to focus on her work. She reached up as high as she could for one last fig on the branch she was working, causing her dress to lie close against her, accenting her body's curves, and rekindling the feelings she had inspired in me when I had first met her.

Donato broke the spell. "What will happen to Troglius if they catch him?"

Moira stopped picking to listen to my response.

"They will be very hard on him." I thought about the deserters I had encountered on my trip from Rome to Croton. "He will be tried for his actions."

"Will they kill him?"

I looked to Moira. She answered. "It's possible, Donato. That's why I'm worried about him."

"Your mother's right. It's possible. I hope he's smart enough to stay away. He's a good friend of mine, and I worry about him."

When we had filled ten baskets with figs, we carried them back to the house and laid them out on wooden racks so that they could dry in the sun. My time had been well spent. I had found out what I needed to know. I wanted to spend more time with Moira. She had remained cool to me. There was no doubt about that, but at times, she had allowed me glimpses of her smile and a few sparkles from her eyes— and it was just enough.

As I was about to leave, she surprised me by asking if I wanted to stay for the evening meal. "You deserve something for helping. It will be simple. Nothing special. I slaughtered a chicken this morning and we have some chickpeas."

"I helped because I wanted to. You don't owe me anything, but I would like to stay."

"Then keep an eye on Rosa and Donato while I put things together."

While I wrestled playfully with the children, Moira roasted the chicken and tended to other things around the house. When we ate, the conversation, much like that in the orchard, was in bits and pieces with long spells of silence in between.

We finished eating long before the sun went down. She walked me to the edge of the property. She thanked me for my help, and I thanked her for the meal. Then I leaned into her and did what I had been thinking about throughout the afternoon. I kissed her softly on the cheek. Instead of backing away she embraced me and hugged me as though she hadn't been held in a long time. I wanted to stroke her hair and kiss her again, but I resisted the temptation and stepped away from her.

Moira bowed her head, then looked up at me. "Come again. The children seem to be more comfortable around you."

"I will," I said, pleased that she too was finally warming up to me.

CHAPTER 52

Scipio's brother Lucius was stationed in Messana. Scipio received a report from him saying there had been more trouble in Locri. Following Scipio's departure and his abbreviated encounter with Hannibal, the Roman garrison, commanded by Pleminius, had become abusive to the Locrian populace. The Carthaginian garrison had already been a plague upon the city, drinking in excess and taking liberties with the women, resulting in repeated clashes with the local men. One would have thought that the Locrians would be in better hands with the Romans. Pleminius' men, however, took the bad behavior to an even greater extreme, as though justified punishment to the Locrians for giving in to the Carthaginians in the first place.

The difficulties reached a head when one of Pleminius' men was caught stealing a silver cup from a Locrian home by two Roman officers. When the officers demanded that the soldier return the stolen cup, a fight broke out. The soldier who had stolen the cup got the worst of it and went to Pleminius, complaining of the two intervening officers. Pleminius, who had been as vile in his actions as any of the soldiers, was furious and had the two officers brought to him. He screamed at them for starting the disturbance, then had them stripped and publicly flogged. If things weren't bad enough, some of the soldiers banded together against what they thought was unjust punishment of the officers. They sought out Pleminius and beat him to the edge of death. That's when word got out, and Lucius called for Scipio to intervene.

What resulted was another two week delay of the campaign to Africa. Scipio went to Locri and held a second trial. Despite the complaints registered by the locals against Pleminius' command, Scipio acquitted Pleminius and ordered the two officers who had stopped the soldier to be sent to Rome for punishment by the Senate.

After Scipio left Locri, Pleminius decided that Scipio had been too lenient on the two men. Instead of sending them to Rome, he had them brought to him in chains. He then personally tortured them until they were dead. Their mutilated bodies were taken from the city and left unburied in the wild.

While Scipio was in Locri, I visited Moira again. I found her weeding her garden. She looked up and actually greeted me with a smile. I got down on my knees and joined her and Donato pulling unwanted green things from between the vegetables, while Rosa played in the dirt beside us.

After weeding, Moira asked me to help her with one of the outbuildings that needed repair. We worked together the rest of the afternoon rebuilding a small lean-to building. We spoke little, mostly about the work we were doing. She was much more cordial to me than during the previous visit, though still somewhat guarded. She asked again about Troglius. Unfortunately my answer was the same. He was still missing.

Moira invited me to stay for the evening meal. This time I dawdled afterward, not really wanting to leave. Moira went about her chores and put the children to bed. She made some tea and we sat outside in the grass, watching the sun slip behind the hills to the west.

Both of us knew that the day had been leading to this moment. I leaned over her and kissed her on the lips. She embraced me and we lay on our sides so that we faced each other in the grass. When I pulled her dress up around her waist and put my hands on her bare bottom, she stopped me by touching me on the nose and looking through the darkness into my eyes.

"Timon, I want you tonight. Very much. But during the time you were in Rome, I was injured on the inside." She ran her finger down my nose to my lips as a signal not to say anything until she was finished.

"I'm not quite the same down there," she said with obvious meaning. "You may have me, but I'm a little tender and you'll have to be gentle." She became even more serious. I could see the stars glistening in the moisture gathering in her eyes. "And I can no longer have children."

I started to speak, but again she pressed her finger to my lips.

"I know that you're leaving for Africa at some point. And that I may never see you again. That's all right. I know that tonight is only tonight."

I started to sputter but she went on.

"You needed to know that I am not fit to be wife." She shrugged her shoulders, her tears running sideways across her face. "If you had any thought of something like that."

I was pressed against her now, my tunic above my navel and our warm bellies touching. "Thank you, Moira. I appreciate your honesty. We both know that we can't read the future or see beyond this moment tonight. Let's enjoy it as though the rest of the world has melted away, and only you and I and this night matter."

Moira leaned into me and kissed me as though there were no tomorrow.

CHAPTER 53

The next two weeks passed quickly as Scipio accelerated preparation for the voyage to Africa. I managed my time so that I could go out to Moira's farm one day a week to help with the work. There were no promises of love and no discussion of what might happen after the campaign in Africa, but Moira never failed to ask about Troglius. Six weeks had passed since the incident, and I still knew nothing. On one of my two trips to the farm she asked me to stay the night. Without daring to mention it, we were growing closer and it was good.

Sempronia, who I had told my mother was the perfect woman for me, now seemed a distant memory. The things that seemed so important in Rome—her wealth, her mother's desire for her to marry a patrician—seemed so foreign in Sicily, especially when compared to Moira's life on the farm, where there were no pretensions, just hard work while the sun was up and sleep at the end of the day. I had no doubt who my mother would prefer if I asked her for advice, but at this point what did it matter? I was going to Africa for an undetermined length of time. My life was on hold until I returned—if I returned. I was in no position to commit one way or another to anyone about anything.

I was in headquarters when Scipio told his staff that the delays in Locri had put the voyage to Africa in jeopardy. He was hesitant to take a large army to sea after the beginning of October. "We must be ready to leave in ten days," he said, "or I will be forced to put the invasion off until the spring."

Two days later, Scipio received a letter from the Senate with more bad news about the state of affairs in Locri. The week after Pleminius had tortured and killed the two Roman officers, a contingent of Locrians slipped out of the city and traveled to Rome. They went directly to the Senate to report what had happened. With tears in their eyes, they detailed the actions of Pleminius and his minions. Not only were their homes looted and trashed, but hardly a woman or a child had not been abused in some way, some repeatedly. They concluded their report by saying that on top of these crimes against the people Pleminius had looted the Temple of Proserpine of its silver and gold. The Locrians emphasized the brazenness of this act of thievery by recounting the long tradition of the sacred temple and its vast treasure, referencing the story of Pyrrhus' plundering the temple seventy years earlier. The Greek general had loaded the silver and gold into his ships and set sail for Sicily. The first day at sea the fleet was overtaken by a vicious storm. Every ship containing any portion of the Proserpine treasure was capsized and washed up on the shore. Pyrrhus, fearing the storm had been caused by the goddess' wrath, returned all the treasure he could recover to the temple. In conclusion, the Locrians claimed that Pleminius' actions were the result of madness induced by Proserpine's supernatural power, and that all of Rome would be similarly cursed if the treasure weren't returned.

This caused a tremendous reaction in the Senate. When given a chance to question the Locrians, Fabius asked them if Scipio had any knowledge of Pleminius' actions and if he, as well as Pleminius, should be held accountable.

They answered yes. Scipio's timely arrival in Locri had allowed them to cast the Carthaginians out, but he was also responsible for putting Pleminius in command, adding that he had even returned to Locri later that summer to address tensions in the city. Instead of recognizing Pleminius' poor character, Scipio had punished the wrong people and allowed Pleminius to remain in command and continue his criminal activities.

In the discussion that followed both Pleminius and Scipio were the targets of severe abuse from several of the senators. Fabius led the attack, saying that Pleminius' actions were symptoms of a lack of discipline in Scipio's command. The consul was unRoman. His attire and his actions were not even soldierly. He wore a toga in camp, wasted his time with reading, and enjoyed levels of luxury unbecoming of a commanding officer. Hadn't Scipio already spent five months in Sicily? When did he intend to make his "glorious" voyage to Africa? The consul, stated Fabius, was not fit for command and should be recalled immediately.

Another senator, Quintus Metellus, agreed with much of what Fabius said, recommending that Pleminius should be brought to Rome for trial and that all the soldiers stationed in Locri should be removed to another garrison. Metellus, however, felt Fabius' call to strip Scipio of his command was going too far.

In the ensuing debate, the Senate agreed that Pleminius should be brought back to Rome, his garrison relocated, and the temple's treasure restored *and* doubled. But there was no majority to strip Scipio of his consulship. Instead, it was decided that the praetor in Sicily, Marcus Pomponius, who happened to be Scipio's cousin, should go to Syracuse as soon as possible with ten members of the Senate and two tribunes of the plebs to hold an inquiry. Scipio's methods of preparation, his discipline, his lifestyle, and the character of his troops would be reviewed. If the inquiry found Scipio lacking in any way, Pomponius would have the authority to remove him from his command. According to the letter sent to Scipio, the praetor and his team would be arriving in Syracuse in two weeks.

I was in headquarters reviewing changes in the map with Scipio, his brother Lucius, and Laelius when the letter arrived. Scipio read it and immediately exploded. "So this must be the work of my dear friend Fabius," he snarled through gritted teeth. "Just enough delay to put the campaign to Africa off until the spring." He had hoped to leave within a week. The inquiry meant no less than a three week delay. The risk of taking troops and the necessary provisions across the sea would increase every day afterward throughout the winter.

Lucius had arrived in camp a few days earlier with more volunteers and five warships. He and Laelius stood back as Scipio stomped back and forth across the tent. I had never seen him so angry or indignant.

"I will have my revenge on that old man," he stated like an oath. "Just wait until I return from Africa with Hannibal's head. He will eat his words. An inquiry on the eve of my leaving! Have I not already proven who I am? Jackals, that's what they are. Come to snap at my heels while I do the deeds of gods."

Scipio suddenly spun around and faced the three of us standing side by side at the map table. "Pleminius! Why did I trust such a man? For that one oversight, my entire ability to command has now been called into question." He stood across from us and slammed his fist on the table. He glared at his brother and Laelius. "How can they do this?"

"Brother, you have always known that the man who dares to achieve the greatest glory, the man who takes on the most responsibility, also takes on the harshest criticism." Lucius was two years younger than Scipio. He had the same fair hair and good looks, but not the sense of destiny that motivated his brother. "Let's turn this inquiry into an opportunity to showcase your talents. Let's prepare such a clear demonstration of military discipline for Pomponius and his jury that they will know their coming here was a farce instigated by a fool. We'll let them know that we were ready to go and that the delay they've forced upon us only works to the advantage of our enemy."

While Scipio appeared to weigh his brother's words, Laelius added to them. "Another six months, Publius. Either we fume at the setback and waste our energy by arguing with the Senate, or we realize that it's six more months to prepare—and more importantly to raise troops. Our numbers, right now, are twenty-one thousand foot and one thousand horse, not including what we might get from Masinissa. When you and I spoke of this a year ago, we imagined taking thirty thousand combined forces to Africa. Maybe this is fortunate. Maybe we can muster another five thousand men in the next six months."

Scipio knew both men were right, but he was not in the mood to be soothed by rationale. He was angry and he shouted them down, but the next day and during the following two weeks, he acted on their words. He would put on a show like no review team had ever seen before, and set his sights on leaving in the spring with a larger invasion force.

CHAPTER 54

I had a free afternoon the following day and decided to go to Moira's farm to tell her that I would be around for another six months. As I left the camp, the guard at the gate told me an old woman had come by asking to see me. He said she was a skinny Greek with a short temper and an ugly disposition. He told her to go away. The guard didn't get her name, but there was only one person it could have been, and she would never have come to the camp if it weren't important. Rather than going to see Moira, I decided to head into Syracuse and find Agathe.

I went straight to the tenement apartments where she lived. I didn't see her right away, but I remembered which building Eurydice had come out of when I was there last. The door led to a narrow hall and an even narrower stairway. Four rooms were on the ground level. I knocked on the first door and got no answer. Before I knocked on the second door, Agathe came into the building.

"Agathe, did you come to the camp today looking for me?"

She nodded, and without a word, led me up the stairs to the second floor where there were four more rooms. She opened the first door on the left and I followed her in. Troglius sat on the floor with Agathe's husband Galatus, a man who had lost his right arm and his left hand in battle. Troglius' crooked face twisted into a wide smile. "I want back in the army," he exclaimed, struggling to his feet. I saw an amphora and two cups on the floor between the men.

The huge man embraced me as he never had before.

"Where have you been?" I asked when he released me.

"I was down in those tunnels."

"I looked for you there."

"I got so badly mixed up in the dark I had to get out. I came here because there was nowhere else to go. I want you to take me back to the camp and tell them I made a mistake."

211

I couldn't help but smile. "The centurion didn't die."

His eyes went wide. "Maybe I will only be flogged!"

"That could be," I replied, then I began to think. "One thing we do know, Troglius, is that Scipio would preside over the trial, and at times he listens to me. I might be able to bend his ear." I turned to Agathe. "Can Troglius stay here a little longer? The timing for Troglius' return would be better if we waited a couple of weeks." I was thinking of the upcoming inquiry.

Agathe balled up her face in her usual ugly expression. "He's been here this long, why not a bit longer. He eats more than the rest of us put together."

"Maybe I can help." I took a few coins from my tunic and gave them to Agathe, who quickly pocketed the money. I looked at Troglius. "Why did you come here?"

Eurydice appeared in the doorway. "He—he came here ask—asking for me."

I glanced at Troglius, who was suddenly staring at his feet.

"But I've been taking care of him," said Galatus, still sitting on the floor.

Agathe looked up at the ceiling. "He gives Galatus someone to talk to."

"And drink with," slobbered Troglius, who I had never known to drink at all.

"And he's not bothering anyone?" I asked, remembering how Hektor had thrown himself at Eurydice when I worked in his kitchen.

"No—no," said Eurydice. "He told us wh-wh-what happened. He's a ka—ka—kind man, and we kn—knew he was your friend. He's been a pleasure."

"Then give me two more weeks, and I'll be back to get him."

Both women nodded. Troglius was staring at Eurydice.

"Troglius?"

He looked at me.

"Two more weeks?"

He nodded several times rapidly.

And so it was. I had found Troglius. I would represent him in his trial and begin preparing for it immediately. I would both present his defense and soften up Scipio—if I could. I excitedly headed back across the city to see if Moira might be in town.

When I reached the edge of the market, I headed to the location where she usually had her cart. I saw her from a distance, but she didn't see me coming. As I got closer I was struck by the beauty of this barefoot brunette in a simple cotton chiton, who worked a fig orchard in the idyllic Sicilian farmland. I had seen more beautiful women in my life—Sempronia was one of them, as was Portia—but none of them exuded the sensuality of the earth the way Moira did. Although I didn't want to say it outright to her, I could not imagine loving a woman more.

Moira looked up from a transaction she was completing and saw me standing a few feet away. She smiled, then finished attending to her customer.

When the customer walked away, I whispered the words, "I found Troglius."

Her eyes lit up. "Is he all right?"

I motioned with my hand to keep her voice down. "He's fine. I spoke to him earlier today. He wants to turn himself in."

Donato heard us whispering and came up close to listen. He held his sister's hand.

"What will happen then?" asked Moira.

"He will be put on trial. With a little luck, he could get off with twenty lashes." I shook my head. "He's a soldier through and through. It's something he's prepared for."

Moira looked at her son, then to me. "Couldn't it be worse than that?"

"Anything is possible after evading arrest for two months." I looked around at the people milling through the market. "I have decided to represent him in the trial—with one goal—to keep him alive. Flogging is all but a certainty."

"Truly, you'll act as his lawyer?"

"He's smarter than most people give him credit for, but he can't speak for himself. He needs help."

"Might they kill him?" asked Donato, who had become enamored with the man, though having seen him only once.

"I hope not, but I think your mother could help," I looked at Moira, " if she's willing to come to the trial."

Moira didn't hesitate. "The man stood up for me. If you're sure I could help, I would be happy to do whatever is necessary."

"I'm not sure of anything right now, but there are only two arguments to make. He stood up for a woman in distress, and he's irreplaceable on the battlefield."

Moira handed me a fig. "When would the trial be?"

"Two or three weeks from now."

"I thought you were leaving."

"That's my other news." I popped the fig in my mouth. "We're not going to Africa until the spring."

"What could be better!" exclaimed Moira with a big grin. "The winter is slow on the farm, but the repairs I've let go are many—and the fig trees need to be pruned. That's all much easier with help."

"I thought you'd be pleased."

A woman came up to Moira's cart and began to assess the fruit. Moira glanced at the woman, then looked at me. "Maybe the Roman army will never even go to Africa."

"Don't count on that. I doubt anything will stop Scipio from going to Africa. But I do welcome the delay—though in some ways I want to get on with it. I want the war to be over. None of us are free of its impact until then."

"Come out to the farm before the trial. I need to know what to say."

"Of course."

The woman had filled a basket with produce. Moira nodded to me, then turned away to assist her customer.

Donato tugged at my tunic. "Don't let them kill, Troglius, Timon."

I patted the boy on the head. "I'll do what I can, Donato. I'll do what I can—and don't repeat a word of any of this to anyone!"

CHAPTER 55

Pomponius, Sicily's praetor, was stationed in Lilybaeum. He met his legal team in Locri on the first leg of their trip from Rome. They spent three days there to ask questions and allow the citizens another opportunity to voice their complaints. When the inquiry was completed, they sent Pleminius and thirty-two others to Rome in chains for imprisonment.

The entire review team, Pomponius, ten senators, and the two tribunes of the plebs, arrived in Syracuse after the two-day voyage from Locri. They were lodged in a large villa in Neapolis. I learned from Laelius that one of the tribunes was Marcus Claudius. His second day in Syracuse he came to our camp and found me.

I lived in a tent with seven other soldiers, just as I would during a campaign. I was sitting at the campfire after the evening meal when he walked up.

I immediately stood and embraced him. I suggested we take a walk. We went out the camp's back gate and into the low hills to the west. It was still daylight, and the sun was behind us. The view to the east was stunning in its clarity. Thick banks of clouds sat off in the distance over the sea.

"I can't tell you how happy I am to see you, Marcus. I didn't know until yesterday that you were part of Pomponius' legal team." I thumped him playfully on the shoulder. "You look well."

"And so do you. I hear the invasion has been put off because of the inquiry. Is that true? Was Scipio really ready to go?"

"We'd already be there if not for the trouble in Locri. I'm not aware of all the reasons for the review, but attention to detail cannot be one of them. Scipio is remarkably organized and knows exactly what he wants to do. Would you really take away his command?"

"We'll see. The Locrians used only the worst words to describe Pleminius, but their criticism of Scipio was relatively mild. They felt he lacked sympathy for their predicament and that he trusted Pleminius too much. They said Scipio was a good man who had badly misjudged his subordinate. Considering how bad it had been in Locri, they were as positive as anyone could expect. It was important that they didn't target him with any specific abuses."

"What do you think of Scipio?"

"I'm a little jealous, but he's proven himself over and over again on the battlefield. I'm not certain if going to Africa is necessary, but if anyone should go, I'd say Scipio is the man—especially if he can show us something in the review tomorrow. Fabius has called him lax and undisciplined. That could lose an officer his command. But you like him."

"He's arrogant, Marcus. You already know that. But he's also extremely smart, and as tough a drillmaster as your father was. You'll see it tomorrow. But no more talk of the military, how is my mother? Tell me that she's well. No news is as important as that."

Marcus smiled. "Your mother and Lucretia have settled in like family. Meda and your mother seem to have become friends. They make a curious pair."

I laughed. "How's her health though? Has her color come back?"

"I didn't know her before the poisoning, but I would say she's still quite pale. Anyone can tell she's recovering from something serious."

"Who knows that she's there?"

Marcus tipped his head. "I've said nothing. I don't believe she's gone into Rome more than a few times since you left, but my mother may have said something. I overheard her talking one day—to the woman who always wears black. I don't know her name."

"Paculla Annia"

"That's the one."

I shook my head. "That's not good news."

"There's been nothing else, Timon. No one has come out to the farm, and there's no reason they would. I wouldn't worry."

Despite his words, I could imagine little worse than Paculla knowing the whereabouts of my mother, especially if Portia had told her that I had called her a fake. Lost in thought, I stared out at the ocean. The sun had slipped behind the hills, tinting the undersides of the clouds a pale orange.

Marcus put his hand on my shoulder. "Your mother will be fine. She's got to be the least of Hannibal's worries. Last I heard both armies in the south have been struck by the plague. Neither Hannibal's army nor Livinius' legions are in any shape to fight. The war in the south has stopped completely."

"What about Mago? I heard he's gathering troops in Etruria?"

"He's contained for now. I don't think he's as dangerous as Hasdrubal. Time will tell—but I must get back to the city before it gets any darker. Will I see you tomorrow?"

"I won't be at the inquiry, but I'll be at the military review. Scipio has asked me to grade the exercises."

"Then I'll see you there. It should be an interesting day."

CHAPTER 56

The inquiry took place in the morning at the villa in Syracuse where Pomponius and his twelve-man team were staying. They questioned Scipio about the events in Locri. I wasn't there, but judging from Scipio's mood when I saw him afterward, it must have gone well.

Following the inquiry, the legal team was taken to the battlements on the south wall of the city that overlooked the Great Harbor. Scipio offered the men chairs to sit in and then directed their attention to the open field between the harbor and our camp. Scipio wore full armor— a dazzlingly bronze cuirass and red plumed helmet, a matching bronze greave on his left shin, and his gladius on his hip. Pomponius, an overweight man with a deep ugly cough, and his team were in togas. It was a breezy afternoon. A few had red mantles draped over their shoulders. Twenty trumpeters, ten on each side of the attendees, stood ready with their trumpets. I was there with my wax pad and bronze stylus.

Scipio, who was his most charming self all day, asked the men if they were ready. When all said they were, he raised his gladius over his head. The trumpeters lifted their instruments. Scipio stroked down and the twenty trumpets sounded. The front gate to our camp opened and four legions of soldiers—two allied, two Roman—just under twenty thousand men, marched out in perfect order and assumed regimental position in the field.

Scipio again raised his gladius to signal another round of trumpet blasts. One thousand cavalry, riding four abreast, came from behind the camp and rode down the slight incline to take their position with the other soldiers.

Using the trumpets as signals, Scipio ran the four legions through a series of maneuvers. Following Scipio's direction, the four legions then split into two groups, each with a Roman legion and an allied legion. They faced off in two lines as though opposing armies with five hundred cavalry on a side. With another round of trumpet blasts, the two armies' velites raced across the field and tossed their javelins at the opposition to simulate the opening of a battle. The tribunes then signaled for their men, who were carrying wooden swords, to advance into a mock battle that demonstrated a variety of troop movements—the advance of hastati, the support of the principes, the reinforcement of the triarii, and a series of sorties on the flanks by the cavalries. All was carried out with enough actual sword play to create the drama and feel of a real battle.

When the two armies retreated back into formation, the thirteen men on the battlements stood as one and applauded. Even I, who had witnessed the long hours of training, was impressed.

After the four legions and the accompanying cavalry had returned to the camp, Scipio directed his audience's attention to the Great Harbor. On Scipio's signal and the blare of trumpets, twenty warships, which had been waiting outside the harbor, rowed into the harbor two abreast, then separated to opposite sides of the harbor. Much as the soldiers had simulated combat on land, the ships enacted battle at sea. The ships drew up side by side. The marines fought across the gunwales, boarded the opposing ships, and engaged in a fairly realistic battle. At one point, one of the ships slid along the side of another, breaking off all the oars, a standard battle maneuver.

The military exercises took all afternoon. The sun had begun its descent when the last of the ships were pulled onto shore and the marines deboarded. All thirteen men on the review team raved about the discipline and precision of both demonstrations. They gathered around Scipio and praised him for his work. After a quick survey of his team's opinions, Pomponius announced that Scipio had nothing to worry about. His command was secure. The inquiry team would present only the highest praise to the Senate.

"I don't believe there was ever a finer looking army in all of Rome's history," stated Pomponius, followed by several watery coughs. "Carthage has no chance, Consul. You are sure to bring glory to Rome."

CHAPTER 57

I spoke with Marcus the day after the review. It was in the evening. His team would leave for Rome the following morning.

"Did you agree with Pomponius' assessment of Scipio?"

Marcus nodded. "I did, but perhaps not as wholeheartedly."

"Why do you say that?"

Marcus chuckled. "Like I said before, envy. No, I was impressed by what Scipio showed us yesterday, but I was not so impressed by his explanation of what happened in Locri. The others accepted it, and I didn't fight it. But he made a critical mistake—the kind of mistake a commander can't make. He trusted the wrong man. Pleminius was the worst of what is Roman. My father would have executed him on the spot. Scipio should have. It was a grievous error. Only Scipio's outstanding record prevented his downfall. Even the Locrians said they admired Scipio despite his mistake. Like many Romans, they believe he's the man who will finally bring an end to the war."

"Do you?"

"Yes. Partly because of his ability and partly because of the circumstances. Rome has been destined to win this war from the beginning. No one would have said that fifteen years ago, but that's how it's played out. And Scipio is the right man, in the right place, at the right time—perfectly positioned to deliver the final blow. Sometimes great actions are the result of many smaller actions coming together at the same time. That's what's happening for Scipio."

"How would you compare him to your father?"

Marcus shook his head. "You're asking the wrong man."

"Then you believe your father was a better general."

He nodded as though there could be no question. "Did you see that Cato is in camp?"

"The young lawyer from the forum?"

"Yes, he came from Messana with Scipio's brother. Hopefully you won't have much contact with him. If he sees you, he'll connect you with me. That could only be bad." His laugh was sardonic. "Are you enjoying your return to military life?"

"Not so much. I just hope that my maps can help Scipio end the war."

"Will you come back to Rome?"

"To get my mother, yes. Will I stay? I'm not quite sure." I wanted to tell him I would return to Syracuse. I wanted to tell him about Moira. Instead I brought up the one topic that divided us. "I would like to see Sempronia one more time. Has she been promised to anyone yet?"

Marcus looked at the ground. "I have no idea."

A silence held between us. It was a bad way to end our conversation.

"Do me one favor when you return to Rome," I said.

Marcus lifted his eyes to mine.

"Tell my mother that others know she's there. Tell her to beware of the woman Paculla Annia."

He smiled. "Timon, your mother is fine at the farm, but, yes, I will pass that name on to your mother."

We embraced and parted. I wished he had told me that Sempronia had a husband. Then I could stop comparing her to Moira.

CHAPTER 58

Four days after Marcus' departure, Troglius, following my advice, appeared at the gate to our camp. He was immediately arrested and put in chains. The court-martial was scheduled for three days later. It was something I needed to talk to Scipio about.

I was in headquarters the next day, working on the map much later than usual, well past sunset. Scipio had been in and out all day, and had just returned. Before I had a chance to address the topic of the trial, he approached me from the other side of the table.

"Timon, I've been so busy I haven't been able to talk to you about the spyglass." He eyed it hanging on my belt.

"Yes, sir, there's been a lot going on."

"I'm beginning to understand what Marcellus went through when he was so intent on defeating Hannibal. Every man with a grudge against you voices an objection. That's all this is now. Lesser men getting in the way of greater, older in the way of younger." He shook his head. "But the review is over. As soon as the seas are safe for travel, we're going to Africa." He grinned. "But that's several months off, and I've finally got a free moment for a change. Let's go outside. I want to look into the sky with your spyglass."

We went out to the stone plinth behind the camp. The night was still and the sky clear. Stars filled the heavens. The moon, a fat crescent, lounged on its backside.

I handed the spyglass to Scipio. "Aim it anywhere you want, sir, but I suggest starting with the moon."

Scipio lifted the spyglass to his eye and gazed upward. He twisted the tubes in and out, taking his time, clearly focusing on the detail of the lunar surface. "The clarity is utterly fantastic—breathtaking," he said as he stared upward through the spyglass. After a moment, he lowered it from his eye. "I know nothing more astounding than this device. I simply don't. Can you explain it to me, Timon?"

"It's geometry, sir. A specialized part of geometry called optics. It gets complicated, but I can tell you the basic concepts whenever you like."

"I would like that."

I pointed to a star in the southwest. "Focus on that exceptionally bright star, sir."

Scipio aimed the spyglass at the star.

"If you can bring it into clear enough focus, you'll see that it's not a star at all. It's the planet Venus."

Scipio had become quite adept with the spyglass and quickly focused on the planet. "By the gods," he muttered. "The planet Venus. Why is it so bright?"

"It's lit by the sun. Just like the moon."

After he took a second look at Venus, I told him to aim the spyglass at the most distant stars. "Try to appreciate the depth of the heavens, sir."

Again Scipio followed my instructions. He was not that much older than I was, seven years. His military success and his over-sized ego, however, could make those seven years seem like twenty. The spyglass tended to reverse that. He knew that my experience with Archimedes was unique, and on rare occasions, he spoke to me like a student to a teacher.

While Scipio gazed into the sky, looking in one direction and then another, I told him the man he was trying in two days was a friend of mine. "I will act as his lawyer in the court-martial."

Scipio lowered the spyglass. "You will represent this brute, Troglius?"

"Yes, sir. He's not particularly well-spoken and tends to silence, especially under pressure. I can't see him defending himself. I was there at the time of the incident. I know what happened. I can clarify what he won't be able to."

"How do you know this man?"

"We were part of the same tent unit during my three campaigns with Marcellus. He was the best combat soldier I saw during those three years. On the battlefield, he fights like ten men."

Scipio tilted his head. "You're not trying to prejudice the judge are you? That could be considered improper prior to a trial."

"I believe the facts of the case will speak for themselves, sir. I trust you in that. But as a general, I just thought you should know who was being court-martialed. You might talk to some of the other soldiers. Not all of them know him, but those who do want him fighting beside them."

Scipio seemed to consider this, then aimed the spyglass at the sky for another look. When he lowered it, he gazed at me through the darkness. "Would you leave the spyglass in my hands for safe keeping if I promise to withhold the death penalty? Not only did the man strike an officer, Timon, but he resisted arrest. It's what he deserves."

This caught me off guard. I hesitated a long time before responding. "No, sir. I believe you are a fair man, and the facts are on Troglius' side. Besides, as long as I'm your scribe, sir, you can have all the use of the spyglass you want. It just remains in my possession."

Scipio laughed. "I admire your confidence, but would your answer change if I told you that Marius Cato has volunteered to be the army's prosecutor?"

"Truly? Cato."

"He will be my quaestor and command the Twenty-third legion. I've already been told he will press for execution." He extended the spyglass to me.

I hesitated taking it. "Maybe I should reconsider your offer?"

"No, I learned my lesson with Pleminius. I will run a fair trial. Make your case. Cato will make his."

CHAPTER 59

A wide belt of unused space circuited the interior of the camp separating the soldiers' tents from the palisades. This space was called the intervallum and was used to assemble the soldiers in marching formation prior to exiting the camp. The court-martial was scheduled for noon and would take place in the east intervallum.

I spoke to Moira the day before and asked her to come early. I would meet her outside the camp so I could escort her in. I told her to come without the children, if she could arrange it, so that she wouldn't be distracted.

I visited Troglius the morning of the trial. I told him that I would ask him only one question—*Why did he strike the centurion?*—and that his answer should be entirely honest—*The centurion insulted a woman in a manner unbecoming a Roman officer.* After practicing this exchange several times, I advised him to be as brief as possible if Cato should ask him any questions. Troglius was more frightened of the trial than any punishment he might receive. At one point he asked me if he could simply plead guilty and get it over with. I told him to trust me and that it would all go well, though I was also highly anxious about representing my first client in a trial—against a man known as the best lawyer in Rome.

I was outside the camp waiting for Moira long before noon. As time passed I found myself staring down the road that led south with increasing anxiety. When the trumpets sounded, signaling the beginning of the trial, I had no choice but to go into the camp without her. I told the guards that I was expecting a young woman as one of the witnesses for the court-martial and that she was late. I asked them to please have someone escort her to the east side of the camp.

Almost all of the soldiers who weren't on duty—I'm guessing about two thousand—were squeezed into the limited space, talking and laughing, eager for the spectacle to begin. The drama could not

225

have been higher for the soldiers. Although Troglius was not well known in camp at that time, one of their own was on trial, and there was quite a bit of curiosity about what punishment he would receive. Striking an officer was a serious offense. He had also effectively deserted for nearly two months by hiding from his superiors. Most expected a death sentence, and the anticipation of an execution always drew a crowd.

I pushed my way through the intervallum to the opening in the mass of soldiers that served as our court. In the center sat Scipio's curule chair, waiting for the consul's arrival. Cato's ruddy face and searing gray eyes were hard to miss. He stood to the left of the chair with the centurion who had been struck and the centurion who had been there at the time it happened. Cato watched me cross the opening and take a position on the right. I had grown a beard since he had last seen me. I couldn't tell if he recognized me or not. I wore my red military tunic and held my wax pad at my side with some notes to myself etched in the wax.

Scipio made us wait. I kept looking around for Moira, worried she had changed her mind about coming, and hoping the guards would bring her into the camp if she hadn't. She still hadn't arrived when the crowd of soldiers parted and Scipio strode into the opening. He would be the judge and jury for the trial. He acknowledged the presence of Cato and myself, then sat down.

Our augur Dilius Strabo appeared with his cage of chickens. He sprinkled feed into the cage and the birds ate heartily, signaling that the gods had given their approval to proceed. Strabo then sacrificed a goat to Justitia, the Goddess of Justice. After opening the goat and inspecting the entrails, he announced that she had given her blessings.

Scipio called for the defendant. Two guards led Troglius through the soldiers into the opening. He was wearing his red tunic with iron shackles on his feet and hands. Troglius gave me a darting glance as he walked by me. I was so nervous I had to force a smile.

Scipio motioned for Cato and me to come forward. "Discipline among the soldiers is one of the military's greatest strengths and greatest concerns. I take this incident very seriously." Scipio looked at Cato. "The prosecution will state its case first. Then the defense will respond." His eyes met mine. "The prosecution will then call forward its witnesses for questioning, then the defense will have the same opportunity. Don't waste my time with long speeches. Make your point and move on."

I stood off to the right beside Troglius and his two guards. Cato strode to the center of the court. He paced back and forth twice before delivering his opening. Despite Scipio's request for brevity, Cato went on and on about the meaning and tradition of discipline in the Roman army before getting to the specifics.

"This case is an easy one," he said, scanning the soldiers crowded all around. Although a young man, only four years my senior, his reputation as a lawyer extended well beyond Rome, and most of the soldiers knew who he was. "A legionnaire," Cato continued, "the man in chains before us, struck an officer at the market in the Tyche district of Syracuse." He motioned to the centurion who Troglius had hit. "Another officer witnessed the incident. There is nothing to prove or disprove. The accused soldier all but admitted his guilt by running from the scene of the crime and staying in hiding for nearly eight weeks before turning himself in. Army regulations could not be more clear. The man has both struck an officer and deserted his duties. A bastinado is called for and that is how I will argue."

A bastinado was equivalent to the death sentence. The guilty soldier was forced to run through a gauntlet made up of the men in his own cohort, meaning two lines of two hundred and fifty soldiers. The soldier would be beaten as he tried to reach the end of the two lines. It was rare for a soldier to make it the entire way, and if he did, he likely died within the next day or two from the beating.

Scipio motioned to me. I took one last anxious look around for Moira, then stepped forward. "Thank you, Consul, for allowing me to represent this soldier." I nodded to Scipio, then Cato. "I have known the accused for almost five years now and know him as one of the most capable soldiers in a Roman uniform." Several soldiers in the crowd disputed this claim with insulting sounds. Scipio raised his hand for quiet.

"The prosecutor has mistakenly said that there is nothing in the case to prove or disprove. I disagree. I was there. I witnessed the incident. It is my intention to prove that it was the centurion whose conduct was improper, not the defendant's. He insulted a woman in the Tyche market, then forcefully grabbed her. The defendant, whom I stood next to at the time, responded in the only way an honorable man could. He protected the woman." Cato looked to the sky, then shook his head. "In fact, I would have done the same if the defendant's sense of honor weren't quicker than mine. What I will attempt to prove in this trial is that the defendant should be commended for his actions, not punished."

Using his fist to cover his grin, Cato took my place in the center of the court.

"Does the prosecution wish to question any witnesses?" asked Scipio.

Cato asked the centurion who had seen the incident to come forward.

"Centurion, for the court, please describe what you saw at the market that day."

"My fellow officer, the victim, and I were at the Tyche market. We stopped at a vendor's cart to view her wares. The defendant and this scribe, I mean his lawyer"—this generated some laughter in the audience—"were also there. When the victim asked the vendor what she had for sale, the woman spit on him. The defendant followed with a punch to the victim's jaw."

"Then in no way," asked Cato, "could it be called an act of self-defense? In fact, as you describe it, the defendant was not part of the original exchange at all. He wasn't personally insulted or even touched by the centurion. All of the victim's words and actions were directed at the vendor. Is that correct?"

"Yes, sir."

"That is all," said Cato.

Scipio looked at me. "Would the defense like to ask the witness any questions?"

"Yes, sir." I approached the centurion standing in the center of the opening. "Sir, would you say that the vendor was an attractive woman?"

Cato quickly objected. Scipio upheld the objection, but the smile on the centurion's face was an obvious yes to my question. I continued. "What exactly did the officer say to the vendor? Do you remember his words?"

The man looked to the victim, standing alongside Cato at the edge of the opening. "I can't say word for word, but it was something like— *What have you got for sale?*"

I nodded. "What if I refresh your memory? Did he say—*What else do you have for sale, sweetie?*" Because of the obvious suggestion in the words, this drew a round of laughter from the soldiers.

Again Scipio raised his hand for quiet.

"Does that sound familiar to you?" I pressed.

"Yes, I think that's right," the man conceded.

"Though his words didn't contain any clear vulgarity, the victim was clearly trying to proposition the young woman. Is that not correct?"

Cato again stepped forward. "He's trying to think for the witness. I object."

Scipio denied the objection and asked the witness to answer.

The centurion scowled. "I can't say if that's correct or not. Ask the man himself."

"He'll get his chance," I said. "But it seems clear from the response of those observing this trial that there was something untoward in his question."

Cato objected again. "He's making suppositions that will influence the court."

Scipio upheld the objection.

"One last question," I said, then turned to the witness. "After the woman spit at the officer, did he not grab her by arm and threaten her before the defendant struck him?"

The centurion scowled at me. "She spit at him. Why wouldn't he have threatened her?"

"But he also grabbed her arm. Is that correct?"

The man reluctantly nodded.

"That's all, sir."

Scipio turned to Cato. "Councilor, do you have any more questions for the witness?"

"No, sir."

"Any other witnesses?"

"I would like to bring the victim to the floor," said Cato.

The man came forward.

"Officer," asked Cato, "is that the man who struck you?" He pointed to Troglius. As everyone turned to look at Troglius, one of the guards from the front gate pushed through the crowd. Moira followed him with Rosa and Donato holding onto her hands. Scipio glared at the guard for the interruption.

"She's a witness, Consul," I said quickly. "She's the woman who was insulted."

"He can't say that," screamed Cato, his red face glowing purple.

Scipio took a deep breath. "Continue with your questioning, councilor."

Cato gave me an ugly look, then repeated his last question. The centurion verified that Troglius was the one who had struck him.

"Officer, did you do anything to this man that merited any kind of retaliation—punch or otherwise?"

"Not in the least. No."

Cato appeared to be done, then he suddenly stopped and asked the centurion, "Is the woman who spit on you here in court?"

"Yes."

"Where?"

He pointed to Moira. Both children looked up at her.

"Did you intentionally insult her?"

The man's brow lowered. "No. Why would I bother?"

This inspired another round of laughter from the audience. I began to wonder if I had made a mistake by having Moira there.

Scipio asked me if I wanted to question the man. When I said no, Cato asked to question the defendant.

Scipio addressed the two guards. "Bring the man forward."

Cato stared at me then turned to Troglius. "Did you strike the centurion?"

Troglius turned in my direction.

"Look at me," snapped Cato. "Yes or no."

"Yes," muttered Troglius so softly that the crowd of soldiers quieted trying to hear him.

"Why did you run away after you hit him?"

Troglius stared at the ground rather than look at me. "I thought he was dead."

Cato turned to the crowd of soldiers, then to Scipio, as though this was a significant admission.

"How long was it before you turned yourself in?"

"I don't know. I didn't keep track," said Troglius to the ground.

"Eight weeks, soldier," sneered Cato. "That makes it desertion by any definition. Do you understand that?"

Troglius was too humiliated to answer.

"Do you understand that you deserted, soldier?"

Troglius muttered a barely audible, "Yes, sir."

"That's all I have, Consul."

Scipio turned to me. "Defense, do you have any questions for the defendant?"

"Yes, sir." I walked up to Troglius. When he lifted his head, I did my best to put on a heartening face.

"Troglius," I said gently, "why did you strike the centurion?"

Although we had rehearsed his answer many times, Troglius hesitated.

"Why did you strike the man?" I asked, urging the words into his head.

Troglius looked down, then up at me so frightened I couldn't believe this was the same man I had seen take on four men at a time in the heat of battle. "The centurion insulted the woman," Troglius mumbled, then added, "in a manner unbecoming an officer."

I looked at Scipio, making certain he had heard what Troglius said. Assaulting women and children had been one of the most grievous crimes perpetrated in Locri during Pleminius' reign of terror. I hoped to the gods that Scipio had not missed that connection.

"Was that the same woman who's in the court?"

Troglius nodded his head.

"That's all, sir."

Troglius was led away to the edge of the opening, and Scipio asked Cato if he had any more witnesses. When he said no, Scipio looked to me. "Any more witnesses for the defense?"

I had no idea what Scipio was thinking. I didn't feel I had made much of an argument. I looked quickly to Moira, then said, "Yes, Consul. I would like the woman involved in the incident to come forward. Her name is Moira."

Scipio motioned to Moira, and she came out of the crowd holding the hands of both her children.

"Moira," I said, "please describe what happened on the day the defendant struck the officer."

Moira was forthright. "I was talking to you and Troglius—the defendant—at my fruit stand in the Tyche market. Those two Roman officers," she pointed to the centurions, "came up to the stand, and the one who was just questioned propositioned me as though I were a common prostitute. I spit on him, and he grabbed me by the arm with who knows what on his mind." She glared at him angrily. "That's when

Troglius came to my aid. It was as clear to him as it was to me that the officer had bad intentions. The defendant made sure that nothing more would happen."

"Did you feel threatened at the time?'"

"Didn't I just say that," she snapped back at me. "Yes, I felt threatened. I always feel threatened when there are too many damn soldiers around." She scanned her rapt audience, making sure they all heard her loud and clear. "All women do. They take liberties only a husband is due."

"Thank you, Moira. That's all I want to ask, Consul."

Cato now had the opportunity to question Moira. He came up close to her and walked around her once, as though he were appraising her value, as though he might be sniffing her and her mongrel children. I immediately knew I had made a mistake.

"Moira," he said softly, "are these your children?'"

Moira knew how bad this man was even without knowing word one about his reputation. She gripped her two children's hands. "They are."

"Where is their father? Or is it fathers?"

The second part of his question was just as insulting as the centurion's remark at the market. Instead of spitting on Cato, she let him have it. "That's a good question, councilor. Their fathers were both Roman soldiers who forced themselves on me just like this man had hoped to. There's lots of children in Syracuse wondering where their fathers are. You tell me. Where are they? I think their children want to know."

No one could miss Moira's spirit. Many of the soldiers cheered her on. Others hid their faces. Cato got more than he wanted, but I'm sure he felt it supported his case.

"That's all, Consul."

"The defense may reexamine," said Scipio.

I shook my head. "The defense rests."

"Make your final statements. Prosecution, you have the floor."

Cato stood in the center of what had now become a rather tight circle, surrounded by many rings of soldiers leaning in close to follow the proceedings, and erupting throughout with shouts and animal sounds. "I restate my opening. This is a simple case. A soldier struck an officer in a public space. He evaded arrest at the scene of the crime, then hid in the labyrinth of Syracuse for nearly two months. Not only is he guilty of the most extreme form of insubordination, he is a deserter.

"Only one argument was made on behalf of the defendant. The defense claimed that he was protecting the reputation of a female street vendor. I think what we just heard from the woman in question renders the point moot. She has no reputation to defend. I would add that it seems highly unlikely that the defendant could even have a sense of honor." Cato turned and pointed at Troglius. "Look at him. See how his head is misshapen. See how his eyes look in two directions. This is no man. He's some mixture of man and beast, with a great talent for killing things. He came close to killing a centurion. And as a deserter, he has revealed that he has no loyalty to Rome. I demand a bastinado. He is an undisciplined freak. He should have been left out to die as an infant. Why not correct his mother's error in judgment now?"

Cato's words prompted a rousing applause, mixed in with shouts for a bastinado and an outpouring of ugly comments directed at Troglius. Those few who knew Troglius were quiet or, like myself, were angered by the method of attack Cato had chosen.

Scipio gave me the floor.

I took a moment to gather myself, then stated my defense. "At no time does a man demean himself more, particularly a soldier in uniform, than when humiliating a woman with rude words or ruder actions. The defendant may have his own unique appearance, but that does not mean he is a man without feeling or honor. He struck the centurion because that centurion was about to strike the woman or abuse her in some way. The defendant stopped a criminal action. At some moral level, rank is outweighed by wrong." I stopped short of saying *we saw what happened in Locri.*

"Implicit in the prosecutor's argument is an admission that the centurion had been improper, but that it didn't matter because the woman had two children out of wedlock and that the defendant didn't have the wits to stand for up for a woman anyway, much less a woman he knew I loved and hoped to marry." Moira's eyes widened. "I contend that respecting a woman, any woman, is part of what it means to be a Roman soldier, and that the defendant did, in fact, put himself on the line to uphold this woman's honor.

"As to his loyalty to Rome, I should remind the court that he won the Mural Crown three years ago for topping the walls of Hannibal's camp outside Asculum. It was the single most impressive act of soldiering I have ever seen. When he came out of hiding, the first thing he said to me was 'I want back in the army.' When the court sentences this man, it's important to remember that the defendant is one of Rome's finest."

A small portion of the soldiers applauded my comments, but the majority shouted for a bastinado. When the uproar quieted, Scipio called for Troglius. The guards brought him forward. The huge man stood head bowed before the consul. Scipio then motioned to Cato and me. We took our places on either side of the Troglius and his guards.

Scipio addressed the entire gathering as much as Troglius, Cato, and me. "As I said at the opening of this trial, discipline is a key element to the success of the Roman army. Discipline in carrying out battle directives, discipline within the camp, and discipline when one interacts with the public. The events in Locri this past summer underscore this last piece. In that regard, it appears that the centurion in question should be more careful in his dealings with the public. That said, however, the defendant overstepped his rank and broke one of the most sacred of our principles, respect for an officer. In that I hold him guilty."

The crowd of soldiers responded positively to the judgment with hoots, hollers, and more barbs aimed at Troglius. Cato had no reaction. Scipio raised his hands for quiet and continued.

"The prosecution also raised the question of desertion. In my mind the only crime worse than desertion is treason. In this charge, I find the defendant also guilty, though the fact that he turned himself in, fully aware of the consequences, does remove some of the ignominy attached to his actions."

Cato nodded very slightly. The rest of the audience held quiet, knowing that Scipio would pronounce Troglius' punishment next.

"Individually, either of these crimes merits execution. The prosecution has asked for a bastinado." Scipio paused to look at Cato, then at me. Troglius stared at the ground.

"Prior to this trial," continued Scipio, "I did speak to a few of my tribunes about their knowledge of the man on trial. Two of the men had served in the Eighteenth legion with the defendant. They both spoke highly of his skills in battle. The defense mentioned his courage in Asculum. One of the tribunes was there and echoed similar sentiments."

Cato's eyes swung my way as mine swung his.

Scipio continued. "I have decided that instead of a bastinado, the legionnaire Troglius will receive one hundred lashes—to be administered at daybreak tomorrow morning. Until then he will be kept in the chains."

The mass of soldiers uttered a disappointed groan, mixed with catcalls directed at Moira and more insults aimed at Troglius. Cato, however, was furious.

Scipio stood from his chair and headed off to headquarters. Cato turned to me. "This kind of laxness is what caused the breakdown in discipline at Locri. Scipio is coming dangerously close to making the same mistake twice." I think it was at this moment that Cato recognized me as Marcus' friend. He gave me a haughty look, turned away suddenly, and stomped off to some other part of the camp.

Troglius finally lifted his head and looked at me. "Thank you, Timon," he muttered softly. "The lashes are nothing, but I could not bear to be beaten by members of my own cohort."

"I did my best, my friend. I had hoped for a better result. I'm sorry," was all I had a chance to say before the guards led him away. I was not so sanguine as Troglius about the sentence. I had seen men whipped fifty times with a brass studded flail. More than half of them had died. I had never even heard of a hundred lashes. What could possibly be left of the man?

Moira came up to me with questions in her eyes. "Did I help or hinder? I'm sorry I was late. Not everything is predictable." Her two children looked up at me.

"It's fine. You did all you could, but I should have done better. We avoided the humiliation of a bastinado, but a hundred lashes? I can't even think about it."

I escorted Moira out of the camp and thanked her again for making the effort.

"Let me know how Troglius fares," she said. "Regardless of this silly trial, he did stand up for me and that means a lot."

That evening I went to headquarters to work on the map. The tent was empty. I lit four of the oil lamps and arranged them for the best possible lighting. The map was essentially done. I had worked like a man possessed to complete it before we left. Now I had six more months to detail it. The first thing I wanted to do was double-check all my earlier calculations. That's what I was doing when Scipio appeared from beneath the tent flap.

Neither of us said a word. He came across the tent. He looked down at the map, then up at me. "You did well against Cato today, Timon. Your talents never cease to amaze me."

I stared back at him. I was angry.

"You should be pleased. Troglius was spared the bastinado. No soldier wants that."

"If I may speak freely, sir. With one hundred lashes the outcome will be the same. He's going to be executed tomorrow. Then you can say that both the prosecutor and the defense got what they wanted. How fair can one expect a judge to be?"

Scipio was the figurehead of Rome, a consul, her most daring young general. One might argue there was no more important man in the world at that moment. I was a freedman. A Greek who owned no property. Not even a slave. The sarcasm of my final comment had overstepped my rank and position.

Scipio did not miss it. He could easily have stuck me for insubordination. Instead he leaned across the table and in a voice just above a whisper said, "He should have gotten the bastinado for desertion alone, Timon. I was easy on him. If Troglius is the warrior you make him out to be, he will survive a hundred lashes. If he does, I will promote him to centurion."

CHAPTER 60

I did not attend the flogging the next morning. I deliberately buried myself in work on the map. I suspect that most of the soldiers not on duty were there. Had the camp been open to the public, a good number of the locals would have come as well. It has always surprised me how people are drawn to an execution or the spectacle of one man brutalizing another. Apparently I am deficient in some basic human ingredient.

The flogging took Troglius to the very edge of his life. A story came out later that the man with the scourge was so overcome by Troglius' courage beneath the whip that he deliberately missed with his last twenty lashes, and that those still present to watch understood. His back was nearly cleaned to the bone of skin. It wasn't clear if he would live. Scipio was aware of Troglius' condition. He ordered the camp surgeon to clean and dress the wound, something never done following discipline for a military crime.

I found Troglius in the hospital tent. The doctor, who was a Greek, wasn't there. Troglius lay on his stomach on a cot, striped of all clothing. The vast open wound—his entire back—hadn't been dressed yet. One look was more than I needed. It was obvious that anything placed on Troglius' wound would adhere and create a bigger problem when it was removed.

Troglius' eyes were closed. His hair was matted to his head with sweat and blood. I whispered his name. His face was sideways on the cot. The upper eye cracked open.

"It's me," I said, uncertain of how cognizant he was.

His eye turned in my direction, but he didn't say anything.

"I can't believe you're still alive."

The eye stared up at me. No other part of his body moved.

"Apparently your courage during the flogging was enough to earn you a doctor. That doesn't usually happen." I wanted to say *consider*

237

yourself lucky, but it seemed too cruel when his life still hung in the balance.

I put my hand on his. "You're going to make it," I said, not believing it.

He squeezed my forefinger.

"Are you still interested in being a soldier?"

Again he squeezed my finger.

"You are a better man than I, Troglius. You are a better man than I."

I stayed until the doctor returned. He was an Athenian by the name of Abrax. We had never met. I addressed him in Greek. "What are his chances?"

"He lost a lot of skin, but no muscles were severed. He might make it through the night," he said. "Beyond that I cannot say."

CHAPTER 61

Troglius made it through that night and the next. Abrax became more optimistic, but had yet to cover the seeping wound. The biggest concern was infection. When I asked the doctor if he would live, the doctor said, "I doubt it."

I made the time to go out to Moira's farm. She saw me crossing the field from the road. She ran out to meet me. Donato ran after her. Rosa toddled far behind.

"Is Troglius alive?" she asked, trembling with anticipation.

I nodded, then embraced her. When I released her, tears were streaming down her cheeks.

"But he's in bad shape," I said. "Each day he survives gives him that much more chance to survive the next."

"You did it, Timon. You saved him. I was impressed by the way you handled yourself during the trial. How did you know what to say?"

I looked at the ground, then up into her eyes. "It's too early to celebrate anything, Moira. And if he makes it, it won't have been through my efforts." I used my fingers to sweep the tears from her cheeks. "His toughness is the only reason he's alive right now. Few men could live through that kind of beating. His back resembles a huge slab of raw meat."

Donato stood beside his mother. He pulled at my tunic. "Did you watch the flogging?"

"No, Donato, I couldn't."

"Why not?"

Moira answered. "It's very difficult to watch a friend being beaten, especially when you can't do anything about it."

"Why?"

I almost smiled at Donato's innocence. Instead of answering, I took Moira's hand and led her back to the house. Donato asked us *why* three more times without getting an answer. I didn't have enough time

239

to stay and help with the chores, but when I left, Moira accompanied me through the fields to the road, stopping several times along the way to pick comfrey.

"Have the doctor steam these leaves." She handed me the comfrey. "He can use them as a compress to cover Troglius' back. They will ease the pain, speed up the healing of the skin, and won't stick to the wound. Try this, please. Change the compress every day until the wound stops oozing."

I thanked her for the comfrey and kissed her on the cheek.

"Thank you, Timon, for coming out here with the news."

"I knew you wanted to know. I had to come." I stroked her hair and gazed into her eyes. I thought about how beautiful she was and the twist of fate that had brought us together for a second time.

"Did you mean what you said at the trial, Timon? Or was that just something you said to save Troglius?"

My look was a question.

"Are you really considering marrying me?"

In the months since I had reunited with Moira, she hadn't asked me for any kind of commitment or inclusion in my future. What I had said at the trial had not been planned, but it had surely come from somewhere deep inside me. "I said that, Moira, to defend your honor in the face of Cato's insults. Do I want to marry you? You and I both know that any plans we might make regarding the future are meaningless until I return from Africa. It's senseless to even talk about it."

Moira looked away, trying to hide what she felt. I embraced her and whispered, "But, yes, I did mean it."

She stood up on her toes and kissed me on the lips, then spun out of my arms and ran back across the field to her children.

When I returned to camp that afternoon, I went to check on Troglius. His condition was unchanged, but he was alive, which was all I wanted to know. Abrax was there. I gave him the comfrey. He didn't seem too interested in using it. I told him the man was my best friend and that I would do it if he wouldn't. Abrax agreed to do it, but he wasn't very convincing, so I stayed to steam the comfrey and help him lay the large soft leaves on Troglius' back.

I skipped the evening meal and went from the hospital tent to headquarters to complete the work I had left undone to visit Moira.

The tent was empty when I entered. I went straight to the map table and resumed reviewing my calculations.

I was nearly done when Scipio entered the tent followed by Laelius and his brother. Scipio was furious. Syphax's envoys had arrived that afternoon while I was at Moira's farm. They had delivered the message that Hasdrubal had requested: Syphax had married Hasdrubal's daughter, and Scipio could no longer count on his support should he come to Africa.

"Say nothing of this" said Scipio to the other officers, then looked at me. "You either."

"Yes, sir."

"If word gets out that I have lost Syphax, it will work against morale and bring yet another barrage of criticism from Fabius in Rome. We'll go ahead as though nothing's changed." He looked at his brother. "Lucius, I want you to stay with the envoys until they leave. Make sure they talk to no one. If anyone asks, say that they came here requesting we come to Africa as soon as possible. Once we're in Africa, none of this will matter. Immediate needs will take over. But until then, I don't want the men dwelling on bad news."

CHAPTER 62

Troglius showed considerable progress in the next few days. I don't know if it were a result of Moira's comfrey compresses or not, but the wound began to dry up and form scabs. When it seemed safe to say he would survive, I felt it was important to tell Agathe and Eurydice. I found some time to go into Syracuse and went straight to the tenement housing where Agathe had lived as long as I had known her.

Both women were glad to see me and were relieved that Troglius had not been executed. I thanked them for allowing him to stay in their home, especially when they could have been implicated in the crime had he been found there. Predictably, Agathe took the news with her usual spit and vinegar; however, Eurydice's emotional, tearful response surprised me. I knew that Troglius entertained the idea of marrying her, but I found it difficult to believe that Eurydice could feel anything beyond ordinary compassion for my misshapen friend.

On my way off the island, I passed the warehouse where Archimedes had supervised the building of the arrays of parabolic mirrors. The building's doors were secured with a large, loose fitting chain. Curious what might remain, I pried the doors open as wide as the chain allowed and peeked in through the opening. The only light in the warehouse came through cracks in the building's siding. I couldn't see much, but it was evident that the floor was still cluttered with bits and pieces left over from the project.

Still curious, I twisted and turned the chain so that I could open the doors a little wider. Then, with great effort, I squeezed sideways through the opening into the building. Five years had passed since Archimedes had quit work on the adjustable array. Its large, unfinished wooden substructure dominated the center of the warehouse.

As I maneuvered through the darkness and debris, my eyes gradually adjusted to the lack of light. I saw several of the parabolic mirrors stacked in one corner. I remembered how much effort had been put into perfecting the three working arrays. Archimedes and his crew and I had spent nearly all of our waking hours for several weeks in this warehouse, trying to be ready for Marcellus' next assault on the city.

I unstacked the pile of bronze mirrors to evaluate their condition. The one on top was badly tarnished, but the others retained much of their original polish. In the process of moving the mirrors, I noticed several dusty scrolls lying on a shelf adjacent to the stack of mirrors. I took one of the scrolls to a place in the warehouse where there was a rectangular patch of sunlight on the dirt floor. I got down on one knee and unrolled the scroll. It was a set of drawings for one of the stationary mirror arrays.

On the day the Romans finally stormed the island, and it was evident the plundering soldiers would soon be coming to the tower, Archimedes had me burn all his notebooks, drawings, and letters before anyone could take possession of them. At the time, I felt it was a mistake. Despite my arguments, Archimedes refused to save a single document. Apparently he had forgotten that some of his drawings had been left in the warehouse.

I collected all the scrolls—four more—and took them over to the patch of light. One by one I unrolled them to see what they were. All were detailed engineering drawings, copied by me for Archimedes many years before. Two of them were drawings of stationary arrays, each with a different focal length. One contained drawings of the adjustable array that was still in pieces, and one was a catapult, which I recognized as one of Archimedes' most advanced designs.

As I realized the importance of what I had just discovered, my hands began to shake. The drawings for the adjustable array were certainly valuable, but they were unfinished and needed some work. However, the designs for the three stationary arrays and the catapult were of weaponry that had already been proven to work—and were of immediate value. Although I would always feel the compound lenses were a greater discovery, men like Hannibal or Scipio would find the catapult and the parabolic arrays considerably more alluring.

My first thought was to take the scrolls to Scipio, then I remembered his reaction to the spyglass. I had worried ever since if showing him had been a mistake. My second thought was to burn the drawings. That would have been what Archimedes wanted. For many reasons I was compelled to do this. Then I thought again. The war was not over. Rome seemed likely to win, but what if something changed? What if Hannibal somehow regained the upper hand? Weapons like these might be the only way to defeat him.

Knowing I could always burn the scrolls at a later date, I rolled them all into one and squeezed back out of the warehouse. When I got back to camp, I separated the five scrolls and put them at the bottom of my stack of maps in the headquarters' tent. During the next three months, as time and privacy allowed, I studied these designs with the intent of teaching myself how to build them all.

PART VI

THE INVASION OF AFRICA

"The bravest are surely those who have the clearest vision of what is before them, glory and danger alike, and yet not withstanding go out to meet it."

-Thucydides.

CHAPTER 63

The ecstatic mood in Rome following the defeat of Hasdrubal in north Italy and the decision to allow Scipio to stage an invasion of Africa had steadily eroded in the time since the discovery of the war crimes in Locri. Along with the arrival of Mago in Etruria, the outbreak of the plague in Bruttium, and the inquiry that postponed Scipio's voyage to Africa, a string of unusual prodigies generated tremendous apprehension for the coming year. Quintus Caecilius Metellus, who had been named dictator in the absence of the two consuls, ordered a ten-man team to consult the Sibylline Books for advice, something reserved for only the most dire times.

During the review of these sacred books, a passage was found that read, "If ever a foreign enemy should invade Italy, the invaders could be driven out if Cybele, the Idaean Mother of the Gods, were brought from the Asian city of Pessinus to Rome." Although Rome had few allies in Asia, four envoys were immediately sent to Phrygia, where Pessinus was located, with the task of acquiring the large black stone that the Phrygians believe represented the Idaean Mother.

On the way to Asia, the envoys stopped at the Temple in Delphi to make an offering to the oracle and seek his advice on bargaining for the goddess. After they had placed two large chests of silver and gold in the temple, the oracle told them to go to King Attalus in Pergamum and that he would help them. The oracle also told them, that should they receive the treasured stone, the goddess should be received in Italy with the utmost hospitality and welcomed into Rome by the best man in the city.

Attalus received the Roman envoys with a warm welcome, and after hearing their request, escorted them to Pessinus, a city in his kingdom. With the king as the envoy's sponsor, the native people declined any payment for the stone and simply gave it to the envoys.

During the time that the stone was in transit from Phrygia, Metellus presided over the elections in Rome. Marcus Cornelius Cethegus, a member of Scipio's clan, and Publius Sempronius Teditanus were chosen as the year's two consuls. Cethegus was given the province of Etruria, with orders to keep Mago pinned in the north, and Teditanus was sent to Bruttium to join forces with Livinius against Hannibal. Scipio was again assigned to Sicily with a nearly unanimous vote of support to go to Africa when he was ready.

On the ides of March, when the two new consuls were inaugurated and the first Senate meeting of the year took place, Metellus reported that the ship carrying the Idaean Mother would arrive at the port of Ostia that week. Following this welcome news, the Senate had a lengthy discussion about who was the best man in Rome. Most likely because of his family connections, Publius Scipio's twenty-two year old cousin with the same name was selected.

On the appointed day, the cousin, whose father Gaius had been killed in Spain the same year as Scipio's father, waited in a small boat at the mouth of the Tiber River for the arrival of the transport ship. Midafternoon the ship anchored in the Ostia harbor. Publius Scipio sailed out to the transport vessel, and with great ceremony and a live sacrifice, received the stone. When he brought the stone ashore, he was greeted by one of Rome's leading women, Claudia Quinta. Claudia had come to Ostia in a long procession containing all the married women in Rome. The women were evenly spaced along the road so that they stretched all the way from Rome to Ostia. Claudia took the stone from Scipio, and carrying it a short distance, passed it to the next woman in line. In this way, the stone was transported to Rome, passing from one woman to next the entire fifteen miles to the city gates.

Everyone in the city came out for the arrival of the stone. The excited populace lined both sides of the bridge over the Tiber, and then created a pathway to Porta Carmentalis and through the city to the top of the Palatine Hill and the Temple of Victory, where the stone was placed. A festival and a feast were held afterward with the hope that the gods had been properly satisfied and that the war would soon end with Rome the victor.

CHAPTER 64

At the end of April, Scipio began the process of transporting his troops to Lilybaeum, where the voyage to Africa would begin. All the soldiers, all the provisions, and all the warships and transports arrived in Lilybaeum a week before the departure scheduled for the ides of May.

By this time Troglius had recovered fully and was ready to go with the troops to Africa. If men had referred to him as a monster before, now he truly looked like one. The shiny layers of scar tissue on his back and shoulders, worn like a fibrous white mantle, made him more reptilian in appearance. With the rhomboid shape of his head, he could have passed for a hippopotamus on two legs. The incident, the trial, and his survival of the flogging created quite a reputation for Troglius among the other soldiers. They held him up as a kind of mythic being—even though very few of them had yet to see him on the battlefield. Scipio promoted him to centurion as promised. Troglius, however, declined the promotion, saying he preferred not to be an officer.

I spent my last night in Syracuse at Moira's farm. I got there late and ate leftovers. After the children were in bed, Moira and I lay on our backs in the grass out front of the house and stared up at the stars.

"I don't know when I'll be back," I said looking into the sky. "It could be two months. It could be two years."

"Timon," replied Moira, "I understand. It's the war. It's all you or I have known our entire lives. We only have what is here and now. We got a lot of work done this winter." She turned on her side, facing me. "Our time together has been good."

I turned toward her. "More than good, Moira. Much more than good."

She grinned. "It seems strange that we should have met twice."

"And fortunate."

We didn't say another word all night. We slept outside. I got up before daylight without waking Moira. I had brought four of the five scrolls that I had found in the warehouse to the farm. Without saying anything to Moira, I hid them in one of the outbuildings. I left the fifth scroll—the adjustable mirror array—at the bottom of the stack of maps in headquarters and would take it to Africa. I planned to work on it when time allowed, challenging myself to complete the unfinished drawings.

I went back to the farmhouse and woke Moira with a kiss. When she tried to talk, I put a finger to her lips. "Whatever needs to be said, we said last night. Let's make this simple. Let's leave it at good-bye."

I lifted my finger from her lips, and with tears glistening in the corners of her eyes, she whispered, "Good-bye, Timon. I'm sure we wouldn't have met twice if we weren't destined to meet again."

CHAPTER 65

For three years Scipio had boasted that he would go to Carthage and draw Hannibal out of Italy. Now he was finally prepared to cross the one hundred and twenty-five miles of open sea to Africa to prove it. People from all over Sicily came to the port of Lilybaeun to watch our departure. Throughout the morning, on a day of cloudless blue skies, crowds accumulated on the wharf and around the harbor's shore. Scipio's campaign held the hopes of all Italy, and to some, marked the beginning of the end of the war. Forty triremes and four hundred transports filled the harbor, carrying some twenty-six thousand infantry and two thousand cavalry, in nearly equal parts of Roman legionnaires and allied levies. Forty-five days of rations and water were included with the freight.

Scipio's flagship was anchored alongside the wharf. Scipio, Laelius, Cato—all in full dress armor—and our augur Dilius Strabo, wearing a hooded, white robe, fanned out across the forecastle. A herald and ten trumpeters stood off to their right. I was on the left with my wax pad and bronze stylus to take notes. Soldiers filled the rest of the deck to watch the ceremony to launch the flotilla. Farther from shore, the other ships were similarly packed with cheering legionnaires, eager to begin the campaign.

Scipio turned to the herald. The herald gave the signal, and the ten trumpets sounded. The herald stepped forward, and lifting his hands in the air, shouted to the enormous, boisterous crowd for quiet. When the thousands in attendance calmed to a muddy murmur, Scipio advanced to the foremost edge of the bow. He looked up into sky and addressed the heavens.

"O gods and goddesses of the seas and lands, I pray and beseech you that whatever things have been done, are being done, and will be done under my authority will bring prosperity for me and for the people and the commons of Rome. And I pray that you bring the victors home safe and sound, enriched with spoils, and laden with the plunder of an enemy defeated. Grant us the power of vengeance to inflict upon the Carthaginian state the same suffering which they have labored to inflict upon Rome."

The huge crowd erupted with resounding cheers and applause, calling for the destruction of Carthage. When the hubbub died down, two priests came to the bow leading a well groomed calf, adorned with red and blue fillets tied to its tail and ears. One priest carried an amphora of wine, the other a sack of mola, a mixture of salt and wheat prepared in Rome by the Vestal Virgins. Dilius Strabo, a short fat man, who would be our augur for the entire campaign, sprinkled a handful of mola along the calf's spine, then used the amphora to dribble some wine on the calf's forehead. He withdrew a flint knife from his robes and removed its soft leather sheath. With one hand on the calf's head, the augur drew a line down the calf's spine with the tip of the knife, only parting the hair, not cutting into the skin, then nodded to the priests. They took the calf by its legs and flipped it onto its back. The augur knelt beside the calf and quickly cut its throat. He allowed the calf to bleed out, then used the knife to make an incision in the calf's midsection from the genitals to the throat. The priests held the incision open while Dilius dipped his hands into the calf's glistening pink innards. One by one, he drew out and cut free the lungs, the kidneys, the gall bladder, the liver, and the heart. As he took out each organ, he inspected it and laid it on the ship's deck. When the last organ had been examined, Dilius stood, his hands dripping with blood, and announced at the full volume of his voice, "The organs show no abnormalities. The gods have spoken. The campaign will be a success. Carthage will be destroyed."

Everyone within hearing range burst out in another raucous cheer. Those farther off knew what the cheer meant and joined in. Starting in close to the flagship and expanding out like a wave, the entire harbor—wharf, ships, and shoreline—swelled with the sounds of jubilation that always accompanied sending a Roman army off to war. Amid this extended cheer, the two priests collected the internal organs from the deck and tossed them into the harbor, followed by the rest of the animal's carcass and three buckets of sea water to wash the blood from the deck and flush it into the sea.

Scipio raised his gladius above his head and stroked down through the air. The trumpets blared again. The ships' captains gave the order

Dan Armstrong 253

to set sail. Five thousand oars dipped into the water and pulled forward as one. A thousand sails unfurled as they were hoisted up the masts, one by one snapping full with a brisk southerly breeze. Slowly, awkwardly, the huge fleet rowed or sailed out of the Lilybaeum harbor into the open sea.

It must have been an amazing sight from the shore, but from the deck of the flagship, watching the ships gradually maneuver into formation was breathtaking. Midday I moved to the stern of our ship and used the spyglass to scan the sea behind us and watch the ships cutting through the waves, five abreast, in a long curving line as far as I could see. Laelius led the flotilla with a squadron of twenty triremes. Lucius commanded another twenty at the rear. Together, they served as escorts for the four hundred unarmed transports in between.

I spent most of my time at sea with Laelius, either on deck or in headquarters looking at our map. When on deck, he and I took turns with the spyglass. The ability to see the entire fleet from the stern of our ship gave him tremendous peace of mind. Scipio joined us off and on throughout the day, and repeatedly remarked on the unique power of the spyglass, especially at sea.

Late in the afternoon of the first day, the breeze trailed off to nothing and fog set in. As agreed upon before leaving Lilybaeum, at night or in fog, each warship would hang one lantern on its mast, the transports two, and the flagship three. By nightfall the fog had reduced our progress to a crawl. As we cut through the dense fog, not a ship in sight, only the faint glow of the lanterns and the steady slap of the oars on the water assured us that we were not alone.

Scipio paced the deck the entire night, never sleeping, fearful that some horrible mishap would bring an end to his dream. With the rising of the sun came a breeze from the northwest. As the fog gradually dispersed, we saw that the fleet had scattered farther during the night than believed. Through the first part of the day, Laelius frantically counted the ships with the spyglass until the flotilla had regained its original formation.

By noon we had been out of sight of land for almost a day and a half, and for myself, and surely everyone else, there was a deep, inherent fear of being surrounded by nothing but water. I was so eager to spot land I hardly took the spyglass from my eye.

The closest stretch of African coastline from Lilybaeum was the peninsula that formed the east arm of the Bay of Tunis, called the Promontory of Mercury, about sixty miles of twisting coastline east of Carthage. Midafternoon I spotted what I was certain was the tip of this peninsula. I immediately told Laelius and gave him the spyglass so I could go aft to inform Scipio.

Scipio was in headquarters when I found him. He came forward as excited as anyone about the sighting of land. Laelius handed him the spyglass and pointed to a spot on the horizon that showed nothing to the naked eye. Scipio lifted the spyglass and quickly found the tiny nub of darkness that was the Promontory of Mercury. When he lowered the device, greatly pleased, Laelius asked him, "Should we tell the crew? Does it matter that we've seen land with the aid of this device?"

Scipio hesitated. I spoke up. "As far as any of the soldiers know, the spyglass is merely a sighting tool. Nothing of its special nature is evident without actually using it. I suggest we go to the crow's nest for a better view, and from there announce that land is in sight."

Laelius and Scipio both agreed. Wanting to be the one to make the announcement, Scipio ordered the man in the crow's nest down to the deck, so that he and I could take his place.

Climbing a mast while at sea can be a harrowing experience. Fortunately the winds had been light and the seas reasonably calm the entire voyage. The ship heeled this way and that, but not like it could, and Scipio and I climbed to the top of the mast with little trouble. Standing side by side on the tiny observation platform above the sail, and holding on for dear life, we took turns with the spyglass.

"Watch the way the land comes into view, sir," I said when he raised the spyglass to his eye a second time. "Notice that we are seeing the top of the ridge that forms the promontory first, and then as we get closer, more of the land below comes into view."

"Yes, I'm noticing that," said Scipio without removing the spyglass from his eye.

"Archimedes said it's proof that the Earth isn't flat."

He lowered the spyglass from his eye and looked at me. "I've heard that certain Greeks have said that, but I've never thought that it was true."

"Keep watching the land. Clearly we are on a curved surface. The Earth is a sphere."

"But isn't water always a flat surface?"

"As Archimedes would have said—only if you're not looking close enough. He proved it to me by pointing out how a ship disappears over the horizon—from bottom to top. It's the same as what we're seeing with the land."

"And he believed that the Earth was round?"

"Yes, and that it was moving around the sun, not the reverse. It's contrary to what our senses tell us, but there are scientists who have proven it by studying charts of the stars and doing the geometry."

Still uncertain, Scipio took another long look through the lenses, then turned back to me. "I find it difficult to believe, but I would have said the same of this device had I not seen it for myself."

"One night when the sky is clear and the moon is something short of full, the spyglass can show you other reasons to believe this notion. I talked many times with Archimedes about it, and still struggle with what it suggests—and yet I believe he was right."

"When time allows, I would like to hear more." He smiled at me, further impressed by the things I knew. "But we have more pressing matters ahead."

"Of course, sir. Let the sailors know we've seen land. There could hardly be sweeter news to them now."

"Land Ho! " shouted Scipio, using the spyglass to point to the south.

Several of the men on deck cheered. Others looked in the direction that Scipio was pointing, but land was not yet visible from the deck.

We stayed in the crow's nest for some time. Scipio was entirely fascinated with the view as more and more of Africa became visible. When we finally climbed down and the shoreline was visible from the deck, Scipio took me aside.

"This spyglass is remarkable, Timon. More than that. The more I use it, the more I appreciate how helpful it could be in warfare. Just imagine being able to see your foe before he can see you. I would love to have this device for myself, but we have spoken of this before. Is there any way to obtain a second one?"

"The key parts, sir, are the large crystal disk, which is rare but not impossible to obtain—perhaps in Alexandria, and the smaller lens, which Archimedes made himself through months of trial and error. Finding two lenses that perfectly compliment each other would be a long, arduous task, but there are craftsmen who know how to work with glass. Maybe one of them could replicate the pair."

"So it's possible, but difficult."

I nodded. "Yes, extremely."

After sighting land, Scipio, Laelius, and I went aft for a look at the map. Laelius pointed out the promontory and its relation to Carthage. Though it would add another day of sea travel, Scipio told Laelius he wanted to follow the shoreline further west past Carthage before striking land. Laelius suggested we beach the fleet at Bizerta, where we had landed the previous year. When Scipio agreed, Laelius stood at the stern to signal the change of course to the rest of the flotilla. Instead of continuing south toward land, we headed west, staying far enough from the coastline that we could not be seen from the shore, except from a substantial elevation—or with a spyglass.

When I had a moment alone with Scipio in the cabin, I drew a picture for him, showing how the advantage of height gave the man in the crow's nest a more distant horizon, then how using the spyglass in the crow's nest added to that distance. Scipio, like Marcus, found the geometry extremely interesting. He had already seen its power in the making of the maps and in the application of optics to the spyglass.

For a year now, I had steadily earned more and more respect from Scipio. I had also gained more insight into him. I respected the man for his attention to detail and his intellect, but I also understood that he was a manipulator; a man who utilized the remarkably charming side of his personality for one effect when in public, but revealed a much more cynical and self-centered side of himself for another effect when in private. Whether it was his desire to own the spyglass or his punishment of Troglius or his barely contained arrogance, I could never quite reach equilibrium with the man, and an unstated tension always seemed to stress between us. And yet, through the ups and downs of our acquaintance, he stood out as the one man who truly recognized the profound nature of the spyglass and understood that it provided just a small glimpse of the vast potential scientific knowledge prophesied. There was a brave new world looming in the future and he, as well as I, could see it through the spyglass.

CHAPTER 66

As we proceeded west, the light breeze that assisted our progress died away to nothing, and again fog settled in around us. As night fell, the conditions became even more dangerous than when we had been farther out at sea. We couldn't be seen from land, which helped, but neither could we see the land for navigation. We ran the risk of drawing too close to shore and grounding any number of the ships. Laelius gave into caution and the entire flotilla was brought to a halt and anchored.

Much like the previous day, the wind came up with the sun and the fog dispersed, revealing that we were much closer to land than we had thought. Concerned that the fog would come up again in the afternoon, we headed to shore and landed at Cape Farina a few miles east of Bizerta. This put us about thirty-five miles of twisting coastline from Carthage—twenty miles as the crow flies, and less than ten miles from Utica, the other large Carthaginian city on the coast, and the oldest of the Phoenician colonies. The region inland was mostly used for growing grains and was tended by the local Libyans as tenant farmers for their Carthaginian landlords. The local villages were small and had little or no protection, meaning they were ripe for raiding and securing fresh provisions.

The arrival of more than four hundred ships could not be disguised in any way and rapidly brought the nearby coastal villages to life. At first large groups of the tribal Libyans came to the shoreline to watch, then as they realized that forty warships were mixed in with the transports and private merchant ships, they ran off to spread the word that the Roman invasion had begun, prompting a mass evacuation of the area. By the time we had beached our ships and begun the process of building a camp, we had to assume that news of our arrival had reached Utica and would be communicated to Carthage by the next day.

Scipio was all business from the moment we arrived. He sent out scouts in all directions to get a reading of the area. The following morning he assembled five raiding parties to establish strategic outposts and scavenge the countryside for food and booty. By the end of our second full day there, ten transports had been filled with plunder. They left for Sicily the following morning.

Scipio's first major objective was to besiege Utica and make it his winter camp. The day the transports left for Sicily, he dispatched a single legion to Utica to establish a position in the hills that overlooked the city. The following day he sent Laelius down the coast with thirty warships to occupy the harbor.

Carthage by this time was in a frenzy. All able-bodied men were pressed into service and armed. Large stores of grain and other necessities were stockpiled within the city walls, which were then sealed up tight as though Scipio could appear at the gates at any moment. Hasdrubal Gisgo, serving a second term as a sufet, and also one of Carthage's most experienced generals, sent a unit of five hundred cavalry to Cape Farina to assess the Roman camp.

The Carthaginians encountered our outposts long before reaching the camp. They engaged our cavalry and were quickly out-flanked and dispersed. More than half of the Carthaginians were killed. Another hundred were taken prisoner. Scipio's campaign was off to an auspicious start.

CHAPTER 67

Three days after the encounter with the Carthaginian cavalry, Masinissa arrived at our camp with one thousand Numidians on horseback. Scipio could not have been more pleased. He met Masinissa out front of our camp, then ordered a guard to find water and fodder for the horses. Scipio escorted Masinissa to headquarters accompanied by Lucius and Cato, both in full armor. I was there working on the map of North Africa when they entered.

Masinissa burst into the tent like a dust devil off the African plains with his long white robe swirling about his feet. A dark blue mantle was wrapped around his head and shoulders, providing a frame for his startling green eyes and disarming smile. He recognized me immediately and strode across the tent to embrace me. "My friend, Timon, I have so looked forward to seeing you again."

Masinissa saw what I was working on and advanced to the edge of the table. "You've upgraded your map." He studied it briefly, looked up at me, then turned to Scipio. "This man is an artist with a compass and a straight edge. How fortunate you are to have him."

He spoke in Greek. Only Scipio and I understood. Cato, who had railed against the "effeminate" Greek culture for years, demanded that we speak in Latin.

I bowed my head as I translated Masinissa's compliment. Scipio smiled. He already knew how valuable I was and echoed Masinissa's sentiments.

"What took you so long to get here, General?" Masinissa was as handsome and confident as Scipio and spoke to the Roman general as an equal. "We have been ready for nearly six months."

Scipio, who wore a toga, enjoyed the man's boldness. "We wanted to give you more time to increase your numbers. We could use twice as many men as I saw in front of the camp just now."

Masinissa laughed, then became serious. "You will have more cavalry in due time, my friend. But first I need assurance that you'll help me regain my kingdom in exchange for my helping you defeat the Carthaginians."

"You have it," stated Scipio. "With Syphax now fully in the Carthaginian camp, any Roman victory in Africa must be accompanied by the defeat of your usurper. Your kingdom as well as his will be yours should things go as I expect."

"Then consider the men I brought today yours. More will be drawn in by our victories." He grinned at Scipio. "Have you a plan?"

Scipio laughed at his bravado. "Of course, I do."

"Be careful, General," interrupted Cato. "Is it wise to tell this man what our intentions are? One barbarian has already reversed his promises to you."

Scipio, two years older than Cato and all too aware that he was a protégé of Quintus Fabius, snapped at him in Latin. "I have every faith in this man, Quaestor. And in no way would I call him a barbarian. He's better educated than you are."

Cato, as stubborn and arrogant as anyone, glared back at Scipio, but said nothing.

"Our first objective, Masinissa," said Scipio, "is to besiege Utica. I would like to use it as our winter quarters."

Masinissa nodded as though thinking through the logic.

"We have five thousand infantry positioned in the hills overlooking the walls as I speak, and thirty of my warships are in Utica's harbor. What can you tell me about the readiness of the Carthaginians?"

"Hasdrubal Gisgo is in charge of all military operations. He is scrambling now to assemble an army of Carthaginian citizens and Libyans. I'm sure he's already reached out to Syphax. Syphax's army will be large but untrained. Siga is a long march from here. It will be weeks before Syphax can join forces with Hasdrubal. You'll have to take Utica before they arrive."

"That would be nice, but it seems unlikely. Is there anything that you need from me?"

Masinissa grinned. "Your word on our agreement and a place for my men to camp."

Cato stepped forward. "Get it in writing, General."

Scipio turned to Lucius then the Numidian prince. "Should we make it formal, Masinissa?"

Masinissa frowned. "Only your hand is necessary, General. A man's word should need no documents to substantiate it."

Scipio extended his hand. "Give us your full support, Masinissa, and you will have our assistance in regaining your kingdom."

Masinissa gripped Scipio's hand. "Agreed."

"Tell your men they can camp on the south side of our camp. Take any water or fodder you need from our supplies." Scipio looked him in the eye. "And you will be expected to follow my command."

Masinissa smiled. "It will be an honor, General."

Before leaving headquarters, Masinissa asked me to come to his camp that night. I was as happy to see him as Scipio was, and following the evening meal, I went to the Numidian camp. With no trenches dug around it and no palisades, I entered the haphazard array of canvas tents with no resistance. I recognized one of the men I had met the previous year and asked him where I could find Masinissa. He pointed to a large campfire surrounded by twenty or so seated men. Masinissa stood up as soon as he saw me and again greeted me like an old friend.

Masinissa suggested we walk. We wandered down to the beach and followed the waterline where the sand was still wet from the receding tide. A three-quarter moon sat low in the sky over the ocean to the east. A band of moonlight lay across the water's surface, riding the waves like a wide silk ribbon.

"How did you meet Scipio?" I asked as we proceeded down the beach.

"I met him in Spain from opposite sides of a battlefield. His tactics impressed me from the first, but he did something early in his time there that made me think he was something special."

"What was that?"

"When I first went to Spain, my cousin, Massiva, not yet fifteen years of age, begged to come with me. Against my better judgment, I brought him, but forbade him to take part in combat. I told him he should first learn the life of a warrior before putting his life on the line.

"I had a position as captain of a contingent of cavalry under the command of Hannibal's brother Hasdrubal. We engaged Scipio near Baecula. Scipio's strategy fooled us badly. We suffered a horrible defeat. Without my knowledge, Massiva had slipped out of camp with a horse and a sword to join the battle. He fell from his horse and was captured while the more fortunate of us made a hasty retreat. I didn't know that my cousin was missing until we made camp in the woods that night. When I went to seek him out, I was told he had been killed.

"A week later Massiva rode into camp on a Roman horse, wearing a new tunic, a gold broach, and a fine Spanish cloak. He told me that when Scipio learned that a young Numidian prince had been captured, he had him brought to his tent. On learning his name, Scipio asked him about me, complimenting my skill on the battlefield. At the end of the evening, he released Massiva because of his youth, then gave him a horse and a new tunic."

"Scipio is an interesting man, Masinissa. He's not your usual Roman. Like you and I, he has been introduced to Greek literature and science."

"I admire the man," said Masinissa with pride. "I feel honored to fight by his side. The way I feel tonight I'm certain I'll regain my kingdom."

We walked on for a short distance without saying anything more. Masinissa was the first to break the silence. "When you were here before, I spoke of a woman, Sophonisba."

"Yes, of course. Isn't that the same woman who has just married Syphax?"

Masinissa looked out at the sea. "Yes," he said with clear resentment. "And it only gives me more incentive to conquer Carthage and take back my kingdom. I would have preferred that she not have shared his wedding bed." Masinissa shook his head sadly in anguish of not being Sophonisba's first lover. "But I still intend to make her my queen." His anger spiked behind the words.

Another long spell of silence passed between us. "What about you, Timon? It may be that my heart is broken, but you had two loves." Masinissa grinned in the moonlight. "Is that three now?"

I laughed. "No, I narrowed it down to one since I last saw you. I chose the farm girl, Moira, if you remember her name. She's as beautiful as the Sicilian farmland where she lives. When the war is over, I will return to Sicily to marry her."

"What of the other woman, whose name was so lovely to pronounce?"

"Sem-pro-nia," I said, saying the syllables one by one, thinking of her alone in Rome. "Her situation is difficult. I'll continue to worry about her no matter how happy I am with Moira."

Masinissa nodded. "Then you are a better man than most, Timon. The men I know care more for the horses they've left behind than the women they've loved."

"Is that how you are?"

"Sophonisba might think so, but it's not true." Again the anger rose in his voice. "You watch. I will be faithful and she will be mine."

CHAPTER 68

The next week was spent moving the camp and our equipment to an elevated location about a mile southwest of Utica. During that time Scipio received a report that the Carthaginians had assembled four thousand cavalry inside the city of Salaeca, twenty-five miles inland, almost directly south of where we were. It seemed the Carthaginian strategy was to gather as many soldiers in the vicinity as possible, in preparation for the arrival of Syphax and his troops.

Scipio sent Masinissa to Salaeca for reconnaissance. I went with him and ten others from his contingent to further detail my map. We left early in the morning with me riding as hard as I could just to keep up with the Numidians. Our first twenty miles covered relatively flat land and we made good progress. As we neared Salaeca from the north, we had to slow our pace. The terrain became rockier and small ridges and hillocks rose up across the African plains like large, awkward animals that had surfaced from beneath the ground.

Our route led us through a narrow pass between two parallel ridges. As we exited from the defile, we spotted Salaeca. The rest of the way to the small fortress was flat and open. Any further advance would put us in plain sight from the battlements. I suggested we seek a position of higher elevation to get as wide a view of the area as possible. Masinissa and I left our horses with the other riders and climbed to the top of the east ridge.

I had promised Scipio that I would not show the spyglass to anyone else, but with the situation so perfect, I decided to give the Numidian prince a lesson in its use. Like all who first used the device, Masinissa didn't quite understand what he was seeing. I believe he thought he was looking at something inside the tubes, but as I directed him to look at different objects, he began to realize that the spyglass was not some kind of magic trick. I told him not to mention it to anyone, even Scipio, and that he could ask to use it whenever he was with me, as long as he was careful not to make a show of it.

I made a few sightings and sketched the topography as far as I could see. We didn't stay long and were soon on our way back to Utica. We arrived in camp at dusk and immediately met with Scipio, Lucius, and Cato to discuss what we had seen.

Masinissa and the other officers watched as I extended the detail of our existing map to include the region we had just scouted. Scipio commented in Latin and Greek as I proceeded with the work. Masinissa interjected his thoughts in Greek. Cato and Lucius used Latin. By the time I had completed my additions to the map, Scipio had devised a plan.

"This terrain gives us the perfect opportunity for an ambush," said Scipio pointing to the two ridges outside Salaeca. "We will leave tomorrow morning with the Twenty-third legion and two hundred of Masinissa's Numidians. We should be able to make it there by midafternoon the following day. We will position the infantry so that they are hidden at the far end of the pass." Everything he said, he said twice—in Greek and in Latin.

"Masinissa, you will take your two hundred men and ride directly up to the walls of Salaeca. Toss your javelins, shout insults, do whatever you can to taunt the soldiers inside, then ride away. If they don't immediately come after you, do it again—advance and retreat. I believe the officer in charge is Hannibal's second youngest brother Hanno. He spent some time in Spain with Hasdrubal. His reputation is nothing like that of his older brothers. He tends to be a bit impetuous. I want you to draw him out—even if it takes ten sorties."

This was what Hannibal had done so many times when I was with Marcellus. The Numidians on their quick and agile garrons would advance to the edge of our camp, toss their darts, then ride away, only to come back to do it again, always stirring up the soldiers and creating a lot of frustration in the camp.

"If Hanno takes our bait, Masinissa, he will gather his cavalry to chase you off. Once that happens, I want you to turn tail and head back to these two ridges. Lead your men and Hanno's right between them. When you reach the far end of the pass, where our troops are waiting, turn and confront Hanno and his riders. We will collapse on them from both sides. Cato, you'll be stationed on the left with half the men." He pointed to the map. "Lucius, you'll be on the right with the other half."

"What if we can't draw them out?" asked Masinissa.

"Keep at it until you do. Take greater chances. Incite them in any way you can. Insult their gods or their mothers."

"This seems like a cheap trick, General," said Cato. "Like something Hannibal might try. I don't believe it's the way Roman soldiers are meant to fight."

Scipio looked up from the map and glared at Cato. "I think we learned a long time ago, Quaestor, that we must fight Hannibal in the same manner he fights us—whether it's Roman or not. In my mind, only one thing is truly Roman in warfare—and that's victory. Any questions?"

"Our time would be better spent investing Utica, General." Cato's hackles seemed to rise every time he clashed with Scipio. "Isn't a secure base for the winter more important than anything we might gain in Salaeca?"

"No," snapped Scipio. "Anything else?"

Cato's red face darkened to violet, but he said nothing and stared at the ground.

"Good," said Scipio. "Inform your men. We leave at the first light tomorrow. We'll march at double time the first day so the second day is not so demanding. Bring plenty of water."

CHAPTER 69

I traveled to Salaeca with Scipio and the Twenty-third legion as part of my continuing effort to know and map North Africa. Troglius, whose tent unit I had lobbied to join, was also with us as part of the Twenty-third. When we reached the two ridges, perhaps two miles of open plain from Salaeca, I climbed the eastern ridge to observe. Lucius and Cato positioned their men behind the ridges. Masinissa led his Numidians through the pass and up to the walls of the fortress. Four times they rode up to the city gates to toss their darts and shout insults at the Carthaginians.

At first the soldiers inside resorted to shooting arrows at the marauding Numidians, but Masinissa only allowed his men to get close enough to be targeted, yet not so close as to be easily struck, before turning and riding away. Each time they advanced, more soldiers came to the walls until it seemed the entire city was standing along the battlements, shouting at the Numidian riders and using anything from small catapults to javelins to counter their sorties.

On the fifth advance, when Masinissa's men made their most daring approach to the walls, the main gate swung open and the entire four thousand horse cavalry burst forth in a wild charge with Hanno at the lead. The Carthaginians' long-striding war horses were faster on open ground than the smaller garrons, but the Numidians knew what they were doing. They zigzagged across the plain in small clusters, not clearly headed toward the pass until Hanno's men had nearly caught up with them. Then they closed ranks and made a quick zag between the two ridges.

Hanno's cavalry was right on Masinissa's tail when they reached the far end of the pass. Our men fell on Hanno from both sides. The numbers were considerably smaller, but the devastation was as complete as Hannibal's ambush on the shore of Lake Trasimene. More than half the Carthaginian force was killed in the initial assault, including Hanno. Another hundred or so were run down as they tried to escape.

Without Hanno, and the majority of the Carthaginian garrison dead or hiding in the hills, Salaeca's city council surrendered to Scipio as soon as we assembled outside the gates. Scipio remained in Salaeca three more days. During that time, he conferred gifts from the plunder upon those officers or legionnaires who had shown the most courage during the engagement. Masinissa received the most valuable gifts and the most praise for his effort. This was the first time he had fought for a Roman general, and it only enhanced his reputation for horsemanship on the battlefield.

The ambush was also Troglius' first action for Scipio, and his first since the flogging. Apparently he had recovered fully. His capacity with a gladius was not missed by Scipio nor his fellow legionnaires. He was another of the soldiers significantly rewarded for his actions in the ambush.

CHAPTER 70

Scipio left a small garrison in Salaeca, then led us through the countryside in a week-long campaign of devastation and plunder. We collected what grain and fruit we could carry, then destroyed the rest of the crops and any small villages we encountered, intent on filling the region with fear at the mere mention of Scipio's name much as Hannibal's name had in Italy.

The ships that had been sent to Sicily with the first load of booty returned to the camp outside Utica the same day we did. They were reloaded the following morning with the plunder we had just collected. I was part of the team of scribes that filled out the shipping orders. We set up a small, open tent on the beach with a table and some stools to facilitate the process. Late in afternoon, when we were nearly done, I noticed an unusually young legionnaire, one of the those who had been doing the loading, coming my way, and looking directly at me as he approached.

When the soldier got closer, I recognized him and stood up. "Rullo! What are you doing here?"

Rullo came up close to me and put his finger to his lips. He had grown to my height and filled out with maturing muscle since I had last seen him. A light dusting of blond hair ran along his jaw line. "When we're done with this work, Timon," he said, taking a quick look over his shoulder, "I must talk to you—in private."

"Of course," I said, wondering how this boy, barely sixteen, had managed to join the military. "Meet me outside the south gate to the camp just before the evening meal."

"I'll be there," he said and walked away to continue working.

I had always liked Rullo, and felt that my friend Marcus should have given more attention to his talented, though illegitimate, son. But that was not for me to worry about now. I was eager to talk to him and see why he was there.

I found him outside the south gate just as planned. We went down to the shore and sat on two large boulders partially buried in the sand.

"How did you get into the army, Rullo? You're at least a year short of seventeen?"

"Quintus Ennius," he said with the crash of waves in the background and the sun low and bright in the west.

"Ennius?"

"He set everything up so I could come here."

"I don't understand."

"Ennius knew he could trust me and that you would too. He also knew I had tried twice to enlist in the army and had been turned away. He got me on a ship in Ostia sailing for Syracuse. From there, I talked my way onto one of these transports as soon as I learned they were coming to Scipio's camp."

"I still don't get it."

"It's about your mother."

"What about her?"

"Ennius saw the woman Paculla frequenting the Community of Miracles. He began to follow her to see what she was up to."

I already knew Ennius felt the same way I did about Paculla Annia.

"He discovered she was looking for Carthaginian agents. They spend time in the community seeking information just like everyone else up there. Apparently she had something for sale."

"About my mother? That she was in Rome?"

Rullo nodded. "And Ennius wanted you to know."

"Is that all? Is my mother still at Marcus' farm?"

Rullo looked down at the wet sand. "No, she was kidnapped and her slave was found dead in the Tiber. That was more than a month ago."

"Lucretia? Dead. What about my mother?"

"Ennius believes she was taken to Hannibal. He didn't say why. Maybe you might know."

This was the worst possible news. I took a deep breath. "Let's just say I have a clue. What about Marcus and the other slaves at the farm—Edeco and Meda?"

"Marcus was sent to Etruria and has been there all summer. He doesn't know about your mother, and I've heard nothing about the other slaves."

"Anything else?"

He gave me cautious look.

"What?"

"Don't tell anyone who I am or my age. I want to be trained as a velite. I want to take part in the war."

"I'll keep your secret if you'll agree to one thing."

Rullo frowned at me.

"I have a friend I want you to meet."

"Fine."

Though my head swam with worry about my mother, I took Rullo to my tent. Troglius was there and I introduced him to Rullo. I told Troglius to keep an eye on Rullo and to make sure he didn't get taken advantage of or killed.

Had it been any other soldier, Rullo would have been insulted. But he sensed something special in Troglius right away, and, of course, Troglius welcomed the chance to do me a favor after what I had done for him.

I arranged for Rullo to be placed in our tent unit, and from that day on, Troglius and Rullo rapidly became friends and were rarely far apart. I, on the other hand, was in a state of utter despair. My mother, it seemed, was either dead or back in Hannibal's camp playing her lyre in shackles. And it all went back to Paculla. Portia must have told her I called her a charlatan and fake, and then she took the information about my mother to the Carthaginians to get even. How she knew Hannibal would be interested, I hadn't the slightest idea, but it was too late now to do anything about it. I just wished I had kept my thoughts about Paculla to myself.

CHAPTER 71

Scipio now focused all his effort on the siege of Utica. It was a well-defended city, and for forty days he tried its walls by land and by sea with no success. By this time, Hasdrubal, who had been doing everything he could to raise troops, had assembled twenty thousand infantry and three thousand cavalry outside Carthage. Syphax had raised another forty thousand foot and ten thousand horse. The two armies joined forces south of Carthage, then marched north to Utica, setting up separate camps two miles from ours.

With this huge enemy force nearby, Scipio could not risk continuing his siege of Utica, and even though his men were vastly better trained than the mass of those collected by either Hasdrubal or Syphax, he decided to pull back to a more secure location to settle in for the winter. The new camp was situated at the end of a promontory that stretched out into the sea not far from Utica. Shaped like a head on a neck, the promontory was wide where we built our camp, but narrow where it met the mainland. Only one rampart across the neck of the promontory was needed to protect us from attack by land. We beached our ships along shoreline for addition protection.

Although the winters were not nearly as cold in Africa as they were in Italy, the war still came to a halt. The two opposing armies made no attempt to engage in combat, and the months grew long with inactivity. I thought often of my mother, fully aware that there was no way of knowing how Hannibal might treat her. Assuming he knew she had been acting as a spy, he was as likely to execute her as keep her in chains. Thinking about all the possibilities made me sick with worry, and I wondered if my leaving Rome had been a terrible mistake. All I could hope for now was that Scipio's strategy would work. That his presence in Africa would bring Hannibal back to Carthage and that my mother would be with him. Then Scipio would have to do what no other Roman general had done, defeat Hannibal. Only then might I see my mother again.

CHAPTER 72

Scipio became obsessed with the mapping of North Africa. Knowing he would be fighting armies native to the region, he was convinced that thorough knowledge of the ground was as essential to his success as the training of his men. Compared to what the other Roman generals were doing, this was advanced military thinking. During the winter, when little beyond an occasional skirmish heated the blood, Scipio would send me out with Masinissa and a squadron of his cavalry to continue the work of detailing the map.

On one of these excursions, Masinissa confided in me while we sat around the campfire after the evening meal.

"If the reports Scipio has received are accurate, Syphax has remained with his army outside Utica. I have heard that he had Sophonisba delivered to Carthage by ship so that he can leave camp on occasion to visit her."

"That doesn't sound so surprising."

"She's staying at her father's house in the city."

We were camped on a hill well south of Carthage. The lights of the city were visible at night. Masinissa stared off in that direction, then turned to me. "My father knew Hannibal's father. Their friendship allowed me to spend several years in Carthage as a youth. I know the city inside and out. I know where Hasdrubal's home is located." He looked off again in the direction of Carthage. "I plan to go there."

"That could be awfully dangerous."

He grinned showing his teeth. "And I want you to go with me."

"How would we get into the city?"

"I know ways."

I hesitated, then asked, "When are you thinking of going?"

His eyes flashed in the firelight. "Tonight. I want to use your spyglass."

"Are you sure? Tonight?"

"Are you willing?"

I stared into the fire, watching the flames lick at unburned chunks of wood. It seemed like a crazy idea, but I had grown very fond of Masinissa. I spent more time with him than either Troglius or Rullo. I faced him, still uncertain.

Masinissa left me no choice. "We should go now before it gets any later." He stood. "I will tell my men that we will be back before daylight."

We left camp almost immediately and rode as fast as the light of a full moon allowed. It was at least ten miles. The ground was mostly level and we made good time.

Carthage was situated at the end of a bulb-shaped isthmus, protected on the north by a lagoon, on the east by the ocean, and on the south by the Lake of Tunis. Surrounded by twenty miles of walls and precipitous cliffs, the only access to the city by land was from the west, where the isthmus narrowed to three miles across and met the African mainland. Three barriers—a ditch sixty feet wide, an earth and timber rampart, and a stone wall, forty feet tall and thirty feet thick—stretched across the Isthmus and controlled entry to the city. The three-story wall also contained barracks for twenty thousand soldiers and stables for four thousand horses and three hundred elephants. Carthage was considered impenetrable, and yet Masinissa's plan involved surmounting all three of these barriers.

We hid the horses in a grove of almond trees at the base of the isthmus. As we approached the first of the three barriers—the ditch—we could see the silhouettes of soldiers patrolling the battlements of the three-story wall up ahead. Our task seemed impossible.

"Masinissa, how will we ever get pass these ramparts?"

"Follow me. The ditch has no guards. We can climb through it. It's easier for two people than an entire army."

He was right. We stumbled down into the ditch, then crawled up the far side. The next barrier was a steep hill of compacted dirt, reinforced with timbers.

"These earthworks are patrolled," whispered Masinissa when we got close. "But the guards are few. We can slip by them if we're careful."

Again he was right. We watched the patrols long enough to predict their coming and going, then at the proper moment, we scurried up the rampart. Masinissa with surprising ease, me with considerable difficulty.

Next was the forty-foot stone wall. The guards were more numerous and we could not possibly climb a vertical wall. "What's the secret here?" I asked

"We'll go down to the edge of the lagoon, where the wall enters the water." He pointed to the north. "Then we'll wade through the water to a small fault in the wall that I learned about as a child. Again, an army can't do this, but we can."

Masinissa led us through the thick reeds that grew along the shore of the lagoon. We trudged out into the water up to our waists and followed the wall for several hundred feet to a shadowy crevice in the stonework. Masinissa squeezed into the crevice with me behind. It was completely dark and we had to feel our way through what was essentially a crack all the way through the wall.

Soaking wet, our legs coated with mud up to the shins, we squeezed out of the crevice into Malqua, Carthage's industrial area, where the fishermen lived and the mackerel they caught were dried for shipping and the murex they gathered were made into purple dye. Soon we came to another stone wall, not so large as the first, but also impossible to scale.

"Now what?"

"This wall only surrounds Byrsa, the plateau in the center of the city. It's the sacred part of Carthage and is deliberately separated from the rest of the city. We don't need to get in there. If we follow the wall this way," he pointed, "it will take us where we want to go."

Again Masinissa was right. He led me north along the base of the wall. The path was uneven, clearly rarely traveled, and at times very steep, but it allowed us to bypass Brysa and enter the city proper. It was late. The moon stood high in the sky. Only dogs and drunks were on the streets. We wound through a labyrinth of narrow streets and alleys, between five and six story tenement housing, steadily making our way north to Megara, where the most wealthy Carthaginians had been building new homes.

Masinissa pointed through a stand of date palms to the outline of a three-story home. It sat on the edge of a cliff, overhanging the lagoon. A six-foot wall enclosed the garden that surrounded it. "That's Hasdrubal's house. I'm sure it's guarded better than the ramparts were."

I handed him the spyglass. He scanned the house without seeing sign of anyone. We slipped through the trees to where the garden wall met the cliff. On the way, we spotted two guards patrolling the outside perimeter of the wall, but there was no sign that anyone was awake inside the building.

We crept to the very edge of the cliff and a one hundred-foot drop to the water. Masinissa tried the spyglass again. A stone balcony extended from the north side of the home and hung out over the lagoon. With only an oblique angle on this side of the house, Masinissa could just barely see that one of the windows off the balcony was lit from inside. He turned to me and whispered, "Listen."

I heard a woman's voice softly chanting in the Punic language, which I recognized but didn't know.

"I'm guessing that's Sophonisba," Masinissa whispered. "She must be in the lighted room off the balcony." Masinissa was so excited his hands shook. He gave me a quick glance. "Take hold of my hand with both of yours."

I gripped his hand.

"Set your feet and hold on tight." With me as a counterweight, he leaned out over the cliff as far as he could, hoping to get a better angle on the window. Stretched out nearly perpendicular to the cliff, he sighted through the spyglass using only one hand to focus—no easy task. After a moment, he lowered the spyglass and whispered, "She's sitting at her dressing table with her back to the window." He lifted the spyglass for one more look, then signaled for me to pull him in.

"You stay here. I'm going up there."

"Onto the balcony? How?"

His eyes gleamed in the moonlight. "Watch me."

"Are you sure?" I asked, but he was already gone.

Masinissa dropped down below the edge of the cliff, then climbed like a spider sideways along the footings of the house. I lost sight of him in the shadows, then saw him reappear on the ground below the balcony. I used the spyglass to watch him.

With remarkable dexterity, he scaled the side of the house, digging his fingers into the mortar and pinching his toes into the creases between the rough stones, steadily moving upward. After what seemed hours, I saw his hand reach the top of the balcony wall. He pulled himself up just enough to get his head above the edge, then swung his right leg over the balustrade. Using his leg as a lever, he rolled himself over the railing onto the balcony. When he stood up, someone inside the house screamed, then screamed again. A guard shouted. Several men came crashing through the garden, calling to each other. Light appeared in two windows, then in two more.

Masinissa hopped up onto the balustrade, glanced down at the water below, then took a long leap to the top of the garden wall, where he teetered, dangerously close to falling, before catching his balance and dropping down to the ground beside me. He grabbed me by the hand and pulled me into a run. I took one last look over my shoulder as we raced away. A young woman stood at the edge of the balcony staring into the darkness. Then we were dodging through the date palms, running as fast as we could.

Fortunately the guards had gone into the house instead of out beyond the garden wall. We were well ahead of them by the time we heard them come out of the house, calling instructions to each other.

We retraced our path out of Megara and into the dark streets of Carthage, winding out way along the edge of Byrsa and down to the crease in the wall. We squeezed through the narrow crack and slipped into the lagoon. We waded through the mud and reeds and water to the west end of the wall, scaled the dirt rampart, and climbed into and out of the sixty-foot ditch. Not until we were in the almond grove untying our horses did we slow down enough to catch our breaths.

Masinissa called to me excitedly as we rode away. "She saw me through the mirror. Only for the briefest instant did our eyes meet, but I now know for certain that someday she will be mine!"

CHAPTER 73

Sophonisba had recited a prayer to Tanit, then had gotten up from her knees to sit at her dressing table. A single, white candle in the center of the table provided the only light. Felicia, who Sophonisba hadn't seen since her marriage, lay stretched out on the floor beside her. Suddenly the young cheetah growled, deep and low. Sophonisba glanced at her cat. Felicia was now sitting up, keenly alert, her small spotted ears upright and turning this way and that, clearly having heard something. Sophonisba stood up to see what it was and happened to glance in the mirror. Masinissa was staring at her in the reflection.

In the adjacent slaves' quarters, Nycea had also heard a noise on the balcony. Zanthia and Gaia, in beds on either side of her, were asleep. She slid from her bed and looked out the window just as Masinissa stood up to peer into Sophonisba's room. Nycea immediately screamed, waking the entire household and alerting the guards. Then she ran out into the hall to scream again.

Zanthia leapt from her bed and went directly to Sophonisba's bedroom through the connecting door. The room was empty and the doors to the balcony were open. Zanthia found Sophonisba on the balcony staring off into the darkness with Felicia at her side. She appeared to be in a state of shock, her eyes were full like the moon and she was shaking.

"Are you all right, Sophie? What did you see?"

Sophonisba didn't answer. She floated, as in a trance, back into the bedroom and stood before her mirror. Felicia remained out on the balcony, anxiously pacing back and forth.

Zanthia came up from behind Sophonisba and placed her hands on her shoulders. "What is it, my lady?"

Sophonisba turned to face her most trusted confidant.

At this same moment, Nycea returned to her quarters looking for Zanthia. First she saw Gaia sitting up in bed, then that the door to

Sophonisba's room was open. She heard Zanthia's voice, and thinking she would go in, walked over to doorway, then suddenly stopped to listen rather than enter.

"I saw a man on the balcony," gasped Sophonisba as though waking from a dream.

"A thief?"

"No." Sophonisba put a finger to her lips. "You can't say a word."

"Of course, my lady."

"It was Masinissa, but he was gone by the time I reached the balcony."

Zanthia understood immediately—as did Nycea.

The clank of armed men sounded in the hallway. There was a heavy knock on the door and it opened. Hasdrubal entered the room, leaving four guards and his slave Vangue in the hallway behind him.

"What's going on? Who screamed?"

Sophonisba quickly gathered herself. "Everything's fine, Father. I believe it was Nycea who screamed. I went out on the balcony, but I didn't see anything."

"And you, Zanthia. Did you see anything?"

"No, sir. I came into Sophonisba's room after Nycea screamed."

On hearing this, Nycea returned to her bed. Moments later, Hasdrubal entered her bedroom without knocking. Vangue stood outside the door. Gaia and Nycea leapt from their beds.

"Who screamed?" demanded Hasdrubal.

"I did," said Nycea, just above a whisper. "I saw a man on the balcony off Sophonisba's room."

"Who was it?"

Nycea lied. "I don't know."

Hasdrubal exploded with a string of curses to the gods, then brusquely pushed past Vangue and rushed out of the house to talk to the guards who were searching the grounds.

Vangue came into the slaves' quarters and glared at the two women. He moved up close to Nycea and grabbed her roughly by the arm. "You lied to Hasdrubal. I can tell." He stuck his face into hers. "Who was it?"

"I—I—I'm not sure."

Vangue took hold of her right breast, covered only by a light sleeping gown, and squeezed. "Who did you see?"

Gaia stood back as tears began to run from Nycea's eyes.

Vangue twisted her breast until she wet herself. He called her a filthy pig, then let go of her. Nycea sank to the floor in pain, holding her breast and sobbing.

"Do I need a flail?" snarled Vangue.

"No. No. It was Masinissa, the Numidian prince. I overheard Sophonisba say that to Zanthia."

Vangue grinned ugly. "Don't say a word to anyone." He shot a hot glance at Gaia. "Either of you. We might be able to use this information to the advantage of all of us."

CHAPTER 74

Meanwhile Scipio had not completely given up on Syphax as an ally. In the days after Masinissa's clandestine trip into Carthage, Scipio sent Marcus Ralla, a recent addition to his staff, to the Numidian camp to ask the king if he would meet with him. Syphax accepted the offer and suggested a neutral site between the two camps. A tent was set up for the meeting. Both men came with security guards, but met alone, except for me to take notes. The only furnishings were a rug, two chairs, a table, and two oil lamps on bronze stands. Scipio wore a toga. Syphax was in his royal robes. A tray of fresh fruit, a loaf of bread, and an amphora of wine sat on the table between them.

Syphax immediately apologized for his change of heart regarding the alliance they had agreed to in Siga. "After thinking hard about your request, General—that I was required to stay out of the war—I realized that was impossible. Knowing I would eventually be drawn into the conflict in some manner, my heart told me that I must fight on the side of Africa. Carthage is not Numidian, but its people have been a part of my tribe's history for ten generations. Many of our families have intermarried, and when Hasdrubal offered his daughter's hand in marriage to me, I understood that my loyalty must be to Africa. I hope you have been able to understand this."

Scipio shook his head and frowned. "I wish that instead of desiring the charms of a woman, you had chosen to honor your word to another man. That's the true measure of a man's character, when his word is stronger than the transient pleasures of the bed. It's sad to me that I must say this to any man, much less one of royal blood. Now you and I, who once dined together as friends, must be enemies. And I don't want that."

"Nor I," replied the king, clearly stung by Scipio's words.

"What might it take for you to reconsider? You must know that Carthage will never win the war, and that in the end, their defeat will have a serious impact on the security of your kingdom."

Syphax appeared to be under great personal stress. I believe he truly admired Scipio, wanted him as a friend, and even understood that he was a superior general who would be difficult to defeat. And yet the temptation to join the Roman cause was countered by the allure of Sophonisba. He couldn't imagine giving her up for anything. Instead of answering Scipio, he poured himself a cup of wine and took a sip.

Scipio seemed to read his mind. "You know, Syphax." He filled a cup for himself. "A man's lust for a woman eventually dies off, but his honor is eternal—even engraved on his tomb. I have heard of the beauty of Hasdrubal's daughter, and I can imagine how she might enchant a younger man, but you have more than forty years. I find it hard to believe that you consider her a more valuable asset than the friendship of Rome, especially when you'll be bedding some other woman before this year is out." He lifted his cup to the king. "Can we raise a drink to Rome and put your change of heart behind us? Or must I, in the days to come, seek you out on the battlefield to repay you for going against your word, a reversal that I had been warned about in the Roman Senate. They said any deal with a barbarian," he let the word hang in the air, "was asking for trouble. But I put my reputation on the line, and said, oh, no, Syphax can be trusted."

Syphax hung his head.

"No chance of a change, Syphax? Are we wasting our time? Should you and I be preparing for battle, not treaties?"

Syphax lifted his head and let out a great sigh. "Scipio, you are a man who is very hard to deny, but maybe there's middle ground. Maybe this talk of an alliance with me should be one of peace between Rome and Carthage?"

"How's that?"

"What if I act as a mediator between you and Carthage? It's the same thing I offered when you and Hasdrubal were at my dinner table. Maybe I can broker an agreement. Wouldn't peace be better for all involved—better than war? That's what I want. That's what's best for Africa, my people, and my kingdom."

Scipio raised his fist to his lips, then spoke. "I feel certain of victory, Syphax. Carthage has no future. The only agreement I would consider is one that names Rome as the victor."

Syphax was no match for Scipio's confidence. He took another sip from this cup. "If the Carthaginians agree to surrender, and order Hannibal and his brother Mago back to Carthage, would that be enough incentive for you to take your army back to Rome?"

"That makes a fair starting place, Syphax," answered Scipio. "But I believe Carthage must also pay an indemnity or an annual tribute. Prisoners on both sides must be released, and certain limitations must be placed on the size of the Carthaginian military."

"I'm in no position to make those kinds of concessions for Carthage. Hasdrubal and the Carthaginian elders must be consulted. Give me a chance to talk with them and perhaps we might come up with something."

"Very well. Tell the Carthaginians that we have opened a discussion for terms of peace. Explain my position. See how they react. Then we can talk again."

CHAPTER 75

Syphax traveled to Carthage with a large armed guard the day after his meeting with Scipio. He arrived late in the day and stayed at Hasdrubal's home in Megara as a guest. Although Sophonisba already occupied three rooms on the second floor, five more were given to Syphax and his accompanying slaves. Intoxicated by thoughts of spending the evening with his wife, Syphax spoke only briefly with his host about the potential peace agreement, then excused himself immediately after the evening meal.

Syphax went directly to his suite of rooms and ordered the first chambermaid he saw to have Sophonisba, whom he had yet to see, come to his bedroom. He pulled off his clothing and lay on the bed naked, fully aroused just thinking about his wife. But she didn't come to him right away or for a long time afterward. The king grew impatient. He sat up in the bed and screamed for Sophonisba. When this got no response, he put on his robe and stormed out of the room. Dealing with Scipio had pushed him to his limits, he wanted the reason for all this trouble in his arms—now!

Syphax entered the women's chambers without announcing himself. He was all set to vent his anger until he saw Sophonisba. She stood in the center of the room in a sheer white gown that was little more than invisible. Nycea stood behind her brushing the queen's hair. Zanthia was across the room sorting through ribbons to give to Gaia, standing beside her. Felicia lay on the floor, her chin on her front paws. She lifted her head to appraise this man she had never met, then hissed and growled showing her teeth.

"Quiet, Felicia," commanded Sophonisba, then she turned to Syphax. "I'll be right with you, my king. Please have patience with your queen. I wanted to look my best for you." Although she smiled, she had no desire to see her husband at all.

His anger dispelled, Syphax returned to the bedroom and paced anxiously in anticipation of Sophonisba's arrival. After another long period of waiting, just as he was about to storm from the room for a second time, the door swung open. Sophonisba entered without a word, swayed across the room, and made herself available to him.

When Syphax awakened in the morning, Sophonisba had already left the bed. His immediate reaction was again anger, then he reflected on the night that had passed. They had made love more than once, but Sophonisba had not displayed her usual passion. Instead of thinking something was wrong with her, he wondered if something had been lacking in him. He chose not to summon her back to the bedroom and ordered his slave to bring him something to eat.

Later in the day, Syphax sought out Hasdrubal, and with no mention of Sophonisba, the two men spent the afternoon discussing the possibility of a peace agreement with Rome. Syphax pushed hard for a treaty, saying it was in the best interest of all of Africa, but Hasdrubal balked at Scipio's desire to dictate the terms as victor of the war. He told Syphax he would discuss the subject with the Council of Elders and get back to him with the Council's response.

That night, when Sophonisba joined Syphax in bed, after another long wait, the king made a determined effort to bring greater pleasure to his wife, performing acts in which he might not otherwise engage. But the result was the same, and her physical indifference again caused doubts in the Numidian king.

Perplexed, and suffering from a lover's woes, Syphax spent the next morning pacing from one to room to another not knowing what to do, now more obsessed with Sophonisba's attention than he had been before.

Vangue did not miss Syphax's distress. He sought out Nycea and pulled her aside that afternoon. "Nycea, how would you like to be Sophonisba's handmaiden?"

Nycea feared Vangue and cowered at his words. "What do you mean?"

"I want you to tell Syphax about last week's intruder. I'll take you to him. Tell him all you know. It will result in something good for both of us."

Nycea was a pretty young woman in her own right. Her aspirations were for something more than being a maid. Syphax was known to tire of his wives. She, like Scipio, didn't believe his infatuation with Sophonisba would last. Nycea hoped that the king might find her a suitable replacement when he grew bored with the high strung queen. She looked around as though afraid someone else might be listening, then said, "Take me to Syphax."

Vangue went to Syphax on his own first. He told him that there had been an intruder during the previous week and that Hasdrubal had sought to hide it from him. He knew little of it personally, but one of Sophonisba's maids had seen the intruder. He thought Syphax should talk to her. Syphax found this information highly unsettling and immediately wanted to know more, wondering if this could be connected in any way to Sophonisba's recent distance.

Vangue brought Nycea to Syphax's room. She fell to her knees at his feet.

"Tell me what you know about the intruder," demanded the king.

Nycea glanced at Vangue, then told her story. "A man climbed onto the balcony outside Sophonisba's room. I saw him and screamed. The guards didn't catch the man, but later on, I overhead a conversation between Sophonisba and her handmaiden Zanthia. Sophonisba confided that she had seen the man and had recognized him."

Syphax tilted his head. "Go on."

"I heard her tell Zanthia it was Masinissa."

Syphax's face darkened with rage. "What does she know of this man?"

"They met once, well more than a year ago. Her handmaiden spoke highly of him, and Sophonisba took it to heart. She has longed to know the man better ever since."

"But there's nothing more than that? A longing?"

"Not as far as I know, Your Majesty."

"And when Sophonisba confided in her handmaiden, did the maid continue with her praise of the man?"

"I believe she did," lied Nycea. "Zanthia has no respect for you or your marriage to Sophonisba."

"And why do you tell me this? Such a confidence might cost you your position."

"My high regard for you, Your Majesty. I am Numidian. My respect for you is greater than my loyalty to the queen."

Syphax was more disturbed by this news than he wanted to show. He turned away from Nycea and went to the room's window to stare at the sky and collect his thoughts. After a moment, he faced her. "Don't mention the conversation we've just had to anyone." He moved up close to her and touched her cheek with his hand. "It would be valuable to me to have ears in the queen's chambers. Very valuable. What's your name?"

"Nycea, Your Majesty."

Syphax smiled. "I will be here one more night, Nycea. Let's talk again before I leave."

After Nycea had left the room, Syphax turned to Vangue. "The same to you, slave. Keep this quiet, and for your trouble I will buy your freedom from Hasdrubal and make you my personal attendant."

Syphax now appraised his time with Sophonisba from a completely different perspective. Another man had tried to intrude upon him. His conflict was not with Sophonisba. She was but a woman. Besides he still found tremendous pleasure in bedding a woman all men would want, yet whose intimacy only he had known. His fight was with the intruder, Masinissa, and there was only one possible outcome. Syphax promised himself that he would kill Masinissa with his own hands. Should the war continue, it would be on the battlefield. Should there be peace, it would be anywhere he could find him. And once the interloper was dead and gone—for good this time, he, the King of Numidia, would certainly be able to rekindle the passion in Sophonisba that made her such a treasure.

Syphax returned to his camp the following day with permission from the Council of Elders to continue talks with Scipio. Before leaving, he had Hasdrubal arrange for a squadron of Carthaginian warships to take Sophonisba back to Siga. Hasdrubal suspected that Syphax had learned about the intruder from Sophonisba, but he didn't ask, and Syphax offered no explanation for sending his wife away. Neither did he say anything about the brooding hatred he now felt for Masinissa.

CHAPTER 76

Two days later, Scipio received word from Syphax that he was ready to talk again. Scipio sent Marcus Ralla with an escort of four soldiers to Syphax's camp the following morning. I was in headquarters when Ralla returned that afternoon. Scipio debriefed him immediately. Lucius was also present.

"Did Syphax have the Carthaginian's response to my terms for peace?" I couldn't believe Scipio really expected or even wanted them to surrender. He was more interested in drawing Hannibal back to Africa and defeating him on the battlefield than immediate peace. He wanted glory, not surrender.

"They are quite willing to call both Hannibal and his brother back to Africa," said Ralla. "And they offered to make a one time indemnity payment for the cost of the war, instead of an annual tribute. But they resisted any effort to limit the size of their military."

Scipio looked at his brother. "What do you think?"

"I'm surprised. They're actually admitting that they have lost the war."

"But it's not enough," replied Scipio. "I want a full capitulation. The military must be restricted. And I want an annual tribute, not a single payment. It keeps them under our thumb." Scipio turned to Ralla. "Is it worth going back to Syphax simply to deny their counter offer?"

"We can learn how much they really want peace."

Scipio nodded, seemingly uninterested. "Anything else, Tribune? Could you make any appraisal of their troops?"

"Both camps seemed quite primitive. The Carthaginians have built their make-shift shelters with wood and woven reeds instead of using leather or canvas. The Numidian camp isn't much different. All they have are little huts of thatch in the shape of beehives."

"It seems like that puts them at risk for fire," said Lucius.

Scipio shook his head at his enemies' ineptitude, then seemed to pause in his thinking. "Maybe you should go back again, Tribune. I'd like to know more about their camps and their numbers. Take two of your best centurions. Have them dress as slaves. Have them snoop around a bit."

"Should I repeat the initial offer?"

"No," said Scipio, clearly turning things over in his head. "Suggest that we are flexible on the indemnity and the way that it's paid. Hold tight on limiting the military, but be willing to take a counter offer. Draw the process out a few more meetings and learn what you can. Who knows what we might do if these peace talks stall."

After Ralla was dismissed, Lucius addressed Scipio. "If the peace talks stall, *who knows*? What are you thinking?"

Scipio leveled his eyes at his brother, a brother he was very close to. "I have an idea, Lucius. Let's see what more we learn about their camps, then we can talk about it."

During this period of negotiation, I continued to work on the maps, but for the most part, things were slow and most of my thoughts were about my mother.

Late one afternoon, I returned to my tent unit to help with the preparation of the evening meal. Troglius, Rullo, and two other tent mates were playing dice in the dirt out front of the tent. The dice belonged to Rullo, and as I later discovered, he had been organizing these dice games once or twice a week. To the chagrin of the older soldiers, the boy had shown a knack for winning.

Rullo noticed me as soon as I walked up to the little circle he had drawn in the dirt. "Timon, do you have a few spare coins to lose?"

The others looked up at me through the eyes of losers, finding nothing funny in Rullo's confidence.

I fished a few asses from the pocket of my tunic and showed them to Rullo. "This enough to get into your game?"

"We turn away no one with money. Sit down and join us." The sixteen-year-old shook the dice in his fist and dared a little grin.

I knelt down at the edge of the circle between Troglius and another soldier, Aurelius, then piled my little stack of coins on the ground in front of me. "What's the game?"

"Craps. Two dice. Camp rules. If the shooter's first throw is a seven or an eleven, it's an automatic winner. If the first throw is double sixes or snake-eyes, it's an automatic loser. If the first throw is some other result, the shooter must match that throw before throwing a seven to win—otherwise he loses. The shooter must bet to win, but the others can bet either way on his throw."

"Good enough. Give me a chance with those dice."

Rullo, who seemed to be in far more control of the game than was healthy, reached across the circle and dropped the two crude cubes in my hand.

When I looked at them, Rullo said, "I made them myself."

I turned to my left. "Are they fair, Troglius?"

Troglius looked at me with one eye while the other diverted to Rullo, who didn't seem too happy with my question. Troglius shrugged.

"What do you say, Aurelius?"

"Not to me," said the soldier, a veteran, maybe thirty-five years old, with a wide, severely pock-marked face.

"Then let's see what they hold for me." I pushed an as into the circle. Rullo, acting as the bank, matched it. The others waited for the outcome of my first roll. I shook the dice in my hand and tossed them into the center of the circle. They bounced and jumped across the dirt, stopping with a five and a three uppermost. I would have to roll an eight before I rolled a seven to win.

Troglius put down two asses on my winning. Aurelius and the other man went the other way, betting against me. I shook the dice and threw them into the circle, a four and a one. No winner, no loser. I rolled again. A five and a four. Again no winner, no loser. The next roll was a five and a two. Troglius and I lost our bets, the others won. I also lost the roll.

I stayed around long enough to lose six asses, then dropped out of the game. Troglius had already lost all his money. He left the circle at the same time I did and got out his whetstone to sharpen his gladius—something he did all the time. I sat down beside him. Neither of us said anything. Had I sat there a full week, Troglius might never have said a word. Troglius was simply not given to talk. Some imagined him dumb because of this, but I had known him long enough to know that wasn't true.

I broke the silence. "How's Rullo doing with military life?"

Troglius continued to strop his gladius, which he kept as sharp as an eagle's eye. "Better than most."

"What do you mean?"

"You saw him with the dice just now. He doesn't need anyone watching over him. He's won everyone's money in our unit and the one next to ours."

I laughed. "Yes, I guess he doesn't need much help here in camp, but on the battlefield he'll be tested in other ways."

Troglius stopped stropping and aimed his right eye at me. "I'm teaching him to use a gladius." He lifted his and inspected its blade. "He's good. And he is stronger than you might think."

I nodded. "He's Marcus Claudius' son by a slave—an Insubrian. You can see it in his hair color and his size. He's already taller than his father."

Troglius tilted his huge head and turned his left eye in my direction. I had learned that he used each eye for specific types of responses.

"That's right," I said. "I expect he might have the temperament of a soldier. Don't tell anyone I told you this. I'm not even sure if Rullo knows."

Troglius looked over his shoulder at Rullo, then leaned in close to me. "What's more astounding is he's not yet seventeen."

"He told you that?"

"And not to tell anyone else."

I laughed. "But you just told me."

He swung the other eye at me. "Telling you is not the same as telling anyone."

"Does that mean I'm a nobody?"

Both of his eyes focused on me. "It means telling you is the same as telling myself."

CHAPTER 77

Sophonisba was one week into the two-week voyage from Carthage to Siga. She and her attendants occupied the captain's quarters of a large Carthaginian warship. Four more ships served as their escort. The small fleet traveled only during daylight and never when the seas were rough. The ships beached on the shore each night and embarked again when the sun came up.

The captain's quarters were luxurious even by a queen's standards, but Sophonisba, who was bringing Felicia to Siga to buoy her spirits, could not have been unhappier. Seeing Masinissa had disturbed her badly. She had succeeded in pushing his memory out of her mind during the early months of her marriage because their one encounter only made him a fantasy, nothing more. But since seeing Masinissa on her balcony, and knowing that he had risked his life to be there, she could not get him out of her mind. When Syphax had come to the house in Megara, she struggled to give herself to the man at all. She even thought that was why Syphax had sent her away so suddenly. She had no idea that Nycea had revealed her secret to the king.

The weather was so mild during the eighth day of the voyage, the captain decided to continue westward after the sun had gone down. Once before, on very calm seas, he had elected to extend the day at sea. This evening was no different. With the sun down and only the slightest breeze, standing on the deck was more pleasant than at any other time during the voyage. Sophonisba, escorted by Nycea, Gaia, Zanthia, and two Carthaginian guards, climbed to the bow to escape the melancholia that had overtaken her in the captain's quarters.

A waning moon hung in the night sky to the east. The stars, never more glorious than at sea, turned the heavens into a luminous mist that sparkled on the sea like a rolling carpet of diamonds. Sophonisba filled her lungs with the sea air and tried to lift herself from the shadow of her marriage. She stared down at the sea, watching the prow of the ship cut through the water spooling with phosphorescent sea creatures. She forced the thoughts of Masinissa from her head and reminded herself why she had married and how she must comport herself. The marriage was politics. Her body and mind must be focused on the security of Carthage and her people, and if that meant she must regain her passion in the king's bed, she would.

Desiring some time alone, Sophonisba went aft to her cabin with the guards, allowing her three slaves more time to enjoy the beautiful evening on the bow. Gaia and Nycea barged into the captain's quarters a short time later, hysterical and babbling over top of each other.

"What's happened? One at a time. Where's Zanthia?"

Nycea, older than Gaia by two years, blurted it out as Gaia cried. "Zanthia fell overboard!"

Sophonisba gasped, then bolted from the cabin to the deck. Her two slaves and the two guards outside the cabin raced after her. When they caught up with her, she was at the stern of the ship, tears running from her eyes, staring into the black sea looking for any sign of her closest friend. She screamed at the guards to get the captain. When the captain appeared, Sophonisba demanded he turn the ship around to look for her handmaiden. The captain fought her request briefly, saying the woman was only a slave. Sophonisba erupted into greater fury and threatened to have him stripped of his command.

Unable to deny the orders of a queen whose husband meant so much to the Carthaginian war effort, the captain ordered the ships to reverse direction. With Sophonisba darting from one side of the ship to the other looking for Zanthia, they plied the waters deep into the night, never finding any sign of her.

When the ships finally beached for the night, Sophonisba collapsed on her bed in tears, beside herself with grief. How could she ever tolerate life with Syphax without her beloved Zanthia. The young queen dropped deeper into the depression that was her political task to disguise.

CHAPTER 78

The meetings between Syphax and Marcus Ralla advanced through two more rounds of discussion. With each exchange, the two sides appeared to get closer to a settlement. This greatly pleased Syphax. He wanted no part of war in Africa. He had already doubled the size of his kingdom and had only two other immediate desires—to kill Masinissa and to spend more time in his palace with Sophonisba.

Scipio, for his part, continued to make preparations to besiege Utica. "Just in case the talks should stall," he told his staff. He had five thousand men in the hills overlooking the city, thirty warships barricading its harbor, and a moat dug across the front of the city fortifying a position outside the city gates. All of this was part of an elaborate deception. Although he had told no one else, Scipio had no intention of besieging Utica should the talks fail. He had something much more incendiary in mind than a siege.

Shortly after the ides of March, Scipio received his orders from Rome. The consuls for the three hundred and sixth year of the Roman Republic, and the sixteenth of the war, were Servilius Caepio and Servilius Geminus. Little had changed in the last year. Caepio was sent to Bruttium to replace Publius Livinius and continue putting pressure on Hannibal. Geminus was sent to Etruria to prevent Mago from going south and joining his brother. Scipio, with renewed support in the Senate, was given the province of Africa for another year. It was exactly what he wanted, and upon learning this, he sent Marcus Ralla to Syphax's camp with orders not to return until a settlement was agreed upon.

When Ralla delivered this message, Syphax believed that a deal was close at hand and that Scipio wanted peace as much as he did. After two full days of discussion with Ralla, Syphax invited Hasdrubal to join the discussion, and an agreement was reached that, it appeared, both sides could accept. Syphax was elated. Ralla returned to the Roman camp thinking his work was done and made his report to Scipio. Scipio told Ralla that he needed the Senate's approval to sign the documents. Three weeks later, Scipio, without having sent any kind of notice to the Senate, called Ralla to headquarters.

"This agreement is fine with me, Tribune, but the Senate has rejected it."

"After all this time and discussion, sir?"

"I understand, Tribune, however, it's out of my hands. Go back to the Numidian camp and tell Syphax that I have conferred with the Senate. They seek a larger tribute payment and demand that the Carthaginian navy be reduced to thirty ships."

"But sir, those are issues we've already discussed. The Carthaginians are sure to refuse."

Scipio nodded. "That could be, but there can be no agreement without the Senate's consent, and without those changes, the Senate won't sign on."

Ralla reluctantly returned to Syphax's camp. Syphax, expecting acceptance of the agreement, was dumbfounded. Still he presented Hasdrubal with the suggested changes. Insulted, Hasdrubal immediately called off any further talks. Marcus Ralla was sent back to Scipio with no agreement. That night, Scipio requested I prepare a map of the area around Utica. He asked me to include our camp as well as the Numidian and Carthaginian camps, plus all the information that had been collected about those camps during the failed negotiations. He wanted the map by noon the next day.

The following morning, Scipio ordered his officers to step up preparation for the siege of Utica. At noon that day, he called a special meeting of his staff, which included Lucius, Laelius, Cato, Marcus Ralla, and Masinissa. I was there to take notes.

"I have decided on a change of plans," said Scipio to his officers. "And repeat nothing of what I'm about to say except to those soldiers who are part of the operation."

Scipio gave his staff a moment to absorb this, then continued. "I had a dream last night in which my father came down from the heavens and spoke to me about the destiny of Rome. He showed me a vision of our enemy's camps leaping with flames and the soldiers running from the exits with their clothing on fire. I didn't know what it meant until I awoke this morning." He made eye contact with each of the officers before him. "We are going to raid the two enemy camps tonight."

"Tonight?" asked Cato.

"Tonight," repeated Scipio. "I know that's not the usual Roman practice, but the circumstances are also not usual. In the next month, we are certain to enter into a pitched battle with the troops across the way. We are greatly outnumbered, and they have us pinned on the tip of this promontory. In my opinion, the circumstances tremendously favor our enemy. Tonight we will do something to better our odds."

Again he gave his staff a moment to let this settle in, then he continued. "We have learned from Marcus Ralla's trips to the Numidian camp that the soldiers of both enemy armies have chosen to build their shelters out of wood or woven reeds. They have been in place almost six months now and are sufficiently dry to be little more than thatch and tinder. After the trumpets for the night watch, we will send the Fifth legion, under the joint command of Laelius and Masinissa, to the Numidian camp and the Twenty-third legion, under my command, to the Carthaginian camp. There will be no moon tonight, so it will be especially dark." He looked directly at Laelius, then his brother. "My plan is to set fire to both camps."

Cato stepped forward. "Sir, do you mean that after three months of talks, you're simply going to discount all honor and burn down the enemy camps? That's goes against all that is Roman. Have you been infected with the local waters and become a Carthaginian? Our duty is to stand and face them like true Romans."

"They rejected our offer, Quaestor. Whatever hope we might have had for peace is gone. Our duty is to conquer the enemy, not to prove that we are more honorable than they are. Is your memory so short that you have forgotten that Hannibal used one trick after another to destroy our armies in Italy? I see nothing different here."

"But you're stooping to their level—even lower."

"They have established the rules of engagement, and from my reading of Hannibal's actions, the Carthaginians have no rules. We will proceed in the same way."

Although Masinissa seemed to be excited by the idea, several of the other officers agreed with Cato. "Sir," asked Marcus Ralla, "were we truly sincere in our efforts to reach an agreement with the Carthaginians?"

"And the preparations for besieging Utica," followed Lucius, "have they all been for show?"

Scipio turned away without answering either question and directed the officers' attention to the map I had only recently completed. They gathered around the table as Scipio pointed out the important details of each camp—the exits, the locations of the officers' tents, and the horse corrals. When he was finished, he dismissed all of them but Masinissa.

After the last of the officers had filed out of the tent, Scipio asked Masinissa for his opinion.

Masinissa grinned. "I think it's brilliant, sir. War is not a moral act. We butcher. We rape. Every higher principle is discarded. We can eliminate their entire army tonight. What more could a general want?"

Scipio seemed tense. I believe there was an element of what he planned to do that went against his own ethics just as much as they went against Cato's.

"Exactly," said Scipio. "I have assigned you to the Numidian camp because you are familiar with their ways. Laelius will listen to you. Don't hesitate to express your thoughts."

"I'm honored by your trust in my judgment, General, and I admire your daring."

CHAPTER 79

The Fifth and Twenty-third legions slipped out of our camp shortly after dark. I was not part of the mission. The two enemy camps were seven miles from our camp and a mile apart. The legion led by Masinissa and Laelius set up a position near Syphax's camp, while Scipio made ready for an attack on Hasdrubal's.

Masinissa and Laelius split their legion into two parts. Masinissa arranged his twenty-five hundred men to cover the gates. Laelius took the same number to act as a second line. At Masinissa's signal, two hundred naptha-coated torches were lit and thrown into the camp. The camp may as well have been built to be a bonfire. The huts that were struck by torches burst into flames. Fanned by the offshore wind, the fire leapt from one hut to the next with such speed that the conflagration exploded across the camp.

The first Numidians to awaken thought the fire had been started by accident. They ran through the camp shouting for immediate evacuation. The soldiers rushed from their huts only partly-dressed and without their swords or armor. The camp had only two gates. Both became blocked by the number of men pushing and shoving to get out. The confusion increased to utter hysteria. Those fortunate enough to fight their way through the gates were met by Masinissa's troops and cut down. The rout was on.

Scipio, a mile away, had yet to attack. He watched from a distance as the Carthaginian camp came to life with news of the fire across the way. Again, the soldiers, never suspecting that Scipio would stage a night attack, thought the fire was an accident. Many of them wandered out of the camp in small unarmed clusters to stand and watch the fire.

At this point Scipio attacked, cutting down those outside the camp and tossing flaming torches within. The scene was a repeat of the first attack. The individual fires soon roared into a single blaze. Those who had not already left the camp now raced for the gates. The

Carthaginian camp had four gates, but that was still not enough. Frantic men piled into snarls at the exits, trampling or smothering each other in their hurry to get out. Those who broke free met the stabbing, cleaving gladii of Scipio's men. The slaughter doubled in ferocity.

The night filled with the screams of burning men, some stuck within the camp, some running off in all directions their clothing and hair on fire. Horses and mules, some aflame, some not, raced around in circles adding to the confusion. The men who understood what was happening fought through the flames and half-burned bodies to get to their weapons. But then there was no way out.

Scipio and his troops remained at the site until daybreak revealed the smoldering desolation of their night's work. Scorched corpses, human and animal, littered the ground for miles around. The smell of burnt flesh and char carried on the wind all the way to our camp. Scipio estimated that more than fifty thousand men were killed that night. The only failure of the mission was that both Syphax and Hasdrubal escaped with contingents of cavalry. Hasdrubal headed to Carthage for refuge; Syphax went inland for protection in the hills. Less than ten thousand others survived. The Roman casualties were in the double digits. It was a tremendous victory. Our camp celebrated as one that afternoon.

In headquarters, Scipio stalked from one side of the tent to the other, fighting with his conscience. I was there as were Laelius and Lucius.

Scipio suddenly stopped his pacing and faced his closest advisors. "Well, was it worth it?"

Neither man answered.

"Was that any different than Lake Trasimene?" snapped Scipio. "Should I be filled with glory or unable to face myself? Am I a bold general or a monster?"

Lucius dared to respond. "It was brutal, brother. But there was nothing that we did that doesn't mirror the nature of this war from its first day. War is no longer a noble endeavor. War is only victory or defeat. The victor can describe his methods in any way he likes. We all know how Hasdrubal infiltrated our father's Spanish allies and convinced them to turn on him and our uncle. That's why you saw our father in your dream two nights ago. He was telling you war has changed."

Scipio shook his head. "I hope you're right, Lucius. I hope you're right."

"It was quite a sight, sir," said Laelius. "And we have delivered a killing blow. I suspect the agreement they just rejected will look awfully good to them tomorrow."

Scipio nodded. "And if not, there will be increased pressure for Hannibal to return to Africa."

To the outside world, Scipio appeared to be a man of the highest honor and the most noble intentions. Like Marcellus, he had a huge ego and even more ambition. Also like Marcellus, he sought the glory of defeating Hannibal. At this time in Rome's history, nothing meant more than that. Were I to compare the two men, I would say that Marcellus was superior to Scipio. But I was biased. Marcellus had saved my life then allowed me to live with his family. But more importantly, Marcellus seemed to be a man of higher integrity. What he said he meant. Deception was not his way. Scipio was considerably more complex, with people and with his command. Since showing him the spyglass, I had realized I didn't wholly trust him. I even wondered if the dream he described to his staff was a fabrication, used as a way to legitimize his unRoman tactics. Yes, he was a great general, comparable to Marcellus for his courage and attention to detail. But Marcellus was a soldier, simple and true. Scipio was an intellectual, a man of education and subtlety, who often hid his motives from others. That was the reason I had yet to tell Scipio about the weapon designs I had found in the warehouse on the island of Ortygia. I still didn't trust the man.

During the meeting just described, however, Scipio did raise himself in my estimation when he revealed some measure of remorse for using fire to destroy the enemy's camps. Not that I felt the attacks were wrong. I felt they were justified for the same reasons Scipio did. This was what Marcellus had said to Marcus years earlier. The rules of engagement had changed since Hannibal's invasion of Italy. I was simply heartened by the fact that Scipio did have a conscience and that he was capable of second-guessing himself.

CHAPTER 80

Taking advantage of the complete absence of Carthaginian troops, Scipio spent the next three days plundering the nearby villages. When the ravaging was over, he distributed the booty among his men to reward them for the successful destruction of the enemy camps. He then refocused his efforts on the siege of Utica without fear of being pinned up against its walls by an opposing army.

Within a day of dispensing the booty, a caravan of dealers, slave traders, and pickers, just like those that followed the armies in Italy, set up shop outside our camp. As quaestor Cato sold all the prisoners that had been captured to the traders. The soldiers exchanged the assorted goods they had received for gold and silver coins. Large numbers of them immediately sought out the swarm of prostitutes who trailed after the caravan.

That night, while many of the soldiers still wrangled with dealers or emptied their purses to painted women, I decided to check on Troglius and Rullo. Troglius was not one to seek out a woman. Rullo I wasn't so sure about.

I heard an excited shout, then a chorus of curses, as I walked down the aisle into a massive dice game outside our tent. Three oil lamps were hung on wooden staves rammed into the ground around a circle of ten soldiers. Another twenty squeezed in behind watching. Rullo, years younger than any of the other men, was running the game. Three tall stacks of gold and silver coins were piled up in front of him.

Troglius, standing off to one side, saw me walk up. I sidled up to my quiet friend. "Why does this not surprise me, Troglius?"

"He's going to win all the money in camp," he whispered.

"That the prostitutes don't get."

"I've never seen so much money in the hands of such a young man."

"He's something, Troglius. You'll have to become his bodyguard in camp as well as on the battlefield with the amount of gold he's collected. I wonder how he does it?"

Troglius looked at me with one eye as though it was obvious. "He's very lucky."

"That's one explanation."

Rullo darted a glance at me as though he might have heard me and allowed a smirking grin. I shook my head and decided to watch the game.

A man across the circle shouted, "My turn to throw!" and grabbed the dice from the center of the circle. The man shook the dice and let them fly. They bounced across the dirt coming to a stop with a five and a two uppermost. That was a winner and Rullo pushed a silver coin over to the man. The man threw a four on his following roll, then a five, then a nine, then a seven to end his turn. He gave up the dice and the small pile of coins that had accumulated as he increased his bet on each roll.

I watched the action through several shooters. Rullo's stacks of coins grew and everyone else's diminished. I knew no amount of luck could produce a winner every time, so I kept a close eye on Rullo's hands as the game progressed and the stakes increased.

I noticed that every now and then Rullo scooped up the dice with one hand but gave the dice to the shooter with the other. On other occasions, he passed the dice with the same hand he had picked them up with. I didn't think much of it until I started keeping track of the rolls in my head. After a short time, I realized that every time he used both hands to pass the dice, a seven was the result of the next roll. At first I thought this might be a coincidence, but the longer I watched the more suspicious I became. He was changing dice between throws.

I didn't watch the game to its conclusion. Like Troglius, I wearied of the action and went into our tent to sleep. I found Rullo the next morning sitting on the ground happily counting his winnings. Troglius stood by, clearly impressed by the young man's talent with dice.

I sat down opposite Rullo and placed two silver coins on the ground. "Give me a chance with the dice, Rullo. It was too crowded last night for me to get into the game."

Rullo looked up from his piles of money as though I was bothering him. "Come back tonight. We'll have another game."

"I'll be busy. One chance with the dice for both of these coins."

"Fine. Let's make it fast." Rullo reached into the pocket of his tunic and handed me a pair of dice.

I shook the dice in my fist and threw a six down between us. I proceeded to throw a five, and an eight. Rullo reached out with his right hand to pick up my eight, then returned the dice to me with his left. He did this very deftly. I barely noticed, but I was certain he had switched the dice. Sure enough, the result of my next throw was a seven. He took my two coins with one hand and was about to take the dice with the other, when I reached out and scooped them out of the dirt.

Rullo's eyes went big. "What are you doing? You said just one game."

"One fair game, Rullo," I said, looking at the dice in my palm. One die had three spots on all six sides, and the other die had four spots on all six sides.

Rullo knew I had seen into his game and began to fidget.

With Troglius there, I decided to keep my insight strictly between Rullo and me. "You know, Rullo," I said, rolling the dice around in my hand. "I think there's something wrong with these dice. I think they're worn out. I suggest you get rid of them or give them to me. Who knows what a sore loser might say if he discovered you were playing with a set of dice that had been overused?"

"I didn't know a pair of dice could get worn out," said Troglius.

"Oh, yeah," I said staring at Rullo. "The corners get round and they become like little balls not cubes."

Troglius shrugged, but Rullo agreed. "Maybe you're right, Timon. I think it's time to retire that pair."

"Yes," I said slipping them into my pocket. "I'd hate to be caught running a game with worn out dice. Someone might get mad—very mad. As a matter of fact, I think I would like my two silver coins back."

Rullo knew he had been found out. He took a deep breath and returned my coins.

Troglius was astounded. "You mean, I could have gotten my coins back if I had noticed the worn out dice?"

I gave Rullo a chance to answer, but he deferred to me.

"I'm guessing Rullo was too smart to be using these dice last night. It was probably an accident he used them here today. Right, Rullo?"

He nodded.

"So be careful tonight, Rullo." I looked right at him. "Troglius will be watching."

"But how do I tell?" asked the huge soldier.

"When Rullo's stacks of coins get too big." I got up and walked away.

CHAPTER 81

Hasdrubal felt certain that Scipio would abandon the siege of Utica and come straight to the gates of Carthage after incinerating the two camps and some fifty thousand soldiers. He took this message to the Council of Elders, demanding that they raise another army to protect the city. His rival Hanno countered by saying the war was over. It was time to sue for peace. Several other councilors wanted to call Hannibal back to Africa. Only with his leadership, they said, could Carthage possibly hope to defeat Scipio.

After three days of fierce debate, Hasdrubal and the Barcid party won out. As impossible as it seemed, they would raise yet another army. Hasdrubal immediately started recruiting Libyans from the surrounding farmland and also sent a messenger to Syphax, who by this time had returned to Siga. Hasdrubal's message was simple: *The war is not over; we need more men.*

Syphax, who simply wanted the war over, resisted the call to arms. He cursed to the gods after receiving Hasdrubal's messenger in the great hall, then stormed out. Sophonisba, who had been seated beside him with Felicia on a chain at her feet, found him shortly afterward, pacing furiously in their bedroom.

Syphax spun around when Sophonisba appeared in the doorway. "I know what you're here for, Sophonisba, but I can't do it. I know that I have agreed to help your father, but this war is nonsense. It cannot be won. Anything that I put into it now can be counted as lost. Your people must realize this. It's time to surrender to Scipio."

Sophonisba had not spent ten months in Syphax's bed to have him suddenly annul the reason her father had given her away. Her first inclination was to scream at him, to call him a coward and confront him on the nature of their matrimonial agreement. Instead she gathered herself, forcing the loss of her handmaiden and her love for

Masinissa from her mind, and assumed the role she had promised herself to master.

"Forget the war for a moment, husband," she said softly, pulling the pins from her hair and shaking it out, so it hung around her like a black cape. "Forget the failed agreement with Scipio and surrender to me." She came up close to him and methodically undressed him despite his clear distraction. She took his hand and drew him to the side of their bed.

Sophonisba laid him down on his back, then used her mouth to gather the king's full attention. Turning on all her charm, she straddled him at the waist and seductively drew her robe up over her torso and tossed it aside. She adjusted her hips so that he was inside her, then she leaned forward, ravishing him with kisses on his neck, while gently rolling her hips to the rhythm that was so natural to her and so overwhelming to Syphax.

When Sophonisba knew that Syphax was near the height of his arousal and had become animal in his own passion, she stopped the movement of her hips and whispered into his ear. "Syphax, my king, my husband, my love, Carthage means everything to me." She eased back up and down on him three times, then stopped again. "Can you imagine how sad I would be if the city of my birth, of my people, were overrun by the Romans?"

She ran her fingers through Syphax's hair and eased back into a slow roll. "All I would be able to do is cry." After a moment, she stopped the movement of her hips again and lifted herself high on her knees so that they disengaged.

Syphax reached out to her, taking her hands and drawing her back onto him.

"Oh please, husband," Sophonisba continued, "you must help my father. Not to do so is the same as hurting me." Her eyes now glistened with forming tears, and she rolled sideways off of him and out of the bed.

Syphax would have screamed at any other woman. He would have struck any other woman. But not Sophonisba. He sat up in absolute desperation, the thing in his groin throbbing for a climax.

Sophonisba went to the window, and leaning forward, stared out at the city, crying softly, her bare bottom poised in the most irresistible of positions.

Syphax climbed from the bed and approached her from behind. "Sophonisba, my queen, my love," he cooed, stroking her roundest curves, "both armies were entirely destroyed by the fire. There's no way to beat this man Scipio. They're calling him a genius."

Sophonisba spoke to him over her shoulder, pressing her rear into his hands, pretending arousal. "It takes neither genius nor courage to light a fire. That bit of intrigue was no measure of his valor, no measure of his army, and certainly no measure of ours. That can only be judged on the battlefield. Scipio has been here almost a year, and there has yet to be a pitched battle. He has shown plenty of deceit, but no real military skill. The war is not over. I married a king. He must be brave and strong." She adjusted her hips to receive him. "I would want nothing else," she mewed as the king slid himself into her and she began to rock with his plunging motion.

CHAPTER 82

Thirty days after Scipio's night attack had destroyed the better part of his enemy's forces, Hasdrubal had hastily amassed another thirty thousand men, including some twenty thousand Numidians recruited by Syphax and four thousand Celtibarian mercenaries. Meanwhile, Scipio, judging that a solid base for the winter was more important than a premature attack on Carthage, had returned to besieging Utica. But when he learned that a large army was camped seventy-five miles south in a region called the Great Plains, he abruptly changed his plans.

Knowing that these troops had been drawn together under great duress and lacked training, Scipio left enough men at Utica to maintain his siege lines and set off for the Great Plains in light marching order with twenty thousand foot soldiers and three thousand cavalry. Until this time Scipio had hesitated going inland with the bulk of his army because of the risk. But now with detailed maps of the region, he was better prepared for the challenge. Five days later, we set camp on a hill four miles from the Carthaginians.

The morning after our arrival, Scipio surveyed the expanse of land between the two camps with the spyglass, once again repeating his praise for the device. After a careful study of the enemy position, Scipio ordered Laelius and Masinissa to probe the enemy defenses with their cavalry and act as a screen while he supervised moving our camp down the hill closer to the Carthaginian camp. This was completed shortly after noon.

I spent the afternoon in headquarters with Scipio. I stood at the map table detailing the ground between the two camps as Scipio paced in the tent, pondering his strategy for the next day—and what would be our first set piece battle since arriving in Africa. Occasionally he would stop at the table and stare at the map, presumably trying to imagine the troop formation he would confront in the morning.

The headquarters' tent had been raised and taken down innumerable times. The weather-beaten leather that was stretched over the tent posts showed the wear and tear. While I worked, I noticed a small hole in the south facing wall of the tent, just a pin prick at shoulder height. By chance, the position of the tent, the position of the sun, the location of the tiny hole, and the dim lighting within the tent recreated the circumstances in Archimedes' workshop when he showed me the image created by sunlight passing through a small hole.

I looked up while running some numbers in my head and saw a patch of light projected on the tent's north wall. On closer inspection, I saw that it was an upside down image of the tents and soldiers outside the south side of the tent. Though Scipio was deep into his own thoughts, I knew he was the curious sort and decided the phenomenon was exceptional enough to interrupt him.

"Excuse me, sir. Do you see that patch of light?" I pointed to the north wall of the tent.

He glanced at the patch of sunlight. "What of it?"

The image was not particularly clear and was difficult to decipher if you didn't know what you were looking at. "Get closer," I said.

Scipio reluctantly moved up close to the tent wall and stared at the patch of light, then at me. "I'm in no mood for this game, Timon."

I doused the oil lamps. "Can you see it now?"

"See what?" he demanded, tilting his head this way and that, trying to understand what he was looking at.

"Keep looking." I crossed the tent to the tiny hole, then removed the large lens from the spyglass. I pinched the lens between my forefinger and thumb and held it over the hole, knowing it would flip image over and make it easier to see. "Does that help?"

Scipio stared at the patch of light while I moved the lens forward and back trying to bring the image into greater focus. Suddenly Scipio gasped. "What is this, Timon?" He turned to me, then back to the wall. "I see an image of our camp! And there are men moving in the image as in a dream!"

"It's the result of the sunlight passing through this small hole." I covered the hole with my hand. The patch of light vanished. I removed my hand and the image returned. "It's a natural phenomenon that Archimedes revealed to me many years ago. He told me not to show anyone because they wouldn't understand, but I thought perhaps you would."

"So what I'm seeing here is happening outside the tent beyond that wall?"

"Yes. And I can't explain why, nor could Archimedes, except to say it was a function of light traveling in straight lines. It's part of the science of optics."

Scipio found it so confounding he went outside to verify what he was seeing. When he returned, he checked the image on the wall and shook his head, dumbfounded. "This is almost as remarkable as what can be seen through the spyglass."

"I agree. And I think they are somehow related, but I don't know how. Watch this." I used the lens to focus the image, then I removed the lens to show the difference.

Scipio was entirely fascinated, as just about anyone would be. He put his hand into the beam of light and saw the image on the back of his hand. Then he ran his finger across the leather as though he might feel the image. He faced me, perhaps with yet another layer of respect. "Who else knows of this effect?"

"Archimedes said Aristotle described it in one of his essays, but I have never met anyone else who knew about it."

Scipio seemed to think about this. After a moment he said, "Let's keep this quiet, Timon. At some later time, I might like you to demonstrate it again."

"I expect the Carthaginians to offer battle tomorrow morning," Scipio told his staff later that day. "We are outnumbered, but our troops are more experienced." He led his commanders, Laelius, Lucius, Cato, Ralla, and Masinissa, to the map table where he had already laid out blue markers in the formation he anticipated from Hasdrubal.

"We will use a single line, containing both of our Roman legions and their accompanying allies, so that the enemy line doesn't overlap ours. We won't deploy until they have." He looked at Cato and put a red marker on the table. "I want the Twenty-third opposite the Celtibarians, their most seasoned troops. Ralla will be on your left with half the allied troops." He put the allied marker in place.

Scipio turned to his brother. "Lucius, I want the Fifth on the far right, with the other half of the allies between you and the Twenty-third." He put two more red markers on the table. "Laelius and Masinissa, you'll have the flanks. Laelius, I want you opposite their Numidian cavalry. Masinissa, opposite the Carthaginian horse." He put those markers in place. "All of this will become more obvious once they've set their formation. We'll make the appropriate adjustments if it differs from what I have here. Any questions?"

"How do you see this playing out?" asked Masinissa in Greek.

Scipio answered him in Greek, then repeated his answer in Latin for the others. "I want the center to hold, while our cavalry strips theirs from the flanks. Once their cavalry has been dispersed, ours will return and attack their flanks. I foresee an easy victory. We'll review all of this in the morning."

CHAPTER 83

Our camp was divided into two parts, as it had been outside Utica. The Roman legions had built the regulation, square camp, surrounded by a six-foot ditch and wooden palisades. Two-story towers stood at all four corners. Masinissa's cavalry had their own camp, not nearly as well fortified and considerably smaller than ours.

I went over to the Numidian camp that night to share the evening meal with Masinissa. I sat at the campfire with fifteen of Masinissa's most loyal men and ate roasted gazelle. Three had been killed that day on the way back from the morning's skirmishes with the Carthaginians. The camp was alive with anticipation for the morning. The meal was a celebration, a time to inspire the warrior in each man's heart.

"I'm excited to finally fight under Scipio's command." Masinissa used his teeth to pull a hunk of meat from a rack of ribs. "I believe he's of the same genius as Hannibal."

"I have yet to see Scipio manage a set piece battle, Masinissa, but I had a few chances to observe Hannibal while I was in Italy with Marcellus. From what I've seen of Scipio so far—his ambush of Hanno outside Salaeca and the firing of the two camps outside Utica, I would say he has learned much from Hannibal."

"Oh, yes, if you are familiar with what Hannibal did when he first arrived in Italy—at Ticinius and at Trebia—it was all about using the cavalry to strip the flanks. Scipio was there at both of those battles, though, I believe, only seventeen years of age. He used variations of those flanking maneuvers in Spain, against Hannibal's brother at Baecula and against Hasdrubal Gisgo at Ilipa. I was there for both. In my opinion, Scipio is Hannibal's best pupil."

"Things will surely get more interesting if Hannibal returns to Africa."

Masinissa laughed with his mouth full. "Interesting to say the least. I hunger for it as much as Scipio does."

"You spent some time with Hannibal in Italy. What did you think of him?"

Masinissa wiped his mouth with the back of his hand. "My time in his camp was short. I never fought a battle with him, but I learned more about commanding a cavalry unit in a month with his man Maharbal than I had in all my previous experience." He used his teeth to strip another hunk of meat from the ribs. "I respect Hannibal. I would be fighting for him right now except that the only way I can regain my kingdom is by joining the Roman cause. And if we are victorious, I will ride to Siga to collect my prize." His eyes lit. "Sophonisba!" he shouted out to the night. The others around the fire knew who she was. They raised their cups and voiced their approval with high-pitched yips and whistles.

On my return to camp, I went directly to my tent. I was tired and needed sleep. Anxiety ran high. No one in the tent unit had gone to sleep yet. Six men and one youth sat around a dying campfire, some sharpening their gladii, some adjusting the leather straps on their armor. For Troglius it could have been any night of the campaign. He always set aside time to work on his gear, whether there was a battle in the offing or not. Rullo sat quietly next to Troglius, rolling a pair of dice from one hand to the other, clearly a little on edge with his first battle looming. He had earned a position in the first line of velites and would be among those that led us into battle.

Rather than go straight into the tent to lie down, I squeezed into the circle and sat between Troglius and Rullo. Troglius acknowledged me with the glance of one eye. Rullo was so tense he didn't even seem to notice it was me beside him.

Wanting to draw him out, I decided to start a conversation. "Troglius, I have always meant to ask you, do you fear going into battle?"

The question caused everyone at the campfire to look up.

Troglius ran his whetstone down the edge of his gladius, held the blade up to admire his work, then answered, seemingly directing his words to his sword. "No," he said flatly. "I was not given a handsome face. Women find me so frightening that only my mother has ever kissed me."

On any other night this might have generated a few rude remarks from the others, but on the eve of battle, Troglius, his reputation in battle now well known throughout the camp, was respected with a grave silence.

"So my love must be to my gladius," said Troglius, turning the blade in the dim moonlight. "And it is consummated when I go into battle. I look forward to using this beauty in the same way some men look forward to bedding a woman." Something like a smile graced his face. "There's more than one way to part flesh for pleasure."

I had not expected such an answer, but like everyone else around the fire, I found it chilling.

Aurelius, also a battle-tested veteran, turned to Rullo. "How about you, young man? Are you ready for tomorrow?"

Rullo had been in the army for more than a year now. He had trained with Troglius every chance available. He had also grown in height and put on more weight and muscle. His beard, which was blonde, had grown into a thick down. He was becoming a man, and though just seventeen, presented a formidable presence.

He looked up at me with worry in his eyes, then turned to Aurelius. "I feel the same way Troglius does."

CHAPTER 84

Dilius performed the sacrificial rites to Mars at dawn. Scipio gathered his staff shortly afterward. When the eye of Jupiter peeked over the hills to the east, the Carthaginian army, totaling some thirty thousand men, filed from their two camps and assembled in battle formation. Scipio rode his horse to the top of the rise behind our camp and used the spyglass to observe the process and assess the enemy's alignment. It was very close to what he had imagined, including the Celtibarians anchoring the center. He saw no reason to change our formation and passed this on to his commanders. The battle trumpets sounded, and our soldiers, twenty thousand foot and three thousand horse, paraded from our camps.

As was typical, both armies sent out small cavalry contingents to probe the opposition. On several occasions during the day, these advance groups engaged in minor skirmishes, but neither general signaled for a full engagement. At the end of the day, both armies retired to their camps.

Shortly after noon the following day, the two armies again paraded from their camps into battle formation, ours with some slight adjustments. At times during the day, the soldiers pounded their shields with their swords or shouted insults at the opposition, but the only action was incidental, skirmishes between contingents of cavalry and a few quick sorties from the light infantry.

The third day had a different feel. Everyone in camp was certain this would be the day for full combat. The armies took the field shortly after dawn, both sides loud and raucous, sifting their feet and pawing at the ground like eager racehorses. Hasdrubal used the same formation he had the previous two days, placing the Celtibarians in the center. A phalanx of Syphax's infantry was placed to the right of the Celtibarians, and a phalanx of Hasdrubal's infantry to the left. The

Numidian cavalry, some four thousand, flanked Syphax's infantry, and the Carthaginian cavalry, nearly two thousand, flanked Hasdrubal's.

Our line held twenty thousand foot, four legions side by side, three maniples deep—hastati, principes, triarii—in the standard checkerboard formation. Masinissa's fifteen hundred horse supported the left flank, opposite the Carthaginian cavalry. Laelius' contingent—another fifteen hundred horse—supported the right, opposite Syphax's cavalry. The velites stood ready in the gaps between maniples.

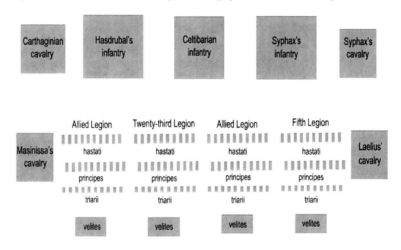

Syphax sat on his horse at the front of his cavalry; Hasdrubal commanded from behind the Celtibarians. Scipio, on his magnificent red war horse, rode back and forth behind the hastati, shouting encouragement to the soldiers and instructions to his commanders. Masinissa, riding his jet black garron Chthonia, pranced back and forth before his loyal Numidians.

Scipio signaled for the battle trumpets before the opposing army made a move. Our skirmishers shouted their battle cries and raced past the hastati directly into the enemy's onrushing light infantry, primarily raw Libyan recruits. Both sides launched their javelins, then retreated, as the two lines of heavy infantry began their steadfast march forward. I watched from the hill behind our camp with the spyglass.

When the two lines met, the Celtibarians stood strong, while the raw Libyan and Numidian recruits on either side of them struggled to hold their own against our more seasoned troops. I scanned the action with the spyglass, looking for Troglius or Rullo. I had seen Rullo in position prior to the start of the battle, but lost sight of him when his cohort of velites rushed forward to begin the fray. Because of his size, Troglius was easier to find. I knew where his maniple was in the formation, and despite the ongoing action, was able to focus on him for short periods of time.

As an hastatus in the Twenty-third legion, he was on the front line from the beginning to the end of the battle, standing toe to toe with the Celtibarian mercenaries, the only truly experienced phalanx in the Carthaginian line. I had witnessed several battles in which Troglius took part, but I had never been able to find him on the battlefield during combat with the handheld lenses. Now with the spyglass I could.

The battle action of a Roman legionnaire in the front line began with his shield, shoving the opposition backward with the knob or swinging it like a battering ram to create an opening. The gladius followed the shield with a straightforward thrust at the height of a man's midsection, or less frequently, with a full swing, hacking at an arm or a neck. Troglius had mastered these moves. I watched him apply them over and over again with an animal-like ferocity. I thought of what he had said three days earlier. Could plunging a blade into a man give the same satisfaction as an act of sex? I couldn't find it in me, but a sense of dominance was surely a part of both.

Despite being outnumbered on both flanks, our cavalry was better trained and more experienced. With the front line fully engaged, Laelius and Masinissa stripped the opposing cavalry from the right and left flanks and chased them from the battlefield, pursuing them into the surrounding hills. No longer protected on the flanks by their cavalry, the Numidian and Libyan infantry began to lose order. While the hastati held firm across the length of our line, Scipio, in a masterful move, ordered the principes to swing around from behind the hastati to the enemy's left flank and the triarii to do the same on the right. Suddenly we were hacking at the enemy formation from three sides, and the rout had begun.

By noon, only the Celtibarians remained on the field for the opposition. Being Iberians in a foreign country they had nowhere to run and were forced to fight it out. When Laelius and Masinissa returned from their pursuit of the enemy cavalry, they went at the Celtibarians from the rear. At that point it was only a matter of time. Although the Celtibarians proven to be a formidable opponent, they were quickly massacred to a man. The day belonged to Scipio.

In many ways, it had hardly been a battle. Too many of the opposition were inexperienced. Both flanks gave way at the first sign of pressure. The Numidian and Carthaginian infantry were then cut to shreds, leaving the Celtibarians on their own. Their determined effort kept the fighting focused on the battlefield, giving the two enemy commanders an opportunity to separate themselves from the action. Hasdrubal escaped with two hundred cavalry and rode off in the direction of Carthage. Syphax broke free from the battle as soon as the right side of the line gave way. He disappeared into the hills to the west to join what was left of his cavalry.

That night Scipio called his staff into headquarters. Although the victory seemed to clarify the hopelessness of the Carthaginian position, Scipio was not in the mood for celebration and focused on the end game. With Laelius, Lucius, Cato, Ralla, and Masinissa standing shoulder to shoulder before him, and me taking notes, he paced from one side of the tent to the other, describing operations for the next day.

"We have them just where we want them," he began. "The two armies, or what remains of them, have been dispersed in opposite directions. Tomorrow," he looked at his two cavalry commanders, "I want Laelius and Masinissa to go after Syphax. His army is scattered and demoralized. He's likely headed to Cirta. Take your entire cavalry and the Fifth legion and try to catch him before he gets there. The rest of us will stay here to bury the dead and collect the plunder. Once that's done, we will sack the local villages before heading back to the coast."

Scipio went over to the map. "We'll set up a base of operations in Tunis," he pointed to a location about five miles southwest of Carthage, "and prepare for an assault on the Carthaginian capital." He looked up at Laelius and Masinissa. "When you have captured Syphax, bring him to me in Tunis—dead or alive. I want him as a trophy to display in Rome."

CHAPTER 85

I got back to the tent late. One of the members of our unit had been killed. The remaining six were shooting dice beside the campfire. None showed any obvious wounds. A torch mounted on a wooden staff had been jammed into the ground to provide light to see the dice. I noticed right away that Rullo only had a few coins piled on the ground before him, but he was laughing and enjoying himself with the others, caught up in the celebration of the overwhelming victory.

I stood in the shadows outside the circle of players for some time watching the game. One thing became clear very quickly. Rullo was not switching the dice, and it was reflected in his winnings or lack thereof. I knelt behind Troglius and whispered over his shoulder.

"How's the game going?"

Troglius, rarely given to smiling, turned to me with a grin and winked his left eye, something I had never seen him do before, then leaned back so that I could see the stacks of coins in front of him.

I acknowledged his winnings with a nod, then asked, "Any serious wounds?"

Troglius lifted his arm to show me a long gash in his forearm that he hadn't bothered to wrap, then pushed two silver coins into the circle, betting against Aurelius who needed to match a ten. Rullo pushed three bronze coins out to bet with the shooter.

Aurelius shook the dice in his fist and rolled them out beneath the torch light. One hit the ground and stopped, showing a six. The second bounced and tumbled to a stop with a one uppermost. Aurelius had lost. Troglius raked more coins into his pile.

Rullo, on the opposite side of the circle, got up from his knees to go into the tent. I intercepted him at the tent entrance.

"I see you survived, Rullo. What did you think of your first battle?"

The seventeen-year-old grinned. "I have never done anything more thrilling."

"Not even winning at dice?"

"There's no comparison. Dice is a game. War is life and death."

"I watched from afar. I saw you enter the battle, then lost track of you."

He nodded, still grinning. "We had them on the run from the start. I threw my two javelins and was never needed again."

"Things don't always go so easily."

"I know that," he said. "But there's no army in the world that can stand up to ours. I've heard others say that we're the strongest and most disciplined army Rome has ever mustered."

"I hope so. If things go as Scipio has predicted, the next battle will be with Hannibal. That will be something entirely different."

"We'll be ready."

"No injuries? No cuts or bruises?"

He extended his arms to show that he had been untouched by the whim of battle.

"It seems you have traded your luck with dice for luck on the battlefield."

He lowered his head, then looked up sheepishly and whispered. "I took your advice, Timon." He glanced around to make sure that no one could hear him. "There's no sense in provoking the gods' disfavor by cheating at dice."

I laughed. "Seems you're getting wiser every day."

"I'm not so sure," he muttered. "I've lost a lot of money tonight, and now I'm going back to my bedroll for more—instead of turning in for the night."

"Tonight is for celebration. Just imagine that you're giving back your ill-gotten gains."

CHAPTER 86

When news of the battle's outcome reached Carthage, the city went into an even greater panic than after the camps outside Utica had been burned to the ground. Hasdrubal warned the Council of Elders that Scipio would soon be at the city gates and that they must immediately begin preparations for his arrival, beginning with arming the populace and rebuilding any portions of the city walls that were in disrepair. Hanno's position had not changed; it was time to sue for peace. But the majority of the Council was against surrender of any kind, and instead voted to recall Hannibal and continue the war. Delegations were immediately dispatched to Italy with orders for both Hannibal and Mago to return to Africa. The Council also gave Hasdrubal permission to assemble a fleet to be sent to Utica, hoping to break the siege before Scipio returned from the Great Plains.

After a week of terrorizing the countryside, Scipio collected his troops and headed back to the coast. The five-day march required eight due to the quantity of plunder weighing down the baggage train. Halfway into the journey, Scipio decided to send the war prisoners and booty straight to Utica to be loaded onto transport ships, so that the rest of the troops could reach Tunis more quickly.

Tunis had been stripped of its garrison to build the Carthaginian army just defeated, and when the populace learned that Scipio was coming, they quickly evacuated to seek protection within the walls of Carthage. Scipio entered what was essentially an empty city and immediately set his men to upgrading the fortifications.

Our first full day in Tunis, Scipio requested I accompany him to the top of the city's highest tower. Carthage was just visible on the far side of Lake Tunis. Scipio used the spyglass to get a closer look at the city he planned to besiege. While Scipio analyzed the city's defenses, he noticed that a fleet of warships—he counted fifty—was preparing to leave Carthage. At first he thought they were coming to Tunis, but when the first ships sailed from the harbor, they turned north.

Scipio immediately realized that the Carthaginian fleet was headed to Utica, where his ships were anchored in the harbor laden with siege equipment and were in no way prepared to enter into a sea battle. Fearing he could lose his warships and his transports, Scipio assembled half of our infantry and one thousand cavalry and took off for Utica at double time.

Following the coastline, the trip from Carthage to Rusucmon Bay, where Utica was located, was nearly twice the distance Tunis was from Utica by land. Unaware that Scipio had guessed their plan, the Carthaginian captains proceeded without the urgency the situation demanded. Scipio raced ahead with his cavalry, while his brother trailed behind with the infantry. Riding fast and unencumbered by foot soldiers, Scipio was there by midnight. Lucius wouldn't be there until the following day.

Expecting the Carthaginian fleet to arrive the next morning, Scipio quickly devised a plan and set his men to working through the night. Rather than risk a sea battle where his warships would be greatly outnumbered, he decided to blockade the entrance of the harbor to protect them. By sunrise he had assembled all his transports and any merchants vessels he could take from the locals into three lines. The masts were dropped and laid across the gunwales to adjacent ships and lashed into place. Long planks were added to the barricade for increased strength.

Midmorning the first of the Carthaginian warships were spotted approaching the entrance to Rusucmon Bay. Soon afterward the entire fleet entered the bay aligned for battle, expecting the Roman warships to come out to meet them. Instead they encountered a floating sea wall, armed with catapults and manned by Roman soldiers. The Carthaginian captains ordered their ships to ram it, thinking they could break right through.

The situation rapidly deteriorated into a mayhem of tangled sea vessels. The Carthaginian warships, though better suited for battle, were not as tall as the transports that had been tied together. The Carthaginians soldiers were forced to toss their javelins upward at their enemy, while the Romans showered them with darts from above.

After battling hand-to-hand in a snarl of lines and broken timbers with no clear progress, the Carthaginian captains instructed their men to throw grappling hooks attached to long ropes into the Roman rigging. With the hooks ensnared in the lines, the Carthaginian warships reversed direction and methodically towed intertwined portions of the barricade out to sea. Unable to stop them, the legionnaires manning these captured ships dove into the harbor to avoid being taken prisoner.

Although Scipio's blockade created enough clutter in the harbor to prevent an all out sea battle, the Carthaginians did manage to sail off with sixty transports. After the two horrible setbacks that Scipio had already inflicted on Carthage, this was heralded in the Council of Elders as a major victory.

CHAPTER 87

By this time Syphax had arrived at the palace in Cirta, accompanied by his new personal attendant Vangue. Syphax knew that Laelius and Masinissa were pursuing him. He had also learned that when Masinissa had reached the ancestral Maesulii territory that Syphax had taken from him, the Maesulii king was greeted by his people as a hero. The puppets Syphax had installed in the lesser cities were quickly removed, and Masinissa was enthusiastically anointed as the rightful ruler. Masinissa added another five thousand volunteers to the troops that had come with him from the Great Plains and continued on with Laelius to Cirta to reclaim the palace that had once been his father's.

The night of his return, Syphax went directly to his chambers to seek out Sophonisba who had arrived the day before from Siga. When Syphax stormed into the bedroom hoping to find sanctuary in the arms of his bride, Sophonisba was sitting at her dressing table. Her new handmaiden, Nycea, stood behind her preparing the queen for bed. Felicia, now an adult cheetah and not yet fully accustomed to Syphax, lay asleep on the bed. She lifted her head to warily appraise the visitor and snarled.

"Get that animal out of the bedroom," snapped Syphax. Nycea quickly put a leash on Felicia and led her from the room.

Sophonisba, who had heard inconclusive reports about the lost battle, abruptly stood. She wore a dark blue robe, and her lustrous black hair lay about her shoulders and down her back. Although displeased by the way Syphax had dismissed Felicia, she spoke softly and with concern. "My king, what has happened? Tell me that what I've heard is not true."

"I cannot lie," Syphax said. "We have suffered another terrible defeat, and even worse, there is an army a few days from here coming after me." He embraced Sophonisba as a dying man embraces the last moments of his life.

"And my father?"

"He escaped from the battlefield as I did. He should be in Carthage by now preparing for Scipio's advance on the city." He shook his head. "It's over, Sophonisba. It's over. It's time for us to give up Cirta and return to Siga."

Sophonisba spun from his arms and angrily strode across the room. "Has Hannibal returned? Has Scipio defeated our greatest general?"

Syphax hung his head in dejection. "No. Hannibal is still in Italy."

"Then he won't be there for long, and your job is not over."

Syphax lifted his head. "No, Sophonisba, there is no reason for me to continue in this war. Your father will certainly ask me to once again strip my country of its young men and come to his rescue, but it will all be in vain. This man Scipio is the equal of Hannibal, and I want no more of this losing effort."

Sophonisba crossed the room and came up close to her husband. "Only the man who does not give himself fully in defeat is a loser," she hissed. "Tell me I have not married a coward."

"Would you prefer a corpse to a coward? You're asking me to die for Carthage, and that I will not do."

Sophonisba glared at him, then quickly snatched the dagger that hung at his hip and stepped away from him. "Then know this for certain. Your wedding bed will go cold without me in it."

Syphax took a step toward her, but she backed away farther and pressed the sword's blade against her breast. "Touch me, my king, and you will lose your queen. Without Carthage, I am nothing. I need not be. I have no need for love. I have no need for passion."

The one thing Syphax knew for certain, amid all the disarray of his kingdom, was that there could be no joy in his life without Sophonisba. He wanted her now more than he had on his wedding night—only because on his wedding night he hadn't known what heights of pleasure such a woman could impart.

Sophonisba raised the knife above her head, set to thrust it into her chest. Syphax dropped to his knees. "I will raise yet another army, my queen. I pledge my life to Carthage."

CHAPTER 88

Syphax's kingdom was vast even without the Maesulii territory. The next morning he sent his officers out into the countryside to conscript any man they found—young or old. After three days he had amassed a force of nearly thirty thousand. He organized his cavalry into squadrons and his infantry into phalanxes, then, having had no time to train these raw recruits, took off to meet the ten thousand foot and three thousand horse commanded by Laelius and Masinissa. He would destroy the smaller army and continue on to Carthage.

The two armies found each other late in the day ten miles from the gates of Cirta. The following morning they assembled in battle formation. Laelius extended the Roman line as far as he could to prevent being flanked by the larger force. As was common, contingents of cavalry on both sides made probing sorties at their opposition to begin the battle. One, then two, then three skirmishes broke out between the mounted soldiers. Suddenly both cavalries were on the battlefield fighting with the infantry in reserve behind.

Although vastly more experienced, Laelius' and Masinissa's cavalries struggled to hold their own against an enemy that seemed to come at them in endless waves. Syphax's riders steadily gained control of the battlefield, despite losing horses and riders at twice the rate of their Roman counterparts.

Instead of retreating in the face of what seemed insurmountable odds, Laelius signaled for the infantry to advance. Syphax's Numidians answered in a swarm, racing forward to confront the tightly maintained rank and file of the Roman legionnaires. The advancing legion cut through the Numidian recruits like soft butter, creating havoc on the battlefield and forcing many of the Numidian riders off their mounts to assist the infantry. The momentum of the battle completely reversed. Fear of defeat spread through the Numidians like a disease. Many began to run from the battlefield.

With the battle turning before his eyes and his queen's words in his ears, Syphax gave a kick to his horse, and waving his sword over his head, raced into the center of the battle looking for Masinissa. If he couldn't have Sophonisba, neither would his rival.

The two men saw each at the same time. Even from a distance, Masinissa could read the hatred in Syphax's eyes. He guided Chthonia through the clutter of dead, close enough to launch a javelin at the Masaesyli king. Syphax's horse took the javelin in the chest. The horse stood on its hind legs momentarily, then went down sideways, throwing Syphax violently to the ground. Masinissa leapt from his horse and held the disoriented king to the ground with the tip of his sword. Six Roman soldiers quickly surrounded Syphax and dragged him kicking and screaming from the battlefield.

The sight of their king being roughly escorted from the battle completed the demoralization of the Numidians. They fled from the battlefield like rats from a sinking ship. The Roman cavalry chased after them, cutting them down as they ran. Some twenty-five thousand Numidians were killed or taken prisoner. The Roman losses were less than two thousand.

CHAPTER 89

The next morning, while the Roman soldiers stripped the battlefield of plunder and buried their dead, Masinissa approached Laelius with a personal request.

"The city of Cirta was once the capital of my father's kingdom. The defeat and capture of Syphax means that Cirta now belongs to the Maesulii tribe and is part of my kingdom. It would be greatly meaningful to me if you would allow me to ride ahead with the cavalry, taking Syphax with us. Think of the sight when I arrive outside their gates with my ouster in chains and demand that they open the city to their rightful king. To me, to the Maesulii, nothing could be more momentous."

Laelius titled his head thinking about the proposal.

Masinissa continued to press him. "You can come at your own pace with the infantry and the baggage. We can secure the city when you arrive, then rejoin Scipio on the coast."

"Fair enough, Masinissa. Leave whenever your men are ready. Expect me to be there tomorrow."

"Thank you. You will be welcomed as a hero."

Masinissa reached Cirta shortly after noon that day wearing Syphax's golden breastplate. Two thousand cavalry, riding two abreast, stretched out behind him with a cart carrying Syphax in shackles at the rear. When the guards in the battlements saw the contingent approaching, they thought it was Syphax returning victorious. A call went through the city to prepare for the king's arrival. Soldiers lined the battlements two deep, and ten trumpets signaled for the opening of the main gate. But before that could happen, a guard noticed that it wasn't Syphax leading the cavalry and shouted out in alarm, "It's not the king! Secure the gate!"

When the contingent of cavalry came to a halt, several of the guards recognized that it was Masinissa and shouted insults at him, laughing at his paltry force, taunting him as though he intended to storm the walls.

Masinissa ignored the ridicule and rose up on his horse to address the guards above the huge wooden gate. "I have returned to take my kingdom back," he shouted. "Open the gates and welcome the son of Gala. I am your king. This is my city."

The taunts and insults increased as others in the city were drawn to the commotion. Some joined the soldiers in the ramparts to shout and jeer. The guard in charge of the gate laughed at Masinissa, calling out, "Syphax is our king, Masinissa. Cirta is no longer yours." Those atop the walls echoed those sentiments, followed by more laughter and catcalls.

"No, you are mistaken!" bellowed Masinissa. "Syphax is my prisoner. His army is defeated. Open these gates. I am your king."

This only brought more laughter. A few of the onlookers tossed fruit and vegetables at Masinissa, mocking his arrogance.

Masinissa turned and motioned to the men behind him. A horse drawn cart, led by a man on foot, made its way up the line to where Masinissa waited on Chthonia.

The sight of Syphax in the cart, stripped of his armor, streaked with dirt and blood, and shackled, brought immediate silence to those along the battlements. One of the guards shouted, "The army has been destroyed!"

This message resounded around the battlements and echoed through the city. Within the palace, Sophonisba, standing at her bedroom window, heard it loud and clear.

As abruptly as the wind can change, the sentiments in the city reversed. Instead of insults, there was adulation.

"Hail to the new king!"

"Hail Masinissa!"

Masinissa raised his right hand, extending his sword in the air. "Open the gates. Your rightful king has returned."

The gates slowly opened. Masinissa led his men into the city and directly to the palace where he had been raised as a child. After ordering ten of his men to take Syphax to a cell in the palace dungeon, he strode up the center of the great hall with his men crowding in behind. Masinissa triumphantly stood on one of the two thrones, and to the cheers of his men, lifted his sword as though it were a scepter. "I am home!" he shouted. "I am finally home!"

Masinissa swept his sword out before him as a gesture to his men. "To you, I give my most heartfelt thanks for your loyalty and for your blood. Without both I could not be here. You will be repaid from the treasure chests of the now deposed king."

Again the men cheered in adulation. Some let out high pitched yips and whistles. Every man there was happy to be home, and the raucous celebration continued as though it might never end. Then, suddenly, a commotion at the rear of the room caused them all to turn around. Silence spread like a rumor from the back of the room to the front. The hall became completely quiet. Masinissa, uncertain of what was happening, watched as the mass of soldiers parted, creating a path to the throne. At the far end stood Sophonisba, wearing her golden diadem and the pale blue gown that was her father's favorite and showed off her body in a way that could make any man's blood run hot. Masinissa stepped down off the throne as Sophonisba swayed like a panther up the aisle, and the awestruck soldiers filled in behind her.

Upon reaching the throne, Sophonisba prostrated herself at Masinissa's feet. With the entire room spellbound by her entrance, she rose up on her knees and looked up at the new king. "The gods' graces shine upon you, Masinissa. You have been permitted to return to your lawful kingdom and your throne. How ironic it is I who you must evict from the royal chambers."

Overcome, Masinissa placed his sword on the throne, then reached out, taking both of her hands in his, and oh, so gently lifted her to her feet, as though she were some creature from the heavens.

Sophonisba looked into his face. "I saw it in your eyes those many years ago, Masinissa—you were destined for great things. I had hoped to be a part of that. Unfortunately the whims of war did not bring us together. Instead we were drawn apart. You are the rightful king. I am your plunder."

Several of the soldiers called for her execution. One shouted out a crude suggestion. A second and third followed with more craven appeals. Many of the soldiers began to laugh. Masinissa held up one hand. The room quieted again.

The dethroned queen turned to the soldiers and then back to Masinissa. "Yes, I know, it was my husband who stole your kingdom and your throne. And for that alone, you have every right to kill me. I will not even trouble you by pleading for mercy. Take me now for whatever pleasure or torture you can conceive, but please, Your Majesty, if there were one thing, one request that I could ask, no matter what else you may do with me, do not turn me over to the Romans." Her passion narrowed to a focus. "You can surely imagine what a Carthaginian woman, the daughter of Hasdrubal, can expect at the hands of the Romans. I will gladly accept what a fellow African determines is my punishment, but do not allow the Romans to parade me into Rome as part of Scipio's triumph. That is a humiliation worse than death."

Masinissa, already madly in love with her, and taken deeply by her words and the spell she had cast, touched her cheek. "Please, Sophonisba, know that your heart-felt request is wasted on me. I have no more intention of giving you to the Romans than I do of killing you. Of all the treasures in Africa, none has more value to me than you. If I may do with you as I like," his eyes lit up and his nostrils flared, "the only prison I would make for you would be my bed. Will you be my queen?"

The soldiers erupted, louder than before, with heartfelt praise for their king and more gratuitous suggestions and vibrant yipping. Masinissa lifted his hand again for quiet so that Sophonisba could respond to his proposal.

"One moment I am the queen of the wealthiest king in all of Africa. The next I am common plunder." Sophonisba squeezed Masinissa's hand as tears ran from her eyes. "Now I am offered that which I have only dreamed of. Whatever pleasures you might seek, Your Majesty, I will give to you with utmost joy for the gift of your hand in marriage."

Sophonisba's words inflamed the passions of an already passionate man. Masinissa, struggling not to take her then and there on the floor of the great hall, contained himself long enough to issue orders to his officers. "Search the city. Seek out every one of Syphax's officials and put them to death. Execute any military officers that you find. Offer any remaining soldiers the choice of loyalty to their new king or the edge of a blade across their neck."

When all but his most loyal bodyguards had filed from the great hall, Masinissa ordered those who remained to secure the palace and to allow no one to enter until further orders. With that, he drew

Sophonisba into his arms and whispered, "I will never give you to the Romans."

Sophonisba finally smiled with all her dazzling radiance, increasing her beauty and further disarming the young king. "If I am to be your plunder, then may it be in my own bed." She took him by the hand and led him up the palace stairs to the royal chambers.

CHAPTER 90

Sophonisba had enchanted Syphax with her beauty and her capacity as a lover solely because of political necessity, meaning every kiss, every act of love was faked and her passions forced. That was not the same woman who gave herself to Masinissa with pleasure, real emotion, and a passion equal to his. The new king and the deposed queen surrendered completely to love, the tender and the animal, a love they had both felt three years earlier, but had never had the chance to express to each other. If ever there was a night given to the throes of Eros, if ever there was a night that the gods might blush, this was that night.

Many hours after disappearing into the royal bedchamber, Masinissa lay awake in the tangled bed sheets with Sophonisba asleep beside him. Lit with love, but also equally troubled, he climbed from the bed and crossed the huge room to one of the windows that gazed out over the city of his youth.

Sophonisba roused from her sleep and immediately sensed Masinissa's absence. She sat up, and looking around the room, saw him before the window. "Masinissa," she said softly, "why are you not by my side?"

Masinissa turned to face her, but said nothing.

Sophonisba slid from the bed, and wearing only moon shadows, joined him at the window. "What troubles you on such a glorious night, my love?"

Grim and silent, Masinissa reached out with his hand and stroked her cheek. She eased into his arms and pressed herself against him, then looking up into his eyes, that were no more than shallow caverns in the darkness, hesitantly queried, "Was I not what you had hoped?"

Masinissa ran his hand down her back to her hindquarters. "You were more than I imagined, Sophonisba. More than I believed possible. No, that's not what worries me tonight."

"You're concerned about protecting me from the Romans." She gripped him tighter, as though it would make them permanently one.

Masinissa sighed. "I have been awake now for some time puzzling over what I might do. Should I hide you in the palace? Should I tell the Romans that I had you executed?" He took her by the waist and held her at arm's length, appraising her beauty, her skin opalescent in the pale light of the moon. He ran a finger over her lips, then down her neck to her left breast. "There is only one answer." He ran his finger tip around her nipple and watched it rise with his touch. "We must be married now, before the Roman forces arrive. Then you are officially my queen and no one, not even the Roman Senate, can take you away from me."

Sophonisba reached up with both hands and pulled his face close to hers. "Yes, to be your wife is my greatest desire. It can't happen too soon." She kissed him on the mouth. They sank down to the floor in each others' arms and made love yet again.

An hour later, Masinissa sent one of his guards to the dwelling of Cirta's highest priest. With only his personal bodyguards and Sophonisba's two maids as witnesses, the lovers were wed. They shared a breakfast of pomegranates and figs, then watched the sunrise from their bedroom window. Sophonisba had Felicia brought to the room so she could introduce her to Masinissa. He stroked the cheetah as he would a loyal dog, and the big cat took to him immediately. Felicia lay on the floor and watched passively when the newlyweds climbed back between the silken sheets to consummate that which they both believed secured them as one for life.

CHAPTER 91

Late in the afternoon of that same day, while the royal couple dozed in each others' arms, a loud pounding on the bedroom door shook them from their slumber. Masinissa abruptly sat up and shouted, "Who dares to interrupt the king?"

"It is I, Laelius," replied the Roman tribune with ten armed soldiers standing at his side.

"Go away, Laelius. I'm not available at the moment." Masinissa turned to Sophonisba to reassure her.

"I have heard things that are upsetting, Masinissa," Laelius called back forcefully. "I order you to open this door immediately."

"A king sees who he wants when he wants to see them!" answered Masinissa, his ire growing. "Go away. I will meet you in the great hall when I am ready."

Laelius turned to his men and pointed to one of the heavy bronze stanchions in the hallway used for holding a torch. Two of the soldiers took hold of it like a battering ram and slammed it into the door.

"You risk your life to enter this room!" screamed Masinissa, leaping from the bed and grabbing one of the swords from the wall.

The soldiers rammed the stanchion into the door again and again until the wood splintered and the door fell from its hinges. Laelius strode through the opening. His men remained outside peering into the vast chamber.

Masinissa stood naked in the center of the bedroom, his sword upraised. "How dare you enter the king's bedchambers? Out or your life!" Behind him Sophonisba lay covered in the bed sheets.

Laelius looked around the room assessing the situation. Masinissa glared at him, furious at the intrusion.

Laelius boldly approached the bed and stared down at Sophonisba as though she were a common whore. "If this is Syphax's queen, Masinissa, she is the property of Rome."

"This woman is no one's property!" shouted Masinissa. "She is my wife. We were married last night."

Laelius ignored him and took Sophonisba by the arm.

Like that—Masinissa's saber was across his neck. "Let go of her, Laelius, if you wish to keep your head. You have no authority here."

The ten legionnaires pushed through the broken door into the room, their javelins pointed at Masinissa.

Laelius glared at the Numidia king. "Have you lost your senses, man! Take heed of what you're doing. The future of your kingdom lies before you. You can't possibly want Rome as your enemy."

Seething, Masinissa wouldn't back down. "Stand away from my queen or I will kill these men as well as you!"

"No, Masinissa," pleaded Sophonisba, pulling from Laelius' grip and running to her husband's side with only her long hair to cover her. "There has been too much bloodshed already."

Outside the room Masinissa's body guards could be heard coming down the hall.

Laelius shook his head at his comrade. "You are making a grave mistake, Masinissa. Married or not, this woman is Roman plunder."

Masinissa stared him down. "Rome may have Carthage, but Cirta and all within are mine. Get out."

Laelius took a quick glance over his shoulder as the Numidian guards swarmed up behind his men. "If you won't listen to me, then you must face the wrath of Scipio. He will not be pleased." He appraised the naked woman at Masinissa side. "We leave for the coast in two days," he said sharply. "Hopefully by then you will have had your fill of this Carthaginian trash and regained your senses."

He abruptly turned. The guards at the door parted and he strode out of the room with his men behind.

CHAPTER 92

Meanwhile in south Italy, the situation remained stagnant. Hannibal had occupied the south for nearly six years as though it were his own private colony. But desperately needing reinforcements, he hadn't entered into a pitched battle in over two years. There had been minor conflicts, skirmishes between foraging parties, and the loss or gain of a few minor towns, but with neither side forcing the issue, Hannibal's only hope for relief was his brother Mago.

Unfortunately Mago remained in the north, blocked from coming south by four Roman legions. He was no closer to his brother than when he had arrived two years earlier, although he had assembled a force of some thirty thousand soldiers and was itching to make a move. Midsummer he was confronted in the Po Valley by two armies commanded by Marcus Cornelius and Quinctilius Varus, a force totaling nearly forty thousand. Tired of preserving his men for a reunion with his brother, Mago accepted the challenge.

The battle went back and forth all day until Mago received a spear in his thigh and was carried from the battlefield. Without his leadership, his troops, almost entirely barbarian mercenaries, gave way, and Mago, watching the battle from a stretcher, was forced to call for a general retreat. Mago and his surviving army huddled in the security of their camp until the middle of the night, when they quietly packed their baggage and left for Genoa. He was met there by envoys from Carthage ordering him to return to Africa.

Hannibal received these same orders from a second set of envoys two days later. Although Hannibal was furious, he had heard of Scipio's victories in Africa and reluctantly accepted his fate.

CHAPTER 93

In times of great happiness or deep depression, Sophonisba sought peace through communication with the goddess Tanit, Mistress of the Moon. On first coming to Cirta, she had instructed a trusted slave to build a temple to Tanit in the palace garden. It became her sanctuary, her place to be alone to pray or write poetry. The day after Masinissa left with Laelius, she went to the temple to contemplate her recent change in fortune and pray that Masinissa's meeting with Scipio would go well.

Gaia found her there that afternoon. "My lady," the slave whispered, entering the temple cella where Sophonisba knelt in prayer.

Sophonisba could be sharp when disturbed, but she faced her maid with a smile. "Yes, Gaia, what is it?"

"I'm sorry to interrupt you, my lady, but this is the only place," she looked out to the garden, "where I can speak to you in private." Gaia was sixteen years old. Four years younger than Sophonisba.

"Come closer, Gaia. What is it you want to say?"

"I saw it on the ship when we were out at sea."

"Coming from Carthage?"

Gaia nodded anxiously. "Nycea pushed her over. I saw it."

"Nycea pushed Zanthia overboard that night?"

"Yes, I saw her do it."

"Why didn't you say something?"

"I was afraid of Vangue."

Sophonisba had not been happy that Syphax had brought this man to Cirta. She had said nothing at the time, but now found her ire rising. "For what reason are you afraid of Vangue?"

"He told Nycea to do it—on orders from Syphax. The king used Vangue and Nycea as his eyes and ears in your chambers."

"Why didn't you tell me this sooner? Didn't you know you could trust me with this information?"

"I was afraid I would be killed if I said anything, but now that the king is gone, I thought you needed to know."

Sophonisba was furious, but contained her anger. "Thank you, Gaia, for telling me this. Perhaps it's time I found a new handmaiden."

Sophonisba dismissed Gaia, then prayed to Tanit for guidance.

The next morning Sophonisba went down to the great hall to conduct the business of the day. She enjoyed the work and had taken care of the kingdom's affairs when Syphax had been gone. Now she did it as a habit and wanted to share this duty with Masinissa when he returned. Gaia and Nycea always accompanied her to the great hall and stood behind her throne. Felicia lay at her feet on a leash. Vangue was also there, presuming to be her advisor.

After receiving several wedding gifts from local merchants, Sophonisba attended to the business of paying bills and collecting fees. In the process of reviewing the numbers with her accountants, a slave dealer was announced by the guards. Sophonisba stopped what she was doing and had the man brought to the throne.

The man was a Cretan with deep-set, unfeeling eyes. His dark hair was slicked down across his head to cover his baldness. "Your Highness," he said with a deep bow, "you requested my presence. How can I help you?"

"I would like you to sell three slaves for me."

"It would be an honor, Your Highness."

Gaia and Nycea exchanged a look. *Who might she be selling?*

Sophonisba glanced over her shoulder at the two women. "These two young Numidians, and the ex-king's attendant." She pointed at Vangue, who suddenly started looking around like she must be mistaken.

"What do you mean? I'm not a slave any longer. I can't be sold," snapped Vangue, stepping up close to Sophonisba.

Felicia didn't hesitate. She leapt at Vangue and took hold of him by the neck. He fell to floor as the cat continued to go at him. Sophonisba abruptly stood, but took a moment to let the cat tear at Vangue before yanking the cheetah off him with the leash. With Felicia pulling at her lead, snarling and snapping at Vangue, the slave dealer came forward with two of the queen's guards and had the Egyptian dragged away.

"I don't expect much for them," Sophonisba said coldly to the slave dealer, as she handed Felicia's leash to a guard. "They are short on loyalty. Make an easy deal—to a harsh master. I will make it worth your while."

Gaia fell to her knees at the queen's feet. "Oh why, my lady, have you chosen to sell me when it was Nycea that killed Zanthia?"

Sophonisba glared at the young woman. "A loyal slave would have told me right away—even at the risk of her life. Now get out of my sight."

CHAPTER 94

Laelius, just back from Cirta, went straight to Scipio's headquarters outside Tunis. Scipio lounged on a divan, wearing a toga and slippers, and reading from a scroll, when Laelius entered. I stood beside the map table, detailing a map of Carthage. Scipio sat up quickly, then rose from the divan.

"Laelius, your safe return is a welcome sight. What news do you bring?"

"We defeated Syphax outside Cirta, sir. He's here now in shackles. Cirta fell without resistance. Carthage's only ally is no more."

Scipio embraced his longtime friend and advisor. "This is the news I have been waiting for. Without Syphax, Carthage is defeated." Scipio paused and stood back from Laelius. "There's something more? I can see it in your face. What is it?"

"It's concern for Masinissa, sir. He arrived in Cirta one day before I did and immediately fell under the spell of Syphax's wife—a young Carthaginian woman."

"Hasdrubal's daughter, Sophonisba."

"He married her the night of his arrival. When I told him the woman was Roman plunder, he refused to annul the marriage."

"Did he return with you?"

Laelius nodded. "He was at the rear of our train. He should be in camp soon, if not already."

"And the woman?"

"I ordered him to bring her with us, but he refused. She's in his palace at Cirta."

Scipio paced twice across the tent, talking as much to himself as Laelius. "I command the movement of tens of thousands of men. I plot and plan to force Hannibal out of Italy. I have Carthage on her knees on the verge of surrender, and this young girl has disrupted my efforts for a second time." He shook his head in disgust and frustration, then faced Laelius. "Have Syphax brought in. I'll talk to Masinissa later."

Laelius ducked out of the tent and called to his men. A moment later two soldiers pushed a chained and weary Syphax through the tent opening. Scipio motioned to the guards to go away. Laelius stood off to one side of the tent as Syphax, his face streaked with dirt, his hair in disarray, attempted to stand up bravely to the man who had conquered him.

"Only two years ago, Syphax," said Scipio with feeling, "I ate at your residence in Siga. It seemed then that we had become friends and had reached a worthy agreement. Now you are in my quarters as a prisoner wearing shackles. I find great sadness in this."

Syphax bowed his head, touched by the sentiment in the other man's voice, then lifted his eyes to Scipio's. "I wronged a good man. I went against my word, and it has cost me everything—my kingdom, my freedom, and your friendship. I am humbled to be in your presence at all."

"How is it that this has happened, Syphax? You pledged your support to the Republic of Rome, then suddenly reversed sides to fight against her. Was there anything in my actions or the actions of Rome to cause you to revoke your word?"

A disconsolate Syphax shook his head. "Only now in this sorry position can I see my madness. I was taken in by the caresses and words of a woman so beautiful I could not look away. For the graces of her bed I gave up my honor and my word. To admit this weakness before such a man as you shames me. I was not fit to be king."

"And what of this woman now?"

Syphax's eyes narrowed. "She has married my rival." The anger that still boiled within him came out in his words. "If there can be anything to gain from my current situation, it's watching Masinissa fall for the same blandishments that I did. If my marriage was a mistake for others to learn from, he missed an important lesson and has now proven to be a bigger fool than I."

"Could such a woman turn Masinissa from an ally to an enemy as she did you?"

Syphax frowned. "You will soon find out. Sophonisba is an aphrodisiac of a woman. She's like poison in a man's blood. Masinissa will not be able to resist her or her wishes."

Scipio nodded to Laelius, then turned away to pace across the tent. Laelius lifted the tent flap and called for the guards. The same two soldiers who had brought the broken king into the tent escorted him out. Laelius started to leave with them.

Scipio stopped him. "Have Masinissa sent to me."

When the tent was empty except for Scipio and me, I spoke on behalf of Masinissa. "Sir, I could not ignore the conversation you just had with Syphax. I believe the situation is different for Masinissa than it was for Syphax."

Scipio faced me. "How so?"

"Masinissa met Sophonisba several years ago. He had hoped to marry her from that moment on. Only the politics of the war prevented it."

Scipio's eyes hardened. "Is this an insight into the nature of love from a man who has fallen for a prostitute?"

I was not expecting this kind of reaction. "The woman in the trial was not a prostitute by any choice of hers, sir. I knew her when she was just a girl, before Marcellus' siege turned her life upside down."

Scipio seemed above it all and turned away from me without a comment.

"War can make people do things they wouldn't otherwise," I said to his back.

Scipio spun around. "War brings out the best in men of character, and the worse in those without. I wouldn't know, but it must be the same for a woman."

Masinissa entered the tent preventing me from saying anything more. Masinissa nodded to me and addressed Scipio. "You wanted to speak to me, sir."

Scipio began by complimenting him on his success against Syphax, then paused and walked off across the tent, as though thinking. After a moment, he turned and faced the Maesulii king. "I believe, Masinissa, that you offered your services to me as an ally against Carthage because you saw some good in me during our first meeting in Spain. But of all the virtues that might have caused you to seek my friendship, there is none in which I pride myself more than self control and superiority to lust of the flesh."

Masinissa bowed his head.

"How I wish, Masinissa, you had added this to your other excellent qualities. For I have seen you in battle, and there are few men with your ability on a horse or your courage in the face of danger. You have been the key to our success on several occasions here in Africa, but with this one human failing, with this one action, wedding the daughter of Hasdrubal, you have put my high praise of you in jeopardy—at a time when all that I'm trying to accomplish is at hand. I anticipate Hannibal's arrival in Africa in the coming weeks, and I don't know if I can trust you. I fear you are under the influence of Hasdrubal's daughter, a known seductress."

Masinissa lifted his head, a passionate man fighting his emotions.

Scipio continued. "I would rather you had thought this over on your own instead of being forced to blush at the mention of your regretful marriage. Believe me, for those who are devoted to a military career, there is no greater peril to their success than being surrounded by the opportunity for sensual pleasures. You have seen what this kind of weakness has done to Syphax. He has been reduced to chains." Scipio sighed and shook his head sadly. "And all of those things that once belonged to him now belong to Rome by right of conquest. That includes not only the city of Cirta and the surrounding region, but also his wife—and would include this woman even were she not the daughter of one of our enemy's commanders."

Masinissa couldn't contain himself any longer. "But General, I promised my queen that I would never give her up to any man, even you. You have now placed me in a position to break a promise that means as much to me as any I have ever made—even equal or surpassing that which I made to you." Tears began to run from Masinissa's eyes.

"Be master of thyself, Masinissa, don't spoil your many fine qualities with this one defect. Don't spoil my gratitude for all your services by surrendering to the most common and base of desires. Hasty moments in a wedding bed mean so little in comparison to the larger thing that we must do. Your promise to this woman cannot stand if you are to remain loyal to Rome. I give you a choice. Either the woman or your kingdom."

Masinissa, who idolized Scipio as a model soldier, as the highest ideal of a man, was undone by his words. "You leave me no choice. I must remain king of the Maesulii. I must retain my kingdom." His voice broke with emotion. "I will renounce my promise to Sophonisba." He looked upward as to his gods. "The things that I did were impetuous and unwise. Please forgive me, allow me to remain in your service to do whatever you request."

Scipio took a step toward Masinissa and put a hand on his shoulder. "Carthage is on the verge of defeat. If they don't simply surrender, a confrontation with Hannibal is as inevitable as the rising sun, and I will need you to lead a contingent of cavalry with all your skill and energy. Now go. Consider all that I have said. Know that this business of war is more important than the flame of lust, which in time always fades. Before the week is out, I will send a contingent to Cirta to bring Hasdrubal's daughter back here to be sent to Rome with Syphax."

Masinissa put his hands together and bowed at the waist to Scipio, then backed out of the tent.

Scipio came over to the map table. "Was I unfair, Timon? Were my words not true—war or no war?"

I didn't believe that the defeat of Syphax was only a victory for Rome, nor did I believe that Rome should control all of the lands that had once been Masinissa's father's. As to Sophonisba, I had never met her. I didn't know what influence, good or bad, she might have on my friend. But instead of defending Masinissa, I bit my tongue and said, "It's not for me to judge, sir."

CHAPTER 95

That night I went to Masinissa's camp. I found him in his tent alone, suffering as much as any man who had broken his own heart.

"I'm sorry for the dilemma you are in, Masinissa," I said, trying to console him. "We have spoken many times of the women in our lives, and in that, I feel we are nearly brothers and that there is nothing hidden between us. Still, though I certainly question Scipio's demands, I don't know what to say to you tonight."

Masinissa looked at me through eyes bleary from crying. "I have every desire to mount Chthonia right now and race back to Cirta to save Sophonisba. Just to say her name makes my heart pound. And now I have promised Scipio that she will not be mine." He put his hands to his face to hide his grief, then immediately dropped them.

"Couldn't I just take her away, Timon? Couldn't I just ride off to the farthest edge of Africa and lay with her on the sands washed by the great sea?" Without giving me a chance to answer, he continued to rip at himself. "But then I forsake my father's kingdom, and my word to noble Scipio. How can I fulfill my promise to Sophonisba and also be the kind of soldier I must be? How can I preserve my honor and also prevent her from being exhibited in a triumph in Rome? I can fight for Rome. I can do battle against Carthage. But give up Sophonisba or give up my kingdom?" Masinissa looked up at me. "I lose no matter which I choose."

I had no answer, no comforting words for my friend. I embraced him, then left him alone in his despair.

That night, unbeknownst to me or anyone else, Masinissa called his most trusted slave, Anir, to his tent. Masinissa, like many kings, carried a vial of poison with him at all times, knowing that should he be captured, death was a better choice than the humiliation of enslavement. He poured a portion of this poison into a small blue vial and gave it and a letter to Anir, with instructions to ride to Cirta immediately and deliver them both to Sophonisba face-to-face, directly into her hands and her hands only.

PART VII

HANNIBAL

"For years they have been trying to force me back to Africa by refusing me reinforcements and money; but now they recall me no longer by indirect means, but in plain words. Hannibal has been conquered not by the Roman people whom he defeated so many times in battle and put to flight, but by the envy and continual disparagement of the Carthaginian Council of Elders. At this unlovely and shameful return of mine, it will not be Scipio who will be wild with triumph and delight, but rather Hanno, whose only way of ruining me and my house has been by ruining Carthage."

-Hannibal, from Livy's *The War with Hannibal*

CHAPTER 96

The capture of Syphax and the third complete destruction of an army he had raised appeared to signal the end of the war. The Council of Elders acknowledged the desperate situation, and though they were aware that Hannibal and Mago would soon be on their way to Africa, a vicious debate ended in the decision to sue for peace. Thirty elders, representing some of the most senior members of the Council, were sent to Scipio's camp in Tunis.

Scipio received them outside the camp with Laelius, Lucius, and Cato. The Carthaginian elders prostrated themselves at Scipio's feet, and in an ugly, if not deceitful, capitulation, blamed the entire war on Hannibal, claiming that Carthage had never wanted war with Rome. In addition to their fawning before Scipio and his war council, they pleaded for the salvation of their city and their people, saying they would accept whatever terms of peace Scipio proposed.

Scipio, clearly disgusted by the display, made the following demands, which I transcribed into Greek for the Carthaginian elders:

- Return all prisoners, deserters, and runaway slaves
- Withdraw all armies from Italy and Cisalpine Gaul
- Stop all activities in Spain
- Evacuate all the islands between Spain and the Italian peninsula
- Surrender all but twenty warships
- Supply the Roman army with five hundred thousand bushels of wheat for the soldiers and three hundred thousand measures of barley for the animals
- Pay an indemnity of five thousand talents of silver

Scipio told the men that they had three days to agree to the terms. If the terms were accepted, a truce would be imposed while envoys from both sides traveled to Rome to have the treaty ratified by the Roman Senate. The thirty elders accepted these contingencies and immediately returned to Carthage.

Two days later, the Council of Elders, again after a vicious battle with the Barcid faction of the Council, voted to accept the agreement. Five envoys were sent to Scipio's camp to report the vote and to verify that Hannibal and his brother had already been ordered to leave Italy. The envoys then sailed with Laelius to Rome seeking a final ratification of the treaty.

CHAPTER 97

Riding as fast as he could, Anir reached Cirta in six days. He had no trouble entering the city or the palace, but access to Sophonisba's chambers required going through her cordon of slaves, including her two new personal attendants—both Numidians—Menna, a gray-haired, older woman, and Illi, a girl of fifteen. Anir got as far as stout and protective Menna by saying he had a letter from Masinissa, but she would not allow him to deliver it directly.

"No man, other than the king, is allowed in the queen's chambers."

"I'm on strict orders to deliver this letter in person," said Anir. A thin layer of dust covered his face and clothing from the two hundred mile-ride from Carthage.

"That's impossible."

"Then bring her to me. I will not disobey the king's orders."

Menna went to get Sophonisba. When the handmaiden returned, she told Anir that Sophonisba would see him in her chambers.

Menna led him to Sophonisba's bedroom. She announced him, then ushered him in. Felicia, laying in the corner, lifted her head and growled softly.

Sophonisba stood in the center of the huge stone chamber. Sunlight through its two windows projected bright trapezoids across the floor behind her. She wore a long maroon robe, embroidered with gold wire at the hem and cuffs. The collar was tight around her neck and studded with rubies. Her hair had just been brushed and braided by Illi. Sophonisba recognized the slave as Masinissa's. She waved her hand. Both Menna and Illi left the room.

"What have you got for me, Anir?"

Anir, with a wary eye on the attentive cheetah, approached the queen and knelt at her feet, hardly daring to look at her in the intimacy of her bedroom. He reached inside his tunic and withdrew the small blue vial and gave it to her.

Sophonisba accepted the bottle, then frowned as she turned it over in her hand. When she looked up, Anir held out the letter, folded in thirds and sealed with Masinissa's signet ring. Sophonisba told Anir to wait outside her chambers. She would have a letter for him to take back to Masinissa.

When the door closed behind Anir, Sophonisba began to cry. She knew what the bottle contained and what it meant. She opened the letter and read it slowly.

Sophonisba,

These past few days without you have been as dark and joyless as any I have known, but the news that I must impart turns all the world black. My heart-felt promise to keep you out of Roman hands is in immediate jeopardy. The Roman general has demanded that our marriage be annulled and that I release you to him—or the next realm of Roman conquest will be my kingdom and all that I have fought so hard to regain. My choice could not be more difficult if I had to tear my heart in half—my love for you is matched against my blood-born responsibility to my kingdom and my people—something no king can deny and still be a king. What many will judge as strength in the years to come feels like weakness as I write the words. With regret piled on top of regret, I must choose my people.

This fateful decision confessed, you must be forewarned. Scipio will send a squadron of soldiers to Cirta within the week to take you into his custody. Expect them within days of receiving this letter. With unfathomable sadness, and apologies for that which I can no longer control, I give you this vial. If I cannot stop them from taking you, at least I can offer you this way of escape—if, as you have said, death is preferable to humiliation at the hands of the Romans. Though our time was short, I can say now that I have known heaven.

Please forgive me for making a promise that I could not fulfill.

I pray that all love is forever,
Masinissa

After a while Menna peeked into the room. Sophonisba lay on her bed sobbing. The handmaiden came into the room and knelt beside the bed. "My lady, what has happened?"

Sophonisba gathered herself and sat up. "Get me a piece of papyrus and some ink."

"What's wrong, my lady?" She used a handkerchief to dab at the tears on Sophonisba's cheeks.

Sophonisba stood and pushed her away. "Just get me what I've asked for. I have a letter to write."

CHAPTER 98

A turma of Roman cavalry led by Marcus Ralla left for Cirta to retrieve Sophonisba four days after Anir left with Masinissa's letter. Upon learning of the turma's departure two days later, Masinissa tore at himself for sending his slave to Sophonisba, knowing he should have gone himself. He paced back and forth in his tent into the night. Near midnight he slipped from his tent, and without telling anyone his intentions, went to the horse corral and whistled for Chthonia. Moments later he was riding southwest at gallop, headed for Cirta, determined to reach Sophonisba before the Roman soldiers.

Masinissa rode through the night, then continued on the entire next day before stopping to rest. The morning of the third day, he saw a cloud dust on the horizon. A horse and rider were coming toward him from the west. He recognized the horse before seeing that it was Anir. Upon reaching each other, they circled around on their horses, talking excitedly.

"Anir, did you see a contingent of Romans on horseback? Have they reached Cirta yet?"

"I saw the riders, but didn't allow them to see me. They were riding at a good pace. By my reckoning, they'll reach Cirta three days from now."

"Did you deliver my letter directly to Sophonisba?"

"Yes, sir, of course. She gave me this letter for you." Anir retrieved the letter from inside his tunic and handed it to his master. Masinissa broke the queen's seal and unfolded the letter. In tears, he read her note.

Masinissa,
  I knew from the moment I first saw you that our destinies were entwined, and yet from the beginning, our lives have been bound up in choices each of us would have preferred not to make.

356

It seems the fabric of our fate contains an unfortunate weave, but also something noble and profound. If my love for you is true and transcendent, then I must also understand that the choice you have made was necessary—and really no different than the one I made accepting the marriage my father arranged for me. In both we chose to deny ourselves because of greater responsibilities. In this we were one.

Now, it seems, our honeymoon must end with a funeral, but that bleak finality will be a thousand times easier to bear than the ridicule I would face in Rome. I welcome your bridal gift in the spirit it was offered. Please remember this when you think of me; I could only die a more dreadful death if we hadn't had those few days together. Thank you for understanding the choice that I have also had to make.

All love is forever,
Sophonisba

"Come with me, Anir. Do your best to keep up. I will not rest until I have seen Sophonisba." Masinissa gave his horse a kick and raced off to Cirta with Anir trailing behind.

Late in the afternoon of his fifth day on the road, not more than five miles from Cirta, Masinissa caught sight of the Roman contingent ahead of him, riding at an easy pace. He was determined to stop Sophonisba from taking the poison. The thirty Romans on horseback were nothing. He could easily assemble enough men to send them back to Scipio empty handed.

CHAPTER 99

The soldiers standing guard in Cirta's battlements saw the cluster of riders coming from the east long before they reached the main gate. Their orders were to let the soldiers into the city, but to also notify Sophonisba as soon as they had been spotted. A series of slaves relayed the message to the palace, finally reaching Menna who rushed into Sophonisba's bedroom with the news.

Sophonisba had deliberately put off using the poison until the Romans were at the gates on the off chance that something in the war could change. She told Menna to have the Romans wait in the great hall when they arrived. She would come down to speak with them when she was ready.

Instead of preparing to meet the Roman soldiers, she went to her dressing table. She removed the vial of poison from the back of the top drawer, along with the letter from Masinissa. She held the blue vial out before her, appraising herself and the poison in the mirror. "What a strange wedding gift," she said aloud to herself, and to Felicia laying on her bed, then pulled the cork from the tiny bottle. "Many dream of being a queen. I only wish to be free to follow my heart."

Masinissa wrapped his mantle around his face so only his eyes were visible and raced past the Roman contingent, now certain of reaching Cirta ahead of them, though Anir was many miles behind.

Masinissa rose up on his horse as he neared the city gates, waving his sword over his head to hail the guards. "Open the gate for your king."

They recognized him immediately and opened the postern gate. He galloped through the gate and into Cirta all the way to the palace, then leapt from Chthonia and ran into the great hall where Menna was awaiting the arrival of the Romans.

"Where is Sophonisba?" he called out, gasping for breath.

"In her chambers, Your Highness. We heard that the Romans were coming for her."

"That's why I'm here."

Masinissa climbed the stairs to the second floor three at a time, sprinted down the hall, and burst into the royal chambers. Sophonisba knelt on the floor with tears in her eyes, stroking her lifeless cheetah. The blue vial lay on its side on the dressing table with his letter.

"Sophonisba! Please tell me I'm not too late!"

Sophonisba wavered as she tried to stand. Masinissa took two long strides and caught her in his arms, then settled down onto the floor to hold her on his lap. She looked up at him through vacant eyes, her life fleeing. Masinissa's tears fell on her cheeks and rolled off as though they were hers. He held her against his chest and rocked her.

Sophonisba gazed into his eyes, puzzled. "My love, how is it that you are here? I was told the Romans were coming."

"They're at the gates now. I'm here to stop them—even if it means losing my kingdom."

Sophonisba managed a weak smile. "I thank you for that, my king." Her eyes turned to the dead cat. "But it seems I've made a hasty mistake. Felicia already leads the way to where I am headed."

Masinissa lifted her into a sitting position. "No, the mistake was mine, Sophonisba, for not realizing soon enough that I valued you more than anything else."

"Merely knowing that, my love, brings joy to my last moments."

"No, you're not going to die. I won't let you." Masinissa called out at the top of his lungs, "Someone come quickly! Help me, someone! Anyone!" Then softly, tearfully, he whispered, "There must be a way to counteract the poison, Sophonisba. There must be." He tried to force his fingers into her mouth to make her vomit, but Sophonisba stopped him.

"No, my king, it's too late. Let us treasure this last moment before it ends. Kiss me one last time so that my final thought is the tenderness I knew with you."

With tears streaming down his cheeks, Masinissa pulled her close and kissed her deeply until he knew she was no more.

By this time Ralla and his men had already arrived at the palace and were waiting in the great hall for Sophonisba to appear. When the wait grew too long, Ralla forced one of the slaves to take him to Sophonisba's chambers.

The tribune and six of his men followed the slave up to the second floor. Illi, unaware of Sophonisba's suicide, tried to stop them at the door to the queen's chambers, but the men pushed past her into the inner rooms. With Illi behind them, shouting for them to stop, Ralla barged into the bedroom with his men. The sight of Masinissa kneeling on the floor, rocking the dead queen in his arms, stopped them cold. Illi and Menna came up from behind and gasped, then fell to the floor wailing.

Masinissa looked up at Ralla and angrily ordered him to leave.

The tribune waved his men out of the room. "I will be returning to the Roman camp immediately." Ralla noticed the blue vial and letter on the dressing table. "I will be taking the woman's body with me."

"Touch her, Tribune, and it will be your life," screamed the sobbing king.

"The general will not be pleased, Masinissa. You will regret your actions." Ralla spun on his heels and stalked out of the room.

CHAPTER 100

During the time that the Carthaginian envoys were in Rome, a convoy of two hundred transports carrying food and supplies for Scipio left Lilybaeum escorted by thirty warships. Upon reaching the African coast, the convoy encountered exceptionally strong winds. The warships were able to maneuver without sails by using their three tiers of oars. The transports, however, relied entirely on the wind and were dispersed down the coastline from the Promontory of Mercury past Rusucmon Bay. More than half of them were tossed in heaps upon the shore in full view from Carthage.

The people of Carthage, having already given Scipio the promised barley and wheat, and being heavily pressed for food themselves, cheered from the walls of the city while watching the transports run aground or break apart on the rocks. Hasdrubal Gisgo, angry about the terms of the treaty, quickly assembled a fleet of thirty ships. He gathered up the supplies strewn along the coast and brought them into Carthage.

Upon hearing what had happened, Scipio was enraged. His first thought was to cancel the agreement, but he had also just received word that the Roman Senate had ratified the treaty and that Laelius was on his way back to Africa. Instead of annulling all that he had worked so hard to achieve, he sent three representatives to Carthage to confront the Council of Elders. They told the Council that the treaty had been ratified, but that Hasdrubal's actions were equivalent to thievery and had endangered the truce and the treaty. The Council repeated the conditions of the agreement and the promises that had been made to Scipio in the name of their gods, then assured the representatives that the goods would be returned.

Certain that Hannibal's return would change everything, Hasdrubal decided to use the issue to spoil the peace. When the ship carrying the envoys left Carthage, Hasdrubal had three triremes waiting for them with orders to attack the diplomatic vessel. The Roman ship managed to escape without being sunk, but was forced to the beach short of Tunis. While some of the Roman sailors lost their lives, the three envoys reached land safely. When the men returned to headquarters with their report, Scipio was livid.*

Two weeks later, when Laelius returned from Rome with the Carthaginian envoys, Scipio informed them that since their departure for Rome Carthage had violated the truce twice, the second time with clear intent to disrupt the agreement. Despite his personal sadness for their failure to secure peace, he could not ignore what had happened and would advise Rome to annul the agreement immediately. At that point, with great care to be respectful to these men—in contrast to the way his own emissaries had been treated—Scipio dismissed the envoys and resumed the war with even greater ferocity than before.

Rather than besieging Carthage, Scipio left the camp in Tunis with his entire army to raid the villages and small towns in the highly productive farmland to the south along the Bagradas River. Much as Hannibal had done in Italy, Scipio became a scourge upon the land, burning the homes, killing the people, and taking the harvest.

---

*I might note that Scipio's rabid indignation over the reversal of the agreement could be called into question. In many ways, Hasdrubal's deceit was no different than Scipio's. All through the peace talks with Syphax, he had planned to set fire to his enemy's camp. In a sense, the two nations had thrown away all honor and had descended into the deepest throes of mutual hatred and distrust.

CHAPTER 101

Scipio had learned of Masinissa's unannounced trip to Cirta in the days after the Numidian king had left. When Marcus Ralla arrived at the Roman camp in the Bagradas Valley, he told Scipio the rest of the story. Masinissa had forced the Roman contingent from the city and remained there to bury his queen. Scipio had already been concerned about Masinissa, but now he worried that he had lost him as an ally, something he could not afford with Hannibal due in Africa any day.

Several days passed with no word from Masinissa. Scipio had just decided to send a contingent to Cirta when he learned that Masinissa had arrived at the Roman camp accompanied by Anir. He immediately dispatched a centurion to find Masinissa and bring him to headquarters.

Scipio was alone in the tent when Masinissa entered, head down, uncertain why he had even bothered to obey Scipio's orders.

"The tribune I sent to Cirta for Hasdrubal's daughter told me that she took poison," Scipio said.

A composed and unusually somber Masinissa nodded absently while looking at the ground.

"And that you were there when he arrived with his men."

Masinissa lifted his head. "Yes, sir, that's correct."

Scipio took a deep breath and shook his head sadly. "In other words, you tried to correct your previous act of poor judgment with a second?"

"If that's how you see it, sir."

"And how do you see it?"

Masinissa, a man who feared nothing, always struggled before Scipio. "I fulfilled the promise I made to my wife."

"She was not your wife. She was the property of Rome. You had no obligation to her for anything."

"I did what I had to do." His composure began to melt away.

"Do you regret that now?" asked Scipio.

"I regret that the woman I loved is dead, yes." His voice shook and tears ran down his cheeks.

"Control yourself, Masinissa. Hannibal is on his way to Africa now. We will soon be facing the greatest challenge of this campaign. Passion, except in heat of battle, is at odds with clear thinking."

Masinissa wiped the tears from his face with the back of his hand.

"Are you capable of leading your men?"

Masinissa glared at Scipio and muttered, "Yes," through gritted teeth.

"Have you any thoughts of taking poison yourself?" There was a hint of ridicule in Scipio's tone.

Masinissa's face tightened. "No."

"Can you, after twice making decisions at odds with your general, be trusted to follow my commands and act according to the interests of Rome?"

"Yes, sir."

Scipio nodded, still unable to read the man's heart. "I cannot deny it, Masinissa, I have lost a large measure of my respect for you. You have revealed the passions of a barbarian, not a military officer. But I also know that when you are right-headed, when you are focused, you are the best man I have. Your capacity as a cavalry commander is unmatched by anyone I have ever seen on horseback."

Masinissa looked down at the ground, furious at the way Scipio was talking to him.

"I promised to give you back your kingdom if you forfeited Hasdrubal's daughter to Rome. You agreed to this, then broke your word. Though the woman is dead and out of the way, there is no reason for me to uphold my end of the bargain. Is that correct?"

Masinissa, his eyes still on the ground, said nothing.

"Is that correct?"

Masinissa lifted his eyes, now nearly spiking with flames from the heat behind. "If that's how you see it, sir."

"Hasdrubal's daughter was only a trophy to me," said Scipio. "Her loss is nothing otherwise. I will still uphold my part of the bargain if you are able to lead your cavalry with complete loyalty to the Roman cause. Can you abide by that?"

"You can count on me, sir"

"Then I will. But don't let me down again. It will cost you everything you have gained, including my friendship. You're dismissed."

Masinissa turned away, then stopped as he lifted the tent flap. "You should know, General, that I have amassed another six thousand infantry and four thousand cavalry. They are on their way from Cirta now. They'll be here in three days. We have a war to win."

CHAPTER 102

News that Hannibal had landed in Hadrumentum—on the African coast about one hundred miles southeast of Carthage—reached our camp four days after Masinissa's return. The reports we had received from Rome said that Hannibal's army had been greatly reduced by attrition in his final year in Bruttium, and that he had been lucky to escape from Italy at all. We also learned that Mago had died during the voyage back to Africa from the javelin wound he received in north Italy. Mago's troops, however, had arrived safely and had joined Hannibal who was now recruiting far and wide to rebuild his army.

Along with Mago's twelve thousand Gallic mercenaries, Hannibal had what remained of his most loyal soldiers, men who had come with him from Spain, now less than two thousand in number, plus another ten thousand mercenaries he had brought with him from Italy. Hasdrubal Gisgo secured another ten thousand untrained Libyan and Carthaginian recruits and eighty elephants and brought them to Hadrumentum.

Hannibal's biggest concern, however, was cavalry, an essential piece in just about all of his tactical maneuvers. He reached out to Syphax's cousin, a Numidian by the name of Tychaeus. Tychaeus answered with two thousand Numidian horse. Little by little, Hannibal was piecing together an army which, though short on experience, was somewhat greater in number than Scipio's thirty thousand veterans.

When Hannibal was ready, he marched from Hadrumetum seventy-five miles west to a place called Zama, not far from the Bagradas Valley. He set up camp less than ten miles from our camp, intent on bringing an end to Scipio's reign of terror.

Finally, some three years after Scipio had been given a consulship and permission to go to Africa, Hannibal and Scipio were positioned to meet on the battlefield.

CHAPTER 103

The day after we learned of Hannibal's arrival, one of our foraging parties caught three of his scouts in the low hills behind our camp. They were immediately brought to Scipio. Rather than imprisoning them or torturing them for information, Scipio ordered Masinissa to give the three Numidians a tour of the camp, then to bring them back to headquarters.

Of course everyone in camp was aware that the scouts had been captured, but the soldiers were stunned to see Masinissa escorting them like guests through the camp. I encountered Masinissa and the three men during their tour. At first I just watched them as they passed, as stupefied as everyone else by Scipio's hospitality. Then I hurried after them, calling to Masinissa to stop so I that could speak to the captured scouts. With Masinissa acting as an interpreter, I asked them if a woman traveled with Hannibal, a woman of forty years with a lovely singing voice. The lead scout, who I'm sure was thrilled not to be in chains, told me what he might not have otherwise. Yes, there was such a woman, a slave, he said, traveling with the army. She was kept in leg irons at all times because of Hannibal's concern that she might try to escape. Though I didn't explain this to Masinissa, I knew the woman was my mother. Now at least I knew where she was, and more importantly, that she was alive.

When the scouts returned to headquarters, Scipio asked them if Masinissa had sufficiently described the workings of the camp, and if there were anything else they wanted to know. Completely disarmed by Scipio's generosity, the scouts said they had no more questions. Shocking these men even further, Scipio arranged for an escort to take them back to Hannibal's camp.

I tossed and turned all through that night thinking about my mother. What would happen to her should we defeat Hannibal? His camp would be immediately plundered, and in the chaos that followed, if she weren't simply murdered by those in the camp, there was no assurance that I would find her before a Roman legionnaire, who would certainly consider her fair game for a soldier's pleasure.

The more I thought about it, the worse I felt. Finally, in the hours before dawn, I concluded that nothing, not the potential battle between Hannibal and Scipio, nor the outcome of the war, nor even my own life, was more important than my mother's safety. That was when the idea struck me.

The diagram for Archimedes' adjustable parabolic mirror array was in headquarters buried in my stack of maps. What if I went to Hannibal's camp and offered him a trade—the drawing for my mother? Instead of giving it to Scipio, a decision I had yet to make, why not use the drawing for my own personal advantage?

Beyond the fact that I might be killed just trying to get close to the Carthaginian camp, what would it mean if Hannibal accepted my offer? How would that impact the war? As I thought this out, I realized that even if Hannibal were able to evade Scipio for a month, as he had Marcellus in Italy, there was really no way that he could build the array and use it effectively against us. I had studied all the designs, but never mastered this one. There were no more than ten men in the world who could even understand the mathematics, much less be available to Hannibal at a moment's notice to make the array operational. The design, in my mind, was an invaluable demonstration of optical science, but in practice, all but impossible to apply to the dynamics of a set piece battle.

After a full night without sleep, I decided to take a chance. I went to headquarters that morning and pretended to work. Midmorning I left headquarters with the scroll containing the plans for the parabolic array. I went to our corral and told the guard that I was going to make some last minute observations of the vicinity to add detail to the map. He knew me well enough to understand that this was something I did, though rarely on my own.

Hannibal's camp was a little less than ten miles away. It was not an easy ride, and I didn't want to be seen. I spotted the camp from a ridge overlooking Zama. Knowing that Hannibal could very well imprison me and take the scroll as soon as I told him what it was, I found a place to hide it. If things went well and I had secured the safety of my mother, I would take Hannibal to the location and give it to him.

I rode down to the Carthaginian camp without a weapon. I was surrounded by perimeter guards before I got anywhere near the gate. I told them I wanted to see Hannibal. When they laughed at my request, I told them I had information that their general would like to know.

They were reluctant, but took me into the camp. That I was a Greek certainly helped. The process within the camp was no easier. I was questioned by a Carthaginian officer and told that Hannibal was too busy for visitors. Fortunately I managed to convince him to pass one simple message on to Hannibal: *Arathia's son is here to talk to you.* The son of a spy, I thought to myself, what had I to lose but my life!

The officer left me in the company of three guards and went off to give Hannibal my message. He was back almost immediately. The three guards took me directly to Hannibal.

I was shaking with fear when I was pushed into the tent by one of the guards. I stumbled and fell on the ground.

"Arathia's son," said a deep voice. "How fortunate we should meet again." Hannibal stood over me and laughed. His cavalry captain Maharbal watched from the far side of the tent. Both men had aged noticeably in the four years since I had last seen them. Hannibal's beard and hair were more gray than black.

"Yes, sir," I said, climbing to my feet. "Quite fortunate for you."

Hannibal frowned. "Why's that?"

"I come from Scipio's camp. I'm his mapmaker."

"What could you possibly know that we don't already? Scipio just gave my scouts a tour of his camp." Hannibal turned to Maharbal. "This is the son of our captured spy. The woman with the beautiful singing voice."

Maharbal seemed puzzled. "Then why is he still alive?"

Hannibal grinned, despite the strain in his face. "Tell me, Timon, why shouldn't I kill you right now?"

"Do you recall, sir, that I said I had been a slave for Archimedes."

"Yes, of course."

"When we met in Metapontum, you asked me about the war machines that Archimedes had used against the Romans in Syracuse. Then you asked me if I could build one of the mirror arrays that focused sunlight into fire."

Hannibal lifted his head in interest.

"I was recruited by Scipio because of what I learned from Archimedes. I went to Syracuse with him and spent a year there before coming to Africa. During that time I returned to Archimedes' workshop and found a few of his documents that had not been destroyed in the siege. One was a set of engineering drawings describing just such a parabolic array, with directions for building it."

Hannibal turned again to Maharbal, then back to me. "Go on."

"I want to trade the drawings for my mother's freedom."

Hannibal didn't hesitate. "Let me see these drawings."

"I don't have them with me. I have hidden them in a location within walking distance of here. They're yours if you allow me to leave here with my mother."

Hannibal was clearly intrigued. He paced back and forth a few times in front of me. "Can you build the device?"

"No. Nor could you without a well outfitted workshop, a crew of top notch craftsmen, and a scholar with exceptional knowledge of geometry."

"Then what good are these drawings?" demanded Maharbal. "We're wasting time with this Greek, Hannibal. I say kill him now. Spies make me nervous." He took his short sword from his belt.

Hannibal raised his hand. "Hold on, Maharbal. I like this young man's bravado." He appraised me with his one good eye. "You have come here at great risk, Timon. You have put your life on the line to free your mother. Even though she deceived me, and used my kindness to draw information from me—to be passed on to Claudius Nero—perhaps by you," his eyes met mine, "I still value her, and even have some respect for her. She's an individual of tremendous courage, as it seems you are too.

"Here's my offer. I will trade your mother for these diagrams. Not because I believe they can help me win this war, but because they are valuable simply as pieces of Archimedes' work—and also because of Scipio's treatment of my scouts yesterday." He smiled. "I have been impressed by this young Roman general. He must be very confident. I would like the opportunity to meet him. I want you to tell him that."

I nodded.

"Good. I will have your mother brought to this tent. Then your mother, you and I, and Sosylus will go to where you have hidden the diagrams. Sosylus and I will review them. If they are authentic, you and your mother will be free to go."

I felt my whole body go weak. "Yes, sir."

He smiled, a genuine smile. "You will take my request to Scipio. Tell him that I would like to talk to him—face to face—alone—before our armies murder each other." Hannibal laughed. "Tell him I have gained a certain admiration for him, and welcome the chance to meet such a man."

"What if he declines?"

"Our arrangement does not hinge on his response, only on your delivering my message in the best possible manner you can. I believe you will be able to do that better than any other emissary I could send. You know the man. Make my offer in a way that allows him to accept it."

"And should you talk to him, I have one request."

Hannibal laughed at my moxie. "And that is?"

"Do not mention the diagrams or my mother. He does not know about the weapon, my mother, or that I have come here on my own. I will have to lie about all of these things to properly deliver your message. I will tell him that I got too close to your camp while working on my map, and that I was caught. You let me go because he let your scouts go. If he learns that I was here to make a deal with you, I will be called a traitor and summarily executed. Can you protect me in this?"

Hannibal chuckled at my request, then turned to Maharbal. "A lad with some rather large ones."

Maharbal found no humor in the situation. "I think we should kill him right now. And forget this talk of yours with Scipio."

"No, that's something I want to do. Scipio intrigues me." He turned to me. "I won't mention a word of our conversation. But how will you explain the sudden appearance of your mother in camp?"

"I don't intend to take her back to camp. I saw a cave on the way here. She is capable of taking care of herself. I will hide her there until—until I can figure something out."

Hannibal had my mother brought to his headquarters. She burst into tears immediately upon seeing me, but we had no time for happy words or kisses or even an explanation of what was happening. Hannibal called for Sosylus and we left the camp.

Carrying my mother's things, I led Hannibal, my mother, Sosylus, and my horse up the ridge to where I had hidden the scroll containing the drawings. Five members of Hannibal's Sacred Band trailed after us for the general's security. I was not at all worried about them killing me. I knew that Hannibal was a man of elevated character and felt quite certain that he would not deceive me.

I retrieved the scroll from beneath a small bush and gave it to Hannibal. Hannibal was highly educated, more so than Scipio. He recognized the quality of the work immediately, and after a moment, handed the scroll to Sosylus. Sosylus, also in a very short time, verified the authenticity of the document and advised Hannibal to accept the scroll in exchange for my mother.

While Hannibal and Sosylus headed back to their camp, I helped my mother onto the horse. I held the reins and led her to the cave I had mentioned to Hannibal.

"How did you know I was in Hannibal's camp?" my mother asked.

"Through the Community of Miracles network. Ennius sent a mutual friend to Africa to tell me. But the information was incomplete. Ennius didn't know if you were imprisoned or executed after the kidnapping. When Hannibal's scouts were captured the other day, Scipio allowed them to view our camp. I asked one of them if there were a woman in their camp with a beautiful singing voice. When he said yes, I knew it was you."

"And Hannibal released me in exchange for that scroll? What did it contain?"

"The secrets of war are changing, Mother. The size of an army or the details of a battle strategy, those are the kinds of information a spy usually seeks. But there are other types of information. Things that are more subtle and are held in even greater secrecy."

"What do you mean?"

"The application of science to war. My experience with Archimedes included knowledge of war machines that no one else could even imagine. The scroll I gave to Hannibal contained plans for such a weapon."

My mother's expression was a question.

"It's a variation of something Archimedes used against the Romans in Syracuse. Hannibal had heard of it. It's significant."

"Will it change the war?"

"No, and Hannibal seemed to know that. The device, or something like it, will surely be a part of warfare in the years to come, but not yet. I believe the real reason Hannibal let you go was that he has strong feelings for you—not love, but respect. I think he sees that the war is coming to an end, and spy or not, he wanted you to have your life back."

My mother nodded. "Yes, I could feel that. Any other man would have had me tortured or crucified. Even as a slave and wearing shackles, I sang for him nearly every night."

"And nothing else?"

"I was flogged upon my return, but only once. Ten lashes. I think he did that for the other officers, not because he wanted to hurt me."

"What happened in Rome? How were you caught?"

"I went to the Community of Miracles. I felt it was important to visit the people who had helped me when I was still a slave. I went there several times and sang at their theater. I owed it to them. Then one afternoon, just after Lucretia and I had gotten inside the city walls, we were surrounded by a group of men and forcefully taken away. I was gagged and blindfolded, and eventually delivered to Hannibal for what I believe was a large reward. I still don't know what happened to Lucretia."

"Her body was found in the Tiber."

My mother turned away and began to cry.

When we reached the cave, I helped my mother from the horse. The cave was shallow, but its opening was partially hidden by a stand of myrtle trees. It was risky, but my mother said not to worry. Hannibal had given her some blankets and a few pounds of wheat. She would be all right. I told her that the Roman camp was less than two miles away and that I would come visit her whenever I got the chance. There was a critical battle was in the offing; its outcome would determine all that came next.

CHAPTER 104

I entered our camp shortly after sundown. I went straight to headquarters. Scipio was there with Cato and Laelius. I told them I had been captured by Hannibal's scouts while mapping the area. Scipio scolded me for going out alone and getting too close to Hannibal's camp, then asked, "Why did Hannibal let you return?"

"Because of your treatment of his scouts. He was very impressed by that. He said he wanted to meet you."

"What do you mean?"

"He wants to talk with you, one on one. I think he has tremendous respect for you."

"What does he want to talk about?" asked Cato, clearly suspicious.

"He didn't say. Part of the reason he released me was so that I could bring you this message. I believe, sir, that he wants to see who you are as a man. I think you should consider this request a compliment."

"A compliment in war?" snapped Cato. "Who needs that? Refuse him."

Laelius echoed the same sentiments, but Scipio was intrigued. He sent two envoys to Hannibal's camp the next morning to agree to the meeting. Later that day, Hannibal moved his camp to a hill about four miles from our camp. The two generals would meet the following day at noon, midway between the two camps, alone except for translators.

CHAPTER 105

With the African sun blazing directly overhead in a cloudless, slate blue sky, a squadron of men on horseback rode out of each camp at noon the next day. The two contingents came to a halt several hundred feet apart. Hannibal and Scipio dismounted and walked toward each other, accompanied by their translators.

I was with Scipio for this remarkable moment in history. The two greatest military minds of that time, with responsibilities equal to those of any king or emperor in the world, both commanding armies near or in excess of forty thousand men, were going to talk. Scipio gave away nothing of his thoughts beforehand. I had no idea what to expect.

The two men, one fair and clean shaven, one dark with a thick, graying beard, acknowledged each other from a distance with their eyes. Hannibal glanced briefly at me then extended his hand to Scipio as they approached each other. Scipio accepted his hand as the two men seemed to appraise each other before opening the conversation. Though both men were capable in Greek, Scipio would speak in Latin and I would translate to Greek. Hannibal would speak in Greek; his aide would translate to Latin.

Scipio initiated the discussion with a compliment. "I don't believe I have ever so wanted to meet any man, Hannibal. This is a great honor for me."

"From what my generals have told me about your campaign in Spain, Scipio, the honor is mine."

Scipio smiled easily. "That's a powerful compliment from a man who has kept Rome in absolute fear for nearly twenty years and never lost a battle."

Hannibal nodded. "If these words between us, Scipio, are truly spoken out of mutual respect and not some facile diplomatic etiquette, then please take what I have to say to heart. You are young. Fortune has been your friend. You have won many accolades on the battlefield.

And from what I have gathered, your military expertise is unmatched by any Roman of any time. Much the same could be said of me as a Carthaginian. I have also been lucky. Fortune shone on me much of my time in Italy. After the battle of Cannae, I was nearly master of the entire peninsula. Four years later, I brought an army to within five miles of Rome, expecting surrender, and wondering how I would exact my terms. Today, I am in Africa wondering what Rome might ask of Carthage, should she surrender."

This was not what Scipio was expecting. A moment of silence held before Hannibal resumed. "Remember that change of fate, Scipio. Do not be overly proud, and I beg you, keep your thoughts on the human scale of things. Follow the course that will produce the most good and the fewest negative consequences. For what man of sense would choose to rush into the danger that confronts you now? If you are victorious, you will add little of importance to your own reputation or to the glory of Rome, but if you are defeated, you will wipe out all memory of the fame and honors you have already achieved.

"I am considerably older than you, Scipio. I have spent more than half of my forty-five years at war. I have seen tens of thousands of men die on the battlefield, both mine and those of Rome. In the last four years, my three brothers have died in the name of Carthage. And, if I am not mistaken, you have lost a father and an uncle."

Scipio nodded that this was true.

"If fate has decreed that I am the aggressor in this war," continued Hannibal, "and that too many times I have fallen short of a final victory, then it is for me, at this time, to ask for peace. I do not wish to see the soldiers perched on these hills," he looked off to both camps, "laid out upon this plain tomorrow in heaps of useless flesh. There is no longer any need for Rome and Carthage to spill blood. That you have forced me home and out of Italy means the war is over as far as I am concerned. Your strategy has been masterful. I would love to show you wrong on the battlefield tomorrow, and yet for my people, for Carthage, there is no sense in going on. So you might ask, why did I request this meeting? I seek peace and offer a proposal for surrender."

Scipio could not help but smile. "That my father should confront you when you arrived in Italy at the beginning of the war, and that I should confront you now, sixteen years later to end it, is a great irony. I never doubted that Rome would triumph in the end, and yet, it still humbles me to receive these words from you, Hannibal. Make your offer."

"I propose that all the territories whose possession we have disputed in the past, meaning Sicily, Sardinia, and Spain, shall belong to Rome, and that Carthage shall never go to war again with her over these territories. All the other islands lying between Italy and Africa shall likewise belong to Rome. Such terms of peace will be difficult for Carthage in the future, but should be considered most honorable for you and all Romans."

Scipio tilted his head as in question. "But where is your concession in those terms, Hannibal? All of those lands you so honorably give away are already in the hands of Rome. I offered your Council of Elders those same terms six weeks ago with the modest addition of an indemnity of five thousand talents of silver. These were terms both your elders and I agreed upon. Envoys from my camp and your council went to Rome to present this proposal to our Senate, and it was accepted. Then, when it seemed that the war was over, your people treacherously violated the peace, most likely because they knew you would soon be in Africa. Put yourself in my position and tell me, should I now strike the harshest clauses from the treaty?

"Had you vacated Italy some time ago, prior to my putting pressure on Carthage, then I would be foolish to reject the armistice you offer. But now, it seems to me, there is a measure of disingenuousness in your offer. As a counter to the previous arrangement, it's not even a compromise, but a retreat from earlier terms that I rejected. Had you included at least part of the indemnity previously agreed upon, then perhaps there could be peace—saving all the blood that will turn this dry desert plain red because you haven't. The fact is you must either put yourself and your country unconditionally into Roman hands—or else fight us and conquer us."

This was not the response Hannibal had sought, but it was not unexpected. "I understand your position, Scipio, and I don't feel any insolence in your reply, but I do not have the power to accept any kind of indemnity without consulting the Council of Elders. My offer today was made in good faith. I accept that it was rejected in the same."

Scipio nodded. "Then what we can not settle peacefully today, we must settle on the battlefield tomorrow."

"So it must be," replied his foe.

The two men turned and walked away. They mounted their horses, and both contingents of soldiers returned to their camps.

CHAPTER 106

Later that day I was in headquarters working on a map of the battlefield when Scipio, Laelius, Lucius, Marcus Ralla, Masinissa, and Cato filed into the tent. I stepped away from the map, and Scipio gathered his commanders at the table.

"I believe we have a force considerably superior to Hannibal's," he said. "He has a number of soldiers who came with him from Italy. I imagine they are his best men, but they are not in great number. The majority of his troops have been raised in the last two months or less. They are untrained and inexperienced. He also has a good number of elephants. We have seen them from camp, more than I have ever seen readied for a battle."

Scipio picked up a few of the markers that were in a pile beside the map. "I don't pretend to know how Hannibal will deploy his troops, but I have such confidence in ours that we will align much as we did against Syphax and Hasdrubal on the Great Plains."

One by one he put the markers on the map. "We will use the standard formation of three lines—hastati, principes, and triarii—but it will be six legions across—three Roman and three allied. Ralla will be on the far right with the Sixth. Cato in the center with the Twenty-third, and Lucius to the left of Cato with the Fifth. Between each of you will be an allied legion, with the Numidian infantry taking the position on the far left. Place your velites behind the lines. They will open the battle as skirmishers in the traditional manner."

No one said anything.

Scipio continued. "Masinissa, I want you on the right flank with your cavalry." He looked at Masinissa and the king's eyes held firm in assent. "Laelius, you will be on the left with the Italian horse."

Laelius nodded that he understood.

"Our strategy will be to repeat what we did on the Great Plains. I want the cavalry to clear the flanks."

"I know Tychaeus," said Masinissa. "His men are nothing compared to ours."

Scipio placed the last of the markers on the map. "Any questions?"

"Maintain rank and order," emphasized Cato.

"Always," added Scipio. "We will meet again at sunrise to review the strategy and make adjustments based on what we see from Hannibal. Prepare your men well tonight. Tell them they are about to make Rome the greatest republic the world has ever known and that they will be her greatest heroes."

CHAPTER 107

That night our tent unit ate in near silence. We all knew that the coming battle with Hannibal, should he actually decide to meet our challenge, was likely to end the war—a war that had been going on for more than half our lives.

The feeling around the fire reminded me of those nights in Marcellus' camp, when our foe had also been Hannibal, and the weight of the world seemed to sit on our shoulders. I had seen Troglius in this situation before. His demeanor never seemed to change. Whether there was a battle the next day or not, he stared into the campfire and ran his whetstone down the length of his gladius.

Rullo, however, was visibly tense, even more so than before the battle of the Great Plains. The war had been going on his entire life and Hannibal's name had become synonymous with death and destruction. Something about him seemed supernatural and god-like. Facing him across the battlefield was like facing Homer's Cyclops or Hercules' Cacus. There was no dice game that night. No horseplay. Everything was business, tending to weapons and armor, trying to shut out the nerves so that at some point sleep might come.

Though not a soldier, I was as anxious as anyone in our camp, wondering about the battle and how its outcome would impact my reunion with my mother. I struggled to sleep and climbed from my bed roll in the middle of the night to go outside. I hadn't noticed that Rullo's bed was also empty. I found him sitting beside the smoldering campfire, staring at the few remaining embers. I sat down beside him, probably just as nervous about the next day as he was.

"Tough night for sleeping," I said at slightly more than a whisper.

Rullo glanced at me, nodded, then continued staring into the fire.

"Are you all right?"

Rullo, who always maintained an air of confidence, even when ill at ease, muttered, "I'm frightened."

"As is nearly every person in this camp."

"Not Troglius."

"As I said, nearly everyone."

"It won't be like the Great Plains," he said.

"Many men on both sides will die tomorrow. That's what war is."

"I don't want to be afraid."

"No one does."

Neither of us said anything for a while. I broke the spell with a question that I had wondered about for a long time. "Do you know who your father is?"

He lifted his eyes to mine in question. "No."

"It's Marcus Claudius."

His eyes widened. "Who said that?"

"Ithius told me."

This was no small revelation. Rullo's eyes darted from side to side, turning things over in his head.

"It happened when your mother and Marcus were young. As you must know, Romans don't acknowledge children fathered with their slaves."

"Marcus is my father? Truly? And you've known all along?"

"For a couple of years."

"Why are you telling me now?"

Despite my own anxiety, I managed to smile. "I thought it might help you tomorrow—to know what your heritage is, what blood runs through you. I think you might be more than you think you are—yet another reason cheating at dice doesn't become you."

"I'm the son of Marcus and the grandson of Marcellus," he said more to himself than to me.

"A grandfather who was elected five times to consul, and a father who will likely be elected to that position a few times himself. Maybe that knowledge will help you believe in yourself—and allow you get a little sleep tonight."

"Or none at all," he said softly.

"I'm going to give it another try." I got up to go into the tent.

Rullo stopped me. "Thank you, Timon. It's important to know what you've just told me, even if Marcus never acknowledges it."

"He may not, but it doesn't change who you are and what courses through your heart." I turned and went into the tent. I heard Rullo come in shortly afterward.

CHAPTER 108

A centurion came to our tent before dawn and roused me from sleep. He told me the general wanted to see me. I had gotten almost no sleep and stumbled out of the tent into the pre-morning dark. The centurion led me to the front of the camp where Scipio was waiting. Four soldiers came out of the camp after us, carrying a folded tent.

Scipio ordered the men to set up the tent, then drew me aside to talk in private. "These men will have this tent up shortly. I want you to help them position it so that you can recreate what you showed me prior to the battle on the Great Plains."

"Sir?"

"The image made of light on the tent wall." Scipio glanced over his shoulder to check the soldiers' progress. "Put a hole in the side of the tent that faces the battlefield." He motioned to the open plain below our camp. "When the sun comes up, I want an image of the battlefield projected on the inside of the tent. Can you do that?"

"The angles of the sun will determine whether it's possible or not, sir. I can't guarantee anything until midmorning."

Scipio looked off at the Carthaginian camp across the way. A few lonely trails of smoke twisted up above the ramparts. After a moment, he faced me. "Do what you can. I will meet with my officers in headquarters at sunrise. Shortly afterward, the troops will assemble in the intervallum. We will make no further move until Hannibal has set his formation. That could be immediately at daybreak or at noon or not at all. In any case, when his troops are in formation, I will bring my commanders here to the front of the camp to discuss last minute adjustments before sending our troops out. I want to use the projected image to help describe our strategy."

"Instead of simply pointing to the battlefield, sir?"

"Using the image will have more impact."

"Yes, I imagine it will."

Scipio nodded, walked away, then came right back, clearly anxious about the upcoming battle. "I also want you to apply the lens to the hole to clarify the image, but don't let anyone notice what you're doing. It should be easy enough. Their attention will be on the image, not you. Any questions?"

"No, sir," I answered, my head swimming with questions.

"Good. Go help the men position the tent. They're waiting."

As I walked away, Dilius Strabo came out of the camp trailed by his two attendants and a calf on a lead. Strabo wore a white, hooded robe that reached to his ankles. He strode directly up to Scipio with all the pretense of his religious arts and pointed to the eastern horizon. The faintest hint of light glowed behind the distant mountains.

The two men conversed briefly. Scipio, a man who always followed the sacrificial rituals perfectly and appeared to view them without cynicism, stepped aside to watch the short, fat augur perform his duties.

Dilius began with a prayer to Mars. Then one of the attendants gave him a small cloth bag of mola. While the other attendant held the animal's lead, Dilius sprinkled mola down the calf's spine. Dilius traded the cloth bag for an amphora of wine and dribbled some of it over the calf's forehead. After running the sacrificial knife along the animal's back, he signaled to the attendants with a tip of his head. They took the calf by the feet and flipped it on its back. Dilius knelt down and slit the screeching animal's throat. The attendants held the animal so that it bled out, then the augur used the knife to open the animal's belly. The attendants held the incision open while Dilius fished out the internal organs one by one for inspection. Scipio stood beside the augur, watching closely, anticipating any hint of the God of War's mood.

Dilius stood. I couldn't hear all that he said, but I did catch his final words. "Mars will bless you with victory today, General. I have never seen such favorable signs in a set of entrails."

Of course this pleased Scipio. Even I, a non-believer, welcomed the auspicious reading. The negative readings before Marcellus' death would never leave me free of these superstitions, but I also knew that Dilius had never given Scipio a bad reading. It seemed that Scipio had attained through soft words what Marcellus had demanded with force—an augur who supported everything he did.

Dilius returned to the camp. The two priests followed, carrying the carcass. Scipio took a moment to look to the heavens. I heard the hush of his voice, whispering a prayer to his father.

Two men with trumpets were standing on either side of the gate, waiting for Scipio's response to the augur's reading. Scipio slid the purple cape from his shoulders and hung it from one of the gate posts. As soon as Scipio disappeared into the camp, the trumpets sounded the wake up call.

On such a momentous morning, the camp came to life quickly. I went back to my tent to get some wheat gruel and flat bread, then returned to the front of the camp to wait for the sun to rise.

Using the spyglass, I could see that Hannibal had hung his blue cloak at the entrance to his camp. It was only a matter of time before the armies would begin to file onto the battlefield to culminate sixteen years of war.

When the sun sat on top of the mountains to the east, and long shadows streaked across the landscape, Scipio came out of the camp with his five commanders. Informed by our scouts that Hannibal had accepted Scipio's challenge, the officers were grim and focused.

Scipio had intended to wait until Hannibal set his formation before giving the signal for our troops to leave the camp, but the early morning passed with no sign of the opposing army. Usually a man of remarkable calm before a battle, Scipio became increasingly agitated as the time passed. Off and on I went into the tent to see if there were enough sunlight to project an image through the hole. Each time, Scipio would look to me for a sign one way or the other. Three times I shook my head, no.

Midmorning Scipio decided not to wait any longer. He told his commanders to give the order to their men to march from camp and align themselves in the formation he had described the day before. On Scipio's request, the commanding officers, who would usually accompany their men, remained on the hill, leaving supervision of the process to their tribunes.

About the time our troops were assembling on the battlefield and the general order of our formation was becoming obvious, we heard trumpets from the opposition's camp, signaling for their troops to align opposite ours. This was also when an image of the battlefield began to clarify on tent's east wall. I passed this on to Scipio.

I was inside, standing beside the hole in the tent, when Scipio entered. He purposely positioned himself so that he blocked the beam of light from reaching the tent wall. As soon as everyone was in the tent, Cato questioned the purpose of the meeting.

"What are we doing in this dark tent, General? What can we learn in here when our opponent's troops are assembling on the battlefield, and there is still time to make adjustments?"

"Aren't we wasting critical time, sir?" seconded Marcus Ralla.

Scipio ignored both comments. "I had a dream last night," he announced dramatically. "I saw the battle take place in a vision on the wall of my tent."

Cato continued to fret. "General, what are you talking about?"

Scipio took a step sideways so that he was no longer blocking the beam of light. "Just like that," he said, pointing to the image on the wall as though it had appeared out of nowhere.

All of the men abruptly turned to the patch of light. Scipio stared at it with such intensity the image appeared to be coming from his eyes. "Yes, that's the vision I saw last night."

The others stood off to either side of the image, staring at it, gradually deciphering, as I worked to bring the image into focus with the lens, that it was the battlefield outside. All of a sudden, there it was—in stunning clarity. The officers, even Scipio, stood back in awe, then leaned in close to watch in amazement as they saw the men on the battlefield in miniature, moving into place like toy soldiers.

"How can this be?" exclaimed Lucius. "Those are our men and Hannibal's moving into formation."

"With his elephants as a first line," stated Laelius aghast at what he was seeing.

"And his Numidians on the left opposite mine," added Masinissa, his eyes wide with the magic of the vision.

"What are we seeing?" demanded Cato.

"My dream," said Scipio. "It's exactly what I saw last night."

"Impossible" said someone under his breath.

Lucius left the tent and came back immediately. "It's identical to what's going on outside. What kind of vision is this?"

All of the officers looked at each other then back to the image.

"Except for the elephants, his alignment matches well with ours," said Scipio. "His infantry stands in three lines with his cavalry on the wings."

"But look at the number of elephants," added Ralla. "How can we fight against so many?"

"Yes, that could be a problem," Scipio muttered.

Laelius approached the image from the side and used his gladius as a pointer. "Look here. If we move our maniples so that they're one behind the other, instead of staggered, we can create lanes in the formation. Some of the elephants might strike our men, but the dumb brutes will seek the openings. I'm sure of it. As they pass through, we can strike them from behind."

"That might work," agreed Cato, still staring at the living image on the wall.

"We'll move the velites forward into the lanes to obscure the change from Hannibal," said Scipio, excited by Laelius' observation. "They can throw their javelins when the elephants charge, then retreat back through the openings."

"And if the elephants catch up with them," added Lucius, "they can dodge to either side—then hack at the animals' hamstrings when they pass."

"Yes, exactly," affirmed Scipio, glowing like some otherworldly creature.

The others were too stunned by the image to say anything more.

"The gods have spoken," concluded Scipio. "We will not be denied. Go instruct your men of the changes. Tell them Mars is with us. Tell them that the war will soon be over and that the spoils of Carthage will be ours to divide. Tell them our next voyage will be to Rome with the glory of Rome's greatest victory." He then purposely moved in front of the beam of light so that the image vanished.

The men, all astounded, and fully convinced that they had seen Scipio's dream, filed out of the tent, talking to each other excitedly.

Scipio turned to me when the last man exited. "Not a word."

"Yes, sir."

"To succeed against a foe like Hannibal, sometimes the men must be convinced that they are invincible. The magic we have just shown my staff will translate into confidence and their men will feel it."

I nodded, absolutely amazed by what he had done—all as a show.

Scipio and I had a difficult relationship. I respected him as a brilliant field marshal, and I appreciated that he recognized my intelligence, but I knew the other side of his graciousness. Despite his disarming manners and natural charm, I didn't like the way he had used a dream to justify his burning of the enemy camps. I also didn't like the way he had forced Masinissa to renege on his promise to Sophonisba. Even worse, I felt he had missed an important opportunity to end the war during his conversation with Hannibal. Instead, he had decided to enlarge upon his own glory by going into battle. All of that said, his use of the image on the tent wall was a stroke of genius. I saw how his officers looked at him afterward, as though he had a direct line of communication with the gods. It would surely inspire them. But it was deception—and very much an insight into the man and his methods.

"Put the lens back in your spyglass," said Scipio as we passed out into the daylight. "I want to use it to further analyze Hannibal's formation."

I did as he said and stood beside him as he scanned the opposition with the spyglass. Below, I saw our commanders ride onto the battlefield to join their men. Cato, Lucius, and Marcus Ralla each commanded a legion. They shouted orders to their men and the accompanying allied commanders. The troops responded to the change in orders like a machine. The maniples moved either left or right out of their checkerboard formation, creating open lanes in the alignment, which were then filled by velites.

Scipio gave me the spyglass, then mounted his magnificent red roan that had been brought to the front of the camp by an aide. I watched him canter down the hill, then gallop into the center of the formation to ride back and forth in the space between the hastati and principes, shouting encouragement to the legionnaires and orders to his commanders.

Across the way, Hannibal, riding the huge black war horse I had seen him on six years earlier, did the same, preparing his men for the most important battle of the war. Two great nations, each represented by tens of thousands men, were now ready to enter into mass murder for the right to claim world dominance.

As the two armies jostled about, settling into order and rank, I used the spyglass to assess the battlefield, thinking, much as I had eight years earlier outside Numistro, that I was there to witness the last battle of the war.

The sun was bright and the sky clear on a day that was already heating up. I counted eighty elephants across the front of Hannibal's formation, all wearing bronze breastplates and sharply pointed iron extensions on their tusks. Each one had a mahout guiding them and a howdah perched on its back, carrying four archers. Amassed behind the elephants were several thousand skirmishers, Balearic slingers and Lusitanian light infantry, supported by three lines of heavy infantry, each containing roughly twelve thousand men.

As best I could determine, the first line of infantry contained the mercenaries that Mago had assembled from the barbarian tribes in northern Italy, a mixture of Gaestate, Boii, and Insubres. These monstrous men were the largest on the battlefield, many standing over six feet tall. They fought bare-chested, wearing only sandals on their feet, and girdled in leather loincloths. Their beards were unshorn, and their hair was long, often blond, braided or secured with pieces of bone. These men, wearing helmets adorned with animal horns or headdresses made from the skins of bears or wolves, were a formidable, but undisciplined, collection of soldiers who fought as individuals, swinging long swords or double-edged battle axes.

The second line contained a mix of Libyans in white tunics trimmed in red, carrying round shields and long swords, and Carthaginian recruits, all very young, in blue tunics with brown leather cuirasses, clutching javelins and rectangular shields. Judging from what I had heard, these were the least experienced of Hannibal's troops.

The third line was made up of Hannibal's most loyal men, his remaining veterans, those who had crossed the Alps with him, and the other soldiers he had brought from Italy. These men stood further back, at twice the distance between the first and second line, as though waiting in reserve.

On the wings, matching the Roman formation, were Hannibal's two cavalries. On the left were the highly trained and proficient Numidians, perhaps two thousand, all riding their garrons bareback, and commanded by Syphax's cousin Tychaeus. On the right was the cavalry mustered by Hasdrubal from the aristocracy of Carthage. These men were recent levies, with no more than a month of training.

Opposite Hannibal's heterogeneous mix of barbarian mercenaries and African recruits stood Scipio's nearly uniform legions in red tunics. Half were Roman citizens, half were allied levies, almost all of which had fought and trained together for three years or more. Three lines of heavy infantry—hastati, principes, triarii—formed our center, sixty maniples across, twenty-four thousand men in total. The velites stood ready in the lanes between the maniples.

On the wings were the cavalry. On the right was Masinissa and his four thousand Numidians. On the left was Laelius with two thousand Italians, a mix of Roman equites and allied levies. By my rough count, nearly eighty thousand men were faced off on the dusty African plain to determine the course of world history.

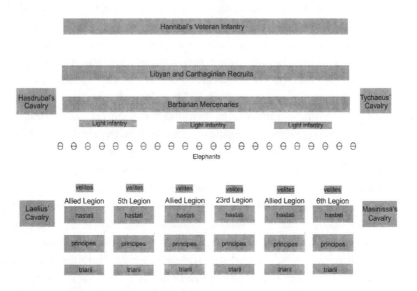

I anticipated a lull, a short break after the commotion of forming battle lines, when both armies stood ready, prior to the beginning of the battle, but Hannibal was still riding up and down his lines, making adjustments in the ranks, when Scipio sounded the battle trumpets. The velites raced forward, javelins upraised, into the open ground between the two armies, while the lines of infantry followed, marching slowly at first, pounding their shields with their gladii and shouting war cries like some huge, screeching machine.

The sudden eruption of sound startled the elephants, causing them to jostle among themselves, some nervously turning in circles. Hannibal quickly shouted his last orders, then waved his sword over his head, signaling for his own battle horns, followed by the multi-lingual battle cries of his mercenaries gathered from ten different nations.

Hannibal had placed the elephants in front to lead his charge and break the order of the Roman line, much as Xanthippus had used them against Regulus at Tunis in Carthage's first war with Rome, but the animals' initial response to the raucous clatter of the advancing Romans spoiled any hope for an orderly attack. While the slingers and light infantry ran mob-like out ahead of the elephants to exchange volleys with our onrushing velites, some of the elephants broke to the left, some to the right.

Elephants were always a risk. In the frenzy of battle, they could stampede in any direction. The elephants that went left saw Masinissa's oncoming cavalry and turned left again, directly into Tychaeus' Numidians. Outnumbered two to one, and scattered by the marauding elephants, Tychaeus' riders were quickly overcome and chased from the battlefield in the opening moments of the battle, with Masinissa's cavalry in hot pursuit.

Some of the elephants that veered right ran between the two armies and off the battlefield completely. Others, pierced by the velites' javelins, turned right again, mirroring what had happened on the left, and thundered directly into the Carthaginian cavalry. These men were young aristocrats with no battle experience. They dispersed almost immediately, trying to avoid the trumpeting monsters that waved their trunks in the air like huge gray serpents. Laelius took advantage of the confusion and routed the cavalry from Hannibal's right flank, chasing them from the battlefield just as Masinissa had done. This repeated what had happened in the early moments of the battle on the Great Plains. Hannibal had lost his protection on both flanks, but for the time being, all cavalry—on both sides—was gone from the battlefield and fighting on the run.

Of the eighty elephants, perhaps forty maintained their course straight ahead into the Roman line. Maybe half of them broke through the first line, trampling scores of men, catching others with their armored tusks, tossing human torsos this way and that as they thrashed about. The others, as Laelius had predicted, raced down the lanes between the maniples. Those that weren't cut down from behind disappeared into the hills behind our camp.

By this time the two armies' front lines were marching resolutely at each other. Our sixty maniples of hastati, ten thousand highly trained legionnaires, against Hannibal's twelve thousand Gauls, who fought as individuals with havoc as a tactic. The ferocity of the giant barbarians more than absorbed our initial surge, pushing the hastati back in a mayhem of slashing blades and severed flesh. But the Roman principes, our second line, swelled up behind the hastati, launching their pila and shouting support to their comrades. With our order reigning in their chaos, the hastati gradually turned the tide, my friend Troglius at the center of it. I could spot him off and on with the spyglass, a windmill with a blade, spraying human parts in all directions.

Hannibal had placed his weakest line second for a reason. They hadn't the courage to be in the first line, and pinned between the first and third, they couldn't run. But they also failed to reinforce the first line when our hastati began to break through. Instead, the young recruits held back and watched the destruction of their fellow soldiers. As soon as the Gallic mercenaries saw what was happening behind them, they turned and in anger attacked their own men. Suddenly the Libyan and Carthaginian levies were fighting both the Romans and the Gauls.

Hannibal must have known that at some point the Roman cavalries led by Laelius and Masinissa would return to the battlefield and attack his men from behind—just as his cavalry had done at Cannae. He needed to make a decisive move before that happened, but instead of bringing his best men into the battle, he allowed his first two lines to be beaten down to nothing, as little more than fodder to wear out the advancing Romans. Soon the entire center of the battlefield was a carpet of corpses, animal carcasses, human body parts, and discarded or broken weapons. The depth and extent of the carnage became an obstacle to our advance. The soldiers had to step around so much bloody muck and human refuse, whole and otherwise, that neither rank nor order could be held.

Scipio, riding back and forth behind the principes, saw what was happening and ordered all three Roman lines to pull back and reform. Though time was wasting for Hannibal, he also took advantage of this lull in the battle to reorder his troops by integrating the survivors of the first two lines into his third. At the same time, the light infantry on both sides cleared the battlefield of the injured as quickly as the situation allowed.

Scipio, anxious for the return of his cavalry, extended his front line, sending the principes to the right flank and the triarii to the left, much as he had at the Great Plains, leaving the hastati on their own to hold the center. Now as the two reformed armies faced off, the Roman line overlapped the Carthaginian line on both ends, a sure problem for the Carthaginian flanks, even without the return of Laelius or Masinissa.

When the battle trumpets blared again, the two armies surged forward. Waves of skirmishers rushed ahead, then quickly gave way to the opposing infantries, trading punch for punch across a heavily contested center line, sometimes pushing forward, sometimes falling back. The roar and howl of the battle echoed through the hills, where bystanders from the surrounding villages stood watching the horror unfold.

Using the spyglass, I scoured the battlefield looking for Rullo, but instead spotted Troglius in the center of the melee, covered with blood, holding the line like a human anchor. He would push forward with his scutum, muscling men out of his way, then cut and slice through the opening with his gladius. To the best of my knowledge, he had been there all day, with only the one break—on an afternoon that was getting long and hot.

Despite Scipio's extension of the front line, our troops could not turn the corner on the Carthaginian line and overrun its flanks. Instead, the two armies held fast, seemingly prepared to fight toe to toe until the last man fell. Then a cloud of dust and thundering horses appeared out of the northwest. Some four thousand Numidians led by Masinissa attacked the Carthaginian line from behind, tossing their darts, then spinning away, only to come back at them again. The arrival of Laelius and the Italian cavalry signaled the beginning of the end. Once the Carthaginian rear was breached, our extended line swung like two gates across the Carthaginian flanks. The enemy was completely surrounded. Except for the brutal butchering of those trapped within, the battle was over.

Dust devils, spawned by the late afternoon wind, spun across the open plain and through the litter of lifeless bodies and animal carcasses. Those few Carthaginians who weren't dead or severely wounded broke for the hills. Hannibal and a small contingent of his cavalry, led by Maharbal, escaped to the south.

While our soldiers straggled back to camp, weary and streaked with blood, Scipio sat astride his red charger, surveying a landscape littered with thirty thousand dead. There was relief, not pleasure, in his face as he contemplated the greatest victory Rome had ever known. A huge weight had been removed from his shoulders. He had accomplished what he had promised to the Roman Senate some six years earlier.

Standing out front of the camp, I used the spyglass to scan the battlefield. Here and there men still fought in small knots of frenzied survivors. Others staggered through the corpses, wildly waving their weapons at anything that moved. I spotted a single legionnaire holding off two of the enemy near the center of the battlefield where the fighting had been fiercest and the dead lay in enormous heaps. As I focused the spyglass, I realized it was Rullo, standing knee deep in corpses, swinging a gladius, and struggling not to be overcome. I didn't take a second look. I secured the nearest horse and a gladius and took off down the hill into the field of human refuse.

I dismounted before my horse came to a stop and ran to Rullo's aid. He stood over a fallen soldier, protecting him from a Libyan waving a sword and a Ligurian hefting a double-bladed battle axe. I raced blade first at the soldier with the axe and pierced him from behind. When the Libyan caught me out of the corner of his eye, Rullo lunged forward and stabbed the man in the stomach. He twisted the blade into the Libyan and pushed him to the ground, then shouted, "It's Troglius, Timon! Help me!"

Troglius lay amid the tangled bodies at Rullo's feet. He was breathing but covered with blood. Rullo and I each took an arm and pulled him from the muck of lifeless debris, then laid him flat on the ground.

Rullo looked at me. "I was on my way back to camp when I saw him staggering out of the carnage. That's when those two men went at him."

I leaned over Troglius and used my tunic to wipe the blood from his face.

"He blocked the first man's parry with his shield," continued Rullo, "then he stumbled backward over a body just as I arrived. The Libyan had him by the hair about to slice his throat when I pulled this gladius from the hand of a dead man and blocked his sword mid-swing."

I could see no major wounds on Troglius' arms or legs, so I loosened the straps of his breastplate, wondering what might be beneath. Troglius muttered something unintelligible as I lifted the heavy armor from his chest and, thankfully, saw no blood.

"Rullo, get the water from the horse!" I shouted, thinking now that Troglius was simply exhausted.

I had Troglius sitting up by the time Rullo returned with the leather water bag. I held it to his lips and dribbled some into this mouth. He tried to gulp it down, so I lowered the water bag to keep him from choking. After another long drink, Troglius reached out and gripped me by the wrist. "You asked me to protect this boy," he turned one eye to Rullo and kept the other focused on me, "but it was he who saved me."

"Yes, apparently the gods were watching. Can you get up?"

He nodded weakly. Rullo and I helped him to his feet. He wavered a moment, then seemed to gather himself. We led him over to the horse and helped him climb on. Rullo led the horse and I walked along beside, making sure Troglius didn't slide off.

When we reached the camp, Scipio cantered up to us on his horse and appraised Troglius' condition. "How is he?"

"I think he's all right, just worn out."

"No doubt. He anchored our front line from beginning to end. Take him into the camp and get him whatever he needs."

"Yes, sir," I said, as Rullo led the horse toward the gate.

When I turned to follow, Scipio stopped me. "You were right about this man, Timon. He was worth any ten soldiers I have. Maybe twenty. Thank you for preventing me from executing him." He yanked on his horse's reins and trotted off.

CHAPTER 109

After the battle, Scipio sent a contingent to plunder the Carthaginian camp. They killed those still in the camp, then looted and burned it. Unless Hannibal took Archimedes' drawings with him, which I doubt he had the chance to do, the scroll was likely lost in the fire.

Scipio sent a second contingent into the surrounding countryside to round up any of the enemy that could be found. The victory was complete. Hannibal's army had been destroyed. More than half were dead, a quarter taken prisoner. The rest sought refuge anywhere they could. Here and there on the horizon I could see the silhouettes of elephants striding slowly across the plain, their empty howdahs displaced to one side or the other. The war was over. The axis of world power had shifted. Instead of a line connecting Rome and Carthage, it was a perpendicular shaft centered at the top of the Capitoline Hill—symbolically a staff in the hand of Jupiter.

That evening after the meal, I took my mother a pot of wheat gruel. She had heard the battle but didn't know the outcome. I told her the camp would be rowdy with celebration and to stay one more night in the cave. I would be back the next morning to bring her into camp and explain her presence to Scipio. No doubt I would have to tell another lie or two.

I headed back to camp in the dark. I could hear both camps, ours and Masinissa's, celebrating long before I reached the gate. Scipio had planned ahead for the victory by procuring a thousand casks of wine in the week prior to the battle. They were quickly distributed throughout both camps. Despite the number of their comrades lost in the battle or nursing wounds, the legionnaires hooted and hollered as I walked down the rows of tents and roaring campfires to my unit.

As I approached our tent, I could see four men sitting in a circle with a torch on a stake flickering over them. I assumed it was another dice game and hoped Rullo wasn't cheating again. Troglius, looking half-dead, lay on the ground at the edge of the circle. Rullo sat beside him. We had lost two men from our unit that day. Aurelius and one other legionnaire completed the group.

I knelt down next to Rullo and immediately jumped back when I saw two scorpions, tails and claws outstretched, stalking each other in the center of the circle. On closer inspection, I noticed that a barrier had been built around the circle to contain the poisonous insects and that stacks of coins sat before Rullo and the other soldiers. They weren't playing dice at all. They were betting on the outcome of a gladiatorial match between the scorpions, one very large and black, the other half its size and a reddish brown.

"Got a bet to place, Timon?" asked Rullo, who had hunted up the scorpions and brought them back to the camp to add some spice to the celebration.

Troglius reached up from his prone position to touch me on the shoulder and offer a weak smile. "I'm betting on the big one."

I gladly accepted a cup of wine from Aurelius, threw a silver stater on top of Troglius' stack of coins, then settled in to watch the scorpions, thankful for Rome's victory, the significance of which wouldn't settle in for another month or more.

CHAPTER 110

After we had buried our dead and packed our train with the plunder taken from Hannibal's camp, we marched back to Utica, where fifty warships and a hundred transports had recently arrived.

Scipio wasted no time in following up his victory. He loaded the transports with booty and sent them off to Sicily escorted by twenty warships under Laelius' command. Scipio then ordered Lucius to take our three legions and their accompanying allied troops to Carthage to establish the siege. Scipio set sail with the remaining thirty warships to blockade the harbor.

Upon reaching the harbor entrance, Scipio was greeted by a Carthaginian merchant ship hung with woolen fillets and olive branches. Ten of Carthage's leading citizens were on board. When their ship came up alongside Scipio's warship, the men called out to Scipio from the deck with praise for his victory, then asked for an opportunity to sue for peace. Scipio told them to meet him in Tunis in a week.

Scipio called off the siege and sailed for Tunis. He sent word to Lucius to meet him there instead of setting up camp outside Carthage. On the way to Tunis, Lucius learned that Syphax's son, Vermina, had scoured the countryside to raise yet another army, determined to save the kingdom his father had lost. Vermina and his fifteen thousand men were headed to Carthage to intercept the Roman forces. Lucius turned south to meet Vermina's army head-on. The ensuing battle matched a confident Roman army against a collection of Numidian rabble. The confrontation was a rout from the onset. Vermina escaped but his army was destroyed.

Lucius joined his brother in Tunis the same day the thirty envoys arrived from Carthage to confer with Scipio. Much as they had a year earlier, the envoys pleaded mercy and blamed the war on Hannibal, prostrating themselves before Scipio, kissing his feet in the oriental fashion of supplication. Although Cato demanded that Scipio besiege the city and strip it of its wealth, Scipio offered them terms for peace, beginning with a stern reprimand for breaking the previous truce, and ending with a much harsher agreement than the first. He doubled the indemnity and asked for one hundred hostages, children from the most powerful families in Carthage, to prevent any further treachery. The final terms of peace were as follows:

- Return all prisoners, deserters, and runaway slaves without ransom
- Withdraw all armies from Italy and Cisalpine Gaul
- Cease all activities in Spain
- Evacuate all of the islands between Spain and the Italian peninsula
- Recognize Masinissa as the king of Numidia
- Surrender the entire Carthaginian fleet except for ten triremes
- Surrender all war elephants
- Supply the Roman army with three months of food and pay the soldier's remaining wages
- Refrain from making war outside Africa except with Rome's permission
- Pay an indemnity of ten thousand talents of silver over a period of fifty years

The envoys returned to Carthage and presented the agreement to the Council of Elders. One elder stood before the Council and shouted them down, telling them that there was no way Carthage could accept such terms. Hannibal, who had returned to Carthage, rushed onto the floor and dragged the man from the podium. The elders erupted in anger at Hannibal. Such a display of force in the Council was against Carthaginian tradition. Had he been at war too long to be civilized?

Hannibal apologized for his actions, saying he had not been in Carthage since he was nine years old and that he was now forty-five. "Yes," he continued, "it was wrong of me to break with custom, but it seems quite beyond my comprehension that anyone who is a citizen of Carthage and has full knowledge of the policies we have adopted against Rome, should not thank his lucky stars that we have obtained such lenient terms. I beg you to not even debate the question, but to declare your acceptance of the proposal unanimously, to offer up sacrifices to the gods, and to pray with one voice that the Roman people will ratify the treaty."

The treaty was accepted. Envoys were sent to Scipio, then on to Rome for the final ratification of the agreement. The war was officially over. After sixteen brutal years of war, Hannibal's daring attempt to conquer Rome had failed.

PART VIII

A TRIUMPH FOR SCIPIO

"Only the dead have seen the end of war."
-Plato

CHAPTER 111

A month after Carthage agreed to the terms of the treaty, Scipio got word from Rome that the Senate had ratified the agreement. His work in Africa was done. The Sixth legion would remain in Africa; a second legion would come from Italy to join it. The Fifth and Twenty-third legions would accompany Scipio back to Lilybaeum. The Fifth, the Cannae survivors, could not return to Italy and would stay in Sicily. The Twenty-third would go on to Rome where Scipio would request a triumph.

Prior to leaving, Scipio gathered all the troops, Roman and allied, outside the camp in Tunis. He stood on a slight elevation before some thirty thousand men and thanked them all as a group.

"Many of you have been with me for four years," he began. "We came to Africa with grand ambitions and many unanswered questions. We leave having accomplished all that we set out to do. We lured Hannibal back to Africa and defeated him, something no other Roman army had done in fifteen years of war. We have relieved the Roman people from a reign of terror, and at the same time crowned our Republic as the greatest in the world. We will return to Rome with a glory unmatched by the deeds of our ancestors, and a military tradition to be built upon by the generations to follow."

The men let out a long sustained roar for Scipio. He raised his hands for silence and continued. "For me, all of this began eight years ago when I was twenty-five years old. The death of my father and my uncle during action in Spain dictated that I volunteer to take their place. Some of you have been with me since that time. The siege of Cartagena, the battle of Ilipa, the battle of Baecula, each step of the way was preparation for the invasion of Africa. But even with those successes, I struggled to get the support of our Senate. Two years were wasted in debate. Another was spent in Syracuse building an army from volunteers and outcasts—outcasts who became the backbone of our infantry!"

A cheer rose up from the survivors of Cannae and Herdonea. They knew Scipio had believed in them from the beginning, much as Marcellus had.

"While it's unfair to single out any one man from an effort achieved by so many, I cannot take leave of Africa without acknowledging her greatest king."

Masinissa stood at the front of the assembly with the rest of Scipio's staff, including Laelius who had just returned from Sicily. Scipio motioned for the Numidian king to come forward. Masinissa climbed the slight incline to Scipio and kneeled before him.

"Masinissa, as a representative of the Roman people, I present you with these gifts as symbols of Rome's appreciation." A centurion behind Scipio handed him an ivory scepter and a beautiful purple toga embroidered with palm fronds. The Roman general placed the toga on Masinissa's shoulders, then bid the king to stand.

"Your skill on a horse and as a cavalry captain are unmatched. No command was more important to our victories in Africa than yours. Rome owes you much for the success of this campaign." Scipio embraced Masinissa then gave him the scepter. "With this ivory scepter Rome affirms your rule of Cirta and all the Maesulii ancestral lands, plus the city of Siga and all the territory that was once ruled by King Syphax."

Masinissa pivoted to face the troops and received a roar of approval that ended only when he lifted his hands out of humility.

Scipio then called Lucius and Laelius forward. Both men had served with him since Cartagena. He spoke to their superior service throughout their time with him. He gave a large gold bowl to Lucius and a gold sword to Laelius. Several other soldiers were also honored for acts of courage during their time in Africa, but Scipio saved the best for last.

"One soldier deserves my special acknowledgment," announced Scipio, raising his voice so that the soldiers in the very back could hear. "Four years ago, when we were in Syracuse, I wrongly punished this soldier to the edge of death for an action that was badly misunderstood, and yet this man never hesitated in his duty to Rome. The hastati who form our first line and must hold that line throughout each battle, theirs is the most grueling work on the battlefield. The soldier called Troglius, from the first maniple of the third cohort of the Twenty-third legion, embodies, in my mind, the ideal hastatus to which all should aspire. To him, I confer the Golden Crown, Rome's highest award for bravery in combat, for defying defeat and being the anchor in the center of our line throughout this campaign. Come forward, Troglius."

Troglius, head down, tilting from side to side as he walked, weaved through the formation up to the front. A centurion behind Scipio handed the general the golden crown.

"Kneel, Troglius."

Troglius removed his helmet and knelt on one knee. Scipio placed the crown on his head. No roar of the day equaled that which followed. I cried as I cheered, thinking of that day I had found him in the doctor's tent, his back ripped down to muscle by a flail. Nothing meant more to me than being able to call this man of so few words my friend.

I sought out Masinissa after the ceremony. He was leaving for Cirta the next morning. I would be sailing for Lilybaeum within the week.

"I'm surprised our general didn't mention his map maker," said Masinissa. We stood by ourselves looking out at the bay of Tunis. The sun had just settled below the horizon. The color of the sky matched the pink of a conch shell. A light breeze from the north carried the smell of the sea.

"What I do is certainly important, Masinissa, but it's nothing compared to combat and what you must do. I've watched many battles and have the highest respect for the individual soldier, the man who puts his life on the line each time he marches from camp."

Masinissa smiled. "But your maps probably saved more lives than any single soldier took." He motioned to the spyglass at my hip. "And don't forget. I want you to come back to Africa to map my kingdom—which is now all of Numidia."

"Oh yes, I will come back, my friend, but I have two women to face. One to deny, the other to marry."

Masinissa looked off. "Yes, be thankful you have such a choice."

"I'm sorry, Masinissa, I shouldn't have said that. I have been fortunate in love. You have not."

Masinissa shook his head, sadly. "I didn't feel you were boasting, Timon. The choices of kings are not those of joy, but of duty. At least

I have one consolation many broken-hearted don't. I had my honeymoon night with the one I loved. Without that, I could not say the name Sophonisba at all."

I embraced him, and he pulled me close. I felt as though he were a brother to me. It would be an honor to return to Africa to map Numidia for him.

CHAPTER 112

Eighty transports escorted by fifty triremes sailed out of the Bay of Tunis past the fortress of Carthage, beginning the two-day voyage to Lilybaeum. I was on the flotilla's lead ship. I had arranged for private quarters for my mother and me. It involved telling Scipio that my mother had been in Hannibal's camp as a spy, and that she was the one who had given me the information that led to Claudius Nero's historic march north. Scipio was stunned by this information, even more so when I told him that I had learned my mother was in Hannibal's camp from Ennius.

Near noon on the second day of the voyage, I stood at the bow of the ship, staring off to the north, anxious for the sight of land. Off and on I would use the spyglass to scan the horizon in hopes of spotting some elevated portion of the island of Sicily. Scipio came up alongside of me and opened a conversation, not as a general to a scribe, but as a general to a valued advisor.

"I didn't mention you the other day when I thanked the troops for their contribution to the campaign, but in some ways, you were as valuable as any man I had, even Masinissa."

Though Masinissa had said something similar to me, I was surprised to hear this from Scipio. "Thank you for saying that, sir. You're too kind."

"No, not at all." He looked at the spyglass in my hand. I handed it to him, and he used it to stare ahead into the distance.

"This viewing device cannot be overvalued. It's absolutely remarkable." He lowered the spyglass from his eye and touched me on the shoulder. "Your maps were a godsend to me, Timon. No thanks that I might give you would be equal to what I gained from your work. Did the maps or this spyglass defeat Hannibal? No. It was the determination of the Roman legionnaire who was willing to give his life for Rome. But for a man like myself, who thrives on preparation, accurate maps are as critical as training. And this spyglass, which some might consider little more than a magic trick, speaks to the grandness of Greek science and a new world yet to come. Not everyone can appreciate this, but I do, and I want you to know that."

"You deserve credit for recognizing the value of a good map, sir. You were interested in my maps long before we met. That kind of forethought, I believe, separates you from the other Roman generals."

Scipio smiled. "Claudius Nero deserves the credit for noticing you. He told me of the work you did for Marcellus. He spoke very highly of you and your maps."

I bowed my head at the compliment.

"I would like to repay you somehow, Timon," continued Scipio. "I don't intend to tell anyone about the spyglass, but I would like to buy it from you. I would like to own it. Name any price."

"It's not for sale, sir. I'm sorry. It was a gift from Archimedes, and it means more to me than gold. I hope to continue making maps. I will need it as a sighting device."

Scipio nodded slowly, perhaps surprised that I had turned him down. "Well, what if I made you part of my family? What if I adopted you? Then at least the device would be in the Cornelian clan."

Adoption was very common in Roman families. Had Marcellus lived, I suspect he would have adopted me. "That's a very kind offer, sir," I answered instead of saying no.

"I heard you have feelings for Tiberius Sempronius' daughter. I know her. She's a very pretty and intelligent young woman, certainly a cut above the Sicilian woman I saw you with at Troglius' trial."

"I plan to marry that woman, sir."

"Don't be naive, Timon. Think of what the Cornelius name would do for you. You would be a patrician. Forget your farm girl. You could ask Fulvia for her daughter's hand in marriage. I have heard the story of her plight with the Vestal Virgins. Fulvia would be certain to say yes were you part of my family."

Even though I had already decided that I would ask Moira to marry me, something in this offer made me second-guess myself. Scipio saw it in my face.

"Give it some thought. I would love to add you—and your spyglass—to my family. It would change your life forever. You could have whatever you wanted."

"Yes, sir, I understand that. Let me think about it. I wasn't really planning on settling down in Rome, but your offer certainly puts that in a different perspective."

Scipio lifted the spyglass to his eye again and scanned the horizon. "I see land," he announced. "Have a look." He handed me the spyglass and pointed.

I peered through the lenses at the horizon. "Yes, that might be the peak of Mount Etna, meaning we're still quite far from shore. I'm guessing it will still be a while before the man in the crow's nest notices."

"And further proof of the device's value, Timon. Think about my offer." Scipio turned away and headed to the rear of the ship.

A short time later, the man in the crow's nest called out, "Land ahead!"

CHAPTER 113

We entered the harbor at Lilybaeum before sunset. The Fifth legion deboarded for deployment in Sicily. Although members of the Twenty-third, both Troglius and Rullo, along with several hundred others, were added to the Fifth to bring it to a full five thousand legionnaires. The rest of the Twenty-third would travel with Scipio to Rome. My mother and I would go with them. I planned to return to Syracuse, but I had unfinished business in Rome to attend to first.

We stayed two days in Lilybaeum before departing for Rome. I sought out Rullo and Troglius, knowing they would be stationed in Syracuse for the next few months. I found them in the Roman camp the afternoon prior to my leaving. We walked down to the harbor and sat on the wharf, watching the tide come in. I told them I would be in Rome only a short while, then I would return to Sicily to live outside Syracuse.

I noticed when we walked and when we were on the wharf that Rullo kept scratching himself, often quite vigorously. I ignored it as best I could, but on the way back to the camp, I asked him about it.

Rullo seemed embarrassed by the question, and only answered after I asked twice. "Something itches down here," he said, as he pressed his tunic against his groin to dig at his crotch in obvious discomfort.

"Is it a rash?"

He shook his head. "I don't know, but it's driving me crazy." He went at himself again.

"Are you willing to show me?"

Rullo scrunched up his face, not at all happy with the idea, but with only Troglius and me there, he lifted his tunic and pushed his loin cloth down low enough to expose his pubic hair. The skin beneath the hair was raw from scratching. I looked closely and saw that there little bugs crawling in the hair. "You've got lice, Rullo!" I pinched one between my fingers and squeezed it lifeless, then showed him the tiny dot of an insect while he straightened his tunic.

He made a terrible face and looked at Troglius who was just as surprised as he was.

"How long has this been going on, Rullo?"

"Too long," he muttered, further embarrassed by my discovery, and again scratching at himself.

"Since right after Zama," said Troglius.

"You didn't go to the prostitutes, did you?"

Rullo hung his head.

I shook my head. "That's where these things came from. Try not to itch. It only makes it worse."

Rullo rolled his eyes like *how can I not itch!*

"Let's see what one looks like under the crystal lens," said Troglius.

I had never shown the lens to Rullo and figured this was as good a time as any. I removed the lens from the end of the spyglass, then demonstrated its magnifying power on the back of Rullo's hand. He was fascinated, but not as much as he would have been had he not been otherwise distracted.

"Now do the insect," pressed Troglius.

I had never looked closely at lice before and didn't know what to expect, but when I drew a focus on the dead one in my hand, I couldn't believe what I saw. "Look at this," I gasped. "It looks like a tiny crab!"

Troglius took a look and immediately stepped back. "I don't want any of those on me."

Rullo bent over my hand, and with a little instruction on the use of the lens, got a glimpse of the source of his scratching. "By the gods!" he exclaimed. "That thing looks like a scorpion without a tail." Badly upset, he lifted his tunic and peered into his pubic hair with the lens. "Oh my, there are hundreds and hundreds of them. How can I possibly get rid of them?"

I looked at Troglius and he looked at me. Neither of us had a clue. "Wash yourself and your loincloth. Do it twice," I suggested. "I don't know what else to do."

"Pick them off one by one," ventured Troglius.

"That would take me the rest of my life!" Rullo looked so distraught I thought he was going cry.

"It's not that bad," I said. "We all know people who have had lice, and they got rid of them somehow. Find someone who's had them. See what they did."

And that was how I left it. Rullo and Troglius returned to their tent unit and I went back to the ship, chuckling to myself at what I imagined had been Rullo's first experience with a woman.

CHAPTER 114

During the voyage from Lilybaeum to Ostia, I escorted my mother to the bow one afternoon and treated her to the use of the spyglass. While she trained the lenses on the Sicilian shoreline, I told her about Moira. I told her that after going to Rome I would come back to Sicily to marry her, and that I hoped that she would come with me and live with us.

"Have you asked her father yet, Timon?"

"No, she's an orphan with two children of her own, but I expect her to say yes."

"What about the young Roman woman you told me about? Wasn't she the perfect girl for you?"

"I plan to see Sempronia while we're in Rome."

"Will you tell her about your marriage plans?"

"I'm not sure. I want to see her and make sure I'm making the right decision."

"I didn't think you had a choice. Wouldn't Sempronia's mother object?"

I nodded. "But Scipio has offered to adopt me. I would become a patrician. That would change things."

My mother smiled at me. "Then you haven't really made up your mind."

"No, I think I have, but I just want to see Sempronia one more time. Is that wrong?"

"No, it's important you're certain before you ask a woman to marry you. But what of this offer by Scipio? Are you seriously considering it?"

I bowed my head. "It's complicated," I muttered.

"No, it's not, Timon. Marry the Sicilian girl. Help her with her children and her farm. I got to know Rome just as you did. I saw nothing in the patrician way of life that I would want. Did you?"

"I saw lots that I wanted nothing to do with, but the Cornelian name would greatly assist me in life."

"You'll do fine in Syracuse with your own name." My mother's smile was in her eyes. "Go see Sempronia. Don't mention Scipio's offer. That will only confuse things. But be clear with her about your intentions. And be clear about your own feelings for Moira."

I embraced my mother. How I had missed her.

CHAPTER 115

Our arrival in Ostia was much like Marcellus' on his return from Syracuse. The celebration at the docks was greater by far, but the process of removing the plunder from the transports, recording it, and packing it into a baggage train for the trip to Rome was the same. It took us three weeks. During that time, Scipio went into Rome to give his report to the Senate in the Temple of Bellona.

Scipio had become like a god to the people. They followed him in hordes to the temple that day. Others lined the battlements and cheered from the walls as he circuited the south side of the city with a turma of cavalry, riding his beautiful red roan and wearing his polished armor.

The Senate welcomed him as a hero, showing none of the hostility that had marked Marcellus' return. There was no debate whether to give him a triumph or an ovation. He had just achieved the greatest military victory in the three hundred year history of the Roman Republic. He had defeated Hannibal and ended sixteen years of terror in Italy. Scipio received extended praise from every Senator present and unanimous support to hold a triumph. Fabius, however, was not there. He had died during Scipio's last year in Africa, only months before Hannibal left Italy. That was a shame. Scipio might have enjoyed a few kind words from old warty.

Although I was busy throughout the unloading of the transports and the preparation of the baggage train, I did manage to take my mother to the Claudian farm. Marcus was in southern Italy, helping eliminate Hannibal's last remaining garrisons. Thankfully Portia was at the residence in Rome. I was afraid what I might say if I saw her. But Edeco and Meda were there, running the farm and taking care of the household. They were relieved to see my mother, particularly Meda.

My mother and the testy house slave had become close friends in the time before her kidnapping. Meda cried at the news about Lucretia.

Edeco accompanied me to the stable. Balius was in one of the stalls. Although it had been three years, he greeted me like an old friend, rolling up his lips and fluttering them in my face when I stroked his forelock.

"How is Marcus?" I asked the man who had once been a king.

"Marcus has done well since his father's death. He spoke often of you. He wished he were in Africa. Like his father, I think he wanted to meet Hannibal."

"I met him."

"Truly?"

"Yes, he impressed me. I wish Marcellus had met him—and I was there to hear them talk. When will Marcus return to Rome?"

"Soon, Timon. Any day. Certainly within a few weeks. He has a surprise for you."

"What could that be? A gladius?"

Edeco actually laughed. "No, it's for him to tell you. I think you will be pleased."

CHAPTER 116

Scipio's triumph took place on the ides of October. Never before or since have I seen such an enthusiastic welcoming for a man. Scipio owned Rome the way Fabius had after the fall of Capua, only more so, because the war was over and the object of derision had finally been defeated.

The Twenty-third legion assembled at daybreak in a long column on the east bank of the Tiber in Mars Field. One hundred trumpeters led the procession through Porta Carmentalis and into the city. They were followed by decorated floats and painted wagons, overflowing with spoils from Africa, including one hundred and twenty-three thousand pounds of silver. Syphax came next, laden by chains. The deposed Numidian king was the target of rotten fruit and vicious insults hurled at him from every direction. Syphax was trailed by twenty elephants, two-by-two, and a long file of captured soldiers, some noble Carthaginians, some dark Numidians, some wild looking men from the tribes of Spain or Gaul. The entire Roman Senate, wearing their ceremonial robes, followed the prisoners of war. Then came ten flamines, each leading a white, sacrificial ox for the appeasement of Jupiter. Twelve lictors preceded the triumph's celebrant. Scipio wore a purple toga embroidered in gold and rode in a gold plated chariot drawn by four white horses. His long blond hair, held in place by a gold wreath, was combed back from his face and fell in waves to his shoulders. He held an ivory scepter in one hand and a laurel branch in the other as he bowed and gestured to the crowd on his way to the forum. He may as well have been king for the day. Tens of thousand of citizens cheered for him. They filled the streets, the hills, and the battlements along the walls.

Last in the procession were the soldiers, led by the officers on horseback, who were trailed by the cavalry, and then the men on foot, proudly carrying their standards, singing bawdy songs, and calling out

417

to friends along the parade route. Music, clouds of incense, and festoons of multi-colored flowers filled out the pageant that turned all of Rome into a grand circus.

The procession wound into the city through the cattle market where the train of plunder and the soldiers halted. The trumpeters continued on to the forum, followed by the members of the Senate, the flamines, the ten oxen, and Scipio.

When they reached the forum, Scipio climbed from the chariot and led the procession to the base of the Capitoline Hill and up the winding staircase to the Temple of Jupiter. The citizens and soldiers followed him until the hill overflowed with people and looked like a giant piece of fruit covered with ants.

Scipio took his place at the temple altar as the crowd filled out before him. Many more were in the forum and the streets below. Others watched from the Palantine and Quirinal Hills. The sound of cheering and jubilation could be heard for miles around, and was probably enlarged upon by the farmers in the fields close enough to hear.

Licinius the pontifex maximus stepped up to the altar beside Scipio and raised his hands for quiet. It took some time but gradually the excited crowd settled down to a murmuring impatience.

The ten flamines positioned the oxen in a line across the front of the altar and adjacent to the ceremonial brazier. A Vestal Virgin came forward with a torch lit from the sacred flame and applied it to the kindling in the brazier. As the fire took hold, she sprinkled wine and incense into the flames, causing the fire to spit and spark. Licinius prayed to Jupiter, then nodded to the flamines. One by one, the oxen's throats were slit, and the animals bled out.

Four of the flamines turned the first ox on its side. One of them opened the beast's midsection with a flint knife. Two others held the incision open as Licinius performed the duty of inspecting the entrails. After a hesitating silence, broken several times by shouts of Scipio's name from the crowd, Licinius stood and raised his blood covered hands in the air and announced that Jupiter had conferred his blessings on Scipio, all of Rome, and the great victory over Carthage. The crowd exploded into another jubilant frenzy of cheers, calls for Scipio, and curses against Hannibal and all Carthaginians.

Scipio, at the altar throughout the ceremony, allowed the demonstration to go on longer than I would have thought. Finally he lifted his hands for quiet. Silence came almost immediately, broken only by the intermittent shout of the victorious general's name. The whole city held still, as in a block of amber, in anticipation of what Scipio would say.

Scipio lifted his eyes to the heavens. "Thank you, Jupiter, for your blessings, and thank you, Mars, for infusing my troops with your spirit and for providing them with the confidence and energy to defeat the most dreaded enemy Rome has ever known." Several more shouts of Scipio's name erupted from the huge crowd.

Scipio faced the audience. "Eight years ago, soon after I arrived in Spain to take my late father's command, I had a powerful dream, which until this day I have revealed to no one because of its impact on me at the time. I was barely twenty-five years old. My experience was that of a young tribune. I had been at Ticinius and pulled my wounded father from the battlefield. I had been at Cannae to witness the lowest point in the war, but I had yet to focus on anything more than the duties of a junior officer.

"On arriving in Spain, my ambitions were still modest. I simply sought to carry out my duties to the best of my abilities. Then I had the dream. It was at a time when I was uncertain of myself. I struggled to find the confidence that a man commanding tens of thousands of men must have and must project.

"In the dream, my father, as a shade, came down from the heavens and spoke to me at length, as though he were still alive, but with the grand vision of the past and future granted to those special few who in death have achieved the highest realms of the spirit world and can confer with the gods as easily as I do with you.

"My father, seeing clearly into my heart, addressed this hesitancy in me, common to a young officer. He told me that he had seen the future, and that he had seen the end of the war. He told me that I would go to Africa, and that by going there, I would force Hannibal to come there also to confront me. And though Hannibal up to that point in the war had never been defeated, my father said I would emerge victorious, and that my victory would bring an end to the war and earn me great military glory. He told me he had seen me *here*, before the Temple of Jupiter, saying these words that I am saying right now—and that I remember as clearly as if the dream were last night.

"I knew then what all Romans know now—and yet, it seemed too remarkable for me to tell anyone at the time. I was a young man, and it would be unbecoming for a junior officer to make such bold predictions.

"Two years after this dream, which so fills me at this moment that I can see my father's face looking down from the heavens right now, I dared to present my plan to go to Africa to the Roman Senate, which our eldest statesmen quickly condemned as naive and certain to fail. I presented this idea to the Senate two more times, each time gathering in a few senators with the wisdom of my strategy. Finally, four years ago, at the time of my first consulship, the Senate, somewhat reluctantly, granted me the province of Sicily and permission to raise an army to take to Africa.

"The going was slow. I spent a year in Sicily, recruiting and training an army. Then another two years in Africa, putting pressure on Carthage, hoping to draw Hannibal back to his homeland. The rest is well-known. Inland from Carthage, two armies of forty thousand men faced off to decide the war, one commanded by the invincible Hannibal, the other by a young Roman. Hannibal is now without an army. Carthage has surrendered, and that young Roman is here before you now, living out a dream that no one in their right mind could have believed but him. Thank you to my troops. Thank you to all Roman citizens. Thank you to the Senate for finally believing in me, and thank you to Quintus Fabius, watching now from above with my father, for forcing me to defend my ideas against the most highly revered military mind Rome has ever known—until two months ago in Zama!"

Those before him, those below in the forum and in the streets, and those on the hills, many of whom surely could not have heard his words, exploded with the excitement of the moment, releasing sixteen years of fear and frustration, and exulting in the rise of the Roman Republic to the pinnacle of world power.

Within that sea of jubilation, amid the hugs and cheers of Roman citizens, and the cries for Scipio Africanus—the name bestowed on Scipio after his great victory—I watched and said nothing, thankful simply to be alive, relieved that the war was finally over, and hopeful that one day I might free my mind of the visions of the dead that the war had imprinted in my memory.

CHAPTER 117

Scipio's triumph was followed by three days of revelry. Rome, a nation that seemed addicted to war and city-wide festivals, surpassed all my previous experience for debauchery during those three days. The streets were filled from dawn to dawn with revelers, free drink, and, of course, the usual collection of pickpockets, prostitutes, and vendors hawking religious trinkets—several selling locks of Scipio's hair at a quantity no one head could support. I'm sure I enjoyed the celebration as much as anyone. *The war was over!*

The second night I went to the Community of Miracles. There, atop the Aventine Hill, the festivities were really no different than any other night, and I pushed my way through the throng in search of Quintus Ennius.

Always loud, invariably drunk—or at least appearing so—Ennius found me first. I felt a hand on my shoulder and turned to face just who I was looking for, looking just as he always did, his toga soiled and his hair sticking out like quills on a porcupine.

"Quintus..." I began before he abruptly interrupted.

"Homer, my friend! Please address me in the manner Rome's best poet deserves."

"Oh, of course, how could I make such a silly mistake," I said laughing. I bowed to him as I would had he actually been Homer, then became serious. "All kidding aside."

"Absolutely not, Timon, there is no greater wisdom than a properly timed joke."

"Or a well-deserved expression of gratitude and appreciation."

"What? Are you about to insult me?"

"Hardly. Whether you know it or not, I did receive your message from Rullo. You could not have done me a greater service."

A drunken woman stumbled up to Ennius with one large pendulous breast exposed. She kissed him on the cheek, then staggered

421

off into the rowdy crowd. "My mother," he said. "On occasion, I'm still in need of nursing."

I laughed again but pressed on with my heart-felt message. "I was able to save my mother, Quintus—Homer. She's here in Rome now, primarily because of the information I got from you. She and I will never forget it."

"But you might if this celebration continues another few days. Drink is known to do that."

"No, no matter how much I drink, I won't forget. Thank you." I embraced him despite his effort to stop me. "And please pass my thanks on to Caelius. He also deserves credit for reuniting me with my mother. I just don't know how you've done it, somehow fooling everyone into thinking you're a fool."

Ennius pushed me away. "Kind sir, you underestimate my talents as an actor." He winked. "Soon I must take up the role of a dedicated member of the Roman military. I hope I can play that part as convincingly."

Before I could assure him of certain success, two men approached him, both also showing no pain. "We're looking for the Mayor," said one.

"You've found him," announced Ennius with a wide grin and a bow. "I'm guessing you'd like me to recite *The Iliad* for you."

"No, no," said the other, taking him by the hand and dragging him off into the crowd. "We want you to introduce us to Caelius. We have Hannibal's sword in our possession. We're looking for a buyer."

"Oh, yes, I'm sure there's a sucker somewhere that will swallow that line," I heard the playwright chuckle before he vanished into the night.

CHAPTER 118

Two days after the celebration had ended, I learned from Edeco that Marcus had returned from southern Italy and that he was staying at the residence in Rome. I rode Balius into Rome the next morning, knowing that seeing Marcus and talking to Sempronia were necessary before returning to Syracuse.

Somewhat hesitant to visit Sempronia's home, I went to the Claudian residence first. I stabled Balius, then went into the house through the peristyle. Laelia knelt beside a flower bed, pulling weeds. She looked up at me in complete surprise.

"I'm looking for Marcus, Laelia. Is he here?"

"He's in Rome, but not here at the house. I'm not sure when he'll be back. How are you? I heard you were in Africa with Scipio."

"Yes, that's right. And so was Rullo."

"What! He ran away. I had no idea where he went."

"You should be proud of him. He joined the Twenty-third legion and fought in the battle that defeated Hannibal. He's a hero in his own right."

"How is he? Is he in Rome?"

"He's fine, but he's not here. He was reassigned to the Fifth Legion and is stationed in Sicily."

"At least he's alive. I thought he'd been killed in the streets."

"No, Laelia. He's a fine young man. I'm going back to Sicily. I will tell him I saw you."

"Timon!" Portia came into the garden from the Atrium. It had been four years since I had seen her. She was still as stunning a woman as ever. She embraced me like a son, while all I wanted to do was pull away and give her a piece of my mind.

"Where might I find Marcus?" I asked as she released me.

"I'm not sure. He may have gone back to the farm. He's been in Rome the last two days."

"Yes, that's what I've heard. I haven't seen him yet." I hesitated, weighing the need to confront her about Paculla.

Portia looked at the floor, then up at me. "I owe you an apology, Timon. You were right about Paculla. She befriended me and my friends to take advantage of us. She was a spy, not a priestess. I think she was responsible for your mother's disappearance, and I feel partly to blame. I'm so sorry. I'm just glad you're back from Africa."

Instead of venting my anger, I pushed past it. "Let me relieve your worries. Paculla did have something to do with my mother's disappearance, but she's fine now. She's out at the farm as we speak."

Portia embraced me again, this time with greater warmth and feeling. I told her the short version of finding my mother and did my best not to reveal the feelings I had harbored against her for the last four years.

I left the house, head down, as into a wind, and crossed the city to Sempronia's home. I approached the front door prepared to knock, but decided against it. I couldn't bear being turned away again. Instead, I went down the alley to the back of the property. Just as I had before, I climbed the rail fence and quietly edged up to the peristyle, hoping that Sempronia might be there.

I didn't see her, so I slipped through the colonnade that surrounded the peristyle and into the garden. No one was there—but the parrot.

"Timon!" squawked Ajax loud and piercing.

Sempronia appeared at the entrance to the atrium as Ajax squawked again. "A squared plus B squared."

We stared at each other from across the garden uncertain how to begin. Dora broke the spell by striding out of the atrium with a broom, set to use it on me. Sempronia stopped her.

"Dora, please leave us alone. I want to talk to this man."

Dora glared at me, muttered something, then went back into the house. Sempronia, now twenty years old and looking more beautiful than ever, a dream in real life, came up to me and cautiously took my hand. She led me to the stone bench where we had reviewed so many geometry proofs. The roses were in bloom. Their fragrance paled in comparison to the sweet smells that encompassed Sempronia.

"You've returned, Timon." She still held my hand.

"As I said I would."

A long silence filled the garden. I fought the urge to compare her to Moira. Sempronia was something different—a fairy, a princess, ethereal and pure, a woman to whom geometry and numbers were as much a joy as they were to me. Clearly she was special in a way that Moira was not. I thought of Scipio's offer to adopt me. I thought of living in Rome at the pinnacle of wealth and society. Then I thought of my mother's words of caution, and finally I thought of Moira and her children and her little orchard in Sicily.

"I need to tell you something, Sempronia."

Sempronia let go of my hand and put her index finger to my lips. "Before you say anything, there's something you must know. It might impact what you want to tell me."

This caught me off guard. "What is it?"

"I have met Marcus."

I tilted my head.

"He was just here. I was taking him to the front door when you came in through the back." She lowered her eyes, then lifted them to mine. "He asked my mother for my hand. We're going to be married." She smiled, clearly pleased, but with just enough sadness in her eyes to suggest she was worried this might hurt me.

"That's wonderful," I said, embracing her as I never had before, truly loving this woman, yet knowing that fate had given us separate paths.

When I released her, I told her I was going back to Syracuse. I told her that I had found a woman in Sicily and that I would ask her to marry me when I returned. Sempronia then embraced me.

At that point Fulvia stormed into the garden. "What's this man doing here?" she screamed. "I thought we threw him out long ago."

Sempronia stood up, and with Fulvia's and my lurid moment in the dark spinning out there in air between us, she told her mother that she had asked me into their home to tell me about her engagement to Marcus. Fulvia frowned, then glared at me and stomped out.

I embraced Sempronia again and said good-bye. I wished her the best in her marriage to Marcus, and assured her that I would return to Rome one day to visit them. We parted as good friends should, happy for each other.

Seeing Marcus was now imperative. Thinking he must have returned to the farm, I hurried back to the stable for Balius. Ithius was there brushing him. I had not seen Ithius since returning from Africa. As soon as I saw him, I knew I could not have left Rome without talking to him.

He asked me about the events in Africa. I told him about finding my mother and Rullo's surprise appearance, and lastly I showed him the spyglass. He seemed to understand the action of the lenses after just a few tries.

"So this must be one of Archimedes' secrets that you were so concerned about revealing?"

I nodded. "I showed it to Scipio and several other people since our talk—what was it, five years ago?"

"Was it right to show them?"

I thought about Scipio's response to the spyglass and his desire to own it. I thought about his using the image projected from the pinhole to deceive his staff. I thought about the drawings that I had found in Archimedes' workshop, and trading one of them to Hannibal for my mother's freedom. "I don't know if it was right, Ithius. I don't. But I did it anyway."

He raised the spyglass in one hand. "You don't think a device like this should be shared?"

"My experience has shown that it depends on the person. For some people, it was simply curious and amazing. To others, like Scipio, it spoke of power and advantage. He wanted it kept secret, but he also wanted it for his own. He even offered to buy it from me—at any price I asked. It may have been a mistake to show it to Scipio, but he was also the only one who saw the spyglass as more than a tool. While it baffled most people, and they thought of it as magic, for Scipio it was a glimpse into a world of possibilities. He saw what the application of science might one day contribute to humankind, and that the potential for such applications was unlimited."

"But he also saw it as an advantage in war."

"Oh, yes. That was nowhere more evident than when we were at sea."

"Did you allow him to use it freely?"

"I did. After we left Africa, he told me it had been of immeasurable help to him."

"So what was wrong with showing him?"

"His immediate desire to keep it secret and for himself."

"Do you think Archimedes was right all along?"

"No, I think you were. Knowledge is to be shared, and yet some knowledge, especially that which can be applied to mass destruction, will always be secreted away or stolen or sold for large sums of money. I can imagine a time when science is pursued as an arm of the military." I recalled Marcellus' dream of seeing long silver projectiles propelled by fire arc across the sky then explode when they hit the ground. "But after watching men among men, and realizing that war is what men do, I struggle to find a reason to give them the tools of science to add to their arsenals. This, I'm sure, was Archimedes' greatest concern. Why give men more ways to kill each other?"

"Yes, of course, but how do you draw the line between the good and the bad? Your spyglass for example. It has military value, but it wasn't designed for war. It's very entertaining and can be used to increase our understanding of the world. That's considerably different than, say, a catapult."

"So you're saying it's complicated. There's no clear *yes* or *no* to the question."

Ithius chuckled. "Exactly, and the only solution is to make knowledge available to everyone, and to hope that it allows men to move beyond war and killing each other."

"Not in our lifetimes."

"What about ten lifetimes?" He grinned.

"Perhaps twenty."

"So what will you do with your spyglass, Timon? Destroy it? Show it to more people? Or keep it secret?"

"Sell it to Scipio for ten gold talents."

Ithius looked at me.

"No," I laughed. "I will keep it, and only show it to those I know I can trust."

"Like me." Ithius laughed.

"Like you."

CHAPTER 119

I rode Balius out to the farm that afternoon. Marcus was in the stable and saw me as I rode up. He immediately came out to greet me and embraced me like a brother when I dismounted.

"Timon! I heard you were here. And your mother is back also."

I told him the story, all but my trade with Hannibal.

"I have something to tell you," he said, grinning in a way he hadn't in a long time.

"You met Sempronia."

"How did you know?"

"I spoke to her earlier today. She told me you're going to be married."

He blushed for the first time since I had known him. "Yes, we only settled it today. I haven't told my mother yet."

"Congratulations, Marcus." Now I embraced him. "I'm so happy that it's finally worked out."

"You were right about Sempronia. I chanced to meet her in Rome before I went south for the summer. She came to the house in Rome with her mother. I happened to be there. And that was all it took. I'm sorry I made it all so hard for you." He suddenly paused to appraise me. "You didn't hope to marry her, did you?"

I shook my head. "I'm a freedman, Marcus." I had no intention of telling him Scipio had offered to adopt me. "Fulvia would never have allowed it. Besides I've found a woman."

"Here in Rome?"

"No, in Sicily. I'm done with the Roman military. I'm returning to Syracuse to be a mapmaker and to marry the Sicilian woman."

"Have you already asked her?"

I laughed nervously. "I haven't seen her in three years. I hope she's still available."

"You'll have to bring her to Rome."

"Of course, but I must marry her first. I plan to leave for Sicily as soon as I'm given my portion of the spoils. Balius will have to stay here until I'm settled, but I'll take my mother with me, and I'll have an entirely new life—without the army."

"I'm happy for you, but I will also miss you. You have been a better friend than anyone I've known. Come, let's go into the house. We deserve a cup of mulsum. I feel like celebrating."

"The war is over!" I exclaimed as though the most important thing to all of us had been forgotten.

"Scipio has done what my father had wanted to do. He has proven to be a remarkable leader. I admire him, and, of course, like any good Roman, I'm a little jealous."

As we crossed the yard to the house, I remembered something I needed to tell Marcus. "Did you know that the boy, Rullo, enlisted in the army?"

"No, I guess I didn't even notice he was gone."

"But you did know he's your son?"

Marcus stopped walking and frowned. "Who said that?"

"I guessed it, Marcus. I saw it in his face."

Marcus looked off to the wheat fields west of the house.

"He was there in Africa, Marcus. I shared a tent with him."

Marcus faced me.

"He made a good showing. You should be proud of him."

Marcus bowed his head, clearly uncertain how to react.

"He saved Troglius' life at the battle Zama."

Marcus hesitated, then asked, "Did he come back with you?"

"No, he's in Sicily with the Fifth for now."

"Does he know I'm his father?"

"I told him before the battle of Zama—to bolster his confidence."

Marcus nodded slowly, then took a deep breath. "Thank you, Timon. I think you've told me something I needed to know." He wrapped an arm around my shoulder and escorted me into the house.

CHAPTER 120

When the spoils were divided, with most of the gold and silver going to the Roman treasury, I received a share. It was more money than I had ever had. I booked passage on a merchant ship to Syracuse for my mother and me. It was at the end of the season and the seas were rough. The one-week voyage took two. I was glad when it was over. When we entered the Great Harbor, I felt as though I were coming home.

The day we arrived I secured an apartment in Syracuse for my mother. The next morning I told her I had some business to attend to outside the city. She knew I was going to see Moira, but refrained from any questions. "Enjoy the walk," was all she said when I left.

I had been ten years old when Hannibal entered Italy. Now I was twenty-six. Well over half of my life had been to the beat of war. During the walk from Syracuse's south gate through the farmland, I finally began to feel that it was really over. For once, I was actually looking ahead and planning a life.

Moira saw me coming down the road. She was in the orchard with her children. She didn't come running. She simply stood there watching me get closer. Donato and Rosa—now seven and five—were at her side.

When I reached the orchard, Donato ran to greet me. Rosa raced after him. I caught them both in my arms and swung them around twice before setting them on the ground. Moira allowed her first smile but had yet to take a step toward me.

The children trailed after me as I continued into the orchard to their mother.

"You've come back," she said as though surprised that I had.

"I said I would."

We stared at each other for who knows how long. The children were a short distance away, picking figs from the ground. I said the only thing I could think of. "Will you marry me?"

Her look was suspicion.

I went down on one knee. "I'm no longer a part of the Roman army. I'm my own man. Will you marry me?"

Finally, finally, she let go and burst into a beautiful smile and a flood of tears. She took my hand and drew me to my feet. We embraced three years worth of missing each other, then kissed deeply into oblivion—until two sets of little hands were tugging at our clothes.

Over dinner that evening I told her that the campaign to Africa had been extremely profitable and that I wanted to buy her grandfather's farm back from the neighbors. I told her we would run the farm and I would also begin a mapmaking business. Depending on how things went, we would stay on the farm or move into the city. Moira could not have been more pleased. I told her my mother had come with me, and that we would go into Syracuse to meet her in the morning.

Moira had led a hard life. Like me, she had known the chaos of war and little else. We spent the night lying on a blanket out front of her house. Sometime around midnight she let it all out, crying like a child. I simply held her and let her cry.

CHAPTER 121

Moira and I walked into Syracuse with the children after the morning chores were completed. I took them to my mother's apartment. Arathia greeted us at the door and was so overcome with joy she began to cry. I left Moira, Donato, and Rosa with my mother. I told her to sing them a song or two while I ran a few errands in the city.

On a hunch, I went straight to Agathe's apartment. From a distance I saw Rullo and Gelo, fighting in the yard with wooden swords and laughing.

"Timon!" shouted Rullo. "What are you doing here?"

"I've come back here to live. I told you that. What are you doing here?"

"I'm with Troglius." He grinned. "The Fifth disbanded for the winter. He suggested coming here before going back to Rome."

"Why was that?"

Rullo rolled his eyes. "Eurydice. Why else? Take a look for yourself."

I followed his eyes. Troglius and Eurydice were walking our way, back from a trip to the market. Troglius carried a basket full of vegetables and fruit. He dropped the basket and nearly crushed me in his arms, blubbering over and over, "Timon, Timon, you'll never believe it!"

Just as I had, Troglius and Rullo had been given a portion of the spoils, and then were given the winter off to return to their homes. Troglius had only thing on his mind. He went straight to Eurydice and proposed. One of the most beautiful women I had ever met and one of the ugliest men I had ever seen were to be wed. Troglius had a small farm outside Rome. After the marriage, they would return to his farm with Gelo. Rullo would go with them. If ever there was a fairy tale ending, to me, this was it.

After Troglius and Eurydice had gone into the apartment with Gelo and their basket of produce, I turned to Rullo. "I've noticed you're not scratching yourself. I take it you got rid of the lice."

He shook his head in embarrassment. "I tried everything—washing, picking them out, simply not itching. Nothing worked." Behind us Agathe came out of the tenement building with a load of laundry. "When I got here, Agathe wouldn't let me in the house with them."

Agathe overheard him. "Had he been Zeus himself I wouldn't have let him in. I told him not to come back until he'd shaved his crotch."

Rullo looked at the ground.

"Then I gave him a little mixture of olive oil statured with rosemary, garlic, and lavender."

Rullo lifted his head. "I put that on every day for a week and they were gone."

"And he didn't even say thank you," snapped Agathe, turning away to hang up the clothing.

"Thank you, Agathe," called out Rullo. He grinned at me sheepishly, then whispered, "She sure is an old hag, but boy, did she save me." Returning to his normal voice, he added, "No more prostitutes for me, that's for sure."

"See that, Rullo? You're getting smarter every day."

A few feet away, Agathe tossed a tunic over the clothes line and muttered, "But not fast enough for me."

On my way off the island, I passed the tower where I had spent so much time with Archimedes. Despite my eagerness to see how Moira and my mother were getting along, I entered the tower and climbed the stairs. When I reached the third floor landing, Plato the cat confronted me coming down from above. I kneeled and held out my hand, much as I had the first time we met thirteen years earlier. Plato hesitated, in the usual cautious way of a cat, then crept down the last three stairs, staring at me with eyes as wide as saucers.

He was an old cat now, a little thin, with a few open patches in his coat, showing scabbed over flea bites. I reached out to pet him. He ducked his head, but I got a few fingers behind his ear and scratched him the way I had so long ago. Plato drew a little closer, looking up at me like he might actually remember me.

Plato followed me to the top floor of the tower. I didn't stay long. I peered out the workshop's three windows, remembering how Archimedes had ignored me for weeks before actually saying something to me. I used the spyglass to scan the ocean to the east, hoping to see a ship appear mast first over the horizon, but none came into view.

I petted Plato a few more times, said good-bye, then left the tower to return to the two women who meant everything to me.

That evening I stayed at the farm. Just before sunset, I went to the outbuilding where I had hidden Archimedes' drawings. My intention had been to burn them, but I couldn't help thinking that Ithius was right. No matter how powerful the knowledge, it must be shared, and humankind must, somehow, learn to live by the lessons it teaches. What would I do with the drawings? I wasn't sure, but I decided not to burn them. I still have them to this day, mementos from the time I served as Archimedes' eyes.

EPILOGUE

The War with Hannibal marked the beginning of Rome's domination of the western world. Already a republic for three hundred years at the time Scipio defeated Hannibal, Rome would command and direct world civilization for the rest of my lifetime (I near my seventieth year as I write these words) and likely for another five hundred years after that.

Curiously, Scipio did not include the surrender of Hannibal in the terms of Rome's treaty with Carthage. Hannibal stayed in Carthage after the war and was elected to one of the two sufete positions the following year. He would remain a public figure in Carthage for six more years, implementing a wide array of civic reforms and proving himself to be a capable bureaucrat

Seven years after the Battle of Zama, Hannibal's strongest critics in Rome learned that King Antiochus of Syria was planning to hire Hannibal to lead an invasion of Italy. Rome sent a delegation to Carthage to look into the matter. The Council of Elders met with the delegation in the afternoon. Hannibal took part in the discussion and even had dinner with the Roman emissaries. But he didn't trust them. Fearing they intended to arrest him, Hannibal left Carthage by horse in the middle of the night. He rode to Hadrumetum and caught a ship for Tyre, headed to the court of Antiochus. In the years to come, he would, in some limited capacity, engage in war against Rome again, this time for the Syrian king.

Hannibal would live for twenty years after Zama, the last thirteen in Asia, too often running from Roman bounty hunters. His final years were spent in Bithynia, where he would serve as a naval commander for King Prusias. At the age of sixty-four, still in Bithynia, Hannibal took poison to avoid murder by a Roman assassin.

Publius Cornelius Scipio became Scipio Africanus after Zama. He was the most acclaimed man in Rome for several years, but his popularity, progressive politics, and fondness for Greek learning worked against him in the Roman Senate. He would serve as consul only one more time. Cato, his quaestor in Sicily, became his most outspoken adversary, culminating in a charge of misappropriated funds against Scipio and his brother Lucius. The acrimony and bitter insults led to Scipio's leaving the Senate. With failing health, he retired to his farm and died the same year as Hannibal, in a self-imposed exile at the age of fifty-three.

There is a story about Hannibal and Scipio meeting by chance ten years after the battle of Zama. Hannibal was acting as an advisor to King Antiochus when Scipio was sent to Syria as a Roman emissary, in an effort to avoid a war. At some point after the negotiations had failed, Scipio and Hannibal had some time alone to talk. Scipio asked Hannibal who he thought was the greatest general. Hannibal didn't hesitate and said Alexander, King of Macedon. He had used a small army to conquer all of Asia and Egypt. Scipio acknowledged this answer, and then asked who would be second. Hannibal replied Pyrrhus, King of Epirus. He was the first to teach the method of encamping and choosing ground. Again Scipio acknowledged Hannibal's choice, then asked who might be third, to which Hannibal replied himself. Scipio, somewhat unsettled by this answer, then asked—what if I had not defeated you at Zama? Who would then be number one? Hannibal smiled, and again said himself. This was in effect, though somewhat backhanded, a compliment to Scipio. Scipio had defeated the man, who short of that one defeat, would have been the greatest general in history.

I should add that my friend Masinissa survived his heartbreak. He is now nearly eighty years old. He rules all of Numidia and is considered one of the greatest African kings of our era. He has had five wives and, last I spoke with him, fifty children. And I did return to Africa ten years after the war to map his kingdom.

To Archimedes, the inspiration for this narrative, go my final words. I went to his tomb many years after the end of the war. Marcellus had the tomb built shortly after the fall of Syracuse. It was carved into the side of the limestone cliffs below Fort Euryalus. I had been there when the scientist's body was interred and had been impressed by the workmanship of the tomb and its meaning to Marcellus.

Even though I knew where the tomb was, I had trouble locating it. Twenty years had passed since Archimedes' death, and no one had bothered to take care of his tomb. It was so overgrown with weeds and brush that only with a very determined effort did I finally find it. As

Archimedes had requested, a sphere inscribed in a cylinder was carved into the limestone above his name. I shed a tear remembering this famous man whom his fellow Syracusans, it seemed, had forgotten.

Much like his memory, Archimedes' work with conic sections and infinitesimal summation did not survive in the years after his death. Greek science continued to be the foundation of all science afterward, but the most sophisticated part of that science—the material that Archimedes, Colon, Apollonius, and Diocles collaborated on—did not advance and gradually disappeared altogether. Perhaps in another thousand years, someone will make the same breakthroughs that Archimedes and his colleagues had and will creep a few steps closer to Pythagoras' dream to unite the form and the figure. For now, however, any worry that mathematics or geometry will spawn some uniquely powerful weapon of mass destruction is hard to imagine. With that hopeful thought, I put down my pen and conclude this account of my experiences during the war with Hannibal.

LIST OF CHARACTERS

Abrax- Greek surgeon

Adeon- house slave in Timon's home in Croton

Aemilus Paullus- senator who died at Cannae

Ajax- Sempronia's pet parrot

Arathia Arathenus- Timon's mother

Aristomachus- Carthaginian agent in Croton

Ava- slave given to Arathia by Hannibal

Balius- Timon's horse

Caelius- King of the Crooks

Carthalo- Carthaginian cavalry officer

Chthonia- Masinissa's horse

Dora- Sempronii slave

Edeco- Claudii slave

Euroclydon- Marcus' horse

Fulvia- Sempronia's mother

Gaia- one of Sophonisba's slaves

Gaius Cornelius Nero- Roman Consul

Gaius Laelius- Publius Scipio's naval commander and lifelong friend

Gala- King of the Numidian tribe the Maesulii, Masinissa's father

Hanno- leader of Carthage's peace party

Hanno Barca- Hannibal's second youngest brother and a cavalry captain

Hannibal Barca- Carthaginian field marshal

Hasdrubal Barca- Hannibal's oldest brother

Hasdrubal Gisgo- father of Sophonisba

Hektor- military cook on island of Ortygia in Sicily

Hiero- King Hiero II of Syracuse

Hieronymus- King Hiero's grandson

Illi- one of Sophonisba's slaves

Ithius- Claudii slave

Julia- Laelia's daughter

Lacumazes- Masinissa's younger cousin

Laelia- Claudii slave

Lucretia- house slave in Timon's home in Croton

Mago Barca- Hannibal's youngest brother

Maharbal- Carthaginian cavalry officer

Marcius Porcius Cato- quaestor for Publius Scipio

Marcus Aemilius Lepidas- Roman senator

Marcus Atilius Regulus- Roman general during the first Punic War

Marcus Claudius- Marcellus' son

Marcus Claudius Marcellus- Roman general and consul

Marcus Ralla- tribune for Publius Scipio

Masinissa- King of the Numidian tribe the Maesulii

Massiva- Masinissa's youngest cousin

Mazaetullus- Masinissa's renegade relative

Meda- Claudii slave

Menna- one of Sophonisba's handmaidens

Moira- Sicilian girl, love interest of Timon's in Syracuse

Nycea- one of Sophonisba's slaves

Oezalces- Masinissa's uncle

Paculla Annia- priestess from Capua

Philip of Macedon- King of Macedonia

Pleminius- captain of Roman garrison in Locri

Pomponius- praetor of Lilybaeum, head of inquiry team

Portia- Marcellus' wife

Publius Cornelius Scipio- young Roman general and consul

Publius Licinius Crassus Dives- pontifex maximus

Quintus Ennius- Roman playwright and poet

Quintus Fabius Maximus- elder Roman senator

Rullo- Laelia's son

Sempronia- Marcus' bride-to-be

Sophonisba Gisgo- Hasdrubal Gisgo's daughter

Syphax- King of the Numidian tribe the Masaesyli

Tiberius Sempronius Longus- Roman senator, father of Sempronia

Timon Leonidas- the Greek narrator

Troglius- Timon's friend and tent mate

Tychaeus- Syphax's cousin and cavalry commander

Vangue- Hasdrubal Gisgo's lead slave

Zanthia- Sophonisba's handmaiden

GLOSSARY

as (pl. asses)- bronze Roman coin, four quadrans make one as

auguraculum- tent in Roman military camp used by augurs

baldric- belt worn over the shoulder to carry a sword

bastinado- gaunlet-sytle military punishment

buckler- shield

cella- main room in a Roman temple

chiton- dress worn by Greek women

comitium- sunken amphitheater in front of the Curia

cuirass- breastplate of metal or formed leather

Curia- Roman Senate House

curule chair- seat for consuls in Roman Senate

decurion- captain of a turma of cavalry

denarius (pl. denarii)- silver Roman coin

equites- second order of nobility in Rome

flamen (pl. flamines)- religious orderly

garron- small horse ridden by Numidian cavalry

gladius (pl. gladii)- double-bladed, short sword of Spanish origin

greave- a bronze or leather shin guard

haruspex- priest trained to read entrails or actions of birds

hastatus (pl. hastati)- soldier in the first row of a Roman battle formation

himation- heavy woolen cloak

howdah- leather and wood tower worn by an elephant or camel

ides- fifteenth day of the month

imagines- wax masks cast from a Roman family's ancestors

imperium- authority to rule

intervallum- space between ramparts and tents in a Roman camp

lictor- bodyguard for Roman consul

mahout- trainer and rider of elephant

mola- religious sacrament made from salt and flour by the Vestal Virgins

mulsum- honey-sweeten wine

nones- the ninth of the month

palla- shawl for Roman women

peristyle- garden in Roman home

pilum (pl. pila)- a spear with wooden handle and extended iron tip

pontifex maximus- highest position in Roman religious hierarchy

poulterer- man who takes care of haruspex's chickens

praetor- governor of Roman province

princeps senatus- president of Roman senate

princeps (pl. principes)- soldier in second row of a Roman battle formation

pugio- small dagger carried by Roman velites

quadrans- smallest denomination of Roman coinage, four equal one as

quaestor- military accountant, quartermaster

quinquereme- a warship with five tiers of oars

scutum (pl. scuta)- semi-cylindrical Roman shield

stola- Roman woman's dress

sufet- one of the two leaders of the Carthaginian Council of Elders

toga praetexta- toga worn by Roman consul

triarius (pl. triarii)- soldier in third row of a Roman battle formation

triclinium- the Roman dining room

trireme- a warship with three tiers of oars

turma- squadron of thirty equestrians

velites- light infantry in Roman legion

via principalis- main street in Roman military camp

ACKNOWLEDGMENTS

I could not have written this book without the love and support of my wife Judith. My thanks to her is always and forever.

Thanks is also extended to the contingent of readers who helped me with this novel: Alice, Jim, Mary, Fast Eddie, Judith, Tim, Chris, and Tyler.

Special thanks goes to Nathan Flis and his wife Ana for permission to use the image on the cover of this book, Cornelis Huyberts' etching of Cornelis Cort's engraving, *Battle with the Elephants,* based on Raphael's tapestry of the Battle of Zama, commissioned by Pope Leo X in 1567.

Although the research for this book occurred over a period of thirty years and included the reading of many hundred books and articles, the historical basis of this book came primarily from the work of two writers, the Greek Polybius (200-118 B.C.) and the Roman Livy (59 B.C.-17 A.D.).

Polybius' *The Rise of the Roman Empire* contains the only contemporary history of the Second Punic War. Born two years after the end of the war, Polybius toured the battlefields, traced Hannibal's route through the Alps, and interviewed men who took part in the war. His book is judged to be one of the masterpieces of classical literature. Written one hundred and fifty years before the birth of Christ, less than half of the original text remains.

Livy's *The War with Hannibal* is another masterpiece. Because Livy had access to all of Polybius' writing, many of the missing parts of Polybius' work are rewritten in Livy's, though with a Roman slant. These two authors deserve my most profound acknowledgment. Without their work, the details of this story would not be known at all.

Another exceedingly helpful book was Gustave Flaubert's novel *Salammbo,* written in 1862. This remarkable love story, set in Carthage after the first Punic War, describing a standoff between Carthage and its unpaid mercenary troops, was the source of many of my images of Carthage and the times. I owe Flaubert a huge debt of gratitude for his seemingly living picture of life in Carthage two thousand years ago.

The crystal lens and the glass bead were known long before 200 B.C., but the use of them together was not. The presence of this concept in the book is not historical.

Primary Sources:

Bauman, Richard A., *Women and Politics in Ancient Rome*, Routledge, London, 1992.

Carey, Brian Todd, and Joshua B. Allfree, John Cairns, *Hannibal's Last Battle: Zama and the Fall of Carthage*, Westholme Publishing, Pennsylvania, 2008.

Cowell, F.R., *Life in Ancient Rome*, Berkley Publishing Group, New York, 1980.

Daly, Gregory, *The Experience of Battle in the Second Punic War*, Routledge, New York, 2002.

Dodge, Theodore A., *Hannibal*, Da Capo Press, Boston, 1891.

Dupont, Florence, *Daily Life in Ancient Rome*, translated by Christopher Woodall, Blackwell Publishers, Oxford, 1989.

Everitt, Anthony, *The Rise of Rome*, Random House Trade Paperbacks, New York, 2013.

Flaubert, Gustave, *Salammbo*, Albert and Charles Boni, New York, 1930.

Herodotus, *The Histories of Herodotus*, translated by Harry Carter, The Heritage Press, New York, 1958.

Jaeger, Mary, *Archimedes and the Roman Imagination*, University of Michigan Pres, United States, 2011.

Laxenby, J.F., *Hannibal's War*, University of Oklahoma Press, Norman, 1998.

Livy, *The War with Hannibal*, translated by Aubrey De Sélincourt, Penguin Classics, London, 1965.

MacLachlan, Bonnie, *Women in Ancient Rome*, New York, 2013.

Miles, Richard, *Carthage Must be Destroyed*, Penguin Books, New York, 2010.

Münzer, Friedrich, *Roman Aristocratic Parties and Families*, translated by Thérèse Ridley, John Hopkins University Press, Baltimore and London, 1999.

Nicolet, Claude, *The World of the Citizen in Republican Rome*, University of California Press, Berkeley, 1980.

Plutarch, *Lives*, translated by John Dryden, The Publishers Plate Renting Company, New York, 1937.

Polo, Francisco Pina, *The Consul at Rome*, Cambridge University Press, New York, 2011.

Polybius, *The Rise and Fall of the Roman Empire*, translated by Ian Scott-Kilvert, Penguin Classics, London, 1979.

Scheid, John, *An Introduction to Roman Religion*, Indiana University Press. 2003.

Taylor, Lily Ross, *Roman Voting Assemblies*, University of Michigan Press, Ann Arbor, 1993.

Warrior, Valerie M., *Roman Religion*, Cambridge University Press, New York, 2006.

The map of Rome at the front of the book comes from *Cambridge Ancient History*, Volume 9, page 70.

Notes:

In several cases, pieces of dialogue in the novel have been paraphrased or repeated word for word from dialogue appearing in Livy's *The War with Hannibal* or Polybius' *The Rise of the Roman Empire*. The most extensive of these passages are identified below.

1. Publius Scipio's and Quintus Fabius' debate before the Roman Senate on the strategy of going to Africa on page 108-113 of the novel comes from the above referenced version of Livy, pages 550-560.

2. Scipio's prayer prior to leaving Lilybaeum for Africa on pages 251-252 of the novel comes from Livy, page 601.

3. Scipio's criticism of Syphax and of Masinissa regarding their relationships with Sophonisba on pages 343-346 of the novel comes from Livy, pages 634-637.

4. The dialogue between Hannibal and Publius Scipio on the plains of Zama on pages 375-377 of the novel comes from the above referenced version of Polybius, pages 470-475.

5. Hannibal's speech to the Council of Elders on pages 399-400 of the novel comes from Polybius, page 481-482.

THE AUTHOR

Dan Armstrong is the editor and owner of Mud City Press, a small publishing company and online magazine operating out of Eugene, Oregon. Information about his books, short stories, political commentary, humor, and environmental studies is available at www.mudcitypress.com.

CPSIA information can be obtained
at www.ICGtesting.com
Printed in the USA
LVOW10s0135020817

543492LV00001B/229/P